A
FEVER
OF THE
BLOOD

ALSO BY OSCAR DE MURIEL

The Strings of Murder

A
FEVER
OF THE
BLOOD

OSCAR DE MURIEL

PEGASUS CRIME

NEW YORK LONDON

A FEVER OF THE BLOOD

Pegasus Books Ltd
148 West 37th Street, 13th Floor
New York, NY 10018

First Pegasus Books hardcover edition April 2017

ISBN: 978-1-68177-345-2

10 9 8 7 6 5 4 3 2 1

Printed in the United States of America
Distributed by W. W. Norton & Company, Inc.

The second one is for Don Raúl and
Doña Enriqueta, very much missed

'Tis at such a tide and hour,
Wizard, witch, and fiend have power,
And ghastly forms through mist and shower
Gleam on the gifted ken;
And then the affrighted prophet's ear
Drinks whispers strange of fate and fear,
Presaging death and ruin near
Among the sons of men; —

Sir Walter Scott
The Dance of Death

1624

31 October

'Open the curtains,' Lord Ambrose demanded, almost gagging from the effort. 'I need to see them die.'

Jane tried to push him back to bed. The man was frail — ancient, some people said — and had been ill for months, but he'd managed to stand up and walk the five feet that separated him from the window. Jane winced at the sheer hatred that moved his old bones.

'You'll hardly see a thing, master. 'Tis new moon night.'

'*Open them, you filthy wench!*' he roared, pulling his arms away, breaking into a fit of coughing, spitting phlegm and blood all over the white nightgown into which Jane had just changed him.

The maid snorted. No matter how often she washed and changed him, the old man constantly reeked of urine and disease; the stench saturated the very stones of the chamber.

'Very well,' she said, wiping his chest and mouth vigorously with a damp cloth. 'But then you'll have a good long rest.'

'Indeed I shall rest,' he grumbled. His bony, blotchy hand was already clenching the drapes. They could hear the cries of the crowd. Jane pushed him aside and drew the curtains at the perfect time. The execution was about to begin.

Through the diamond-paned glass they saw the castle and Lancaster's main square, where roaring torches cast ominous shadows over hundreds of heads. The gallows were ready and people clustered around them like restless ants.

The old man unlatched the window, and a blast of icy wind filled the room.

'Here they come,' he said, straining to see.

The six witches were marching miserably across the main square, their feet shackled, dragging heavy chains that rattled on the cobbles. Centuries would come and go, but the echoes of those rusty links would linger, for the hags' souls would never find rest.

Dressed in rags, their faces soiled, their hair grey and greasy, they were the very image of wickedness, and the crowd showed no mercy: men, women and children shouted, mocked and threw rotten vegetables at the sentenced women.

Jane squinted in disgust, hating that multitude of morbid, heartless bullies who'd be attending church the following morning, calling themselves good Christians.

The witches' backs were crooked and their feet bare, but they still reached the gallows with some dignity. They did not beg, moan or cry, not even when the executioner covered their faces with filthy hoods that still reeked of previous victims. He slipped the ropes over their heads, tightening the knots, as the bishop prayed and offered them pardon.

Lord Ambrose did not blink or breathe, clutching the windowsill with trembling hands. He let out a faint gasp when he saw the witches drop into the air.

They did not die right away though.

For a ghastly moment their bodies writhed like worms on a fishing line, as the mob cheered wildly. Then, even as they convulsed in agony, the witches' arms rose slowly, straight like masts, all six pointing at the same spot, somewhere in the crowd.

People instinctively stepped aside, as if the bony fingers were about to spurt fire. One man, however, remained petrified. An imposing man swathed in beaver fur.

'Is that your son, master?' Jane breathlessly asked Lord Ambrose, even though she knew too well. 'Is that Master Edward?'

'We should have burned them,' Lord Ambrose whispered. There was terror in his eyes, a terror such as Jane had never seen.

From under the filthy hood of one of the agonized witches – nobody could tell which one – resounded a horrid voice, deep and howling despite the ropes around their necks.

All Lord Ambrose could hear of the curse was the number thirteen. But the crowd heard it in its entirety, and the terrified townsfolk began to rush away.

The arms rose further still, this time pointing at the highest level of the town's largest house.

Jane shivered. The witches were pointing at them, directly at the open window, their eyes apparently seeing through their cowls and blindfolds.

Right then, as if pushed by invisible hands, Lord Ambrose fell backwards, his bones cracking as he hit the floor. He knocked over his chamber pot, spilling its nauseating contents all around himself.

The most illustrious and powerful lord of the house of Ambrose, whose great-grandfather had fought alongside kings in the Wars of the Roses, was now expiring in a puddle of his own filth.

Jane nearly uttered the name of the Holy Virgin. She wanted to cross herself, but the window was wide open with hundreds of Protestant partisans to see.

'Witches hanged on a new moon night,' she muttered, looking down at the square and remembering it was All Hallows' Eve.

1882

2 December

Dr Clouston could not help feeling like a thief, slipping away like this in the middle of the night.

He stroked his beard and contemplated the distant glow of Edinburgh, the city diminishing as the carriage drove him quietly into the frosted wilderness. Tom was doing a good job of keeping the horses as quiet as possible, but the price was moving at a frustratingly slow pace.

A sudden noise made Clouston jump in his seat. Turning so quickly that he hurt his neck, he saw that it was the flapping of an approaching raven. The bird squawked loudly, almost sarcastically.

Clouston took a deep breath, trying to compose his shattered nerves, but his anxiety combined with the icy weather made him shiver. From the moment he began his studies in psychiatry, almost three decades ago, he had known that his profession would take him to the darkest of places, that he would witness not only the indignities of the mentally ill but also the occasionally horrible reactions of his patients' kin. Madness was a terrible thing; it brought the best and the worst out of people, and tonight, sadly, he was about to face the latter. Such cases usually flocked to him, but this one was different. This one he'd brought upon himself.

Why had he accepted this shameful deal? It was not the first time he'd done something of the sort. His compassion had been stronger than his good sense, he now understood; or rather his weakness of character had prevailed, as his wife had remarked. Clouston wanted to tell Tom to turn around and take him back, but he'd given his word, even if a gentleman's word meant less and less as the years passed.

Tom tapped the side of the carriage as they stopped in front of a low stone wall, half buried in snow. Some twenty yards beyond it there was a small, derelict farmhouse. Its crooked walls made it look rather like a beaten pile of straw, and the only sign of life was a faint light coming from a narrow window.

Clouston took a deep breath and opened the door, but he didn't even get to set a foot on the ground.

Ferocious barking filled the air, and three enormous hounds seemed to spring out of nowhere to run wildly towards him. He closed the door an instant before the first dog reached it, and through the window he had a disturbing glimpse of wet fangs and angry little eyes.

The dogs swirled around the carriage, barking and growling, but soon they were silenced by a single gunshot and retreated with their tails between their legs. The bulky shadow of a man patted each of them as he approached Clouston's carriage.

He held a bull's-eye lantern but the light was very dim. Clouston could not make out his rough features until the man stood right in front of the carriage door. He saw weather-beaten skin, flaccid cheeks, a broad nose and eyes as small and fierce as the dogs'.

'I – I have an appointment,' Clouston said after a painful gulp; his formality sounded jarring even to himself. 'I have come to meet Lady –'

'*Don't speak her name!*' the man snarled. 'Get out and follow me.'

Clouston hesitated for a moment, but then he saw Tom jump down to the ground, rifle in hand, in a sudden movement that made the man take a step back. It was reassuring that his most trusted orderly was as intimidating as this towering stranger.

'The mistress is inside,' the man said as he walked briskly towards the house.

Clouston gave Tom a quick nod and they followed.

The old door emitted a piercing creak as the man kicked it open and made his way in. Tom entered first and took a quick look around.

'She's here, Doctor.'

The night was bitterly cold, so Clouston was not too reluctant to step inside. The interior, however, offered little consolation: the room was small and dark, the plaster of the walls was falling apart and the floor was covered in straw, leaves and rubbish. The house had evidently not been inhabited in months.

There was an improvised fire, its weak flames keeping the temperature barely tolerable, and the only furnishings were a cracked table and two chairs. Seated on one of them, and visibly uncomfortable, was Lady Anne Ardglass.

Clouston's first impression was that of a fairy-tale crone. Thin, tall and imposing, Lady Anne was in her late sixties, but she looked much older; the fire cast sharp shadows on her wrinkled face, accentuating her deep frown and tense lips.

She'd tried to make herself look common by wearing a simple black dress and a cheap taffeta hat, but the effect was rather theatrical. She could never hide her poise: her back proudly straight, her chin raised high, her long hands, protected by lace mittens, demurely folded on her lap. And the hat did not completely conceal her silver hair, arranged in the most intricate of braids.

'Have a seat, Doctor,' she offered in a clear, commanding voice.

As he sat Clouston perceived an odd mixture of lemon verbena and brandy in the air. He – like everyone in Edinburgh – knew that Anne Ardglass was nicknamed Lady Glass, and looking closely he noticed the dark, veiny rings under her eyes which spoke of a lifetime of heavy drinking. She probably tried to conceal the scent of alcohol with herbal sachets and perfume on her clothes.

'As you can see, I have brought all the paperwork,' she said, pointing at a stack of documents on the table. 'All we need is your signature.'

Clouston perused the papers. He'd warned Lady Anne that he would not help unless she followed the law. According to the Scottish Lunacy Acts, no one could be declared insane unless two independent doctors examined the patient and agreed on the diagnosis. It appeared that Lady Anne had obtained a certificate from some unknown psychiatrist in Newcastle. The quality of the report revealed the incompetence of said doctor, and under other circumstances Clouston would have firmly refuted its validity; nevertheless, the insanity of Lord Joel

Ardglass was far from debatable. Lady Anne's only son had attempted suicide on a number of occasions, and it had been weeks since his last coherent speech – not to mention that ghastly violent episode.

'Doctor,' said Lady Anne, 'before you take my son, there is something I need to ask you.'

Clouston wanted to slam a fist on the table and shout that he had not even started the first favour yet, but he opted to take a deep breath instead.

'What is it, ma'am?'

Lady Anne looked at her servant, and he produced a crumpled envelope from his breast pocket. Lady Anne pulled out a single sheet, which she unfolded on the table. 'Will you please sign this as well?'

As she spoke her servant brought ink and pen.

Clouston had only read the first few lines before he snapped, 'Lady Anne, are you seriously asking me to sign this?'

'Indeed. You made me look at the law and I did so thoroughly. There is no act to keep doctors from telling everyone about their patients' affairs. There was only one case my solicitors found: some London physician divulged how one of his patients aborted an illegitimate child. The trollop's husband heard about it and divorced her. She then successfully sued the doctor. The court deemed his statements to be "libel and defamation" – despite it all being true.'

'And by signing this I admit that if I ever speak out on this matter I'll be defaming you,' Clouston read.

'That is correct. The very words used in that precedent case. That would save us much time in court if this were

9

ever made public. To the world, my son died this afternoon on his way to Belgium.'

Clouston snorted. 'I thought you had a higher opinion of me and my professional practices.'

'And I do, Doctor, but I need to make sure that the name of my family is not tarnished. I am sure you will understand.'

Clouston kneaded his temples.

'You make me crawl in the shadows like a delinquent . . . we are signing patched-up documents to pretend this arrangement is within the law . . . and now it is *I* who must agree to *your* terms? You high-born are more merciless to your mad folk than us poor commoners.'

Dr Clouston knew that all too well. Insanity was a shameful business for the aristocracy: for them it implied weak blood, wicked ancestry, or even a curse or demonic possession.

Lady Anne produced a fine hunter flask from her small purse, together with a little silver cup, and demurely poured herself some drink. Clouston wanted to believe she was ashamed of herself, but he was not sure she was capable of that feeling.

'Do you want more money?'

'Lady Anne, there are things your money cannot compensate for.'

She had a rather long drink, gulping twice before lowering the cup. 'I know.'

'What if I refuse to sign?'

'I will be forced to seek help elsewhere, and you know what that will be like.'

Sadly, Clouston did know. No other respectable doctor

would agree to her terms. She would end up dealing with one of those tricksters who ran dreadful asylums with methods that were downright medieval. They would not even attempt to understand or improve Joel's condition; they'd simply keep him out of sight, slowly rotting to oblivion.

Lady Anne fixed her empty gaze on the fire. It was the only time her voice came out as a whisper.

'Don't make me beg, Doctor.'

The fire crackled in the hearth, and for a moment there was no other sound in the room. It felt as if the entire world had halted, waiting for the doctor's answer.

Clouston rubbed his face in utter frustration. 'Something tells me we are all going to regret this . . .'

He finally snatched up the dip pen and signed so angrily he almost gashed the paper.

Outside, one of the dogs howled. The others followed, and very soon there was a cacophony of barking.

'What the hell?' shouted Lady Anne's servant as he opened the door, letting an icy draught in. He and Tom went outside, while Clouston stood in the doorway.

He had to squint to make out what was happening. The dogs were running to the road, and amidst their piercing barks Clouston heard the frenzied galloping of a horse. It took him a moment to actually see it, for it was a jet-black mount – as black as the hooded figure that spurred its hindquarters riding . . . side-saddle?

'Put that down,' Clouston told Tom, who was nervously pointing the rifle.

It was a horsewoman, and a very skilled one.

She reined in with perfect control and hopped down.

The hounds howled and jumped around her, but kept their distance. Lady Glass's brute of a servant ran back to the house, almost knocking Clouston down.

'She's here, milady!'

'For goodness' sake, tell me a name, Jed!'

He didn't have the chance. The hooded woman had already arrived, walking in with confident strides.

She pulled off the hood and Clouston saw the pretty face of a nineteen-year-old girl. He recognized the bone structure of Lady Anne: the long face, the soft jaw, the pointy chin. On the other hand, her skin was smooth and unblemished, and her brown eyes glowed with turbulent determination. She was also rather short, or appeared so next to the enormous Jed.

'Caroline!' Lady Anne stood up, walked briskly towards the girl and in a swift movement slapped her hard across the face. It sounded like a whip cracking.

Clouston instantly planted himself between the two women. 'Lady Anne, I will not see such savagery!'

'She is my granddaughter; I shall do as I see fit!'

'Touch her again and I will leave you to deal with this misfortune on your own.'

Lady Anne's eyes were bloodshot, her nostrils swelling like bellows as she swallowed her anger. She looked at the girl over the doctor's shoulder.

'Who the devil told you we were here? Was it Bertha?'

Caroline nodded. Despite the vicious blow the girl showed no hint of tears.

'I knew it,' Lady Anne grunted, returning to her seat. 'That old nag is not to be trusted. The beating I'll give her when we return —'

'Don't!' Caroline said. 'I forced her to tell me. It is my fault, I had to be here.'

'You had to be here!' Lady Anne mocked. 'Whatever for?'

'*He is my father!*' It was then that a single tear rolled down Caroline's cheek, but Lady Anne simply downed another sip of spirit.

Dr Clouston ignored the usual formalities and gently placed his hand on the girl's shoulder. 'Pray, calm down, Miss Ardglass. Have a seat.'

She took a step towards the remaining chair, but then shook her head. 'No – no, I need to see him.' She looked up at Clouston with imploring eyes. 'Please, Doctor, where is he?'

Clouston looked at Lady Anne.

'The second bedroom,' she said, and Caroline immediately ran to the staircase. Clouston heard her frantic steps above, and then a sudden burst of weeping.

'What a brutal way to treat her at a time like this,' he said, casting Lady Anne an infuriated look.

She took another drink, this time from the flask itself, most likely to drown the words she really wanted to utter. Lady Anne was one of the most powerful women in Scotland, unused to having her will or methods questioned by anyone.

'Jed, bring him down.' She cleared her throat. 'We have signed the documents; nobody needs to stay here any longer.' She chuckled bitterly. 'Not after that scandalous entrance of hers.'

Jed went upstairs and fetched Lord Ardglass. The poor man was tightly wrapped in a woollen blanket and swayed almost as if he were drunk . . . or perhaps he'd been purposely intoxicated to keep him docile. Joel was a slender man, like his mother and daughter, and his long face was much like theirs, but tonight he lacked the firm gaze of the two women. Tonight he was a sad, broken figure. Clouston looked at his grey hair and his grimace; the most hopeless expression he'd seen in a long time.

Caroline came behind them, holding a wadded handkerchief to her mouth to muffle her sobs.

Joel tilted his head, and after mouthing the words he managed to speak in a dreamy voice. 'My poor creature . . . you must love me so much.'

He caressed Caroline's face, and she pressed her father's hand against her skin for an instant, before Jed dragged Lord Ardglass outside. Caroline tried to follow, but Lady Anne grabbed her by the arm.

'He is in good hands now,' Clouston whispered, but he knew that no words could console the girl at this time. He also knew she would not be allowed to visit her father; no girl of good society could ever be seen at a mental institution. All in the name of propriety.

'I will pay you a visit soon,' Clouston said as he and Tom walked out. He looked directly into Lady Anne's eyes. 'To make sure the girl is all right.'

The only reply he received was a groan, but it was enough to tell him that Caroline would be left alone. Clouston had gained some power over the mighty Lady Anne – and he would wield it.

Tom saw that Lord Ardglass was settled comfortably in the carriage and they were soon on their way back, the howling of the hounds fading slowly into the distance.

The doctor finally relaxed.

He thought he was through the worst, but he could have never imagined for how long this night would haunt him, how many lives would be wrecked or how many death sentences he had just signed.

1883

24 June

Adolphus McGray felt the pain long before he noticed the soft rocking of the carriage, before he heard the sound of the horses' hooves, before the morning light filtered through his eyelids.

It was a stinging, burning pain in his right hand. Dr Clouston had said it would go away soon, but perhaps he had simply lied. Adolphus would not blame him: the doctor had tried to make things easier, but there were some blows no kind deeds could soften.

When the carriage finally halted the doctor spoke gently. 'Adolphus, we've arrived. I've brought you home.'

Adolphus pretended not to hear. He did not want to wake up to that world. Not yet.

Dr Clouston sighed. 'All right, I will help Amy first and then I'll come back.'

Adolphus heard him descend. His little sister – nicknamed Pansy, as her wide, dark eyes and thick lashes resembled her mother's favourite flower – had travelled in a second carriage, knocked out by Clouston's most potent laudanum, her hands and feet tied up with bandages.

Just thinking of that made Adolphus weep, and a nasty shudder ran through his body. He instinctively raised his right hand to wipe the tears, but then he saw the bulky bandaging and the blood stains.

He still had that image imprinted in his memory. Not of his dead parents, or of his sister stabbing his hand, but of that – creature.

It could not be real. None of it.

He thought he would wait, just for a moment, to calm down, and as soon as he pulled himself together he would step out and help Clouston carry Pansy into the house. It would take one minute.

Unfortunately he did not get the chance. He heard a third carriage enter the square of Moray Place, its horses galloping and neighing wildly.

Adolphus caught a glimpse through his carriage door, and saw that it was a large coach: an elegant landau, lustre black, with its bellows top folded back. It was, despite his misfortunes, a fine summer morning.

Immediately he heard yelling. George, the old butler, was cursing and even the refined Dr Clouston was shouting furiously.

'*How dare you?*' Adolphus heard him yell. 'How dare you come right now?'

A female voice he knew well retorted, and Adolphus had to shake off his grief.

As he jumped down Adolphus saw the tall figure of Lady Glass, still dressed in mourning. Her adult son had died some six months ago, and even though she conformed to the colour etiquette, she also sported the widest hat adorned with black plumes and stuffed birds.

Alistair Ardglass, her very chubby nephew, was helping her down from their carriage. The old lady seemed as anxious about exposing her ankles as she was about damaging the ostrich feathers of her flamboyant fan.

'What d'youse want?' Adolphus cried, even though he knew. He felt a surge of burning rage ascend from his stomach; they were already coming to scavenge his family estate.

The old woman's eyes fixed on Adolphus's hand. She fanned herself as if trying to cleanse the air before her nose. 'Young man . . .'

'Don't give me that condescending shite. I'm twenty-five years old.'

Lady Anne smiled sardonically. 'Very well, *Mr* Adolphus Mc– Oh, silly me! You are now the *only* Mr McGray.' She basked in those words. 'I come to regain possession of this residence.'

'*Fuck off!*'

Lady Anne faltered, as if the words had been a physical blow.

'What's the matter?' Adolphus said. 'Have ye been lifting yer flask this early, Lady Glass?'

'This property still belongs to my aunt,' Alistair intervened, his tone even more arrogant than the old woman's. 'Your father paid her less than half, and since he's passed away we are within our rights to repossess.'

'We can afford to pay it off, ye fat bastard!'

'That is not the point,' said Lady Anne. 'I want my property back. I regret ever offering it to the likes of you.'

'And I'm sorry my dad ever made business with such a drunken bitch.'

Alistair jumped up. 'Don't talk to my aunt like that, you filthy shack-dweller.'

Adolphus thrust a punch right into her nephew's chubby face. Alistair fell backwards on to Lady Anne's bosom, and would have received a good beating, but Adolphus had thrown the punch with his injured hand.

'*Damn it!*' he yelled, feeling the stitches burst. He nearly lost his balance, but Clouston caught him.

The doctor's voice was a deep, menacing growl. 'Lady Anne, you should leave now, if you know what's best for you!'

'Doctor, do not force me to be impudent,' she said, barely noticing her bleeding nephew. 'This matter does not concern you. As Alistair said, we are within our legal rights to –'

'Oh, don't throw that legal waffle at me again!' Clouston snapped. 'If you really thought this was legal, you'd have brought your lawyers to witness it.'

The woman drew her fan close to her chest.

Clouston pulled Adolphus away, staring fixedly at Lady Anne. 'Go away and do not bother this family any more. I will not have you try anything against them.'

'Doctor' – Lady Anne stepped towards them – 'you cannot interfere in my affairs. You cannot do –'

'Lady Anne, you know damn well what I can do!'

She stopped, her face livid, as if she'd hit a brick wall.

'You would never dare,' she whispered, her chest swollen, her bony hands clutching the black feathers.

'*You*,' Clouston said, edging closer, 'would not dare risk it.'

Few people had ever intimidated Lady Anne – and she'd been in the world for a good many years – but for the briefest of moments she looked as meek as a cat.

Adolphus let Clouston drag him into the house. He was about to ask what had shaken Lady Glass so badly, but then he saw that old George was struggling to lift Pansy.

Despite the excruciating pain in his hand, Adolphus rushed to lift his sister and carried her inside. He did not want the neighbours to see her in such a sorry state.

The McGrays would not hear from Lady Anne for a good while.

'There you go,' Clouston said, tying up the last end of the fresh bandages.

Adolphus turned his head back, for Clouston had made him look away while he worked. The bandaging looked as bulky as before, but the cloth was clean and the bleeding had finally stopped.

It had been the ring finger of his right hand: chopped off less than cleanly, leaving only a phalange. It would be an eternal reminder of that terrible night.

And the news would travel fast, eventually becoming part of the city's lore. From then on, everyone would know him as Nine-Nails McGray.

'At least I can still give Lady Glass the two fingers,' he said, smiling bitterly.

Dr Clouston did not laugh. If possible, he looked even more miserable.

'What is it?'

Meticulously, the doctor placed his instruments back into his case, and then he looked at Adolphus with almost fearful eyes. 'I need to take her to the asylum.'

Adolphus could barely reply. His voice came out as a gasp. 'What? She's not a lunatic!'

'Just for the time being. You know she needs proper treatment.'

Adolphus jumped to his feet. 'Ye cannae take her there!'

Clouston could not look him in the eye. 'Please, don't make me say out loud what she's done.'

Adolphus felt a nasty chill. It was as if those words opened the box he'd been trying to keep locked. He frowned, his lip trembled, and for the first time in his adult life he burst into tears in front of someone else. He sank back into the seat, covering his face in utter shame and sobbing like a young child.

A sharp, cold realization of the full weight of the tragedy had struck him.

Amy had murdered their parents.

It materialized as an icy pain in his chest, a physical distress that would not go away for months.

Clouston squeezed Adolphus's shoulder and gave him a few minutes to grieve.

'I will take good care of her,' he said at last. 'You know that, don't you?'

Adolphus used the clean bandages to wipe his tears. 'Aye, I ken.' He looked up at the doctor and asked an unnecessary question: 'When d'ye want to take her?'

'Right away, I'm afraid.'

Adolphus nodded, his eyes lost, and stood up before the sorrow overwhelmed him again. He realized it would be better not to think.

Just move, he told himself. *Don't think, just move.*

He dragged himself to the small study, the room where his father had liked to lock himself with a book or a cigar. Adolphus pushed that image away.

Pansy was still sleeping on the sofa where he had carefully placed her. Betsy, their old servant, had changed her into the first clean garment she'd found: a blue summer dress of thin silk, so the girl had curled up to keep herself warm. Her long eyelashes quivered in her troubled slumber.

Adolphus forced himself to look away. If he saw his sister's young face, he could never let Clouston take her. He steeled himself to pick her up, gently wrapping her in a woollen blanket that George had brought.

The few steps from the study to Clouston's coach were the hardest Adolphus had ever taken, and when the girl was secured on the seat he did not want to leave her.

Clouston closed the carriage door. 'Is there anything I can do?'

Adolphus shook his head. 'Ye've done all ye could.'

Again Clouston patted him on the back. 'I shall come back and check on you very soon. Is that all right?'

Adolphus didn't really hear the question. He only reacted as the doctor was about to leave. 'Wait!' he gasped.

Clouston looked back. 'Yes?'

'What was it she said? Before she attacked ye?'

The doctor cleared his throat and swallowed with difficulty. It would be useless to conceal the truth; old George had heard her too.

'She . . . Well, she mentioned the Devil.'

'But she was delirious,' Clouston had added promptly, almost as a sort of apology. 'She could have said anything.'

Adolphus had spent all day in his late father's study,

with nothing in his head but that short sentence. *She mentioned the Devil* . . .

He only became aware of the hour when George came into the room to light the candles, but that was not enough to stir him. He stayed in the armchair, motionless, deep in thought.

What had it been? Had his senses failed him? Had his own mind snapped as well?

He shook his head.

No.

He *had* seen it. He knew it so well he could not fool himself; he could see it every time he closed his eyes, as if it were scarred on to his retinae: the silhouette of a deformed, twisted figure, moving spasmodically as it made its way towards a window.

And that silhouette had horns.

I

1 January 1889

When summonses come at three in the morning on New Year's Day, you know that you have hard times ahead.

It took me a while to hear the banging at the front door, for I was sleeping deeply, still recovering from my rushed trip back to Edinburgh. I had spent Christmas at my uncle's estate in Gloucestershire – a trip which had not ended well at all.

I realized I'd been dreaming of my late mother, something that had not happened in years. We lost her to a virulent bout of typhoid fever. In a blink she was gone. Even though I could not remember the dream itself, I was left with a vivid, lingering sadness. A remnant of the pain we had endured during her last few days, which had become a recurrent ache throughout my life, like one of those memories triggered by a familiar smell.

In the dream I had been in London, which I missed dearly, for I'd not visited my home city since November, when the most ghastly affairs had forced me to Scotland. I had left the capital in apparent disgrace, under direct orders from the prime minister himself, and unable to tell the complex facts to anyone.

The world still thought I had been jilted by my fiancée, demoted and forced to take on the most humiliating and ridiculous post the British CID could offer. I would be assisting the newly formed Commission for the Elucidation of Unsolved Cases Presumably Related to the Odd and Ghostly. Yes, such a preposterous department indeed exists, and it does *exactly* what its name suggests.

So there I was, exiled from my beloved capital, in a new post which gave me hardly any joy. A sad resident of *Edin-bloody-burgh*, a city where I knew no one except my younger brother Elgie – who would in fact be leaving in a few months – and where the days were even greyer than London's. And yes, dear reader, that is indeed possible.

Now I belonged nowhere.

Just as I thought of that, the thumping on the door resounded in my head, like an insistent nagging, telling me exactly where I was: Moray Place, Edinburgh, at the house of Adolphus 'Nine-Nails' McGray, lying on a hard bed that was older than my housekeeper, who did not hear my calls.

'Joan?' I grunted, rubbing my eyes. *'Joan!'*

No reply.

I sat up, suddenly realizing that it was not a usual knocking; someone was desperately hammering at McGray's door. Why was Joan not answering it? It was not a noise one could easily ignore.

'George!' I called even louder, but McGray's ancient butler did not reply either.

A horrendous realization hit me: for the first time in my thirty-one years of existence I would have to descend to the lowest of the low and answer the blasted door *myself*!

I cursed and cursed as I threw on my dressing robes.

The CID clerks were supposed to arrange proper accommodation for me, but now, nearly two months after my initial transfer, I was still sharing lodgings with the most outlandish, vulgar, infamous man that Scotland has ever spawned.

As I reached the entrance hall I saw the man himself emerging from his library: red-eyed and yawning, yet fully dressed in a pair of his gaudy tartan trousers with a mismatched waistcoat. While I am a little taller and perhaps thinner than the average man, McGray is a towering, broad-shouldered, imposing fellow.

'*The one damned night I manage to drift off!*' he roared, making me jump. 'I'm gonnae punch someone to a pulp!'

I could not tell whether he meant that figuratively – mere minutes after I'd first met 'Nine-Nails' McGray I had witnessed him break a man's arm.

'Frey, where the hell's yer lazy maid?'

'Why, this is *your* bloody household. Where is that old sack of bones whom you call a butler?'

Then we heard a giggle and the swish of clothes. Joan, a stout middle-aged widow, was coming from the back room, wrapping herself in a shawl, with an odd grin on her face. We instantly understood the source of her jolliness: George came right behind her, smoothing out his dishevelled grey hair with one hand and with the other buttoning up his old breeches.

Their smiles vanished as soon as they saw us.

McGray's square jaw dropped to the floor.

Joan, usually the quickest chatterbox in the house, was paralysed with shock. The very corners of her mouth, however, were still tilted upwards.

'Sir . . . shall I get the –'

'*Too* –' I snapped, '*blasted – bloody – late.*'

'Get away, youse kinky rascals!' McGray yelled, but as soon as they were gone he let out the loudest of cackles. *'Joan and auld George!* Frey, did ye ken they were dancing the blanket hornpipe?'

I shivered. 'Yes. I, well, sort of – sort of saw.'

Another shiver, this time shared by McGray.

The banging had become, if anything, more desperate.

'I suppose I'll answer that,' I grunted, pulling the door handle. Icy wind and snowflakes hit my face. The moonless sky was still pitch black, and the only light was the golden gleam of the street lamps, barely enough to recognize the elongated features of Constable McNair.

The scrawny lad seemed to have one of the most unfortunate posts in the Scottish police, being summoned at the most unearthly hours whenever required. That night he looked positively mortified.

'McNair! Are you trying to pulverize this door?'

'Sorry, sirs,' he said, panting. Despite the flickering snow there were trickles of sweat on his temples. 'Superintendent Campbell sent me to fetch youse right away.'

'Someone better be dying, laddie,' said McGray, making the young officer gulp in distress.

'Oh dear,' I groaned, reading his distorted face.

McNair fell silent. We were expectant, but he fixed his eyes on the floor.

'And?' McGray urged.

McNair looked at him rather fearfully. 'It's a young lass – in the lunatic asylum. She *is* dying.'

2

McGray was aghast. He grabbed his moth-eaten overcoat and ran to the small stables.

Tucker, McGray's golden retriever, appeared to understand his master's fear: the dog came from the library and followed him, barking nervously.

I barely had time to throw some clothes on, for McGray had rushed me with unintelligible spurts of Scottish abuse (note to self: purchase Grose's *Dictionary of the Vulgar Tongue*).

Joan apologetically handed me a small cup of black coffee. I gulped it down in one go, wrapped myself in my thickest overcoat and stepped out into the bitter cold of the Edinburgh night.

When I reached the stables McGray was already on Rye, his sturdy chestnut horse, holding a large bull's-eye lantern. The stump between his middle and little fingers was evident under the light.

'Will ye hurry, ye carbuncle face!'

Few times have I seen him so scared, so I ignored the verbal lashing and jumped into my saddle. Philippa, my white Bavarian mare, did not welcome the early ride, and carried me with sulky strides.

I lifted my fur-trimmed collar, resenting the icy wind, but McGray was so anxious he could have ridden through a hurricane and hardly noticed.

I knew what was in his mind. He was imagining the worst.

Pansy, his young sister, could well be the girl in question.

It was difficult not to contemplate that possibility. I'd seen Miss McGray merely a couple of times, but her story was so sad and terrible it moved me whenever I thought of it. To McGray the wound was still sore – perhaps it always would be – and I felt for him as he led the way in a frantic gallop.

We must have been like a thunderous dart through the deserted streets, our horses' hooves and neighing cutting the silence along with Tucker's barking. We crossed the Old Town under relatively good lighting, but beyond it the gas lamps became sparser, and soon I felt as if I were riding through a black wilderness. The asylum was at the southernmost extreme of the city, where a mere handful of large estates sat. Occasionally we would come across a pair of glimmers at the gates to extensive grounds, which under a full moon would have been enough to illuminate that road; unfortunately, that was precisely the darkest night of the lunar calendar, and the only constant light came from McGray's lantern.

How he found his way to the asylum I do not know, but we soon saw the glow of its many windows. That was not a good omen: if almost all its rooms were lit at this odd hour, the place must be in commotion.

We passed through the main gates, where a couple of officers had just a split second to greet us, and we found another two men guarding the main entrance. Another bad sign.

'Why would Campbell send so many people?' I asked out loud, but McGray was not listening. He was already dismounting and I had to run to catch up with him.

'Inspector McGray,' said the officer standing by the door, 'the doctor's waiting for ye.'

'How many o' youse are here?' McGray asked, silencing Tucker's barks with a brief gesture.

'Nine, sir.'

'Nine!'

'Aye. Two at the gates, us two, another one at each o' the two back gates, and three guarding the room where they have the lassie.'

'Jesus,' McGray murmured, making his way in. He knew the corridors of that building like the back of his hand, and again I had to trot to match his pace.

The asylum was indeed agitated: nurses and orderlies ran everywhere, and the eerie shouts of countless inmates filled the place like an army of ghouls.

'Something terrible has happened,' I said, feeling a sudden chill.

'Mr McGray!' A haggard-looking nurse came up to us. 'Thank goodness ye got here so quickly!'

'Miss Smith,' McGray answered, 'what's going on? Was it –'

'Follow me, sirs.' She was already walking briskly. 'Dr Clouston says every second counts.'

She guided us to the west wing, where the most affluent patients stayed. I saw McGray frowning, and I soon understood why. I remembered these corridors too.

'We seem to be going to Miss McGray's chambers,' I said.

'Aye,' said Miss Smith, but as we turned a corner we saw that the girl's door was shut. The adjacent room was open, and three officers were standing nearby, wincing at the horrible, guttural screaming that came from within. 'It's not Miss McGray,' Miss Smith added, pointing at the wide-open door. 'It's all happening in there. Please go in.'

I saw a hint of relief in McGray's eyes as we entered, but it did not last, for that room was an assault on the senses: a deeply upsetting scene, repulsive smell and icy temperature.

The window had been shattered, the very frame ripped out of the walls, and there were glass shards scattered all over a Persian rug. A relentless draught had been slowly killing the fire, and a pathetic glow was all that remained in the hearth.

There we found Dr Clouston. As soon as he saw us he let out a long sigh. His usually neat beard was dishevelled and his ever-assured eyes were sunken.

'Adolphus, Inspector Frey, you are just in time!'

He pointed at a four-poster bed; it was not a humble thing at all, decked with a thick velvet canopy and curtains. The screams came from behind them.

I could not contain a shudder when I saw that poor woman, partially concealed by the drapery.

I cannot say that she lay on her back. She was face upwards, but her spine was contorted brutally, forming a ghastly arch – her chest in the air, her weight resting on her hips and shoulders. Nobody's back could bend like that without breaking a few vertebrae.

Her arms were twisted in odd directions, her hands stiff and her fingers set like claws. To complete the disturbing picture, her eyes were bloodshot and her mouth was wide open, unleashing a succession of horrendous cries.

The room stank of vomit, and I saw that the bed sheets were a repulsive mess. However, that was not the only smell; there was also a chemical trace in the air.

'She doesn't have much time left,' Clouston said, just as the woman's limbs contorted in uncontrollable spasms.

'Oh my . . .' McGray muttered, stepping closer. I knew that somewhere in his mind he must be already considering it a demonic possession. That bent spine, however, was an unmistakable symptom to me.

'Strychnine?' I asked.

Clouston nodded, sombrely. 'In a terrible dose; there's nothing I can do.'

There was nothing *anyone* could do.

McGray pulled a chair from a corner and sat by the bed. His blue eyes flickered over the dying woman, and he spoke in an almost fatherly tone. 'Lassie, who did this to ye?'

'There is no use,' I said. 'She is in the last stages of –'

She roared then, a deep, animalistic sound.

'*Lord . . . Lord . . .*'

She did not manage to speak again. With a last spasm, her back twisted further. I heard bones cracking and then her roaring stopped, followed by a ghastly gagging as she struggled to breathe. Her chest heaved, but I knew no air could reach her lungs now.

Her last exhalation came out in a long, raw-throated croak, and then her chest relaxed, unlike the rest of her body: her spine remained arched and her fingers stiff.

It was only her eyes that suddenly showed peace, as if welcoming the numbness of death. She was gone.

There was a long silence. Nobody dared even move. God knows how long we would have remained thus, but then I felt . . . something.

It was a tingle creeping up my leg and sending a shiver through my body. Everyone looked at me as I contorted to reveal I'd stepped on a trail of ants.

I had not entirely composed myself when I heard a soft noise behind me. As I turned around I saw a large raven pecking at splinters of the window frame. It was barely a glimpse, for after a strident caw the bird flew away.

3

McGray poured a double whisky and handed it to Clouston.

The doctor had dropped into the leather chair behind his desk, and was covering his brow with an exhausted hand.

'Here, Doc,' said McGray, offering him the glass. 'Wet yer whistle, ye'll feel better.'

'At least warmer,' Clouston answered, welcoming the drink with a slurp.

McGray poured another two whiskies and we both sat at the desk. We savoured our drinks for a silent moment, and once the fire in my throat had partially restored my spirits, I was the first one to speak.

'Well, Doctor, can you tell us what happened?'

Clouston stared at the tears of whisky on the sides of his glass. He was so tense the tendons were standing out from his neck. 'Gentlemen, I must have your word. Nothing I'm about to say can leave this room.'

'Ye ken ye can trust me,' McGray said. 'And if this London cock goes out singing, I'll personally cut off his – crest.'

'That shan't be necessary,' I retorted in my most phlegmatic tone. 'Doctor, speak freely. Nothing shall ever pass my lips.'

Clouston still stared at his glass, then took a deep breath and downed the remaining drink in one swift gulp.

'The woman you saw die was Miss Greenwood,' he said, putting the glass down. 'Wonderful nurse, very hard-working. Twenty-four years old. She'd been with us five . . . six years, the poor thing.

'She was doing the night shift. Miss Smith was supposed to be going home, but I believe she forgot something and came back. When she did, she heard screams and rushed to the room. She saw the shattered window and . . . well, Miss Greenwood lying on the floor, crying she'd been poisoned. She could not speak much sense after that.'

'Do you have any idea who did this?' I asked.

'It could only have been one person, Inspector. The inmate she was tending to. The man who smashed that window and ran away.'

He looked down as he uttered a name that would become our curse.

'Lord Joel Ardglass.'

McGray lifted his head, as shocked as if he'd heard a hex. '*What?* That cannae be true! The one Joel Ardglass I've heard of is dead. He's been dead for years!'

Dr Clouston sighed and picked up his glass. 'That's why I need your silence. And I am also going to need another one of these . . .'

I cannot find a word to describe the shock on our faces. The doctor's mouth had run dry at almost every sentence, and by the time he'd told us the entire tale there was hardly any whisky left in his decanter.

'How could you accept such a deal?' I asked.

'I've told you, Inspector. I could not find any other possible way to help that man and his daughter. Do not believe I don't regret it. I know now that I was a damn fool.'

'That bitch, Lady Glass!' McGray hissed, pacing manically around the room. He had not managed to stay in his chair for half the story. 'How could she mock me and my sister when she herself had a lunatic in her viper's nest?'

'It wasn't all to your detriment,' Clouston said. 'Your house in New Town, she was set on taking it from you. It was my blackmail that prevented it.'

McGray pressed a hand to his forehead. He was gripping his empty glass fiercely.

'Dr Clouston!' I said, half smiling. 'I'd never have thought you had that in you!'

Clouston smiled wryly, pouring the last drops of whisky. 'I never thought it myself.'

'Are you certain it was Lord Ardglass who poisoned her?' I asked.

'Oh, there's no doubt about it, Inspector. You heard the girl herself trying to say *Lord*. We have a few quite affluent patients, but not any other with a title. Some inmates called him the Lord of Totty Head, others, Lord Bampot.'

'She could have been delirious,' I said.

'Why would he run away if he hadn't poisoned her?' McGray snapped. 'Which reminds me, Doc, have ye sent anyone to look for him?'

'I didn't think it sensible to send people out – it is too dark and the man is too dangerous. I sent one of my orderlies, Tom, a very strong man, to warn the neighbouring estates.'

'Ye thought well.' McGray nodded. Then he called

some of the officers in and sent them out to look for Lord
Ardglass. 'It's likely to be useless,' he said, finally sitting
down. 'As ye said, it's too dark to find a bloody elephant
out there, but we must at least try.'

'In the meantime, there is a lot to do,' I added, thinking
of a similar case I'd seen in my early days at London's Scotland Yard. 'Doctor, I need you to ask your staff to check for
any missing items. I am looking for materials Lord Ardglass could have planned to use for his escape: weapons,
money . . . Count your horses, of course. And also, please
ask them to check particularly for missing rat venom.'

'Is that where you think he got the poison?' McGray
asked.

'Most likely. Strychnine is usually the main ingredient.'

'Now I remember,' said McGray. 'Wasn't that what the
Rugeley Poisoner used?'

'The very thing,' I said. The Rugeley Poisoner had been
executed decades ago, but he was still fresh in the nation's
memory, particularly since his list of victims included
some of his own children.

Clouston rang a bell to summon the head nurse. 'Anything else you need, Inspectors?'

'The patient's full history,' I said.

'And we need to question yer staff,' McGray jumped in,
'and have a proper look at that room.'

'We also need to take the body for a post-mortem,' I
said. 'Dr Reed is going to have a very nice New Year's
Day. Oh, and I must send an urgent message to Superintendent Campbell: as soon as we know whether Lord
Ardglass got away on horse or foot we can establish the
extent of the area to search. And we will have to inform

the press – people in the city will need to take precautions if we cannot find him soon.'

Clouston cleared his throat. 'I'm afraid that won't be possible.'

'Excuse me?'

'I have just told you, Inspector, that there is a damning legal statement I signed . . .'

I chuckled. 'Doctor, you *cannot* be serious!'

'I'm afraid I am. Nothing must leave this room.'

'Are you trying to protect Lady Anne's reputation?'

Clouston jumped to his feet and I regretted my derision.

'*Of course not!* I am trying to save my career and the salary that sustains my family! I am head of this great institution and a respected lecturer. I have written and preached much about the rights and treatment that people with mental illnesses deserve, yet I admitted an inmate without thoroughly checking his sanity certificate. And this is not a man to go unnoticed: people will revel in gossip and my name will inevitably come out. Lady Anne would as soon sue me for libel. I could lose my medical licence. I curse the day I let him in, but there is nothing I can do to mend that now.'

'A demented man is at large,' I insisted. 'Are you telling me you are willing to leave the entire city at the mercy of a lunatic for the sake of keeping your good name?'

Clouston pressed a tired hand to his forehead and sank back on to his seat. I felt truly sorry for him, suddenly cornered by his own desire to help others.

'You must excuse me,' I said, 'but surely you understand that we need to conduct a thorough investigation. We cannot let this man walk away at his leisure.'

'Frey,' McGray intervened, 'I won't argue with ye right now. Ye've had a couple o' drams; drinks get ye too bold for yer own good.'

'As much as I appreciate your attempt at wit, this is *murder* we are dealing with. I must insist that we put these feeble scruples aside and –'

McGray grabbed me by the arm and dragged me out of the office. 'Sorry, Doctor. Ye don't need to hear what I'm gonnae tell this dandy.' He banged the door and whispered irately: 'Keep yer sanctimonious police procedure shite to yerself! I won't let ye ruin Clouston's career.'

'Sanctimonious! Is that not too long a word for you?'

I thought he was going to punch me. 'It's not a bloody joke, Frey.'

'You owe your loyalties to Clouston and I understand that. In fact, I understand it too well. Which makes me think it would be best for everyone if you were not involved in this case.'

'How could I not be?' McGray rubbed his face in frustration. 'When my sister and me were in the worst way he stepped in. Haven't ye just heard? He even saved the bloody house where yer staying now!'

'Not because I want to, I may add –'

'Of course I bloody owe him!' McGray banged his fist on the wall. 'Now that he needs help, I'll do anything I can, even if it takes me all the way to hell.'

Then he turned and went back in, slamming the door mightily.

'I'm sure you will,' I said with a sigh, 'and you will drag me with you.'

4

While we waited for our forensic man to arrive, Clouston let us use his office to make our preliminary enquiries. The first person we called was the head nurse, Cassandra Smith.

An unassuming woman in her late thirties, she could not have been called handsome, with her brittle hair, dull skin and wrinkles around her eyes. Her hands, long and lean, had been mercilessly roughened by work. Still, there was a certain sharpness in the way she talked and held our stares. That, and her immaculate apron, told me she was a very intelligent, diligent person. She was, understandably, very stressed, but seemed to compose herself rather well: she must have seen things as grim as this before.

'I must apologize for those ants,' she said before we had a chance to ask her anything. I could tell she was suppressing some of her Scottish dialect for my benefit. 'That entire corridor has been infested for a while. We've tried everything, but not even the winter's affected them.'

She was looking at me with rather motherly concern, and I had to clear my throat in embarrassment.

'It is quite all right, miss,' I replied as I jotted her name in my pocket notebook.

'Clouston tells us ye weren't supposed to be around,' McGray said.

'Aye, Mr McGray,' she replied with some familiarity; she must know him well, after looking after his sister for five years. 'I was taking the morning off to see my father. He hasn't been well – very auld, the poor man.'

'Sorry to hear that, hen. So why did ye come back?'

'I thought I wouldn't need my hat. Very silly of me – in the small hours on a winter's night.'

I frowned a little. 'What time was that?'

'I'd say past midnight, sir.'

'Were you heading off that late?'

'Aye, sir. That's when my shift ended.'

'Do you live in the city?'

'Aye, sir. Not far from the Meadows.'

I frowned a little more. 'Was it safe to go home on your own, at that time, on such a dark night?'

'Oh, I wasn't alone, sir. Tom was leaving as well and he has a cart, y'see. I usually try to match my shifts with his or other people's, Dr Clouston included. Sometimes it's not possible; then I simply spend the night here.'

I nodded, making a quick note to question this Tom character too.

'Tell us what happened when ye came back,' McGray asked.

For a moment Miss Smith fixed her dark eyes on the wall, her lips tense. 'Well, as I told youse, it was too cold so I asked Tom to come back. I went to my desk, in the nurses' quarters, and it was then that I heard a noise. Shattering plates – I've heard it so many times when the patients throw their meals at us. Then I heard her screaming. I didn't recognize her voice at first; she sounded odd. I guess she must have been choking.'

'Did you go directly to the room?'

'Well, no. First I ran back to the entrance; I was going

to call Tom. I knew something was wrong and I didn't want to go up there on my own. We have a number of violent patients.'

'Did you manage to call him?'

'No. I hadn't reached the door when I heard the window smashing. It was an awful sound, sir, and Miss Greenwood sounded in anguish, so I turned on my heels and went directly to her.'

'That was bold,' Nine-Nails said.

'Aye, Mr McGray. I probably shouldn't have, but when I found her I was glad I did. The poor girl was shaking and – well, youse saw her.'

'Dr Clouston said she mentioned poison.'

'Aye. She said the word "poisoned". Once. I'm surprised she managed to talk at all when youse were there. She had convulsions and then vomited, and –'

She swiftly produced a handkerchief and covered her mouth. There were tears pooling in her eyes.

'Were you close to her?' I asked.

'I try to be close to all the girls,' she said with a certain pride, 'but Miss Greenwood was particularly quiet. She kept a lot to herself.'

'Can you tell us anything about her personal life at all?'

'Well, a little. I know that she had no kin in Edinburgh. She was born in Cumbria and apparently she had to come north after some . . . awkward family affair.'

I looked up. 'Do you know anything about that affair?'

'Not really. She wasn't keen to talk about it, and it's not my place to speculate. If youse want details about her life, the best person to talk to would be Miss Oakley.'

'Another nurse, I assume?'

'Aye. She's one of the most recent hires. In fact, Miss Greenwood was in charge of her training. They became very close.'

'Can ye call her?'

'I'm afraid she's been ill for the past couple of days, but I can give youse her address. She's a very well-mannered lass, and I'm sure she'll answer all your questions.'

She was already reaching for a pen and paper from Clouston's desk. When she handed me the note I saw how swollen and reddened her eyes were.

'One last thing,' I said. 'Did anything else odd happen yesterday? Anything at all, no matter how inconsequential it may seem.'

She twisted her mouth almost wryly. I sensed trouble coming.

'Indeed, sir. Two things. Well, one is rather silly.'

'Tell us.'

She hesitated, but in the end she did speak. 'I mention this simply because I know youse will hear it from some of the girls. The moon.'

McGray leaned forwards. 'The moon? D'ye mean the lack of it?'

'Aye, sir. Some patients have told us they've seen ... ghosts, apparitions ... lurking around, always on new moon nights.'

McGray's eyes widened. His pupils cradled that spark that I've come to fear.

'Silly indeed,' I said in a monotone, 'but I shall take note of it anyway.'

'What d'ye ken about those ghosts?' McGray was angling now.

Miss Smith shrugged. 'Not much, sir. I've heard a few patients and orderlies talking about dark, shadowy figures, apparently wandering through the corridors and sometimes the gardens, but only when there's no moon in the sky.'

'Take good note o' that, dandy,' McGray told me.

'You mentioned two things,' I prompted, trying to put an end to the talk of ghosts. 'The second is . . . ?'

Miss Smith looked intently at McGray. 'That's a wee bit more . . . delicate.'

'Go on.'

'Youse noticed that all this mayhem happened in the room right next to Miss McGray's.'

I could see Nine-Nails slowly clenching his hands, his entire body becoming tense. 'Aye.'

'Well, sir, that's not by coincidence. They were – sort of friends.'

'*Friends?* What d'ye mean?'

'Mr McGray, as you know, Pansy – excuse me for talking about her with such familiarity – she never said a word after Dr Clouston brought her in. After her violent fits receded, she became what youse see now: silent, barely aware of her surrounds; all she does is stare out of the window . . .'

McGray turned his face away.

'I'm sorry, sir.'

He shook his head. 'Don't apologize, hen. Go on.'

'Well, Lord Bampot – you'll excuse me, we came to call him that because of the privacy issue – he liked his books. They seemed to be the one thing that kept him from another suicide attempt – he suffered acute depression – so we encouraged him to read aloud for other patients.

Pansy was still rather unstable, but she seemed to find his voice soothing. And then, when she finally became quiet but absent, those readings had the opposite effect: where everything else had failed, they appeared to bring her a little nearer to us. I could see the life coming back into her eyes. I could almost swear that I saw her leaning forwards or gripping the arms of her chair whenever Lord Bampot read an exciting passage of Wilkie Collins.'

'How come no one told me?' McGray asked.

'Oh, sir, I never thought much of it. It was all so faint. I'd compare it to her reactions when you come to visit: a slight tilt o' the head, a flicker in her eyes, a squeeze when ye hold her hand, that sort of thing.'

I arched an eyebrow. 'So why do you think it is relevant now?'

Miss Smith's mouth was tenser, fine wrinkles deepening around her lips.

'I'm sure I heard them talking.'

I saw McGray's chest swell, and I could almost feel the heartbeat he'd skipped.

'What! When?' he asked, gasping.

'Last night, a few hours before it all happened, I'd say. Lord Bampot was in Pansy's room; I took him there to read for her. I stayed around as usual, but I had to leave briefly for an emergency. I left the door ajar, of course, and stayed close enough to hear if anything happened. I came back a few minutes later, and just as I was about to reach the door – I heard them.'

McGray stood up and began pacing as before, covering his mouth with his bad hand.

'That I *was* going to tell ye, Mr McGray,' Miss Smith added. 'I was going to ask Dr Clouston to send ye a message the next morning – well, today.'

McGray meditated for a moment, stroking his stubble. 'Yer absolutely sure?'

'Aye, sir. Not a shade of doubt.'

'Could ye . . . hear what they said?'

She sighed, frowning. 'I'm sorry. They were whispering. I couldn't make out a word. I didn't want to interrupt them, so I stood by the door until they were finished, which was very soon. Then I waited a good while, and only walked in when I was sure they wouldn't resume.'

'What happened then?' I asked.

'It was suppertime, sir, so I took Lord Bampot back to his room to be fed. After that I made a note to tell Dr Clouston first thing in the morning. I thought that, if Mr McGray agreed, of course, we could repeat the experiment: pretend to leave them alone and see if the lass spoke again.'

McGray turned around and stepped slowly towards the window, simply to stare out in silence.

I looked back at Miss Smith after a moment. 'Had you left them alone before?'

'Oh, occasionally, sir, but never for more than a couple of minutes and I'd always be within hearing distance. However, I don't tend to them the entire time. It could have happened that a more junior nurse or an orderly left them alone for longer.'

'We should probably question them too,' I said, but there was a sombre look on Miss Smith's face.

'Well, sir . . . one of those nurses youse just saw die.'

5

My pocket watch showed a quarter past five when Dr Reed arrived, his face lined with pillow marks.

I still cannot believe he is the chief forensic for Edinbugh's CID. The chap is in his early twenties but he looks sixteen; with his plump cheeks, childish eyes and totally hairless chin he always reminds me of a fidgety cocker spaniel. The young man is smart and capable, that I cannot deny, but as a fresh graduate his practical experience can only be described as limited.

I sighed impatiently as I saw him lean over Miss Greenwood's dead body, his eyes open a little too wide for my liking.

'It does look like strychnine poisoning,' he said. 'Typical arching of the back and . . .'

'Can you perform a full post-mortem?' I urged, for I knew all the symptoms by heart. 'And I need you to look thoroughly; do not let the obvious signs distract you from other possibilities.'

'Aye, sir.'

The body was taken away then, covered with a thick blanket that could not conceal the dreadful contortion of the woman's back.

McGray and I were left in the wrecked room to do our own search. I was about to kneel down to look under the bed when someone knocked at the door. It was Sergeant

Millar, a young man with possibly the fieriest ginger hair I have ever seen. He was struggling to catch his breath.

'Sirs, we found this trail of footprints in the gardens. Youse should come and see it.'

'Once we've inspected this room,' I told him, but the young man faltered.

'What is it?' McGray asked.

'Well – sirs, it's snowing hard. The trail will be gone soon.'

McGray and I turned to the window and immediately understood the urgency: the large snowflakes were not fluttering but falling hard. I calculated that we had a matter of minutes before every mark on that lawn was covered.

'Come on, Frey. The laddie's right.'

I drew nearer to McGray as we walked to the gardens. 'We need more hands, McGray. This is becoming too complex to handle on our own: we have people to question, a room to inspect, Lord Ardglass's medical files to go through, the surroundings to search . . . and then your sister to –'

McGray stopped, a hand over his mouth, the stump of his missing finger standing out. 'Yer right,' he groaned. 'And it bloody annoys me when yer right. It gets ye all giddy.'

'McGray . . .'

'Send a note to Campbell. Tell him we need an extra couple of DIs, but *I* will assign their duties. Understood?'

He and Millar were away before I could respond. I asked a nurse to bring me pen and paper, and hastily scribbled a message to the superintendent. On my way out

I gave it to one of the officers guarding the entrance, to be delivered immediately, no matter where Campbell was.

'Frey, here!' McGray shouted as soon as I stepped out. I saw him following Sergeant Millar, who lighted the grounds with a large lantern.

As I approached I saw the sharp shadows of a messy trail. I could imagine a grown man stamping and kicking the snow as he marched northwards.

'No missing horses,' Millar was saying, his hair alarmingly orange in the light. 'He went on foot.'

'Which means he might still be close,' McGray said with a note of excitement.

We followed the footprints to the limits of the garden, where a thick, tall brick wall stood.

'Did he climb over?' I asked, but then Millar shed the light on a small servants' gate. The oak was old and worn out, with a rusty iron latch that had been ripped off.

I nearly leaped forwards but Nine-Nails held me by the shoulder.

'Don't play the heroine,' he said as he unholstered his revolver. As soon as I followed his example he kicked the shabby gate open.

Millar panned the light from left to right as we walked into the impenetrable darkness of the surrounding fields.

'How could anyone find his way like this?' I muttered, straining to see any hint of light ahead of us.

'Guard our backs,' McGray told me. 'Lord Bampot might still be around.'

As soon as I turned I understood the vulnerability of our position – and how remote our chances of finding anything were: the lantern could illuminate a few yards around us, but the world beyond was all silence and blackness.

'We should go back,' I said.

'Grow a pair, Frey.'

My head turned back and forth, both watching out and trying to keep pace with them. 'This is reckless! We are not going to –'

'*Och, shush!*'

I said no more, not because of McGray's grunt but because the snow was falling into my mouth; it was becoming a downright blizzard.

Nine-Nails quickened his pace, trying desperately to follow the tracks. I heard him and Millar panting, and saw my own breath as bursts of steam. I could see the footprints becoming ever smoother, and within minutes I hardly recognized any trail other than ours. A gust of wind swept past us, as if the very elements were determined to erase any trace of the killer.

McGray went on nevertheless, until the snow on the ground was totally even, and then quite a few more yards. He finally spat out every imaginable curse – and a few I had never heard – and kicked the snow in frustration.

'There is more we can achieve in the asylum,' I said, but Nine-Nails did not reply; he simply turned and started to make his way back, his chest heaving.

I understood his anger all too well. If a man is not caught quickly, it is most likely he will never be found. We might have just lost our best chance.

6

Almost as if to compensate for our defeat, McGray went straight to see his sister. It was nearly six o'clock and he persuaded Miss Smith to wake Pansy an hour earlier than usual.

'Dr Clouston doesn't like to disrupt the patients' routine,' she was saying as she led the way, a breakfast tray in her hands. I was glad she did not call them *inmates*. 'A predictable timetable seems to help soothe the mind.'

'This has hardly been an ordinary morning,' I said, looking at McGray out the corner of my eye.

'And that is the only reason I'm agreeing to this,' Miss Smith replied. 'The poor girl must have heard everything . . .'

We reached Amy's room, where Clouston was waiting for us.

'I've found a carbon duplicate of Lord – Lord Bampot's file,' he said, handing me a thick folder. 'You may keep it for as long as you need.'

McGray was still rather agitated, so I took the papers. 'Excellent, Doctor. We appreciate it.'

'We were going to see Pansy,' McGray jumped in.

'Oh, so Miss Smith has told you?'

'Aye. Was she . . .' McGray lowered his voice. 'Was she scared?'

'I'm afraid so,' Clouston said, looking down. 'I checked

on her, right before I sent for you. She was crouching in a corner of the room, covering her ears. I had to ask one of the nurses to give her something to make her sleep. A very mild dose, of course.'

McGray nodded. 'Thanks, Doctor.'

'She should be all right by now,' said Miss Smith, dextrously holding the tray with one hand and unlocking the room's door with the other. 'I'll stir her so you can visit her.'

'Thank you,' I said, stepping forwards, but Nine-Nails instantly turned to me and pressed his hand against the door frame, his thick arm blocking my way.

'I'm sorry, Frey. This is private.'

Had things been different, I would not have even attempted to step into the room. I knew the full extent of the McGrays' tragedy, and after the dreadful night the girl must have had, I actually wished I could let Nine-Nails have some time with her. However, there was much more at stake.

'I wish it were private,' I said as gently as possible – I knew he'd not hesitate to beat my face to a pulp if I confronted him, 'but your sister may be a crucial witness. I need to be present.'

He glared at me, though the rest of his features seemed unaffected. I do not understand how it happens: those eyes of his can turn from playful to bloodshot within a blink.

'Please yerself,' he spat out in the end. 'But let her have some dignity. Let Miss Smith get her out o' bed.'

I took a small step back. 'That I cannot deny her.'

McGray, Clouston and I waited in a moody silence.

A few minutes later, Miss Smith said we could enter. I saw she had lit the oil lamp, for the winter morning was still as dark as the middle of the night.

The room felt a touch warmer than the corridor, and it smelled of lavender. Somehow those little details made me feel awkward, as if I were truly invading, and the feeling worsened as soon as I caught a glimpse of Nine-Nails' sister. I had seen her before, but I felt a pang of commiseration as painful as that dreadful first time. I wondered if McGray experienced it every time he visited.

Miss Smith was helping Pansy to sit at a little table by the window. She'd wrapped the girl's thin body in a soft dressing gown, and had also refreshed her face and carefully netted her dark hair into a chignon.

She was a very pretty thing to behold, with alabaster skin, soft features and delicate lips, and there was a certain ... lightness about her, as if she were for ever floating in a limbo unreachable to anybody else.

I knew that she was in her early twenties, and it hurt me to think that she ought to be out in town, going to dances, giggling with other young women and making men sigh. Instead, she was wasting away her youth in that institution.

Her wide eyes, as I remembered, were strikingly similar to her brother's, only that instead of blue, hers were dark like obsidian, and they stared at everything with an intensity that was rather disturbing, seeing but not seeing. Right then they were gazing at the breakfast tray.

'You have some visitors, miss,' said the nurse, after laying a napkin on the girl's lap. As ever, there was no reaction, and I had the instant feeling that our efforts would be wasted there.

I purposely stood at a distance, produced my little writing pad and pencil, and let McGray take charge. This was his arena.

He kneeled on one knee before his sister, and his premature winkles softened immediately. He took one of her small, pale hands with a gentleness no one would have expected from him.

'Pan? Pansy, it's me.'

I noticed a slight tremble in Amy's hand, which McGray must have felt.

'Are ye all right?'

Amy blinked, but that was all.

'It must've been michty scary, all that noise in the other room. I want to make sure yer all right.'

Again, no reaction. McGray took a deep breath, then spoke most carefully, as if treading over broken glass. 'I have to tell ye – a young lass died behind that wall.'

All our eyes were on her, trying to detect any twitch or shiver, but nothing happened. I could tell that all her muscles were tense, particularly her slender neck.

McGray softly squeezed her hand.

'Yer friend, that Lord Bampot . . . we think he did it.'

Initially nothing happened, but a few seconds later, finally, we saw some movement.

Pansy's chest began to swell. She inhaled and inhaled, slowly, making the faintest hiss, until her lungs were full. She held the air in, and then my eyes fell on Dr Clouston. The man looked horrified, his eyes wide open, his hands clenched tight, and his lips quivered as if he were mouthing words to himself. Could he be expecting Pansy to have another fit of violence?

A moment later she breathed out, much to the doctor's relief.

At least she seems somewhat aware of what has been said, I wrote, the rubbing of my pencil sounding terribly loud in the sepulchral silence. When I looked up I nearly gasped, for Amy's head had tilted towards me.

She was not looking at my eyes but at my chest, perhaps at the notepad and the source of the noise. Her face, though, was as impassive as usual.

'We think Lord Bampot did it,' McGray reiterated. 'Nae, we're almost certain, Pan. No one else could've done it.'

The girl's eyes remained fixed in my direction, however unfocused.

'Miss Smith tells me he used to read for ye. All the time. Is that true?' Again, no reply. 'Pansy, if ye ken anything, ye must tell us . . .'

Even a sane girl would have felt daunted, I thought, with the inquisitive eyes of her brother, a nurse, a doctor and the brooding, visibly intelligent stranger fixed on her. What could we expect from such a frail creature who had spoken only once in five years?

McGray was growing impatient. 'Pansy, he has *killed*. That lass had a horrible, horrible death. We saw it happen and I can tell ye, nobody deserves that. Now that man's out there and we've no idea what he could be up to. Can ye help us?'

I almost winced at the futility of the question – and McGray's eyes, full of useless expectation.

'We need to find him. If there's anything ye ken . . .' McGray looked down, rubbed his forehead in despair.

When he lifted his face his eyes glimmered with pooling tears and a dark, ominous rage he could barely contain. 'Ye talked to him. *Why won't ye talk to me?*'

The longing note in that phrase made me feel terribly sorry. For both of them. That little scene might have been frustrating to me, but I knew I could not possibly imagine McGray's anguish, after spending the last five years yearning for a response.

I started to make another note, but then there was a sudden rustle. I looked up to see that Pansy had drawn her hands away and was now grasping the green velvet of the chair's arms. In a spasm she pushed herself upwards, rising from the seat and making Miss Smith squeal. McGray and Clouston were so shocked they could not move; all they did was follow Amy with perplexed eyes.

She came to me, her soft steps barely making a sound, her dark eyes fixed on the pad. Once more I had the impression of her floating like a phantom.

I stirred a little, unsure whether or not to move, but then McGray and Clouston raised their hands in an almost identical gesture, bidding me to stay still.

Very slowly, as if it were immensely heavy, she lifted her arm. I suddenly realized how small she was; her eyes were level with my chest, and she had to bring her hand high to reach the pencil. She pulled gently and I let her have it.

I thought she would also take the pad out of my hands; instead, she wielded the pencil, holding it as if it were a dagger, and drew shaky squiggles while I held the paper. Her hand obscured whether she was tracing shapes, words or anything meaningful at all.

Then, accidentally, the back of her hand touched my fingertips. It was the briefest of contacts, but enough for me to feel how cold her skin was.

We both started. She let go of the pencil, which fell between us, and then dropped her arm as if it had become lifeless.

Nobody moved, blinked or breathed for a seemingly endless moment, none of us sure quite what had just transpired. McGray's jaw had dropped, and Clouston's face had never been graver.

We still held on after the initial shock passed, waiting to see if she would move again, but it did not happen. Miss Smith was the first to react. She went to Amy and tenderly led her back to the armchair.

'There, there,' she said. 'I'm going to give you some breakfast now.'

Miss Smith tried to put the spoon in Pansy's hand, expecting her to hold it as she had the pencil, but the girl's fingers would not grip.

If anything, she looked more lost, more absent than ever. An empty vessel once again.

As soon as we left the room I took a deep, soothing breath.

I was expecting Nine-Nails to look utterly drained, but I was mistaken. He snatched my notebook and scoured it as if his life depended on it.

Clouston came up behind him and peeped over McGray's shoulder.

'How extraordinary,' he muttered.

'What did she do?' I asked, for I'd not had a chance to look at the scribble myself. McGray showed me the pad.

Over my regular hand there was a mess of meandering lines, as if scribbled by a toddler. Nevertheless, the pencil undeniably spelled a twisted word:

Marigold

Our faces hovered over the page, all frowning in incomprehension. When I looked up I found McGray leering at the writing, his face so unsettled I feared – no, I *knew* – he was about to drag us into very dark waters.

'All the words in the language,' he whispered, an eerie tremor in his voice, 'and she chooses this one. Why? What can she mean?'

'If anything at all,' I added, shattering the mysticism of the moment, and he cast me a bitter look.

Clouston was about to say something but a young nurse came up, panting and babbling about a patient having a fit.

'You'll have to excuse me,' he said, and disappeared swiftly down the corridor.

I welcomed the brief privacy and whispered to Mc-Gray, who was assessing every curve and smudge on the paper with a rather manic expression, 'McGray, are you absolutely certain you want to take on this case?'

He raised an eyebrow. 'What d'ye mean?'

'You might regret it,' I said, rather prophetically. 'You are far too involved, personally involved with all of these people. An inspector must have all his faculties at his disposal or else –'

'Don't get so twitchy, Frey.'

'Twitch– How can you assure me you will make sensible decisions?'

'I don't need to assure ye of shite, Frey. I'm the commanding officer.'

'Please, leave this case to me! I give you my word, I will do everything . . .'

'*Leave this case to ye!* Do yer black-pudding brains seriously think I'll step aside right now? She's spoken, Frey! *Spoken!* And ye see this writing? This is the most promising thing she's done in years!'

'I rest my case,' I said. 'You are not thinking straight already.'

'And what d'ye expect me to do? Take up knitting?'

'Do you not still have that case of the old woman frightened out of her wits in her cellar? Or those will-o'-the-wisps you wanted to investigate before the weather is too warm?'

McGray snorted. 'Do *not* mock me now, Frey.'

'I am not mocking. I simply think that you should take your mind off this case. It will not do any good to anybody that —'

I did not manage to finish, for somebody at the end of the corridor called our names.

It was Constable McNair, who'd gone back to the City Chambers after summoning us early that morning. Now he was pallid, breathless and shaking, and his hair and shoulders were covered in snow. To my astonishment, the young officer I had sent to Campbell with a message came running up behind him, equally agitated and snow-dusted.

'What are you doing here?' I snapped. 'I told you to deliver my message immediately!'

'And I did, sir,' he cried, 'but —'

'The superintendent sent us back,' McNair interrupted. 'He needs youse in New Town.'

'What – right now?'

'Aye. There's been an attack . . .'

'We're still working on the last one, laddie!' Nine-Nails shouted.

McNair himself looked utterly puzzled.

'I know, sir, but the superintendent said youse would understand. He said youse must know that the victim was that stuck-up auld woman – Lady Anne Ardglass.'

7

We galloped in a mad race across the city, our backs and faces lashed by the growing snowstorm.

Despite the darkness and dismal weather, Edinburgh was slowly coming to life. As we crossed the slums of the Royal Mile merchants, fishermen and factory workers descended from the towering tenements that flanked both sides of the street, ready to start their long working days. Some of them would labour in crowded factories well into the night, earning but pennies for their efforts.

I knew well where we were heading – I'd had the misfortune of meeting Lady Anne the previous November, when she had most unceremoniously offered me the hand of her granddaughter Caroline. Despite the dreadful news of the attack and the million thoughts about the asylum murder revolving in my head, a part of me was silly enough to fear an awkward encounter with the feisty young woman.

Nine-Nails would not be too pleased to see the Ardglass clan either. Their troubled history with the McGrays – as far as I understood it – ran a fair way back.

Soon we arrived at the elegant end of Dublin Street, which Lady Anne owned in its entirety. The corner house – the one with the widest, most lavish Georgian facade – was her main residence; the other four or five adjacent properties she'd let to aristocratic families for a small fortune.

All the mansion's windows glowed from within, large chandeliers visible through fine lace curtains, and there was an impressively stiff butler waiting for us at the entrance, standing stoically despite the blizzard, snow melting on his face. He bowed when he saw us and called a footman to take care of our horses. Not wasting a second, he let us in.

I'd visited the house before, for a formal ball, when all the halls had been bustling with guests, chatter and music. That morning, however, it looked like an entirely different place, its ample rooms barren, our voices and steps echoing beneath the high ceilings. Even though there were a dozen fires well distributed throughout the property, they were barely enough to keep the enormous corridors at a comfortable temperature in this weather.

A short, plump maid with silver hair appeared, carrying a cut-glass decanter. She had large, gentle eyes but a deep fold had long ago set in her brow. She looked rather shaken, as if she'd not slept in days, yet still managed to smile warmly at us.

'Gentlemen,' she said, 'thank youse for coming so soon!' She looked at the butler. 'Forster, I can lead them now.'

'Is that the police?' asked another female voice, coming from one of the back rooms.

Caroline Ardglass herself.

She was an attractive creature, I must admit, with full lips, pointy nose and chin, and dark eyes with a spark I can only define as cunning. Her elegant, hourglass figure was wrapped in a perfectly fitting black velvet dress, and she walked with total poise.

When she saw me her eyes opened wide. It was only for an instant, and then she hid her surprise with sourness.

'Why, my future husband!'

McGray's perplexed eyes went from her to me. 'Future what?'

I rolled my eyes. 'God, I do not have the patience to go through –'

'Och, lassie,' McGray told her with a cackle, 'ye don't wannae touch this giddy goose with a bargepole! He'll be a greater pain than one o' those whimsy poodles ye have to keep grooming all the bloody time.'

Caroline looked at my fur-trimmed collar. 'We'd certainly fight over wardrobe space.'

I cleared my throat, surprised by how quickly they'd teamed up against me.

'We have come to investigate the attack on your grandmother,' I said before the conversation became even more twisted. 'Is she well enough to talk?'

'I will take it from here, Bertha,' Caroline whispered, taking the decanter out of the maid's hands.

'Are ye sure, miss?'

'Yes. Bring me some breakfast, please. And the gentlemen may want tea.'

The woman retreated reluctantly, not without squeezing Caroline's arm with affection. It was one of those gestures that reveal a person's entire character; Bertha must love Caroline like she would her own child.

'Follow me, please,' Miss Ardglass said, walking towards the staircase. 'My grandmother is a little disturbed, but I'm sure she will answer your questions once she's had her morning drink.'

She seemed overly calm, all things considered. Whether it was genuine detachment or calculated concealment, I would soon be able to tell.

'Miss, did ye see or hear anything?' McGray asked.

Caroline chuckled. 'You might say so, sir. I saw it all, but it is probably better that you question my grandmother first.'

She led us to the master bedroom and knocked on the door. 'Grandmama? The police are here.'

It was an old man's voice that replied. 'Do come in, Miss Ardglass.'

So we did, and as soon as the door was open we were hit by the scents of Earl Grey mixed with a heavy hint of wine and spirits. These were the chambers of a heavy drinker.

Lady Anne was prostrated on a velvet chaise longue, but as we walked in all I could see were the embroidered folds of her skirts and a bony arm, stretched out and holding a squat brandy glass that waited to be filled.

A middle-aged physician obscured my view of the rest of Lady Glass, leaning over her as he spoke soothingly.

'There, there, my lady. You have been very brave.'

'*It hurts so much!*' she replied, her voice a weak wail. 'Dr Wyatt, make it stop!'

'I am almost done, almost done. This arnica will help the skin heal.'

McGray cleared his throat so loudly I feared he'd regurgitate a globule of something nasty. The doctor took the hint, and as he moved aside we had our first glimpse of the old woman's face.

Four long fingermarks were clearly imprinted on her

left cheek – fresh welts, for the reddened skin was beginning to turn purple. I could tell that her aged skin would bruise mightily.

The instant she saw us Lady Glass flipped from frail to manic.

'*You two!*' she yelled, so loudly and so earnestly that I immediately knew her injuries were less than life-threatening.

'Lady Anne, we have been sent to –'

'I ask for protection and they send me vermin!' she cried, biting her knuckles in the most theatrical way. Dr Wyatt was leaning down to comfort her, the fake sobs filling the room until McGray yelled: 'Shut that hole in yer face, ye auld hag! Else I'll get yer cheeks even!'

Dr Wyatt was appalled. '*Sir!* How can you possibly talk like that to a fragile –'

McGray took a powerful step towards him, and the little man nearly fell backwards.

'How can I what?'

'I shall wait outside,' the doctor muttered, and then trotted to the door on his shaky legs.

'Get my cheeks even?' Lady Anne said, her eyes shooting venom. 'For that you would need a full set of fingers.'

I saw that McGray was ready to verbally destroy her, and I spoke through my teeth. 'Save it. The sooner they talk, the sooner we can leave.'

His fists were clenched and shaking with rage. 'All right. Make 'em talk if ye can.'

Decidedly callous, he sat on a Chippendale dressing table that cracked under his weight, his hips knocking over perfume bottles and jewellery boxes. He crossed his arms and began whistling 'Strip the Willow'.

I pulled up a chair and sat close to the old woman. 'Lady Anne, I know we all in this room have our history, but —'

'*History!* Rejecting the richest heiress in town — you were as despicable as you were stupid.'

I rolled my eyes and looked away. To my surprise, I found that Caroline was pulling the exact same grimace.

'Lady Anne, I am not here to discuss that. Would you rather be questioned by Inspector McGray?'

Nine-Nails whistled a little louder, and Lady Glass could only grunt in defeat.

'Besides your face,' I said, 'do you have any other injuries? Do you need more medical attention?'

'No,' she said, gently touching her bruised skin. 'Dr Wyatt has been quite thorough.'

'Good. Now, I must ask you — was it who I think it was? Was it your son?'

It was as though I'd thrown a carcass on to the carpet.

'How did you know?' Lady Anne gasped. 'We sent an urgent message to Mr Campbell not five minutes after the affair. He is the sole person in the police who knows about our calamities. I hope he has not betrayed our confidence?'

McGray made as if to speak, but I raised a hand and, miraculously, he restrained himself.

'Lord Ardglass,' I said, 'was sadly brought to our attention earlier today. We have just come from the lunatic asylum.'

The two women had never looked so much alike. Their jaws dropped instantly as they gave terrified gasps.

'So you know?' Lady Anne muttered.

'Yes. We know it all. We were summoned because he escaped from care soon after midnight. Dr Clouston had to explain your son's situation. Now it is obvious that your residence was Lord Ardglass's immediate target.'

'Did the doctor tell you as well that this matter is entirely confidential? *He signed –*'

'Ma'am,' I interrupted, 'we have not come to discuss your family secrets. Before we waste any time, I would like you both to tell us what happened here. Please, do not spare any detail.'

The women exchanged uncomfortable looks.

'Here,' Caroline said, pouring Lady Anne a most liberal amount of brandy. 'Breakfast.'

Lady Glass proved worthy of the nickname and took the drink in one solid gulp. Then she extended her arm for a second round, which she would sip more leisurely.

'I was sleeping,' she began, suddenly unable to look me in the eye. 'Trying to sleep, I should say. I rarely sleep deeply; I didn't even when I was young. I had been tossing and turning all night, and when I was finally drifting off I thought I heard steps coming up the stairs, very slowly. At first I thought it was Bertha. She knows of my insomnia and sometimes brings me tea. It did sound like her, trying not to disturb anybody.

'Then I heard my door opening, very slowly as well. I – I cannot explain how, but I knew there was something untoward. Perhaps the door moved a little too sharply or . . . I do not know. I sat up and –'

She paused, her veined eyes suddenly looking at nothing. She raised the glass to her mouth and took a short sip.

'There . . .' she pointed at the door, 'there he was, standing . . .

'He said, "Mother, have you not missed me? Have you not missed your only child?"

'I would have thought it was a dream, had I not been struggling to sleep all night. I could not say a word. I could not even scream when I heard him walking closer to me . . .'

She was staring now at the foot of her four-poster bed, as intently as if Joel Ardglass still stood there. I noticed how strikingly similar that bed was to the one in the asylum – perhaps his bed had been a token of motherly regret.

'He said, "I've come for you. I know that –"'

She shuddered, then tapped the rim of her empty glass with shaking fingers, and Caroline poured her her third measure of the morning.

'Pray, go on,' I said. 'What did he tell you? What did he know?'

Never would I have thought I'd see tears glistening in Lady Anne's eyes, but there they were, the hard stare buoyant with the most troubled mixture of feelings. She swallowed with difficulty and blinked the tears away, before any could roll down her cheeks.

The tone of her voice shifted slightly. 'He said he knew why I'd sent him to the asylum. How – how it had been more important to me to keep our good name . . . I screamed for help and it was then that he –' She drew her fingers to her bruised cheek but did not quite touch the skin.

'Was he armed?' I asked, and Lady Anne nodded.

69

'He carried a knife. He was wielding it when Caroline came in.'

I turned to her. 'You came in, Miss Ardglass?'

'Yes, Inspector. I heard my grandmother's scream and rushed here. As she said, I saw my father standing by the bed, with the knife held up high, ready to . . . well . . .'

'He would have never done it,' the old woman jumped in.

'On the contrary,' said Caroline in a monotone, 'I believe he was determined to.'

There was an odd quality in her voice when she said those words, some cold finality, yet Lady Glass shook her head dismissively. 'Silly child. Your poor father never had the constitution.'

I studied their faces. Caroline's mouth was slightly open, as if to reply to her grandmother's remark. Both women were certain of their arguments; it was impossible to tell whom we should believe.

'What happened then?' I asked.

Caroline looked down and turned away to put the decanter on the bedside table. She was perhaps trying to conceal tears. 'I recognized him as soon as I saw him,' she said, 'even though it was so dark – and I haven't seen him since I was nineteen. I think I called out his name – I'm sorry, it was so quick; it is all a blur in my head – I yelled . . .'

'You yelled, "What on earth are you doing here?"' Lady Anne said.

'Is that right, miss?' McGray asked, suddenly sympathetic.

Caroline nodded. 'That is right. The last person I expected to see was him . . . holding a knife and about to kill his own mother. I told him to leave her alone or I'd never forgive him. He turned to me, ran towards me . . .'

'I thought he was going to strike her,' Lady Anne admitted, rather matter-of-factly, 'but he only pushed her aside and ran away.'

'Did he hurt ye?' McGray said.

'No,' Caroline answered, but her self-control was beginning to fail. 'Although for a split second I thought he might.'

'Lady Anne,' I said, before she had the chance to make another sly comment, 'do you know how he managed to break in?'

'No, I do not. However, he spent the first twenty years of his life in this house, and after he lost his wits he managed to escape from here a couple of times. He must know every nook and cranny.'

'How did he leave?'

'Through the front door,' Caroline answered. 'I saw him through the window, running down the street.'

'In which direction?' I asked.

'Along Duke Street. South.'

I took note of that, while McGray looked at the steamed-up window glass; the snow was falling as thick and heavy as when we'd arrived.

'Pointless looking for tracks,' he said. Then he looked at me. 'Should we tell them?'

I took a long, deep breath. 'They must know.'

'Know what?' Lady Glass demanded.

'As I told you, ma'am, we heard of Lord Ardglass's escape before coming here. We had a brief chance to inspect the asylum, but – before your son ran away . . .' I swallowed, my eyes falling briefly on Caroline, and her distressed face made me hate saying every word that followed. 'He murdered a young nurse.'

The glass slipped from Lady Anne's hand, fell on the carpet and spilled brandy all around.

Caroline covered her mouth, thunderstruck.

'No . . .' she whispered, slowly sinking on to the bed, all colour drained from her flesh.

'You cannot be serious!' Lady Anne cried. 'I know him; he would never gather the courage!'

Caroline lifted her chin, her eyes suddenly burning with hate.

'*This is all your fault!*' she roared, looking fiercely at Lady Glass. 'You old witch! You locked him up there so he'd lose his mind!'

I was relieved that she'd dropped her glass, otherwise Lady Anne might have thrown it at the girl's face.

'Stupid, ungrateful brat! I did it all for you! *For you!* So that you could have a future! Who in his wits would marry the daughter of a lunatic? Did you want people pointing at you? Thinking that you could be equally mad? Or that your womb could one day breed that kind of spawn?'

Caroline's face was distorted, her eyes shedding enraged tears as she walked up threateningly to face Lady Anne.

I had to stand up, fearing she'd thrust herself against her already battered grandmother. To make matters worse, Lady Anne's speech had also offended Nine-Nails.

'Spawn?' he echoed. 'Ye mean *yer* own spawn! Perhaps yer the one with the infected womb!'

Caroline gasped, Lady Glass showed her teeth and the

room then became a cacophony of yelling and swearing. I had to stand up and shout my lungs out: '*Everyone stop it!*'

Nine-Nails grasped my collar, but I managed to stand my ground.

'McGray, we are here to carry out an investigation,' I said. 'Save your rants for the public house.'

For a moment the room was so quiet we could hear the snow kissing the window, until McGray let go of my coat.

I turned to the women, desperate to end the questioning as soon as possible. 'Do you have any idea, any hint at all, as to where he might have gone?'

Caroline was still pale and would not talk. It was Lady Glass who answered. 'Of course not. He'd been in that asylum for six years. The few friends he had have either died or moved out of town. The one place I would have expected him to run to is – well, here.'

'Can you think of any reason he could have had to attack the nurse?'

'None at all,' Lady Glass snapped. 'Before today we hadn't seen him in years.'

Caroline shook her head as she wiped her tears. I thought she was going to add something, but then McGray asked one last question.

'*Marigold*,' he said with quite some emphasis, but then paused, as if probing the air with the word. 'Does it mean anything to youse?'

The women's faces were expressionless. Caroline seemed genuinely at a loss, but Lady Anne was looking away. Whether she did know something, or was merely dismissing the question because it came from Nine-Nails, I did not know.

73

'I understand you are both upset just now,' I said, 'but if you happen to remember anything later, please let us know.' I produced my card from my breast pocket. 'Here. Send for us at any time.' Lady Anne took it reluctantly. 'Now,' I went on, 'we need a portrait of your son. Preferably a photograph.'

Lady Glass nearly squealed. 'To print hundreds of signs and scatter them all across town?'

McGray stamped his heavy foot. 'It'd help us a wee bit to ken what the lad looks like.'

Caroline was already looking through her grandmother's drawers. She handed us a small photograph kept within the pages of a Bible.

'It is an old one. From before the asylum.'

McGray and I studied the picture for a moment. It was a sharp image of a man in his early forties, very thin, with dreamy eyes and a soft jaw. I could more readily accept Lady Anne's opinion of his weak character: a sadness and vulnerability exuded from the photograph. I could almost see his lower lip trembling whenever the old woman spoke to him.

I looked through the window, at the outlines of countless buildings barely visible under the emerging daylight. I thought of the thousands of corners, closes, slums – of all the alleys and shadows where Lord Ardglass could skulk. Would he decide to hide? Would he try to run as far as possible? Would he come back and make another attempt on his mother's life?

Would anyone ever see him again?

8

No matter how urgently we wanted to leave that house, McGray and I were forced to linger for a while. It would have been very irresponsible to leave the two women and their mostly elderly staff unprotected. They had only one muscular servant, who was already guarding their back doors. I never saw him, but McGray told me he was an elephantine, very vulgar man they called Jed. Such a large mansion would definitely need more than one manservant to guard it, so we sent a note to the CID requesting two more officers to help. It took some convincing but Lady Anne finally accepted the need for a police presence – the threat of her son coming back was very real. To protect her secrets, the neighbours (most of them her tenants) were simply told that the house had been robbed.

While we waited for the peelers to arrive, McGray and I had a brief chance to talk. Bertha offered us a cup of tea so very sweetly that we could not refuse, and the kind woman offered us a seat in a small breakfast parlour.

As soon as she left us alone I put an elbow on the table and rubbed my forehead, a torrent of information almost overwhelming my brains. 'Where shall we start, Nine-Nails? We have a dangerous lunatic at large, not the slightest idea where he might have gone, two crime scenes to investigate, two lots of people to question, a set of mental-health records to read, a dead body being analysed . . .'

'Och, stop it! Ye sound like a peacock with its balls being squeezed.'

'To say that with such conviction you must have handled a great many avian testicles.'

McGray cackled. 'My, oh my! The kitten's learned how to play! Yer right, Frey. There's so much to do, and if Lady Glass wants to keep the affair secret, I can tell ye Campbell won't spare any more men.'

'Indeed. She will be rewarding him handsomely, I am sure. It is a shame it is New Year's Day and Campbell holds his holidays sacred; if he were here, I could at least try and talk some sense into him.'

'Aye, but he'll be in his office tomorrow and ye can work yer charms on him then. I won't be joining ye for that, though.'

'Indeed you shall not,' I agreed. Superintendent Campbell, despite being the head of the Scottish police forces, was among the many people in Edinburgh who had become intimately acquainted with McGray's angry fists.

'We'd better split up this morning,' said McGray. 'Cover as many lines of inquiry as we can while they're fresh.'

'Yes, and to save everyone some grief, I'd suggest you carry on the search at the asylum while I investigate here.'

Right then we heard Lady Anne screaming for another brandy.

'Couldnae agree more,' said McGray, and within a breath he was on his way.

All the servants I questioned were wearing black, as Miss Ardglass did, and I recalled they were still mourning Alistair, Lady Anne's nephew and former head of

Edinburgh's Conservatoire. I had witnessed the very instant of his death, and it would be a long while before the thought of the circumstances ceased to make me shiver. People would soon start murmuring that the Ardglass clan was cursed.

The penultimate person I summoned was Bertha. She had been very busy and only came when I said I could not wait any longer.

'It appears to me that you have been employed here for quite a while,' I told her, noticing a slight agitation in her. 'Am I correct?'

'Aye, sir. Before Miss Caroline was even born.'

'I see. So you got to know Lord Ardglass quite well, I should assume?'

'Of course.'

'See, I have two conflicting statements as to his character. How would you describe him?'

She smiled. 'Oh, he was very gentle, very gentle indeed, sir. And generous. Before he lost his mind, of course.'

'How was his relationship with his mother?'

Bertha shifted on the chair, visibly uncomfortable. 'Well, I cannae tell ye it was easy. She was very strict, as ye can imagine, as hard on her son as she was on her business associates. I always thought he was a wee bit scared o' her, but I could've never imagined that one day he would go this far.'

I took note of that. 'Now, I must ask you a rather blunt question and I do apologize beforehand – would you say he was capable of murder?'

Poor Bertha had to produce a handkerchief and cover her mouth. I did not rush her.

'Quite frankly, sir . . . no. Never.'

I looked intently at her. 'Never?'

She hesitated, which on its own would have been informative enough to me, but then she added: 'Well . . . who am I to judge such things, sir? I always thought he had a big heart, but if his child – or his wife, when the good Lady Beatrice was alive – were under threat . . . who can tell?'

A most interesting statement, that was. I wrote her words down, adding a large question mark.

The last person I interrogated was the dim-witted cook, from whom I could extract nothing useful. Forster, the stiff butler, came to me just as I finished, announcing that the additional officers were waiting for me at the entrance.

As I walked to the main hall I stumbled across Caroline. We stared at each other for an awkward moment, after which I bowed and turned to make my way out, but the young woman stopped me.

'Mr Frey, what is going to happen to my father?'

I looked back. 'Do you mean, what will happen if we find him?'

She nodded, and I thought of telling her a soothing lie; however, I knew she was too clever for that.

'If we find him,' I sighed, 'we will have to escort him back to the asylum and he'll have to go to court. Given his mental health, I doubt he would be sentenced for homicide, as long as Dr Clouston can prove he was insane when he – committed the murder. And in that case I doubt he'd ever be allowed to leave the asylum.'

Caroline bit her lip. 'Thank you for your honesty,' she said, a quiver in her voice. Then she looked at me, and again I thought she was about to tell me something, but instead she looked down and walked to the staircase.

I felt a twinge of sorrow for her, especially when I saw her squaring her shoulders as she went upstairs. What dreadful times she must have gone through.

I shook my head, trying to focus on the practicalities of the case. I went to the entrance and saw that among the guards they had sent us McNair again. The poor man could not believe his bad luck.

'Worst New Year's o' my life,' he said as he took his place near the main gate.

'And it is early still, chap.'

It was mid morning, to be precise, and despite the dull winter sun the city was gleaming. The Georgian buildings were covered with a thick layer of snow, as white as the misty sky. The worst of the blizzard had passed, but a few tiny snowflakes could still be seen fluttering down.

I rode Philippa back to the City Chambers, although it took far longer than I expected, for the Royal Mile was in chaos: the snow had piled up in the narrow street, leaving but a fraction of the pebbled road fit for transit. Philippa's white coat was like a beacon against that filthy street. Her hooves constantly skidded on the murky slush, which did not help her temper. Right before arriving at the police headquarters, I heard a throaty scream from above, and by mere luck did I manage to dodge the ghastly contents of a chamber pot, which a large hag had thrown from her fifth-floor tenement.

'How I love this place,' I grumbled, knowing that the view would not be greatly improved when I reached my office.

The Commission for the Elucidation of Unsolved Cases Presumably Related to the Odd and Ghostly, the ludicrous subdivision instigated and led by Nine-Nails McGray, had its lacklustre headquarters in an abandoned cellar, the only space the CID was willing to spare for such nonsense. A moth-infested, damp-plagued pit, I fondly called it 'the dumping ground', very evocative of what was happening to my career.

I walked in between the towers of books and artefacts crammed into the place: treatises on the occult, crazy pharmacopoeias, witchcraft reports, zoology compendiums for the gullible mind – those were the sort of titles that McGray had collected over the years. I dodged a precariously balanced pile of old books, on top of which sat a formaldehyde jar containing some shapeless specimen, and found my sad, cramped desk. I sat down on my woodworm-infested chair and opened the convoluted medical history of Lord Joel Ardglass.

I was in for a riveting read.

The man had suffered severe depression, with several suicide attempts throughout his adult life. The earliest entry talked of a quiet child, with a natural predisposition to sadness, but other than that quite normal: intelligent, with an aptitude for languages and mathematics, and an avid reader.

Everything had changed by his early twenties. There were citations from a couple of London physicians, mentioning a first attempt at suicide in 1858, when Joel was twenty-three – he'd ingested rat poison. There was no mention as to what had triggered the incident, only details of the treatment undertaken to purge his system. I imagined

Lady Anne already pulling strings so that the records remained purely medical.

After that brief treatment, I found a long list of medicines prescribed and shipped to France, Bavaria and Italy. I supposed that Joel had embarked on a long trip around Europe, perhaps to escape whatever had been tormenting him . . . perhaps instigated by his mother in order to avoid gossip. From the dates, I gathered that the tour had lasted around three years, maybe four.

This must have been followed by Joel's marriage to that Lady Beatrice mentioned by Bertha. The files did not specify it, but there was a rather long gap in the records, which I could only attribute to a brief period of family bliss. Caroline, now around twenty-five years old, must have been born during that period. The next entry concerned another suicide attempt and, contrary to the record of the first occasion, this one did mention a possible cause: the death of his wife. This record was dated 1868 – I calculated that Caroline would have been five years old at the time. She might remember something. I made a note to question her again.

Then there was a long hiatus in the records, spanning almost fifteen years. It was after that that Dr Clouston's entries began, and he detailed Joel's sanity plummeting like never before. He had behaved aggressively towards his servants and mother, and had disappeared on several occasions, to be found days later at unlikely spots in Edinburgh and the surrounding countryside, as well as having attempted to take his own life not once but thrice. This had ultimately forced Clouston to confine him in the asylum.

That terrible spree of violent episodes seemed to have been as unexpected as the very first suicide attempt – assuming, of course, that the absence of recorded incident indeed meant a long improvement in his mental state, rather than further concealment.

I closed the file and tossed it on to the desk, rubbing my eyes and feeling as if I were about to plunge my hands into a pool of dark sludge. Joel Ardglass had led a most complex life – clearly there was so much more to him than his family wanted to tell us, and their frustrating reticence would certainly make solving this case all the harder.

My eyes began to itch from tiredness. In vain I tried to go through my notes or reread the more technical entries; my eyelids were heavy and without knowing I dozed off.

I could have slept well into the evening, but McGray's heavy steps awoke me and I nearly fell off my chair.

'Och, sleeping yer crow's feet away as soon as I leave ye alone? Did ye get a wet shave and a rose-scented bath too?'

'I was resting my eyes,' I said, noticing an unprecedented numbness in my derrière.

'Aye, course ye were.'

As I abandoned myself to an unashamed yawn I saw that McGray was carrying a large leather bag. He had a suspicious look on his face.

'Dear Lord,' I moaned, 'what have you brought in here now? I hate it when you carry leather bags!' The last time he had been carrying a human hand, as casually as he would a loaf of bread.

Before I could protest he tipped the contents out on to my desk. Dozens, if not hundreds of black ants poured

forth, running anxiously in all directions, and I instinctively jumped up, suddenly awake, feeling as if the insects
were crawling under my sleeves. Then something round
and dark fell out of the bag, thumping on to the wood,
and then a handful of white powder.

I had to rub my eyes again. The blackened ball turned
out to be . . . a red onion. Old and dried, half-shrunken,
its surface pierced by shiny pins and nails.

'What the dickens is that?'

McGray's eyes were glowing above a six-inch grin.

'Witchcraft, laddie. Good witchcraft.'

Nine-Nails dumped an ancient-looking tome on his desk,
the covers as dusty as a mummy's veil, and speedily leafed
through it. Amidst his countless books and trinkets he'd
known the exact spot where that title sat.

'Where did you find this mess?' I asked, stamping on
the ants that had invaded our already shambolic office.

'Joel's chambers. Under a floorboard right underneath
his bed. I followed the trail of ants that got you squealing
and twisting like a wet kitten. Now I understand why
Miss Smith couldnae get rid o' the constant infestation.'

'Remind me how you get hold of these sorts of books.'

'Black market, bribes and lots of luck,' he said as he
perused the pages. 'Witches are very cautious; they don't
like to put their secrets in writing, and when they do they
either use codes or keep everything so vague it only makes
sense to their inner circle. This book is a rarity. Let's see.
Onion . . . onion . . . *Onion!* I stepped closer as his eyes
flashed across the lines, his frown slowly deepening.

'Well?'

'Mmm . . . I'm confused. It seems that onions and sugar are healing amulets. Also used for exorcisms and . . . protection.'

'Protection?'

'Aye. They're supposed to absorb diseases and hexes.' He turned the page. 'Mmm, count the pins.'

Gingerly, I lifted the rotten vegetable, flicked away a remaining bug and looked at all its faces. 'Jesus, this is going to turn you smug beyond belief . . .'

'*How many?*'

'Thirteen.'

Another grin. 'That is revenge, it says here: "Take thirteen needles or nails and pierce a large onion which shall be purple; leave it and as it dries away so does the life of those who wronged thee."' Again he turned the pages. 'Damn it, it doesn't say how to direct the jinx. What a careless witch, the bloody hag who wrote this!'

'What do you mean?'

'If ye do the jinx wrong, it can fall on yerself or yer own folk.'

I threw the onion back into the bag. 'Do you honestly believe that you can kill someone by sticking a few nails into a bloody turnip?'

'What d'ye care what I believe?'

I shrugged. 'I do not, but whoever put it there believes it, and with a good deal of conviction. Red onions are an expensive treat, not something the average fishwife throws into an oxtail stew. It looks as if it had been there for a long while too. What about the sugar?'

'What? Now ye want recipes?'

'Rather, to understand the point of it. Your book

mentions healing and protection, as well as revenge. It is somewhat contradictory to say the least.'

'It's not "contradictory". It's one or the other. We just have to figure out which.'

'You suggest that either someone was trying to protect Lord Ardglass or damage him?'

'Aye.'

'Yet another question . . .' I blew out my cheeks, looking at the primitive sketch of a winged devil on a corner of the page. 'That is the last thing we need right now.'

Dr Reed drew the sheets away to show us Miss Greenwood's body.

There is something almost unbearable about the sight of a woman's corpse on an operating table – perhaps it is the horrendous memory of my mother on her deathbed, still playing in the back of my mind, regardless of how many years have passed. Whatever the reason, the instant discomfort I felt then was the exact feeling I'd experienced in the Oxford operating theatres, during my unfinished studies at the faculty of medicine.

It could have been much worse though. Reed, notwithstanding his youth, was clearly skilled. He had done a neat job, the post-mortem incisions stitched up meticulously, the body not entirely robbed of its dignity. I had a more conscientious look at the deceased nurse while Reed fetched his paperwork. Miss Greenwood had been rather beautiful, with soft features, dark wavy hair and a pointed nose. Between her slightly parted lips there were teeth as white as pearls.

'Mid twenties,' Reed began, reading from his report.

'Generally in good health. There were some recent bruises on her legs and arms, but they are most likely from the final convulsions.' He turned the page and pointed at the woman's chest, which was still contorted upwards. 'Broken spine –' Reed gulped, then said, 'again, from the strychnine poisoning.'

'So ye found nothing out o' the ordinary?' McGray asked, but Reed immediately wrinkled his nose.

'Well . . . I don't know how out of the ordinary you'll find this . . .'

'Yes?'

'She gave birth – at least once.'

'She what?'

'There's no doubt, sir. It didn't happen recently, but the signs are undeniable. Hips, belly, breasts, cunny . . .'

'Oh, shush!' I snapped. 'I know how the clock ticks.'

'*Do* you?' McGray jumped in. 'I thought youse ladies in waiting only found out on yer wedding night.'

Even Reed sniggered. 'Perhaps he left Oxford before that lesson.'

I blushed. 'Upon my honour! Watch your mouth, Reed. I can ask Campbell to discipline you.'

'The first thing you did when you arrived,' Reed retorted, 'was to ask Campbell for my dismissal – yet here I still stand, sir.'

McGray almost did a little dance, overjoyed by the young doctor's insolence.

'I liked you better when you were a mousy graduate.' I turned to McGray and changed the subject swiftly. 'Do you remember what Miss Smith said? That Miss Greenwood had come to Edinburgh after an *awkward family affair*?'

'Aye, that's what she said. D'ye think she got into what youse all-michty arses call *trouble*?'

'It is possible,' I muttered. 'Whether it is relevant to the actual murder, we cannot tell yet. We may find out more about Greenwood from that other nurse, the one she was training and sharing lodgings with. Miss Smith did tell us her name.' I turned back the pages of my notebook. 'Miss Oakley. We must question her as soon as possible.'

'Anything else ye can tell us, laddie?' McGray said.

Reed was already nodding. 'Aye. One thing.' He pointed at Greenwood's inner thigh, so high up that the young doctor blushed, despite his degree and the fact that the lady was no longer alive.

From where I stood it looked like a reddened spot, but on closer inspection it revealed itself as a scar. One of the most disturbing marks I'd ever seen.

It was a snake, tangled in on itself and biting its own tail, resembling a Celtic knot. Somebody had once engraved the skin with a blade as thin as a scalpel. It was an old wound, but made so deeply that time could not erase it.

9

We had tried to show Joel's portrait to the ground officers, asking them – off the record – to keep their eyes open. We had mixed reactions, however. Although Campbell had sent his most trusted men to clear the scene at the asylum as inconspicuously as possible, he'd also ordered them, most emphatically, not to become involved any further. Men like Constable McNair, who had a good relationship with Nine-Nails, had agreed, but the majority would not risk unleashing the superintendent's wrath.

Both of us knew there was nothing else we could do until Campbell returned to the office, so we had to curb our frustration and head home. It was already early evening, as we were going through the shortest days of the season, so the city was as dark as if it were midnight, the yellow glow from the gas lamps painting the piles of snow that had still not melted or turned into slush.

As we passed the crowded tenements the smell of stew and boiled potatoes filled the air, making my stomach growl. I realized that all I'd ingested during the day was a rushed coffee and a cup of Bertha's tea.

McGray was thinking the same.

'I'm bloody starving,' he said, and then his eyes glowed. 'Och, they might still have some mince 'n' tatties left at the Ensign. Mary makes the best in town.'

I blinked aloofly. 'Please yourself.'

'I'd ask ye to come along,' he said, 'but I ken that just hearing a word like *tatties* can make a Southron dizzy.'

Before I could come back with some of my dry humour he turned his mount and headed back to the High Street, to his favourite pub, the Ensign Ewart.

Throughout the short ride back I ruminated on the intricacies of the case, McGray's obsessions and Campbell's intransigence. I ended up gripping the reins so tightly my nails could have torn my leather gloves, and my mood did not improve until I sat back in the ragged armchair in my room and was free to kick my boots away. It was not the most comfortable of seats, with a couple of springs sticking up from strategically annoying points, but I was so tired a goosefeather cushion could not have offered more comfort.

'D'ye want these polished, master?' Larry asked, picking up my muddy footwear. The twelve-year-old had changed dramatically within a couple of months. When I'd taken him on as a footman, right after his drunken father had given him a merciless beating, he'd been a scrawny, filthy chimneysweep. Joan – who'd cheekily instigated my decision to hire him – had been feeding him heartily with bread, milk and boiled ham, and by now had almost managed to get him to wear shoes every day. I still feared his father might one day appear, looking for him, but fortunately that had not yet happened.

'Yes, please,' I said, looking at the battered leather. 'I do need a new pair though. Oh, and tell Joan I'd like my supper now.'

'Aye, master.'

Minutes later Joan arrived with a tray. Roast chicken, carrots and potatoes smothered in gravy, and a good portion of buttered bread.

From the moment she came in, Joan prattled away at an unthinkable speed, the never-ending sentences spurting out without pause. Perhaps she'd not had a chance to chatter throughout the day. I focused on the tender chicken and her wholesome gravy, not even registering what she said, but then, as she rambled on and on, I felt one of my eyebrows rise to a perfect arch.

'Joan?' I jumped in.

'Oh, sorry, master. I know you don't like my tittle-tattle.'

'I do not, but . . . right now I need some of it.'

'I beg your pardon?' She seemed rather alarmed. 'If 'tis about this morning with George, master, I swear I'll –'

'No, no, no,' I interrupted, still trying to cast that unsettling picture out of my head. I shifted in my chair, the epiphany now fully formed. 'It is something else. I need you to tell me everything – and I mean *everything* – you know about Joel Ardglass.'

From her mouth came a sizzling noise, as if she were staring at a juicy joint of beef. 'Oh, master, 'tis a most dreadful affair! How come you want to know?'

I shrugged. 'Just to . . . have something to gossip about at the New Club. The conversations have run dry of late.'

'Well, I do know a wee thing or two.'

'Wee? Why, you are swiftly becoming a Scotswoman!'

Joan blushed slightly, but then dived straight into the gossip. 'I had it all from Gertrude, one of the washerwomen who work for that nasty Lady Glass. We both like to buy our soaps at Mr Oleander's. He sells those nice scented bars you like so much; you know, the one made of oats for sensitive skins?'

'You may spare me those details – well, at least I know that your gossip comes from a good source.'

'Indeed, sir, but you mustn't tell *anybody* you heard all this from me. I swore to Gertrude I'd take it to the grave!'

'As I am sure she did too.'

'Well, do you know how the gentleman died?'

I cleared my throat. 'No, not really. Tell me.'

She poured some more gravy on my chicken. 'Made a very good batch of this, master. I had some scrapings from that roast –'

'Joan, please focus! How is he su–' I had been going to say 'supposed to have died', but managed to hold my tongue. Joan, like everyone else, thought him truly dead.

'Shipwreck, master. Well, so Lady Glass claims.'

'Oh? Why would it be in doubt?'

'Well, after it happened folks naturally asked questions and looked at the newspapers. Very soon they realized that – you won't believe this – there were no shipwrecks on the day Lady Glass claimed her son died! Not a single one!'

'You shock and astound me.'

'*Indeed!* Some of the servants say the poor lad killed himself, jumped overboard when crossing the Channel or something like that. Others even say Lady Glass . . . well, did it herself! She was nowhere to be found in the days after Lord Ardglass set off for Europe.'

I nodded, thinking that the truth was far more shocking than people theorized. If only Joan knew . . .

'Why would she do such a thing?' I probed. 'Then again, why would Lord Ardglass commit suicide?'

'That's what Gertrude was most reluctant to tell me.' Joan would not scruple to spill it out though: 'Not long before the affair, Lord Ardglass had a mighty quarrel with his mother. They cursed and yelled horrible things at each other; everyone in the house heard. Apparently Lord Ardglass even tried to strangle the old woman. It was a dreadful affair. After that fight he became very withdrawn, very withdrawn indeed. It was then that Lady Glass decided to send him to some fancy country on the Continent.'

'What was the quarrel about?'

'Do you like them spuds, sir? I did think they needed a touch more salt. I can bring you –'

'Joan, will you forget my dinner until you are done with the story?'

Then Joan said the single sentence that would explain it all: 'Oh, everyone knew that he never wanted to marry the gal he married. He did so to please Lady Glass. Gertrude told me she was this petite, sickly creature from some fading aristocratic family. Most folk were surprised she even endured a full pregnancy; she died when her child was only four or five years old.'

'I see . . .' I muttered, bringing my fingertips together. 'That frail woman was Miss Ardglass's mother, I suppose.'

'Aye. Lady Beatrice . . . Remburn, I think. And Gertrude said her death was a blessing in disguise. She couldn't have been happy, you know, with a husband that didn't want her and that pesky drunkard as a mother-in-law.'

'Perhaps that Gertrude woman is right. Did she mention why Lord Ardglass objected to the marriage?'

'She wasn't sure, master, but Miss Ardglass's old nanny told Gertrude once that the man's heart was elsewhere.'

'Elsewhere?'

'Yes. And if she's right, having to wed another must have destroyed him.'

'That is interesting,' I said, my eyes fixed on the ceiling. I remembered Lord Ardglass's earliest and apparently unjustified suicide attempt, before his trips to the Continent. Could that have been triggered by his doomed love?

'Did she tell you this other woman's name?' I asked. 'Or how they met . . . or anything about her?'

'Oh, I did ask her,' Joan said with frustration, 'but Gertrude didn't know herself. That's all I can tell you, master.'

'Thank you, Joan. It was in fact more than enough.' Having such an avid gossipmonger under my roof was finally paying off.

She curtsied and left me with my thoughts.

Lord Ardglass's character was beginning to make sense in my mind, and his tribulations were so close to my own it was painful to admit.

It was not something I liked to discuss, but I had been jilted myself, and quite recently. That was the matter that had pushed me away from Gloucestershire, the reason my Christmas holiday had ended so abruptly.

It was no secret to anyone that Laurence, my eldest brother, had won the heart of Eugenia Ferrars – *my* former fiancée. I left London the day after she curtly broke our engagement, and I have not been back since, but I am sure the gossip has been industriously disseminated throughout our social circles. I have come to dread the day I return to the capital, which partly explains why I did not push for my reinstatement in Scotland Yard too much.

While I was no longer sure I had truly loved her, Eugenia had certainly stirred powerful emotions in me. I had seen her as the most angelic, most perfect of all creatures, and I had undoubtedly looked forward to our future together: raising children, sharing meals and quiet evenings.

Now it was uncomfortable to even think about her, a dark mixture of disappointment, jealousy and bitterness. I could easily imagine similar resentment brewing in Lord Ardglass's mind. He was a broken-hearted, frustrated man. Those episodes of depression I'd read about now had an explanation. Even his attack on his own mother, the woman responsible for his grief, would have made some twisted sense in the man's vengeful mind.

Had he spent thirty years dwelling on his lost love, until he finally erupted? If so, what had triggered his rage now?

I shook my head, telling myself I would have plenty of time to reflect on those matters in the morning. Besides, the rest of my chicken was getting cold.

IO

Superintendent George Campbell was around sixty, but despite his age and rank he much resembled a wild, scruffy lion, with his grey hair fluffed up, a thick moustache and the corners of his eyes tilted slightly upwards. His sullen face had very recently healed from his last *friendly* meeting with McGray: the ghastly, greenish bruise around his eye had taken weeks to vanish, and the words *Peach-skin Campbell* could still be heard throughout the CID corridors.

I was not expecting him to be in a terribly good mood, it being very early in the morning, but his mouth was twisted into a most unusual shape, his lower lip almost quivering from the contained tension when he saw me.

Campbell could never forgive that an Englishman had been forced into his ranks. As he'd once put it, my presence proved that the high commissioner in London thought of him as 'poor, provincial folk', and the most sympathetic adjective he'd ever used to describe me had been *frivolous-looking*.

Needless to say that the hatred was mutual; nevertheless, I had to make my best effort to appear deferential, for that morning I had something to ask from him.

'I suppose you haven't caught the rogue yet,' he said, or rather yawned.

'Indeed we have not, sir. Not being able to deploy

officers to conduct a proper search has been quite a hindrance.'

Campbell exhaled noisily. 'I knew you'd come here moaning about that. I had to give my men strict orders; I've not forgotten the havoc you and McGray caused in New Town back in November. The last thing the department needed on New Year's Day was an avalanche of complaints from the Queen Street Gardens gentry. If I must endure condescending upper-class peacocks telling me how to do my job, I would rather it is only you. Whom I can ignore. Very easily.'

'We may have missed our best chance to find Lord Ardglass,' I insisted. I would not let his mockery undermine me. 'Sir, this secrecy around him is ridiculous. We have his portrait; the family can surely provide us with a few more, perhaps a more recent one. It would be a routine assignment for a few ground officers to take such pictures and ask around town who has seen him, while McGray and I investigate the other aspects of the –'

Campbell was already leafing through some other documents, deaf to my words. When the superintendent finally deigned to look at me again his eyes were frustratingly vacant. 'Why do you insist on bothering me, Frey? You know what my response will be. Our discretion was kindly requested by Lady Anne; by now you know how delicate this entire affair is for her family.'

'By *kindly requested* do you mean ... handsomely rewarded?'

Campbell's mane seemed to stand on end. It was no secret that he was more than willing to turn a blind eye to procedure when the right bribe came along.

'Any other complaint, Frey?' he snapped. 'Any other aspect of the case you believe I am grossly mismanaging?'

In fact . . .

'Sir, I wanted to respectfully propose –'

'Oh, here we go . . .'

'To propose that Inspector McGray is taken off the investigation.'

'For goodness' sake, Frey . . . My face has barely healed!'

'I do not have the authority to remove him from the investigation, but you do, sir.'

'Frey, it's really difficult to feign interest when all you do is request the same gibberish over and over like one of those Brazilian parrots . . . What are they called?'

'Sir, I am serious. It was nearly impossible to keep McGray and the Ardglass women from eviscerating each other; he is the last person I'd assign to find Lady Anne's son. And if that were not enough, there is the issue of McGray's sister.'

Campbell's eyes opened just a little wider. 'The lunatic girl?'

'The . . . ill girl, yes,' I remarked; I have never liked the blunt term *lunatic*. 'Lord Ardglass was overheard talking to her but a few hours before the murder.'

Campbell sat back. Suddenly I had his full attention. 'You must question her.'

'We tried already, sir. Miss McGray has not said a word in five years. She –' I was about to mention the *Marigold* scribble, but decided not to. 'Even if she could communicate something to us, I doubt the testimony of a mentally ill person would be admissible in court.'

97

'But McGray doesn't see it that way, I would guess . . .'

'Precisely. When his sister is involved Nine-Nails cannot possibly discern the trivial from the meaningful. If Miss McGray blinked or sighed or shook her head, Nine-Nails would see it as some miraculous hint of recovery.'

Campbell nodded. 'I do appreciate your point about McGray's clouded judgement. That's precisely why I want you to assist him. Dr Clouston requested specifically that you two handled the case. Now that you've mentioned McGray's first-hand experience with madwags Clouston's request seems quite logical.'

'With all due respect, I doubt Dr Clouston's judgement can be fully trusted right now. He is deeply involved in this case too, and despite being a reasonable man he shares this nonsensical idea of keeping things quiet . . .'

'Because of his borderline illegal arrangement with Lady Anne. I know that.'

'Indeed. You must also know that Clouston has given excellent treatment to Miss McGray for the past few years, and because of it Nine-Nails feels compelled to protect him. I am more inclined to believe that is the reason Clouston wants McGray in charge. To secure his own reputation.'

'Complicated situation, Frey,' Campbell muttered, now seemingly in deep thought.

'Far more complicated than necessary, sir. To make matters worse, we found traces of witchcraft in Lord Ardglass's room, and –'

It was as though I'd pulled his chin up with a fishing hook.

'Witchcraft!'

I stammered, realizing how stupid I had been to

mention that detail. 'Well, only a fool would believe that those trinkets were actual –'

'Well, I had my reservations, I have to admit; but if there is witchcraft involved in the case, that makes it McGray's field of expertise.'

'Sir, forgive me for asking this, but did you not hear a single word I have just said? It is *dangerous* to leave this in McGray's hands. He will not have a level head; he might make painful mistakes and drag us all down with him.'

'Oh, don't be so bloody melodramatic.'

'Melodramatic! A woman has died and another was attacked. This is beyond your regular penny dreadful.'

By then I knew myself defeated. All power had slipped through my fingers and I had voluntarily handed it to McGray.

Civility would have been too much for me – especially since Campbell was again leafing through his documents as if I were not there – so I simply turned on my heels and stormed out.

I found McGray in the Dumping Ground, his feet on the desk, perusing the tattered witchcraft book. He was wearing the same clothes as the day before and his stubble looked slightly darker. He had probably spent the night at the public house, drinking ale and gorging himself with haggis and other Scottish unmentionables. At least he looked rested enough.

I saw with disgust that he'd casually left the rotten onion on my desk; a couple of ants were still roaming over my paperwork.

'Morning, yer highness,' said McGray. 'How come yer in this late?'

I looked at my pocket watch, surprised by how long I'd been in the superintendent's office. 'I have been here for a while but I went to see Campbell. He wanted a general update.'

'Aye. What did ye tell him?'

'Nothing you do not know already.'

McGray grinned. 'Och, so ye asked him to get me out o' yer way.'

I cleared my throat. 'Yes. I.told you that myself. I do not think this case is –'

He closed the book so hard it sounded like the thump of a mallet. 'I don't give a shite what ye think, Frey.'

'I am aware of that.'

He pointed at me, the book still in his spoiled hand. 'What I do care about is ye telling on me like a wimpy schoolboy. It's not the first time ye've done that.'

'McGray . . .'

'I'm in charge and I'll see it to the end. If ye don't like it, *ye*'d better leave. Understood?' To underline his author- ity, he concluded: 'And the first thing we'll do now is to consult Madame Katerina.'

I took a deep, angry breath. Madame Katerina was Nine-Nails' clairvoyant of choice, and the prospect of meeting her again irritated me even more than sitting on top of an anthill. Protesting would be like preaching to the walls, so I focused on more important matters. 'I have found out a thing or two about Joel Ardglass that Lady Anne *forgot* to comment on.'

That immediately shifted McGray's attention. 'Did ye! How?'

'Chatting to Joan. She is part of a network far more efficient than the bloody *Scotsman*.'

I quickly briefed him on the gossip I'd heard the night before, and I saw his eyes light up when I mentioned Lord Ardglass's unrequited love affair.

'Doesn't surprise me. I told ye once, these people only marry commoners to avoid harelip – not that I need to say that to a Siamese from a similar litter. What does surprise me is that after all these years even her own servants haven't heard the laddie's real story. The auld bitch has done a terrific job at keeping her cards close to her saggy chest.'

'I cannot blame her. See how easily the homicidal mother theories reached our ears. In fact, it shocks me that . . .' *the Ardglass story is not as famous as your sister's past*, I nearly said, but managed to hold myself back and amend the sentence: 'It shocks me that Lady Anne would rather have people murmuring she is a murderer than admit her son lost his wits.'

'The lie might have gotten a wee bit out o' her hands.'

I tilted my head. 'Although that Bertha woman did seem nervous when I questioned her. She must know much more than she admits.'

'Aye. I should try and *persuade* her to talk.'

'McGray, I will not let you beat the truth out of an elderly woman!'

He laughed earnestly. 'Don't worry. The only auld hag I've ever wanted to beat is Lady Glass, and her son's already done that for me.'

II

Madame Katerina owned a most peculiar establishment in the southern slums of the city: the ground floor was a thriving alehouse, while on the upper storey she hosted her 'divination sessions'. The woman was supposed to be *the* most gifted clairvoyant in all of Scotland – how good a recommendation that was, I sincerely cannot tell.

Her sad premises looked directly over the filthy square that serves as Edinburgh's cattle market. To my disgust, it was auction day, so the stench of a thousand flea-ridden cows and sheep hit my nostrils, as powerful and offensive as a physical blow.

Philippa became agitated as soon as we approached, the mooing and bleating too much for her ears. She halted stubbornly, neighing and snorting, and I had to spur her hard until she finally deigned to move. I tethered her next to McGray's Rye, the chestnut horse as unaffected as its owner.

Madame Katerina's fat clerk met us at the entrance to the brewery, where he was tending to three very drunk livestock farmers.

'Jesus, it is not even ten in the morning,' I mumbled, as the clerk led us upstairs, to what the portly man insisted was the 'world-famous' divination chamber.

I sighed in resignation, for I knew what awaited us behind that door.

The small room stank of incense, mixed with sickly herbs and spices. The tatty tapestries that covered the walls had absorbed those ghastly smells for years. I suspected that Katerina's intention was to make her customers slightly ill and thus more malleable.

She was already waiting for us, seated at a small round table where a collection of multi-coloured candles burned with flickering flames.

The woman was as outlandish as her surroundings. Short and of medium build, she liked to clad herself in absurdly colourful cloaks and veils, which she then covered with all manner of chains, adornments and charms, so that she jingled like a Christmas sleigh with every move she made. Her features, chiselled and angular, were another collection of trinkets: her eyebrows, ears and aquiline nose were all pierced with either rings or pendants.

However, all this was overshadowed – not at all metaphorically – by the largest, most vulgarly hoisted breasts in the city, which she liked to show off with an indecent, plunging neckline.

She spread her hands on the table, drumming her alarmingly long black-painted nails. With her overdone make-up and sardonic smile, she looked like a stout Cheshire cat.

'Oi, Adolphus!' she said in a rather strange hybrid of Glaswegian and Eastern European accents. 'What can I do for you, my boy? I can see a horrid shadow over you; something's troubling you.'

McGray and I sat in front of her. Despite my best efforts to toughen up, I had to produce my handkerchief and press it against my nose. 'Something is definitely troubling *me*.'

McGray smacked the back of my head. 'Ignore the dandy. He's been whinging non-stop since his lass left him for his brother.'

I could not repress a gasp. *'How on earth do you know about that?'*

Madame Katerina was laughing, a low snuffle which was far more scornful than a candid cackle.

'Indeedy, hen, we've just come from –'

'Stop there,' she said, a claw-like hand held up high. 'That shadow I see . . .' she leaned forwards, studying McGray's face. 'It's so dark. So, so dark. My poor boy.'

I chuckled. McGray's stubble was fuller than usual, the skin around his eyes was puffy and darkened. A child could tell something was wrong with him.

'I'll deal with you later,' Katerina told me, her undivided attention on McGray. 'This is about dear Pansy, isn't it?'

McGray assented. 'Partly.'

'Oh, I'm sorry to hear that. I can see this gloom around you . . .' Her eyes flickered in my direction. 'Around both of you.'

Katerina stood up and came nearer, her protruding breasts thankfully just avoiding rubbing against me. She examined my face so closely I could see every clot of mascara around her eyes. 'Milk of magnesia,' she said. 'You should get some. Soon.'

'I am not ill,' I said, but she went back to her seat and did not mention the matter again.

'I see there's a pressing question in your mind,

Adolphus. Do you have something for me to read? I can feel you do.'

Again I chuckled. 'Of course he has something for you. Yours is not a place I'd come simply for a cup of tea and a chat.'

McGray was pulling Lord Ardglass's portrait out of his pocket. 'Aye, I want ye to tell me everything ye can from this. Everything, and if the English numbskull makes fun o' ye, I'll hold him and look away while ye punch him. And if he goes crying to our bosses, I'll tell them he tripped.'

Madame Katerina extended an arm, opening and clos-ing her fingers as if she were warming up the muscles. She held the photograph, but as she drew it closer to her face she closed her eyelids, showing the thick layer of bright purple make-up on them. I thought I saw the candle flames flicker, but I prefer to believe I imagined it.

Katerina inhaled, paused, then inhaled again, and as she breathed out she slowly opened her eyes. She stared at the photograph as if suddenly frozen.

It took her a while to react. I was going to say some-thing but McGray elbowed me in the ribs. Finally, Katerina did move, but in a way I had not expected.

She bit her lip, and slowly a frown etched its way across her face. It was not an angry frown though; it was pure sorrow. She was not blinking, and tears began to pool in her eyes. She gulped, and when she finally blinked, tears rolled copiously down her face. She wiped them with a quivering hand, smearing her thick mascara.

'Ye all right?' McGray asked, as dumbfounded as me.

'This has never happened before,' she said, looking

slightly embarrassed by her crying. 'What a sad man. All around him is sadness . . . and despair.'

My first thought was how closely that matched Lord Ardglass's clinical records.

'Do you know who that man is?' I asked. I was looking at the back of the photograph, making sure it was not labelled in any way.

Katerina shook her head. 'Never seen him. I can tell he's well off.'

'Can ye tell us anything else about the lad?'

Again, Katerina looked embarrassed, and the tears kept flowing. 'No, I'm so sorry. There is a very strong imprint here . . . but it's very old. It's a pain that has lingered and lingered. And guilt and . . .'

Katerina had to lay the photograph on the table, and without saying another word she left the room, through a back door concealed by a heavy tapestry.

McGray's eyes were wide open. 'I've never seen her like that!'

'I thought she was as hard as nails,' I added. 'Should we . . . go?'

McGray shook his head and we waited. Katerina came back a few minutes later, her face freshly washed, only the thickest lumps of mascara still clinging on. Even though she'd managed to control her tears, her eyes were as red as before. She regarded the photograph as if it were a poisonous spider.

'I'm sorry, Adolphus. I can't tell you much about him. That grief overpowers everything else. Please don't ask me to try again.'

McGray nodded and reached out for the picture, which

Katerina would not touch again. He gave me the photograph and I put it in my breast pocket.

'We have two other things for ye to see. I hope yer all right to do so?'

Katerina assented, but she continued to take deep deliberate breaths. McGray showed her the leather bag, with a few live ants still crawling inside, and pulled out the dry onion and the sugar.

The gipsy woman started, her bosoms bouncing like undercooked puddings.

'I've not seen one o' those in years!'

'Witchcraft?' I asked.

'Oh yes.'

There was a glimmer of hope in McGray's eyes. 'I've been looking at my books. Cannae tell what this is for.'

'I'm sure you did. These are dual charms, Adolphus, as you probably know already. Can be used for good or evil. I could only tell you which if I'd been around when they were cast.'

'Why, an ambiguous response,' I said, rolling my eyes. 'How unexpected, from you.'

Katerina's eyelashes seem to stand on end. 'If you found a scalpel dripping blood in the street, could you tell if it had been used to slit someone's throat or to cut a baby's cord?'

I smirked. 'No, but I thought your eyes could see . . . *beyond!*'

McGray slapped the back of my head again. 'Ignore the bastard, hen. I was expecting you to say that, but thought ye might see something I'd not.'

Katerina was looking at the pins, counting them. Then

she pulled one out and examined its slightly rusted tip. 'You use new, shiny metal for self-protection, and rusty nails for spreading curses.'

I rolled my eyes. 'What difference does that make?' I asked, and Katerina mistook my sarcasm for actual interest.

'Metals are noble, magical substances,' she said, her eyes wide, 'each with a particular blessing to offer. Iron is strength, command, a ward against ghosts and dark powers. If you use it as a talisman, it's like a well that catches any evil coming your way. But evil is like everything else around us; it doesn't disappear, it only turns into something else, and when it sinks into a talisman our eyes see it as rust. Witches collect dark energy that way, twisting the kind properties of iron, and then project all that accumulated wickedness against someone or something. That's how they curse you.'

I shook my head at that absolute nonsense.

Nine-Nails arched a brow. 'Those pins could have been rusty to begin with . . . or been rusted by the onion's juices.'

I took a deep breath, my patience thinner by the minute. 'Do put that blasted vegetable away; it looks like it will take us nowhere.' I crushed a stray ant on the tablecloth. 'If you are finished discussing your accursed trinkets, I suggest we go.'

McGray did shove the onion back into the bag, but then tossed the bundle on to my legs, spilling a few alarmed bugs on to my clothes for his own puerile amusement.

'Show her the writing,' McGray said, rather gravely.

I took my time to brush the blasted ants off, then produced my notepad and opened it at the page with Pansy's scribble.

'D'ye have any idea what that could be?' Nine-Nails asked as I passed it to Katerina.

She hesitated. 'Does it belong to you?'

'Aye,' McGray answered for me. 'It's the scribble we're interested in.'

Katerina took the notebook by a corner, only touching it with her black fingernails. She used two of those claws to pin it down on the table, and then, very carefully, ran a fingertip along Amy's squiggly lines. She never allowed her skin to touch any of my writing.

'I sense witches all over this,' she said very soon, very assuredly. 'They're like rotting flesh, impregnating everything around them with their stench.'

McGray could not have looked more confused. 'My sister wrote that!'

Katerina did not seem to hear that. She was mumbling nonsense. 'Witches like to come out of their lairs in the darkest of nights. They like it that way; it shrouds their dirty jobs.'

I thought of Cassandra Smith talking about those figures in the asylum, only seen on new moon nights.

Madame Katerina continued. Her voice had gradually become deeper, her Eastern European inflections smoothed out until she did not sound like herself any more.

'Beware of the witches. They're dangerous folk. Very dangerous. They say they can curse you simply with their eyes; one glare and you're lost. The most powerful of them can turn into animals, birds and balls of fire. And they hide in every nook and cranny, everywhere in the land. Beware of them, my dear.'

Then she lifted her head, blinking and taking deep breaths. It was as though she'd been sleepwalking, and then awakened in an unexpected location.

'Somebody died?' she asked, and before I could mock her divination skills McGray replied, 'Aye. A Miss Greenwood, a young nurse.'

Katerina nodded, now running her fingers along the pages. Her eyes moved from side to side, as if hearing something and trying to pinpoint where the noise came from.

'Find out more about her, Adolphus,' she said. 'Listen to her story . . . That will answer questions you two don't even know you should be asking.'

12

We immediately thought of Miss Oakley. She was our best chance to learn more about the late Miss Greenwood.

She lived in the south-west part of Edinburgh, near the Union Canal. It was further from the main roads than I would have expected, but within a reasonable distance of the lunatic asylum.

It was in fact a very nice cottage. Its two storeys over-looked a long front garden, which in the milder months must be a vegetable patch. When we arrived, however, the ground was totally covered in white, and there were very few traces of vegetation: only some frozen stalks of tall, withered foxgloves.

I tripped over a spade and shears, and the rattle must have been quite loud, for a young woman came out imme-diately. She was not handsome, her features a little rodent-like, but her lean face was quiet and self-controlled.

'May I help you, gentlemen?' she asked, wrapping her-self tightly in a shawl. Her voice surprised me: it was a pleasant, well-modulated speech that could only come from an educated girl. She was – to both my relief and my delight – not Scottish.

McGray showed his credentials. 'Inspectors McGray and Frey from the CID. Are ye Miss Jane Oakley?'

'Indeed I am,' she replied with raised eyebrows. 'Are you . . . *the* Mr McGray? Miss McGray's brother?'

Nine-Nails chuckled bitterly. 'Aye. I can tell ye've not been at the asylum very long. Can we ask ye a few wee questions?'

She placed a hand on her chest. 'Is it regarding . . . ?'

McGray nodded sombrely. 'Aye, yer friend Miss Greenwood. I'm so sorry.'

Miss Oakley could barely respond. She took a deep breath and I thought she would burst into tears. She managed only to wave us in, leading us into her small parlour.

The room was unostentatious yet immaculate. A small fire crackled in front of a very old but perfectly polished table, and in the air I perceived the slight aromas of apple and sage.

What a pleasant change from Katerina's dreadful lodgings. McGray looked at the quilted cushions and the embroidered fire screen with slight discomfort.

'Does the lack of grime insult you?' I asked in a whisper.

'Do be seated, sirs,' said Miss Oakley. Despite her polished diction she could not hide a hint of Lancashire inflection – I was well trained, having listened to Joan for seven years.

McGray and I took the two chairs by the tiny table, and Miss Oakley pulled up an old rocking chair for herself. After she was seated I took a moment to discreetly inspect her. Her eyes were rather sunken from lack of sleep, and the tendons of her slender neck looked tense. Her hands were roughened by work, but not nearly as much as those of Miss Smith or Joan; the girl had been working for only a short while.

She was the first one to speak.

'Was it painful?' she asked with a splutter. 'Did she suffer much?'

I had a flashing memory of the vomiting, the broken spine and the anguished screaming.

'It was not an easy passing,' I said in the end.

Miss Oakley's chest began to heave. She looked away as the first tear rolled down her cheek, and I saw her anxious hands squeezing her apron.

'Ye all right?'

She gulped, nodding, but we could tell how distressed she was.

'We understand you two were very good friends,' I said. 'We are very sorry indeed.'

McGray leaned forwards. 'I guess it was all too sudden, wasn't it?'

It seemed a harmless, almost empty question – but Miss Oakley's eyebrow twitched. It was an almost imperceptible movement, yet undoubtedly there.

'Were you expecting anything bad to happen?' I asked. The silence dragged on, so I had to speak again. 'Did Miss Greenwood have any quarrels with her patients?'

'Not quarrels as such. She just . . . Well, neither of us liked working there. It is a ghastly place.' She instantly looked at Nine-Nails. 'No offence, sir.'

'None taken, hen,' he lied.

'Some days were terrible, with all the screaming and the inmates throwing their food at us and calling us names . . .'

What followed was rather haphazard: I brought out my notepad, and as I flicked through the pages to find a blank one I went past Amy's scribble. I saw McGray looking at it and I knew that something was brewing in his head.

'Lass, does the word *marigold* mean anything to ye?'

Her eyes opened so wide I feared they'd fall off her face.

'Marigold?' she repeated. 'Do you mean – the flower?'

There was a trace of a smile in McGray's expression. 'I'm not sure what I mean, lass. Ye might be able to explain to us.'

She blinked. 'Excuse me, why do you ask me that?'

McGray did not reply, and I waited, my pencil ready to take notes.

'Well, sir . . . I'm afraid I don't understand you.' She looked around, now a bundle of nerves. 'Oh God, where are my manners? I shall bring some tea.'

'Ye don't have to, lassie,' McGray said. 'We won't be here much longer.'

'Oh, please, do accept it,' she insisted. 'It's bitterly cold outside and you must have ridden a long way,' and she hurried to the kitchen before we could refuse again.

McGray whispered as soon as the door had shut. 'Looks like *marigold* does mean something.'

'I am not sure.'

'Yer not – Did ye nae see her face? What are the chances the word Pansy wrote would upset this lass?'

'I did, McGray, but you must admit it was a very random question.'

His face began to colour. 'Ye condescending turd!'

'Before you upset her with rose and gladioli questions,' I said hastily, 'please let me ask her about Miss Greenwood.'

'Ask all the shite ye want. Then I'll follow.'

It was not long before Miss Oakley came back with the tea set and some shortbread. She seemed a little more composed, and even attempted a smile as she poured the brew.

'I wanted to ask you,' I said, 'about one patient in particular. Were you familiar with the patient they call Lord Bampot?'

'He did it, didn't he?' she said quickly, almost startling us.

'So ye've heard o' him?'

'Everyone who's worked there has. The man was quite a character, and nobody was allowed to ask questions.'

'How did ye ken we suspect him?' McGray asked.

'Miss Smith came to visit last night and she told me what had happened. She didn't mention the details – I was very distressed, as you can imagine – but she did say it all happened in Lord Bampot's room and that he was nowhere to be found. She also said I must not tell anyone, but you, gentlemen, I assume are aware of it all.'

I took a sip of the tea, which had been brewed very strong. 'Miss Smith was right. We are looking for him, and if there is any piece of information you could provide, however inconsequential it might seem, we'd be very grateful.'

She fixed her eyes on her still-full cup of tea, thinking. 'I couldn't possibly tell you, sir. As I said, I knew nothing about him, not even his real name.'

I wrote that down, thinking that it fitted perfectly with Lady Anne's obsession with secrecy. 'Now I would like to ask you a few questions that you definitely should be able to answer – about Elizabeth Greenwood.'

'That I might be able to help with,' she said, just before McGray slurped his tea as if attempting to be as loud as possible. She cast him an uncomfortable look.

'I understand this is, or rather *was* Miss Greenwood's house,' I said.

'Indeed.'

'How did you come to share lodgings?'

'We had a few acquaintances in common. When they knew I was coming to Edinburgh they suggested I contact her. She was very kind to receive me.'

'Can you elaborate on these acquaintances?'

She shook her head. 'Oh, it is somewhat convoluted, sir. More tea? There you go. You see, my late father was a landlord, and one of his tenants was the cousin of a very good shoemaker in Lancaster. One of his regulars was this spirit merchant, who happened to know Lizzy's – Nurse Greenwood's – milkman.'

I gave up on jotting that down. 'I see, that is convoluted. So you moved here very recently.'

'Yes, last summer.'

'Yet you and Miss Greenwood became very close friends.'

'Oh yes. She was very kind to me. She took me on, refused to be paid any rent – my finances would not have worked out otherwise – and she also taught me a lot about her work. I could not have coped without her help.'

'You are a long way from your home in Lancashire,' I said, which appeared to surprise her as much as the mention of marigolds.

'Did you notice my accent?'

'Yes. My housekeeper is from Burnley.'

She wrinkled her nose. 'Not a very nice place.'

'I have never been, but can undoubtedly take your word. What made you come this far north?'

'It was a very long, sad affair. My father went into debt, lost the family home and then unfortunately died – I shan't go into the detail of it. My only choice was to find some employment elsewhere.' She looked down, visibly affected. 'I preferred to come here, where nobody knew me. Mr Frey, you look like a fine gentleman; you must know how humiliating it is to be whispered about in one's own circle.'

I nodded. 'Sadly, I do know.' I took a deep breath, blocking my too-fresh memories. 'I am sorry to hear you have had hard times.'

'I appreciate it, sir.'

'So you and Elizabeth became very close . . . This will be a very uncomfortable question but I must ask it. Were you aware of Miss Greenwood's pregnancies?'

If she'd appeared nervous before, that was the question that utterly threw her off balance. She spilled some of her tea before hastily placing the cup back on the tray. Her cheeks were as red as ripe tomatoes.

'How could you possibly know about that?'

I downed my cup of tea before replying. 'A post-mortem was needed. It was not difficult to tell.'

'Of course,' she whispered. 'There is no point in denying it now. She had a child before coming to Scotland. She didn't like to talk about it . . . understandably.'

'It would help us if you could tell us any details.'

'Details? Well . . . there are very few I know for sure. She left home when she couldn't hide her state any more and gave birth in some rotten village. Her family would not have her back, so she had to leave the child there with an old matron. Poor Lizzy had to work hard and sent money to support her daughter.'

'Where does the child live now?'

Miss Oakley looked down. 'Oh, well . . . the poor creature died. Lizzy never brought her up in conversation.'

I wrote down the story. It was as sad as it was common; families turning their back on their daughters when they got themselves into trouble.

'Thank you for that,' I said. 'Inspector McGray may have some . . . additional questions. Please bear with him.'

He'd already set down his cup, spilling some tea since he'd drunk very little. It was impossible for him not to notice Miss Oakley's sudden apprehension. 'Don't worry, lass. I won't bite. How often would ye interact with Lord Bampot?'

'Very little, sir.'

'Really?'

'Yes. Well, I was supposed to take over some of Lizzy's patients. He was going to be among those, but I was still familiarizing myself with his case.'

'I see. Ye forgot to tell us that when we mentioned him a moment ago.'

The girl looked sideways. 'Indeed. I do apologize.'

McGray crossed his legs and stroked his stubble, distractedly looking at the low ceiling. 'Miss, tell me what ye could do with an onion 'n' some sugar.'

By then Miss Oakley would not have been surprised by anything he said. She laughed earnestly.

'I do not know, Inspector. Onion marmalade?'

*

'Everything we asked seemed to upset her,' McGray said as we left the front garden.

'I find your attitude shocking. You were the one who told me not to upset our witnesses. Now that girl thinks you are as lunatic as one of the inmates she tends to.'

'D'ye think I give a rat's arse?'

My stomach churned a little. 'You should. You never know when a witness will turn out to be crucial.'

As we walked away we saw that next to our horses there was a black carriage. It must have arrived a few seconds ago, for its horse was still catching its breath. We saw a man alighting, and were astounded to see Dr Clouston himself.

'Why, Doctor!' I said. 'This is quite unexpected.'

'Hello, Inspector. Yes, I wanted to check on Miss Oakley. Last night I sent Miss Smith to give her the bad news. I wanted to see how she was faring.'

'She looks a wee bit shaken,' McGray said. 'I'm sure she'll appreciate yer visit.'

A sudden gust of wind brought tiny drops of sleet. The doctor gulped, and instead of walking on he stood there, planted in the snow.

'Are you all right?' I asked.

Clouston did not look up, but fixed his eyes on his shoes as he spoke. 'I should have remembered this earlier . . . I think I can help you in your quest.'

'Help us?'

'Yes. I believe there is a place I forgot to mention. Lord Bampot might have decided to go and hide there.'

McGray and I were flabbergasted.

'And you forgot to mention *that*?' I snapped.

McGray leaned closer to him. 'Tell us, Doc.'

Clouston's eyes were now on the house. From the corner of my eye I could see Miss Oakley standing in an upstairs window, watching us.

The doctor took a deep breath. 'Well, it is purely intuition, but there is this small farm in the outskirts of Edinburgh ... I believe the land still belongs to Lady Anne.'

13

The wind was blowing mightily by the time we saw the farmhouse appear. The building was borderline derelict, the windows boarded up and the walls invaded by blackened ivy and hardened moss. However, I reckoned the place would make a luxurious shelter for a fugitive.

'We'd better leave the horses here,' McGray said when we were a good hundred yards away. We tied the reins to a pine tree and walked on. I picked up my lantern, anticipating that the place would be very dark. It might have been the harsh wind, or the season's thick cloud, but there was a looming, oppressive presence in the air. I could feel it with every breath.

McGray unholstered his weapon but kept it hidden in the folds of his overcoat, his eyes alert.

As we drew closer we could see that the main door was ajar. I drew my gun as well, just as a black cat jumped on to the house's tattered fence. Its bright-green eyes followed us as we approached the entrance.

Nine-Nails opened the door as quietly as he could, just enough for him to pass through, and after a careful look he stepped in.

I followed, and the smell of damp hit us. Only a few streaks of dull sunshine filtered through the boards at the window, so I lit the lantern, which gave us a much better view of the interior. A cracked table and a broken chair were the only furnishings. There was a small fireplace so encrusted with cobwebs we could hardly see the bottom of the grate.

'So this is where Lord Ardglass last saw his daughter,' I muttered, thinking of the sad episode narrated by Dr Clouston shortly before we departed Miss Oakley's residence.

McGray pointed down. The floor was so dusty it almost looked white, and a trail of footsteps stood out as clear as an ink stain. They were irregular steps, smudged in places, as if whoever made them had been dragging something.

The narrow stairs creaked under our feet so loudly I thought they might give way. They took us up to what should have been a landing to two rooms, but all the partition walls had been stripped, the entire storey now a single wide area.

I looked around, my eyes following every shadow projected by the lantern. My heartbeats quickened; I expected a dark figure to jump from the filthy corners and strike us.

'Nobody home,' McGray said with a rather disappointed sigh. There was another mucky fireplace where we saw fresh ashes, and right in front of it lay a bundle of clean blankets.

McGray kneeled down to inspect them. 'He spent the night here.'

'*He?* It could have been anybody. This place has been abandoned for quite a while.'

McGray rummaged through the blankets. 'Breadcrumbs, cheese crust, apple core – nice supper he had, but nothing to tell us for certain this was left by Lord Bampot.'

He took the lantern out of my hands and we carefully searched every nook and cranny of the room. The place was so bare that we soon satisfied ourselves there were no further traces.

We returned to the ground floor, where the thick layers of dust seemed disturbed only around a chair at the corner of the shabby table. Again, there were smudged tracks here and there, showing how someone had sat at that table without placing a single item on its surface.

McGray shed light on a particularly dark corner, and our eyes instantly fell on a removed floorboard. The half-rotten wood had been tossed aside, revealing a shallow hole.

'Look at that!' McGray said. We kneeled down and the first thing we found was a clay bottle, corked and sealed with wax. It looked as though it had been buried there for centuries. 'Could that be a –'

'A what?' I asked, as Nine-Nails picked up the bottle and shook it.

'Yer not gonnae like this, laddie.'

'Do you think it is something we should collect as evidence?'

It might have been, but McGray banged the bottle's neck against the edge of the table. The cork broke off as if cleanly cut with a sword.

'Is that your best tavern trick?' I said, but could not elaborate on the joke, for the acrid stench of ammonia hit my nostrils and instantly made my eyes tear. *'Gosh, that is urine!'*

Even Nine-Nails seemed repulsed. 'Very auld piss, I'd say.'

He poured the contents on to the floor before I could protest. I expected to see pure urine, but the liquid that came out was dark red and viscous – it made me shudder. Then I heard metallic clinking and saw a handful of nails falling out, all bent and rusty, followed by a couple of blackened woody sprigs.

I had to cover my nose and mouth with my handkerchief, but that only slightly mitigated the horrendous stench. 'What on earth is that?'

'A witch bottle,' McGray said, observing the items with fascination. 'They use 'em for protection. When ye move into a new house, ye bury one o' these. They're supposed to trap any harm coming to the folk living in the building.'

'When you say harm, I suppose you mean . . .'

'Hexes, spells, jinxes.'

'Is that urine? Blood? What on earth . . . ?'

'I've read the main liquid has to be the urine of one of the occupants, preferably the head o' the house. Some witches add expensive wine as a kind of offering.'

'And the nails?'

'It's like Madame Katerina said. For witches metal is like a well for – bad things. That's where all the black magic is trapped.'

I rose and walked to the still open door, trying to find some fresh air. As I took a deep breath I saw the same black cat pacing around the front garden. To my surprise, the animal looked directly at me before it turned around and walked away.

'Are these . . . artefacts something you find at witches' houses?'

'Not witches alone. The hags can charge good money for making one o' these for people's homes. They've been used since the Middle Ages. They work as long as they're left undisturbed and strangers don't ken where they are.'

'Why would someone come looking for that?'

'Mmm . . . Perhaps this isn't all they were looking for.' McGray plunged his four-fingered hand into the ground and had a quick rummage. He pulled out a dusty leather bag and shook it. I thought it was empty, but then a single penny rolled out. 'Aha! This must be what he came for.'

'Money?' I ventured.

'Aye. It's no surprise they're in the same place: ye'd keep yer witch bottle well hidden, just as ye'd do yer gold.'

I pressed my handkerchief a little harder against my nose. 'If this house and land are Lady Anne's – do you think she knew about that bottle and bag?'

'I cannae tell about Lady Glass, but I'd bet yer tetchy nostrils Lord Bampot was here. Those leftovers looked fresh, and there's no others, so I'd say the place was disturbed only last night. The night after he ran away. It cannae be a coincidence.'

'Sounds logical. He comes here for shelter and to retrieve his money.'

'Which he'll definitely need if he's on the run,' McGray concluded, clapping the dust off his hands.

He glanced around, suddenly looking lost.

I shared the feeling. 'At least we now can reasonably believe he is heading away, and not lurking around town preying on somebody else.'

'He might be preying on somebody else *out* o' town.'

McGray made his way out, utterly frustrated. I was

about to close the door, but then something half hidden behind it caught my eye, something that looked almost glossy against all the dusty surfaces.

It was a thin cardboard folder, of a type I recognized immediately.

'Nine-Nails, wait,' I said, leaning to pick up the file. 'This looks exactly like the file Clouston gave me! The one containing Lord Ardglass's medical records.'

McGray snatched it from my hands and looked inside. There was a single sheet of paper, torn from a ledger and with a couple of lines hastily jotted in pencil.

'What does it say?' I urged.

Nine-Nails' face had turned white. 'We've just been there! It's Miss Oakley's address!'

14

We retraced our steps at a wild gallop, sleet lashing our faces, the horses moving so fast their steaming breath trailed behind.

'We might have even crossed paths!' McGray grunted.

'Nonsense. These are open fields. We would have easily seen –' I stopped there, realizing precisely what I was saying; Lord Ardglass could have seen us too, and he would have known we were heading to him. I winced. 'What might he want with Miss Oakley?'

McGray grunted. 'He won't be going there for a cup o' tea.'

Our worst fears were realized when we reached Miss Oakley's cottage. The door was wide open, and on the snow there were fresh marks of thumping steps.

We dismounted and rushed in, guns in hands; the place could not have looked more different from our earlier visit. The table was upside down, its legs broken; the tea set was shattered, pieces of china all over the floor, and in the tumult the wet tea leaves had become mixed with the stuffing of ripped cushions.

I opened my mouth to speak, but McGray raised his hand, asking me to listen.

There was a rustle of papers coming from the kitchen.

I took a sharp, involuntary breath.

We drew closer, as quietly as we could, but then I stepped on something, and before I could realize it was a tiny shard of china the blasted thing cracked loudly under my shoe.

The ruffling stopped immediately, and I saw the fury in McGray's face. He hurled himself at the kitchen door and kicked it open.

The room was in a greater mess than the parlour, but I barely noticed – my eyes fell on the black cat grooming itself on a working table, a pile of crumpled papers around it. There was nobody there.

'Don't move, gentlemen.'

My heart stopped. I felt a hint of queasiness. The deep, imperious voice had come from behind us, sending blasts of ice-cold fear piercing through my body.

McGray tried to turn around, but then a gunshot resounded and I saw the bullet hit the wooden floor right between his feet.

'I said don't move, Nine-Nails.'

I did not attempt to turn; if the man wanted to shoot us he would have done so without giving warning. I could see him, however, reflected in the pane of the window in front of us.

The man himself – Lord Joel Ardglass.

Pointing a large-calibre handgun at us.

I recognized his face from the picture I still carried in my breast pocket, but at the same time it could have been an entirely different man: the skin around his eyes was darkened and wrinkled, and his jaw appeared broader, as if his very bones had grown harder. He was clad in a thick black travel overcoat.

'It's fortunate you like your tartan trousers,' he told McGray. 'I'd recognize you three miles away.'

'Where's the lass?' Nine-Nails snapped.

'I just missed her. Drop your weapons. *Now.*'

We could do nothing but oblige, though we both tossed the guns as close to our feet as possible.

'You, the pretty boy. There's an envelope under that cat's arse. Give it to me – and don't try anything funny.'

I hesitated for a bizarre moment. My breath, my thumping heart, the beads of cold sweat rolling down my temples, they all felt amplified.

'I don't have all day, son!'

I slowly moved forwards. The table was only a yard away, but time stretched as if I'd moved a mile. The cat, oblivious to our situation, was still meticulously licking its coat. I thought it was the same animal I'd seen before, but being closer I saw this one's eyes were yellow. I pulled out the small brown envelope, while the cat hardly acknowledged the movement.

It was as though the paper burned my fingers. Lord Ardglass needed it, but why?

'Kneel down and slide it across the floor.'

I did so, slightly twisting my torso as I threw the envelope. I managed to catch a glimpse of his muddy boots and the leather bag sitting next to them. It was engraved with a much-embellished letter A.

'Look away!' he yelled. 'And don't try to run after me. I'll be watching my back. Don't make me kill you both.'

We heard him pick up the paper and take a first step away. McGray's chest was now heaving and he could not contain himself.

'What did Pansy tell ye?'

Lord Ardglass stopped. From that angle I could no longer see his reflection, but in the absolute quiet I could hear a shift in his breathing. Was it agitation? Anger? The briefest of glances would have let me know. I nearly growled in frustration.

'You would kill to know, wouldn't you?' Joel Ardglass said, not a trace of emotion in his voice. 'You'd kill for her.'

'It would be a noble kill,' McGray responded. 'Not like poisoning a poor lass just 'cos yer bitch mother didn't let ye marry that trollop ye liked.'

I flinched as he spoke, expecting a bullet to stop his reckless baiting at any time.

Lord Ardglass said nothing for a seemingly endless moment, and then I heard a burst, so sudden a gunshot could not have startled us more. He had erupted into laughter, loud and earnest.

'That trollop I liked!' he finally said, an eerie pleasure oozing from every word; the very voice of madness. 'You're a stupid fool, Nine-Nails McGray. You really know nothing! If only . . .'

We were expecting him to say more, but all we heard was him moving again, and then pushing the door open, letting the icy wind inside. The blasted man was getting away and there was nothing we could do.

I feared McGray would turn and attack him. All his wrath came out in his voice: 'What does *marigold* mean?'

Joel Ardglass cackled again. It was not crazed, delusional laughter but rather bitter . . . understanding, and when he spoke his words were chilling: 'Don't follow me, boys. The worst thing you can do to yourselves is find it out.'

Then we heard the door slam. McGray instantly picked up his gun and sprinted out at striking speed, roaring.

I reached for my weapon and jumped up. The door was flapping against the wind, obscuring my view of what was happening outside, and before I reached it I heard a deafening shot, and McGray howling.

I pushed the door open and thrust myself towards the front garden, where I caught a glimpse of Nine-Nails' horse falling into the deep snow.

Lord Ardglass was already on my mount, spurring on the terrified Philippa, forcing her forwards.

McGray was running after him, shooting an aimless bullet, but all we could do was watch my white mare gallop away, carrying Lord Ardglass, disappearing into the distance.

15

'*Shit!*' McGray bellowed, his voice cutting the gusts of wind.

He ran back and we both kneeled down to look at his horse.

The body was still warm, a trail of breath still coming from its nostrils, but poor Rye was gone. He had been shot cleanly in the head, the bullet entering exactly between his eyes with chilling precision.

McGray placed a soothing hand on the horse's mane.

'*No . . .*' he said in a broken whisper. 'He was a great beast. Didn't deserve this, the auld brute . . .'

'It was very quick, McGray,' was all I could say. 'Rye must have hardly known.'

McGray gulped. 'My father gave me this horse . . .'

His eyes glistened and he tried to blink the tears away. I looked up – that was all the privacy I could offer him – and gave him a moment to grieve, but I was already thinking desperately what we could do. There was nothing in front of us but miles of open field, we had no mounts or a carriage, and as the seconds passed Lord Ardglass rode further and further away.

McGray had realized all that too. He cleared his throat, gave Rye a last affectionate pat and then jumped to his feet. 'The nearest place is the asylum,' he said, already heading that way, pushing me back. 'Yer too slow, dandy.

I'll head there and borrow a cart or something. Ye stay here and search the house.'

He was running, kicking up snow in his wake, before I could reply. I was left kneeling by the dead horse, still stunned by how quickly it all had happened; it must have only been minutes since we'd arrived at the cottage.

I stood up slowly, looking at the disturbed snow. Despite the blustery weather I reckoned this time we had a good chance of following Lord Ardglass's trail. The snow was deep and it would take a while for the wind and sleet to erase the sharp hoof prints. It all depended on how quickly McGray managed to return.

I decided to use that time wisely and ran back into the cottage. I made my way to the stairs, but then, without warning, a most unpleasant wave of shivering overcame my chest, shoulders and arms. I had to halt for an instant, taking a deep breath before I could climb the first step.

'What on earth was that?' I mumbled, grasping the handrail. I did not have time to dwell on it though.

I found Miss Oakley's bedroom as messy as the rest of the house, but it was the only place where I could tell there were missing items.

The old wardrobe was open and half empty, some garments still crumpled on the bed. Among them I saw a little wooden chest, wide open and containing a meagre handful of copper pence and a small earring without its pair.

Everything screamed that Miss Oakley had been packing, and in quite a rush. She must have fled the house before Lord Ardglass arrived; then again, how would she know he was coming? When we first called on her she'd not even seemed up to leaving the house, let alone embarking on a trip.

I remembered Dr Clouston sending us to the farm. Had he told her something? Warned her? It would not be the first time he had kept information to himself . . . but if he knew she was in danger, why would he have sent us away?

The room offered one more clue. I looked under the bed and found a familiar item: another red onion, sitting in a bowl full of brown sugar. Had Miss Oakley meant something when she'd said *onion marmalade*? She must have known about that onion under her bed; unlike the one McGray had shown me, this one was still fresh, no ants crawling on it yet. I did not even touch it.

I had a quick look through the window, but there was still no sign of McGray, so I went back to the ground floor to inspect the kitchen. The blasted cat was still there, now grooming its paws, indifferent to the world, yet it did screech when I flung it aside. I looked through the small heap of papers on which it had been sitting.

I found useless bills and merchants' notes, but then a telegram and a newspaper cutting. It was a corner of the *Scotsman*, dated that very day, and listing train timetables.

'Things are beginning to take shape,' I said, as the telegram revealed her intention to travel:

Too late. Come.

The cryptic signature was simply *Miss R*, without any sender's address. Fortunately the telegraphist had noted the office that transmitted the message: Lancaster.

And Miss Oakley hailed from Lancashire. Hardly a coincidence.

I looked at the timetables again. Near the top were the services to Manchester, and Lancaster Castle Station was one of the main stops.

'I have you now,' I said out loud, pulling the chain of my pocket watch. To my dismay, the day's last service would leave Edinburgh's Caledonian Station in exactly forty-five minutes.

'Nine-Nails, you'd better hurry . . .'

I shoved the papers into my breast pocket and rushed to the front door. After a most frustrating wait, I finally saw a shape emerge in the distance. I recognized Clouston's carriage, the one we'd seen earlier, but this time it was pulled by two horses.

Soon I saw Tom, the hulking orderly, lashing the beasts, and McGray's face shouting through the window.

'Hop on, lassie!' he yelled as soon as they halted.

'Could you please stop calling me that?' I barked as I took my seat. I noticed Dr Clouston only when our shoulders clashed. I snapped again: '*You* have some explaining to do.'

'I beg your –'

'Not now, Frey.' McGray banged on the outside of the carriage and Tom instantly drove on, taking us north in a frantic race. 'Follow that trail!' McGray shouted, half his torso sticking out of the window, pointing ahead.

The carriage lurched madly and I had to yell over the rattle of the wheels: 'I know where Miss Oakley is going!'

McGray did not even register my words, focused on nothing but the tracks ahead of us.

I turned to Clouston, suddenly feeling angered. 'What did you tell Miss Oakley? Did you prompt her to leave?'

'*Prompt her?* I don't even know what's happening. Adolphus appeared out of the blue demanding a transport. He's not explained –'

'Miss Oakley fled.' I was too impatient. 'She packed her bags in a rush. From the look of her lodgings, she must have started doing so but minutes after we left her. Which makes *you* the last person she talked to – that we know of.'

'I do not understand . . .' We rode over a pothole and the doctor bounced, banging his head hard against the roof.

'You must have told her something!' I said.

Clouston stammered. 'I told her nothing! I hardly spoke to the girl. As soon as she opened the door she said she was late for some appointment. She was rather curt, so all I did was give her my regards and leave.'

'You do realize how suspicious this all seems.'

'Indeed I do, but I assure you, I didn't even enter the house.'

'You better be telling the truth, Doctor, or else –'

McGray roared, then banged the door with both fists and kicked it too. All of a sudden the carriage was slowing down.

'Lost the trail,' Tom yelled.

The carriage was still moving when McGray jumped out and ran ahead.

Clouston and I stood up at the same time, our heads bumping against each other. I pushed the doctor aside and alighted first.

The carriage had stopped by the bridge that crossed

the Union Canal, right in between two enormous factories, crammed with tall chimneys and columns of black
smoke. There were carts, horses and men running to and
from the workshops, never allowing the snow to settle.
The cobbled road was but a brown, muddy mess.

I wrinkled my nose at the stench of rubber that came
from the factories. Once more, I had to cover my face
with my handkerchief, for the smell was making me terribly queasy. None of the others seemed affected, McGray
least of all, pulling his hair in frustration.

'What now?' he thought out loud. He glared at me and
my handkerchief, and I could not repress a gag. 'Och, pull
yerself together, ye look like an anaemic poodle blowing
into a trumpet. We've real problems here!'

I had to swallow and take a deep breath. 'Lord Ardglass may be following Miss Oakley,' I managed to say,
despite my acute discomfort.

'*He what?*'

I handed him the telegram and the newspaper, and
described Miss Oakley's bedroom as he read them
through.

'The telegram came from Lancaster,' I concluded.

'Miss Oakley does have connections there,' Clouston
said, and he immediately felt my suspicious stare. 'She was
part of my staff; I interviewed her and telegrammed her
references.'

'Caledonian Station . . .' McGray mumbled. 'Up to
here, Bampot's trail could well have been going there . . .'
His eyes flashed between the factories, the trampled road
and the bustling packs of workers. 'This mayhem also
looks like a paradise for hiding in . . .' It took him less

than a blink to decide. 'We better check on that train first; then we can come back with a bunch o' laddies and search these bloody factories.'

'We'd better hurry,' I said once we were all back in the carriage. 'If we allow them to leave the city, this chase will become a living hell!'

In fact, my own omens would turn out to be more accurate than Madame Katerina's.

16

Tom drove at an incredible speed. He took us through some filthy alleys I had never seen, and we ended up rushing through a steep close, so narrow the damp brick walls flew past only inches from us.

I checked my pocket watch, infuriated by not knowing where we were. 'We have less than ten minutes.'

Just when I thought Tom had got us hopelessly lost, the alley opened into Lothian Road, alongside Goods Station and its reeking coal yards. Adjacent to them was the ghastly sight of Caledonian Station, a hastily built wooden structure that served half the city, since the actual station – scheduled to open ten years ago – was still being built.

Tom dodged carts, carriages and pedestrians, and halted right in front of the Princes Street entrance. The station did not even have proper gates, let alone a roof. The ticket offices were improvised sheds, and the platforms on either side of Scotland's main lines were creaking stands of smoked planks that looked terribly frail.

McGray kicked the carriage door open. 'Which platform, Frey?'

'We should alert the station's constables.'

'Alert the vicar of St Giles if ye want, but tell me the fucking platform first!'

I glanced at the cutting. 'Six,' and McGray ran frantically through the crowd.

'Bloody fast Scot,' I mumbled, readying myself to follow him.

'Can we assist you in any way?' asked Clouston, but I did not have a chance to reply. I could barely see McGray amidst the sea of people, and with the noise of engines and steam whistles he could not hear me shouting after him.

One of those whistles was piercingly loud, so much so it made me see stars. I covered my ears, stunned by the horrible sound, yet nobody around me seemed even slightly bothered.

I turned to the source of the whistle: a large, roaring locomotive a hundred yards ahead of me, and when the steam dissipated I found it was the train at platform six.

The engine was already starting, a thick column of smoke above it, and its wheels beginning to roll in an initially sluggish motion. I had to elbow my way forward, and a second later I saw McGray's head, sticking above the crowd as he pushed past everything that stood in his way.

He reached the very last carriage, a first-class one, then hurled himself at the door, grabbed the handle and nearly ripped the whole thing off its hinges as he opened it. As soon as he jumped on to the moving train a thin ticket boy tried to stop him, but McGray pushed him aside as if the lad had been made of paper.

'McGray!' I roared, now running in desperation. I saw the wheels speeding up, gaining momentum much faster than I ever could. Another deafening whistle resounded in my skull, somehow making everything around me appear blurred. 'Get off! We are not going to Lancaster!'

'I saw him hop in!'

Had I not felt dizzy, or had the train been moving but a smidgen more slowly, I would have let McGray go; but without time or clarity, my first impulse was to sprint faster, run until my legs burned, and then I grasped the hand Nine-Nails offered. He lifted me into the air and I landed precariously on the very edge of the carriage's steps, waving my free arm to keep my balance. I felt my shoes slipping on the wet steel, but McGray managed to pull me in just in time.

As soon as my feet were firmly planted on the train's floor another chill took me by surprise, this time spreading to my stomach, which had been aching since we left the rubber factories. I had to lean forwards, my hands on my knees.

'Ye all right, laddie?'

I muttered something but then two tall train guards came up, yelling. One of them shut the velvet-padded door.

'CID,' McGray snapped, showing his credentials. He and the men argued while I took long, deep breaths, slowly coming back to my senses. The swaying of the train did not help my queasiness, so I tried to focus on where I was: the first-class carriage, with a red carpet, oak panelling and brass fittings on the doors.

I managed to follow McGray's explanations, and then one of the guards said: 'Shall we stop the train, sir?'

At once, McGray and I respectively yelled *No* and *Yes*.

'We need to stop now!' I insisted.

'What for? To give Ardglass warning, so he can jump out through a window? He didnae see me get on. We can catch him off guard.'

I looked through the windows; the train was accelerating slowly but steadily, and I grunted. 'Blast, you might be right. It will be far easier to catch him now that we have him in a confined space.'

'Warn the driver,' McGray told one of the men. 'Tell him we need the train to go faster than usual – soon. And no one else can hear we're on board, youse understand? I don't want people whispering that there's a pair of peelers around.'

The guard nodded and left.

'We should hide until the train is moving at full speed,' I said, and the second guard showed us to an empty compartment.

I sat back, fearing I would not have a second to rest ever again, but McGray was pacing in the narrow space like a caged lion.

'Are you absolutely certain you saw him?' I asked, realizing it was a little too late to question the fact.

'Aye. He nearly missed the train. I saw him jumping into one of the front cars.'

'A third-class?' I asked, scowling, for I'd never ventured so close to a train's forepart. The noisy, smoky wagons right behind the engine were usually reserved for cargo and the poorer folk. McGray assented.

We were moving south-west, faster and faster, and in a matter of minutes Edinburgh's blackened buildings gave way to flat, snowy fields.

'He would *not* try to attack someone right now . . .' I mumbled, 'would he?'

McGray looked sombre. 'Nae. Lord Bampot seems to have very clear targets.' He looked at me with a raised eyebrow. 'Ye sure yer all right? Ye look all yellow.'

'I am sure I will survive,' I said, checking that my gun was loaded and ready. The train was now running at some speed, and there was nothing but white fields on either side of the track. 'I believe it is time.'

'It'll be a pleasure,' McGray answered, making his way to the corridor. He was about to open the door to the nearest compartment, but I stopped him.

'Let me do it,' I whispered. 'I might be a tad less conspicuous,' and I pointed at his flamboyant tartans. Luckily he nodded.

I held my gun under my coat's collar, so that it looked as if I was looking for something in my breast pocket, yet the weapon was ready to be drawn. After a deep breath, I opened the door.

There was an elderly, very elegant couple inside, but no one else.

'Oh, do excuse me,' I said, 'I thought this was vacant . . .'
And before they could reply I moved on to the next door.

I searched the rest of the carriage in this manner, while McGray kept watch in the corridor. We crossed to the next carriage and found one of the guards.

'Boss, the driver did as you asked,' he told McGray. 'Anything else youse need?'

I searched my pocket and found Lord Ardglass's portrait. 'This is the man we are looking for. Have you seen him?'

The young man stared at the photograph. 'Uh, I cannae be sure. There's a lot o' people on board.'

'Look for him – *discreetly* – and come back to us if you happen to see him. Do not talk to him or try anything yourself.'

The chap bowed and left.

I felt the sweat on my hands, the tension building up as we moved forwards along the train.

We reached the dining car next. I looked through its door's small window before I opened it, and saw the neat lines of tables with their shiny cutlery, the leather-lined seats and the waiters walking around with silver platters.

I looked at Nine-Nails. 'You cannot walk in there; you will go as unnoticed as a baboon clambering over their dining tables.'

'So will ye,' he retorted, staring at my now scruffy overcoat. 'Yer as sweaty and soiled as me.'

'Just let me inspect the bloody place before you go in,' and before he could remonstrate I entered.

To my surprise, I did attract curious stares. A middle-aged lady with a plumed hat glared at me as if faced with a tray of manure, and then covered her nose with her napkin. I soon understood why. My nostrils were hit by a hint of ammonia, and I realized I must have stepped in urine from the witch bottle.

It was barely a waft but it triggered a most unexpected reaction: I went from queasy to utterly nauseous, feeling a horrible oppression in my chest, pushing upwards, and then my mouth started to salivate, preparing itself to receive vomit.

My legs trembled and I had to lean on the nearest table. I knocked a decanter over, the noise of breaking glass mixing with the general gasp.

In the mayhem I heard a female cry, and looking up I saw a thin, somehow familiar figure standing up like an uncoiling spring, covering her face with a menu and running away.

'*I see you!*' I yelled, but right then I lost all control over my body: strong chills shot across my torso, my hands, already icy, went totally numb, and I felt pins and needles in all my joints. I gagged, vaguely aware of McGray's cry: 'Are ye all right, Frey?'

He did not look well either, his skin as yellow as bile. The very thought made me retch and my entire upper body heaved forwards, expelling an uncontrollable explosion of vomit.

Everything became a blur. I barely felt McGray's hands holding me by the shoulders, and the alarmed shouting of the passengers came to my ears muffled, fading more and more until all my senses abandoned me.

17

Vague shades of colour danced in front of me, and there were moments when I surfaced close to reality. I recognized glimpses of McGray's face, the sunlight flashing through my eyelids, the sounds of a busy train station, and then I relapsed into a nasty dream where I was vomiting a constant stream of foam, my insides burning. After the dream everything went quiet and peaceful, but it did not last.

The worst part of awakening was the real discomforts hitting me again: the surroundings were still fuzzy, yet nausea and shivers overwhelmed my numb brain, and I wished only to sleep again.

'He seems to be coming around,' a stranger said. Then, much to my relief, I heard McGray.

'Ye sure, laddie? He looks terrible.'

I shuddered, suddenly coming back to life. I was in a whitewashed room, the smells of laudanum and ethanol telling me that I was in a hospital.

'What happened?' I asked, my voice almost a grunt.

'Take it easy, Inspector,' said the stranger. 'You've had a difficult journey.'

He was young – I calculated he'd be in his late twenties – and his white coat told me he was a doctor. He had a bushy blond beard, a bony face and eyes magnified by round spectacles.

'Say hello to Dr Riley,' McGray told me. 'It was lucky he was on the train.'

Through the window, all I could see was a patch of grey sky. 'Where are we?'

'Lancaster, dandy.'

I abandoned myself to a long moan. 'Blast! Did you not manage to stop him? The case will now be a bloody tangle of red tape. English, Scottish, all trying to wash their hands of –'

'Och, shut up! I pulled you out of a pool of yer own sick and this is how ye thank me? I thank my lucky stars I wasn't involved in the sponge bath.'

Indeed I was clean – even the smell of cheap soap was a blessing – and my clothes had been neatly folded and hung on a chair nearby. I noticed a menacing-looking hose lying on the side table.

'I did not require . . .'

The doctor smiled. 'Gastric lavage? No. Your vomiting expelled most of the poison before it caused serious harm.'

I sat up a little too quickly and felt my head pounding. 'Poison!'

McGray was taking a spoonful of charcoal powder, and the doctor handed him a glass of water.

'That's correct, sir. You both had clear symptoms of poisoning by cardiac glycoside.'

I pressed a hand to my forehead, futilely trying to ease the ache. 'Glycoside? But how? Whe–' And then it hit me. 'Digitalin?'

'Oh, I see you are familiar with the substance. Yes: foxgloves. I've seen these symptoms many times, but it's usually in summer – and most of the time it's children who've eaten flowers from their mothers' gardens. You two were lucky; if ingested over long periods of time it also impairs the vision and causes wild hallucinations.' Dr Riley pulled up a chair for himself. 'Now, I find it very odd that two grown CID inspectors managed to consume a flower that is not in season. Can you think of any way you might have come to do so?'

It was not a difficult question.

'The tea . . .' I mumbled.

'Aye,' said McGray. 'That Oakley bitch poisoned us. I even remember there were foxglove stems in her front garden.'

That very image was in my head. I also remembered Madame Katerina's words: *Milk of magnesia. You should get some. Soon.* Milk of magnesia would not have prevented the poisoning, but the symptoms would not have been as harsh. How could she have known? I'd rather not dwell on that or give the woman any credit.

'Wait, wait,' I said, thinking now of the tea. 'We both drank from her pot. Why did I pass out while you became only slightly queasy?'

Dr Riley stroked his beard. 'Well, the toxin usually has more severe effects on people of a delicate disposition.'

Nine-Nails cackled so hard I had to hold my aching head. 'Aye, this is definitely a fainting one!'

'He does not mean that,' I protested. 'He means –'

'Auld folks? Dainty ladies? Wee children?' McGray asked with uncontained glee.

'All of those,' Riley said, 'and also the anaemic and the undernourished.'

McGray laughed even harder.

'Doctor,' I groaned, 'could you give us a moment? We have some matters to discuss.'

He assented. 'Of course, Inspector. I have some paperwork to do.'

McGray spoke as soon as the door was shut. 'The guards saw Lord Ardglass.'

'Did they?'

'Indeedy. He was in the third-class wagon, but that was right before ye decided to carpet the place with spew. We never found him after that.'

'Did you search thoroughly?'

'Aye, course we did, but we lost precious time making sure ye weren't dead. The laddies took me to where Ardglass had been sitting – no need to hide after yer wee scene – but he wasn't there any more. We found an auld chap in the next seat; he told us that he'd seen a middle-aged man, with a very fancy coat for third class, but that he stood up and left the carriage as soon as someone yelled there were inspectors on the train.' McGray shook his head. 'I ken ye were a spectacle, but how could they tell we were CID so soon?'

I sighed. 'I think I know. Right before I passed out I saw Miss – this Oakley woman in the dining car. She saw me first; she was running out, trying to cover her face.'

'D'ye think she was the one who told everybody?'

'I cannot think of any other explanation. Oakley and the guards were the only people on that train who knew who we were.'

Nine-Nails shook his head. 'Why? First it looks like she was running from Lord Ardglass . . . but then it looks like she was warning him . . . None o' this makes sense.'

'I am glad I am not the only one at a loss. And we do not even know why she decided to travel all of a sudden.'

McGray began to pace. 'So we went to see her, she poisons us, and for no apparent reason she decides to run away, right before Lord Bampot comes by and makes a wreck o' her house.'

'And takes an envelope,' I added.

'Aye, and we have no idea what that was . . .' He paced a little longer. 'It's clear she was running from him. We must have said something that warned her.'

'Assuming, of course, that such warning did not come from Clouston.'

'I heard him tell ye Oakley didn't say much.'

'Yes, but –'

'Then I believe him.'

'I will not argue about that right now. I'd be more interested to know why Oakley had to run from Lord Ardglass. Some sordid affair nobody has told us about? She knew he was coming . . .' I clicked my tongue. 'Yet if that is correct, why would she not tell us? Why would she poison us, if we were the very ones who could have protected her? And then why would she appear to warn him, as if she did not want us to catch him?'

As I spoke I saw a glow of understanding in Nine-Nails' eyes. He stopped at the window, staring at the dark clouds. 'D'ye think she might've done something . . . something she shouldnae?'

'What do you mean?'

'We are chasing Ardglass, assuming he committed the murder – what if he didnae?'

'Do you mean to say –'

'What if Oakley did it? And now Ardglass is chasing her 'cos he's been framed?'

I pondered that.

'That petite young woman . . . she does not look like a murderer; then again, I have seen odder culprits. I remember when I cracked the case of Good Mary Brown, the tiny woman who poisoned –'

'Half a dozen husbands right after buying them life insurances. Don't ye ever get tired o' telling that story? Yer like a great-granddad boasting he was run over by King Willy's carriage, or –'

'Jesus, I am *trying* to say that you might actually be talking sense. Let's say you are right and Oakley – for some reason I cannot fathom right now – did murder her apparently good friend Miss Greenwood and managed to frame Lord Ardglass. If that were the case, how come he is on the run? Why would he not come to us and explain what happened?'

'The chap's insane,' McGray reminded me. 'Who kens what goes on in his brains?'

'Very true,' I said, massaging my sore head. 'This is not how investigations are supposed to go: we started with one suspicious fugitive – now we have two.'

'And we're in bloody England. Things *are* turning to shite!'

Things became even worse when Dr Riley came back with his bill, and the man refused to take our credentials as a guarantee.

'If you don't mind, sir, I would like to keep you under observation until tomorrow morning,' he told me as he counted the money.

'Tomorrow is a luxury I cannot afford right now,' I said,

buttoning up my jacket, which still gave off a slightly sickly smell, and feeling my considerably lighter wallet.

'Ye cheap bastard,' said McGray when we reached the corridor.

'Cheap! I will have you know I have little money left, and we still need to secure a train back.'

'Don't think o' that so soon, laddie. We're not leaving 'til we find either Oakley or Ardglass.'

I snorted. 'Oh, are we not? How much money do you have on you?'

'Nothing.'

'*What!*'

'I never carry any. I hate my pockets jingling like a baby's rattle.'

'Then how do you buy . . . your pints, or your drams or those ghastly platefuls of haggis that you are so fond of?'

McGray shrugged. 'I tell them I'm CID and folks gimme stuff for free. Haven't ye tried?'

'No. I have never *needed* free stuff.'

'Och, everyone can use a free dram every now 'n' then.'

'Well, we – no, *I* will run out of money very soon, yet you want us to stay here indefinitely? How do you plan to get by?'

'Take it easy, Frey. We can get money wired to any telegraph office; this isn't the Stone Age.'

We left the hospital at twilight, and as we stepped out I fully realized that we were in an entirely different town. Thick layers of stormy clouds shrouded the brown stone buildings of Lancaster, and the old houses, richly fitted with Honduras mahogany, reminded me of the wealth the borough had attracted in the last hundred years. The port was one of the most important on England's west coast, second only to Liverpool. Cotton, precious woods, ivory and many other costly commodities (slaves included, before the Abolition Act) were imported through the waters of Lune Bay. Some said the town's heyday would soon fade, for the waters of the river were slowly silting up; for now, however, trade still thrived, as proven by the many carriages and horses coming and going, seemingly oblivious to the bitter weather.

Lancashire's salty air should have been a few degrees warmer than Scotland, but I did not feel it. The roads and roofs were covered in snow as deep as Edinburgh's, and I had to wrap myself tightly in my overcoat after a blast of icy wind. I still felt rather unwell and the cold air was like daggers stabbing my head.

'Ye still have that photograph, don't ye?' McGray asked.

'Yes. Why?'

'We're going to see if the local peelers can give us a hand in our search.'

I nodded – reluctantly. 'I am astonished. You actually had a very sensible idea.'

The very narrow street ascended a gentle slope towards the heart of the town, where the ancient castle – in fact a working prison and court since medieval times – sat.

We approached the main gates, an imposing display of oak and wrought iron, but there was something else that became fixed in my memory: a gnarled, majestic yew, its trunk so thick that three men's outstretched arms could not fully embrace it. The ancient tree was infested with a large murder of crows, all perched on the knotty branches like black leaves.

I somehow felt that the birds were watching us, their eyes casting a strange spell on me. I had to shake my head to clear it, and then noticed that McGray was talking to the guards, who told him that the police headquarters were housed there too.

After enquiring three times, showing our credentials to five different officers and clerks, and waiting in a dingy, damp-smelling room, we were finally led to a cluttered office. The plaque on the door read *Chief Constable P. T. Massey.*

The oak panelling was dusty and battered, there were enormous piles of documents so old the folders looked discoloured, and the bin by the desk was overflowing with newspaper sheets soaked in grease.

The man behind the desk was lounging on his chair with his feet up, and picking his teeth with a used match. He had a very angular jaw, his dry skin seemed stretched tight across his bones, and he gave the impression of being about to fall asleep.

'A couple of foetuses in formaldehyde,' I whispered in McGray's ear, 'and this could be our Dumping Ground.'

'Can I help you?' the man asked, so lazily that I felt he drained half of my own energy.

There was a solitary chair on our side of the desk, which McGray took immediately, showing his badge. 'We're CID from Scotland.'

'Obviously,' the man said, his eyes on McGray's bright tartan trousers.

I sensed Nine-Nails growing edgy. 'We're after a very dangerous man. Frey, show him the picture.' So I did. 'His name's Lord Joel Ardglass and he escaped from an asylum after murdering one o' the nurses that took care o' him. We have reason to believe he's following a lassie, a Miss Jane Oakley.'

The chief constable dragged his arm out to lift the portrait. 'How do you know he's in Lancaster?'

'We saw both o' them on the afternoon train from Edinburgh.'

'The very train in which we arrived,' I added.

A languid eyebrow was raised. 'The very same train? And you didn't manage to catch him?'

'We had problems on board,' McGray groaned. His limited patience was wearing thin.

'Oh, how inconvenient. Well . . . what do you want with me?'

'Help us find the bastard,' McGray answered, his fists now clenched.

'Do you want me to deploy some of my men and search for this man?'

'Aye.'

'A Scottish gentleman?'

'Aye.'

'Who has committed murder . . . in Scotland?'

McGray made to stand up and I had to seize his shoulder. 'That is correct. Can you help us? We will participate in the search and provide all the information you require, of course. You must understand this man is very dangerous and the murder he committed was a most ghastly affair . . .' We were far away from Campbell and Lady Anne's grip, so I went on to freely describe Miss Greenwood's awful death: her convulsions, her vomiting and her horribly bent spine.

Chief Constable Massey put his feet down, sat straight and interlaced his hands on the desk. 'That's all very sad, but I'm afraid there's nothing I can do. This is a Scottish affair. If you want us to cooperate, we need a formal request from Edinburgh's CID.'

'*Are ye crazy?*' McGray shouted, jumping to his feet.

'McGray –'

'Every fuckin' minute counts, and yer asking us to fetch ye some bloody paperwork?'

The chief constable had barely moved, as calm as if he were sitting down to a picnic. 'It's like I told you. Scottish crimes are out of my jurisdiction. Unless a crime takes place on English soil, I can't intervene.'

McGray was leaning in to grab him by the collar (as he'd once done Campbell), but fortunately I managed to pull him back. 'Hold on!' I hissed. 'He may be a sad-looking waste of space, but he can still imprison you for assaulting an officer.'

Nine-Nails took a deep breath, his homicidal fit scarcely contained. 'Frey, help me here. I need ye to give this shitty pile of snot some o' yer michty arse's Chancery Lane legal slavers.'

I sighed in frustration. 'I am afraid he is right. If he decides to be the most insufferable, uncooperative, by-the-book sack of dead weight, we cannot force him otherwise – unless, of course, we persuade Campbell to instigate a formal request, but that could take weeks to come through.'

'That's *if* the bastard's willing,' McGray said. 'Things as they are, I don't think he'll even consider it.'

Chief Constable Massey leaned forwards. 'Oh? Why is that?'

McGray jumped in. 'Sorry, unless ye ask the question on Scottish soil I'm only allowed to tell ye to stick the longest object ye can find in yer darkest cranny.' He pointed at Massey, the stump of his lost finger sticking out oddly. 'If anything happens, or if this laddie gets away, ye'll be the one to blame.'

And he stormed out of the office.

Massey had gone white.

'Can you believe the man?' he cried as I retrieved Joel's photograph.

'Usually not,' I said, 'and when I do it affrights me. Can you at least give us directions to a respectable inn?' I asked before Massey had time to reflect on my words. 'I doubt we can do much more at this hour.'

'There's always rooms at the King's Arms, down on King Street.'

'What an imaginative name,' I said, and then followed in McGray's footsteps. I found him just around the corner, kicking a poor postbox until the steel bent.

'Better that than a chief constable's face,' I granted. 'Or mine.' I let him kick it a few more times before speaking again. 'Very well, you have had your amusement. We should find some lodgings and have a rest.'

McGray shook his head. 'Nae. Ye go have some sleep, ye still look shaken. I'll go on.'

'What do you plan to do? March through Lancaster looking in every house and alley?'

'If I have to . . .'

'Fine. In the meantime I will drop a shilling into the River Lune and try to fish it back. It is likely to do as much good.'

McGray rubbed his forehead with his maimed hand, his eyes flickering.

'I cannae sleep if he's out there.'

'I understand,' I told him, looking as sincere as I could, 'but you *must* realize how unlikely it is you will achieve anything. Even if we both spent all night searching.' I saw a hint of understanding in his face, coming with an equal measure of frustration. 'Save your energy, McGray; that is the best you can do for everyone right now.'

He deliberated for a moment. Finally he inhaled deeply and looked down, which I took as acceptance, and we moved on.

I counted the few notes left in my wallet and growled. I'd have to have money wired from one of my personal accounts in London. We passed the telegraph office, but it was already closed.

'At least we know where to come tomorrow,' I sighed.

The King's Arms was not too far, and in fact it was a very respectable-looking place, one of those very successful inns that had flourished along with the railways, which brought a constant flock of passengers needing a bed and a roof.

With a recently restored facade and a thick stone arch above its main door, it could well have stood proud next to the hotels around St Pancras or King's Cross.

A middle-aged man, chubby, bald and red-nosed, greeted us.

'Evening, gentlemen. How can I help you?' His Lancashire accent made me think of Joan and the hearty dinner she would have been cooking if we had stayed in Edinburgh.

'Two rooms, please,' I said. 'And we might need them for several days.'

He looked at his books and whistled.

'Is everything all right?' I asked.

'I'm so sorry, I only have one room left. T'other one went not fifteen minutes ago. But it has two beds – you'll be quite comfortable.'

I could not help sneering at McGray. 'Thank you, but I'd rather go and try my luck at the port's inns.'

'By all means, sir, but them two ladies that came right before you said they'd been looking for rooms all day. Town's full.'

'Give us the room,' McGray said. 'I'm not walking any more. If his majesty wants his own privy, he can sleep by the river.'

'Said by the man whom I had to force to have a rest!'

McGray ignored me. 'Can ye arrange some food too? And good portions, don't ye get stingy with me.'

The innkeeper assured us he would send us a wholesome dinner and then showed us the way upstairs.

I sighed with relief when I saw the room. It was not big but at least the linen looked clean, and a small hearth kept it at a very comfortable temperature.

The walls, unfortunately, were very thin, and we could hear the muffled voices of some women arguing in the next room.

McGray hammered on the wall so hard some of the old plaster fell off. '*Och, shut it!*'

Instant result.

Not a few minutes later a young maid knocked on our door, bringing a large tray. I feared she'd offer us tripe

boiled in milk, or some other equally charming Lancashire delicacy, but fortunately it was only stewed mutton,
boiled potatoes, tea and plenty of bread.

The girl wrinkled her nose as I tipped her. 'Would ya
like me to wash them clothes?'

As she said it I smelled the trace of vomit that still came
from my coat and jacket. 'Will they be ready in the morning? We will set off very early.'

'Course, sir.'

I gave her the garments. Before leaving she pointed at
McGray's ancient overcoat, which he'd tossed on a chair.
'That one too?'

McGray was already devouring his meal loudly, so I
simply mouthed: 'It does need a wash.'

'Och, wait!' Nine-Nails said, seeing that the coats were
being taken away. 'Ye have Lord Bampot's picture
with ye?'

'Of course I do,' I retorted. 'Do you honestly believe I
am so stupid I would send the one portrait we have to the
laundry?'

Nine-Nails shrugged, and as soon as he had turned
back to his plate I discreetly retrieved the photograph and
other papers from my jacket's pocket. The maid bundled
it together with McGray's rags, then curtsied and left.

I went to the little table and looked at the food. My
stomach was still a little upset, but I forced myself to swallow some bread and a few swigs of tea. After that I
remember only resting my head on the soft pillow, for I
instantly dozed off, still in my clothes on top of the
blankets – I was so tired I could have slept on a timber
board in a fishermen's alehouse. It was a deep, refreshing

slumber, which was sadly interrupted by loud banging on our door.

I opened one eye, croaking. It was still dark, but with the winter weather it could have been any time of the day. I reached for the side table and looked at my pocket watch: it was early morning, only a few minutes past five.

McGray was already up. He'd probably slept his usual one or two hours, yet he seemed completely unaffected as he opened the door. I sat up and saw the innkeeper, and next to him a grubby, red-eyed police officer.

'What?' Nine-Nails burst out in a hoarse morning voice.

'Sergeant Thatcher, sir,' the officer said. 'I have an urgent message from the chief constable.'

He handed us a note, which McGray snatched and unfolded. He let out a wrathful groan.

'Och, the bastard did it again!'

I stood up and swayed towards him. 'What is it?'

I was aghast yet not entirely surprised when I read over McGray's shoulder:

Murder in the castle. Terrible. Need your help.

C. C. Massey

18

I was still yawning as we dashed downstairs. The young maid was waiting for us with our overcoats, now clean and neatly folded.

'My, did ye sleep at all, hen?' McGray asked as I wrapped myself up.

The girl blushed, looking a little afraid as she gave Nine-Nails his tattered overcoat, which looked only a tad less scruffy. 'I'm so sorry, sir. Your coat's really old and the lining got torn when I tried to rub them grease stains out.'

I laughed with spirit. 'Unavoidably!'

'But I stitched it all back!' the girl promptly added.

'It's all right,' McGray said. 'Better than running round town in shirtsleeves.'

As we walked out of the inn we all shivered. The temperature had plummeted and even my warm coat, which the maid had surely left to dry by a fire, did not feel thick enough.

Fortunately we did not have to walk too far: we were at the castle within minutes. The yew was still covered in black birds, but they were a little livelier now, fluttering and pecking around for food.

We passed through the imposing gates and I saw that the castle was in fact an uneven collection of buildings, walls and towers built one after the other across the centuries. One could see mismatching stones and tell the newer from the medieval ones.

Thatcher guided us across the main yard to one of the oldest-looking areas. The sandstone bricks were weathered and blackened, the walls cut by very few narrow windows. Just as I thought how ominous and depressing the place looked, the caw of a large raven startled me. I looked up, but the sky was still too dark to spot the bird.

'Witches' tower.'

At first I thought the words had come from my own head, but they'd actually been uttered by the sergeant.

'E-excuse me?'

'That's the witches' tower. Haven't you heard about t'Lancashire trials?'

McGray's eyes widened. 'D'ye mean the 1612 trials?'

'Aye, and not only those. They brought witches here for prosecution all the time back then. There were dozens of trials, some more famous than others; my granddad told me all them old tales when I was little. Th'old hags usually stayed in this tower for months before trial. Down there.'

He was looking at a boarded-up gate, framed by a stone arch that seemed rather sinister to me. However, that was a very mild prelude to what we were about to see.

We followed Thatcher into the depths of the castle, to a dingy block of cells. The main corridor was dimly lit by yellow gas lamps. It was not the first prison I had visited, but it was one of the most depressing: the place stank of all manner of human filth, the plaster on the walls was crumbling and the floors were peppered with grime.

There must have been at least a dozen gaolers posted between the barred doors, and I could see they kept order with an iron fist: the only movement was a lonely rat running around a heap of rubbish, and the only noise was a dull murmur coming from one of the furthest cells, where a small group of guards clustered. I saw only a couple of convicts, but they were both crouching in the corners, perhaps not allowed even to glance at us.

'The inspectors are here,' Thatcher announced as we reached an open cell, and all faces turned to us.

Chief Constable Massey was there, not a trace of indolence in his face now. He was deathly pale.

'Has it happened on English soil?' McGray asked, unable to contain his bitterness.

Massey nodded meekly and pointed into the cell, where a photographer was installing a bulky tripod. As he moved aside we saw a white sheet on the floor, almost glowing under the light from the guards' lanterns, covering an eerily familiar hump.

McGray kneeled down and lifted the cloth, revealing the gruesome face of a rough man in his forties. There was froth at the corners of his mouth, his lips were purple and his eyes were still wide open with the most disturbing expression.

As McGray pulled away the sheet we saw the full extent of the tragedy. The man's back was bent in an even more horrifying way than Greenwood's: he rested on both shoulders, but then his body twisted both upwards and sideways, forming an arch that ended at his right hip. His inmate's uniform was stained with vomit and bile, and despite his broken position it was evident that he had been a tall, muscular man – had he been alive he could have passed for another gaoler.

'This seems to have been a more severe poisoning,' I murmured.

The chief constable stepped forwards. 'I recognized the symptoms you mentioned last night, and it couldn't be a coincidence to see them only a few hours later. I wasn't sure you'd be at the inn I recommended; it was very lucky to find you.'

'Not lucky enough for him,' Nine-Nails said, gesturing at the crime scene. 'Ye'll have a lot to answer for, Messy.'

The chief constable cleared his throat. 'It's Massey.'

'Don't ye correct me, ye messy sack of —'

I jumped in before Nine-Nails began beating anyone up. 'Do not mind Inspector McGray. We need you to tell us everything you know.'

'His name was Harry Pimblett,' Massey said. 'He'd been locked up here for the past five years.'

'What for?' McGray asked.

'He attacked a customs officer, and after that it transpired he'd been running some smuggling at St George's Quay.'

'I want to see his full file,' I told him, and one of the guards went off to fetch it.

'How did it happen?' McGray asked. 'I doubt the poison fell accidentally into his porridge.'

Massey swallowed. 'Well, he had a visitor last evening.'

'Let me guess,' said Nine-Nails. 'A very fine gentleman? Around fifty? Lean face?'

Massey could not look at him in the eye. 'No need to describe him. He gave the guards his name: Joel Ardglass.'

'That was bold,' I said.

'It was well past visiting time. The gaoler allowed him in only because he claimed himself a lord – and he had the gold to bribe his way in.'

'I suppose the genius who let him pass is here?'

'T'was me, sir,' said one of the guards, blushing.

'Do you usually grant access to whomever tosses sterling at you?'

'No, sir. Course not! I mean, the gentleman did tip me, but he seemed honest.'

McGray clicked his tongue. '*Honest?*'

'Yes. He said Pimblett had been his butler long ago. I knew the lad; he'd told me once about this Ardglass family he used to serve.'

I certainly took note of that.

'Did Lord Ardglass say why he was visiting?' I asked.

'Yes, when he was trying to convince me to let him in. He said he was about to go on a long trip, wouldn't be back for years, and wanted to thank Pimblett for his services. He brought him a bottle of one of them foreign wines . . .' I raised a hand to my mouth. 'It looked very expensive, sir. With a golden label and all. How was I s'posed to know it would be poison?'

I turned to Massey, rolling my eyes. 'See that this man is properly disciplined.'

'But sir –'

'*Shut yer sauce box!*' McGray snapped. 'Messy, ye've shat on yer career badly enough already. If ye don't want us to make it far worse, ye'll do as we say. Ye heard me?' He did not wait for the chief constable to reply. 'Gather as many peelers as ye can. Youse are going to start the search we wanted last night.'

'And arrange for an urgent post-mortem,' I added. 'Your best physician.'

'Och, and Messy,' McGray said just before the chief constable left, 'be a good boy and fetch me a cup o' tea. Nae sugar.'

Twenty-five constables were lined up in front of the castle's chapel, and McGray walked slowly to and fro, showing them Joel Ardglass's picture.

'This is the man we're looking for. Last time he was seen – by one o' yer most pathetic colleagues – he was wearing an expensive black coat and carrying a leather bag. Memorize his face. He might have gone to the quays – youse three check there – or the train station – youse three check there. The rest of youse spread out evenly across town. Remember this bastard is dangerous and armed.'

I evaluated them while McGray spoke. Massey had put together a very heterogeneous group: some of the constables seemed fit and sharp, but a few others (many more than I would have liked) were undeniable, blatant slobs. A couple of them had swollen beer bellies and I could swear I saw one of the younger ones actually drooling.

'I would not expect much,' I told McGray as soon as he had dispatched them. 'Although I have seen worse cavemen guarding the House of Commons.'

'Did ye find anything new from the other guards?' McGray asked.

'A little.' I had questioned them while McGray and Massey arranged the search. 'Apparently Pimblett did not have many visitors. The ones who came, however, did so quite frequently.'

'Did they keep a record o' their names?'

'Yes, they register the names of all visitors. The book is very long, as you can imagine; I have one of the guards going through it as we speak.'

We walked back to the main yard, where a few shackled inmates were sweeping snow and spreading rock salt. I saw a young clerk running towards us. The poor chap slipped on the wet flagstones and fell right on his rump; after standing up and smoothing out his jacket, he spoke with grovelling enthusiasm: 'Sirs, I've collected Pimblett's files. They're all in the library.'

He led us there, an airy room of high ceilings and large windows, its walls entirely covered by shelves of leather-bound law acts.

'There,' the clerk said, pointing at a wide round table, where a bundle of folders lay. 'I have separated the court proceedings and Mr Pimblett's personal documents. I also took the liberty of signalling the ones I considered particularly relevant.'

McGray sat on a very ornate chair, its arms so wide it looked more like a small bench.

'That seat was custom-made for Her Majesty,' the young man told us, rather eager to please. 'Queen Victoria honoured us with a visit in the year –'

'I don't care,' McGray interrupted. 'Go away.'

Befuddled, the man looked at me. I just waved my hand, but he did not leave until McGray threw him a fuming glare. On his way out he banged his shoulder against the door frame.

'That could be yer son,' McGray said, already leafing through the files.

'I hope not . . . although I must admit he has marked useful facts . . . Pimblett was born in some place called Slaidburn, somewhere in –'

'Lancashire?'

'Indeed. Have you heard of the place?'

'Aye. Long story. Go on.'

'He came to Lancaster as a young boy and worked here and there doing hard labour, until he was employed by a Miss Redfern.'

'Redfern . . .' McGray whispered, pensive. 'Wasn't Oakley's telegram signed by a Miss R?'

'Indeed!' I made a note of that and continued to read. 'Pimblett left her to go to Scotland – presumably that was the period when he served Joel Ardglass. He returned in early 1883, and a few months later he was prosecuted for smuggling.'

McGray sat back, wearing a deep frown. 'Does it mention more specific dates?'

'He left in 1875 and came back in January 1883.'

'It was around that time that Ardglass went to the asylum . . .'

I checked my little notebook. 'Indeed, and that makes sense. If Pimblett was his personal butler, his services would no longer have been required.'

'There's something here that feels odd . . .' McGray said, looking now at the court proceedings, which were not very long. 'The court files are dated June 1883 . . .'

I saw him shudder and by then I knew him well enough to tell why. That was the date he hated the most: the month when his sister had gone mad and he'd lost his finger. A mere coincidence, that was clear, but a bitter reminder nonetheless.

'If I remember correctly,' he said after clearing his throat, 'Ardglass was locked up in December 1882. Pimblett arrives here a month later . . . and within five months manages to get himself in jail. Chief Constable Messy said he'd been imprisoned for five years, didn't he?'

'Yes.' I pointed at a paragraph underlined with pencil. 'His sentence was seven years; he would have been released eighteen months from now.'

'Unlucky bastard,' McGray said. 'That's a long sentence; he must have been smuggling serious shite to get himself in such dire straits so soon.'

'The records will say.'

We leafed through, read and reread, but found only a one-line explanation: *Under oath, Mr Harry Pimblett confessed to charges of unlawful trade.*

'*Is that all?*' I was indignant. 'What kind of judge passes a ruling like this? It makes you Scots look almost civilized.'

McGray went back to the first page. 'Judge Matthew Spotson.'

'Let's forget it. I doubt his sentence will have anything to do with Lord Ardglass.'

McGray was looking intently at the name. 'I'm not sure, Frey. Pimblett was Joel's auld butler *and* he turns out to have a cryptic file . . . It doesnae feel right. We should dig a wee bit deeper.' He whistled loudly, as if calling for his golden retriever.

Immediately the young clerk rushed back in, and I suspected he'd had his ear pressed against the door all this time. 'Yes, sirs?'

McGray handed him the folder. 'Laddie, we want to ask a few questions to this judge, Matthew Spotson. Can ye help us find him?'

The servile expression on the clerk's face vanished, as did the colour in his cheeks.

'Everything all right?' I asked.

'Yes, sir. He retired last year, but –'

'We need to find him, laddie. Can ye arrange that?'

'Oh, of course, sir. He – he happens to be my grandfather.'

I could but chuckle. 'You must be joking.'

'Oh, not at all, sir. He's the reason I work here.' As he spoke he dropped the folder, its sheets scattering everywhere, and after clumsily picking them up he banged his head against the edge of the table.

I sighed. '*That* I can believe.'

The Spotsons might be in want of wits, but they were certainly not short of money. The old judge lived in a large townhouse in Church Street, one of the most desirable addresses in Lancaster.

His clumsy grandson – Crispin – had guided us there reluctantly, sulking all the way. Fortunately the house was a few minutes' walk from the castle; otherwise I would not have agreed to join them. I could not see the source of Nine-Nails' hunch.

There was a black cat seated by the doorstep, looking

almost regal as it watched us arrive. It did not move at all when the door opened and a wave of heat came out. A plump, very loud maid received us.

'Master Crispin! You home so early?'

'These gentlemen want to speak to Grandpapa. Is he up?'

The woman bit her lip. She seemed wilful and rather vulgar, and wore long cotton sleeves even though the house was kept a little too warm for my taste. Her blonde and white curls caught my eye: they were so tight they looked like spiralling wood shavings. 'He is awake, but . . . Are you sure, master?'

'Take us to him,' McGray said, in a tone that did not admit contradiction, and we walked in.

We found the old judge seated in a small yet very elegant parlour on the first floor. His leather armchair was conveniently placed in front of the wide window, giving him a panoramic view of the street.

His age was evident: he was as wrinkled as a prune, with sparse white hair and golden spectacles that magnified his eyes to three times their size. He was settled on the armchair as if someone had pushed him down, or – more likely – as if he sat there for hours and hours every day, until the leather cushions had become moulded to the shape of his frail body. He wore a thick dressing gown and his legs were snugly wrapped in a blanket; rather unnecessary, given the warmth of the room.

Crispin announced us, but the old man only inclined his head slightly. He was staring at his hands, the fingertips of the left touching each of those of the right, as if he were counting, and he also mumbled unintelligibly from time to time.

'Do be seated,' Crispin said, and we sat down on a leather sofa. The maid soon came in with a silver tray and a shiny set of china.

'Tea, gentlemen?'

I touched my stomach. 'No, thank you.'

McGray refused as well. It would be a while before we accepted tea from strangers again.

Crispin did take a cup, with milk and three lumps of sugar.

I looked dubiously at the old judge. His stare was vacant and he had not acknowledged our arrival.

'Mr Spotson?' I said. 'May we ask you a few questions?'

He did not even slightly move his head in our direction.

'It's about Mr Pimblett,' said McGray.

Spotson's fingers became still, the tip of his index fingers pressing against each other, but then he resumed his counting.

I looked at Crispin, all impatience. 'How long has he been like this?'

Crispin dropped his cup on the saucer and half the tea spilled. 'S-sorry?'

'Ye heard the dandy,' McGray intervened. 'It's not yer grandfather's fault. How long's he been in this state?'

Crispin had to put his dripping china on one of the side tables. 'Well . . . two or three years.'

'Is that why he retired?' I asked.

'Yes, sir. People were beginning to mock him at the courts – even the convicts.'

'So he could not tell us much about Pimblett's case.'

'No . . . I don't think so. He has his moments; from

time to time he speaks and he makes sense, but they're fewer every day.'

I was about to say what an awful waste of time the visit had been – Crispin could have told us about his grand-father's condition before we came – but I felt sorry for them. I could imagine the frustration the old man must feel in those rare moments of lucidity; a once powerful, respected public figure reduced, in the end, to such help-lessness. My brother and father had made their careers in Chancery Lane, so I knew very well how merciless the court halls could be. People surely made tasteless jokes about the senile judge whenever the name Spotson was uttered.

'I am sorry to hear that.' My manners took over, mak-ing it impossible to excuse myself and go without feeling terribly guilty. A most uncomfortable, awkward silence seemed to be preferable.

McGray was about to do the sensible thing and leave, but then we heard Mr Spotson grunt.

The man leaned forwards, his shaky hands grasping the armrests, and as he rose we heard his knees cracking. The blanket fell and then, with faltering steps, like those of a toddler, he made his way out. We all looked at him in puzzlement, even Crispin. Just as the old man crossed the threshold he paused and turned to give his grandson an eerie smile. His voice came out in a throaty, spine-chilling whisper: 'Pim-blett ...' He inhaled. 'I remember Pimblett ... and his frogs ...'

'Frogs?' I echoed.

Spotson nodded, making vague figures with his hands. 'Yes, frogs ... Hideous little things ...'

Crispin flushed. 'Grandpa, please . . .'

McGray raised a finger to his lips and the old man started fidgeting once again.

'Frogs. And little snakes . . . He worked for the witches, you see . . .'

Then silence.

A death threat could not have had a greater impact. I was left open-mouthed, McGray gasped and Crispin spilled what was left of his tea all over himself.

Nine-Nails leaned forwards. 'Witches, ye say?'

Spotson nodded, looking directly into McGray's eyes. He stood still, then pulled at the collar of his dressing gown, as if suddenly aware of the house's heat. It was an instant before his gaze became vacant once more, then he dreamily turned on his heel and was gone.

'Told ye I had a funny feeling,' McGray was saying, exhilarated, as we walked back to the castle.

'*He worked for the witches*,' I quoted, very conscious of my face looking as if I were smelling rotten eggs. 'The words of a senile man. I would not take them as gospel.'

As soon as we entered the gates we were told the post-mortem had concluded, so we rushed to the morgue.

The mortician was a very old wisp of a man, and he must seldom leave the depths of his workspace: his skin was so pale there were blue veins running along his neck.

When we walked in he was scribbling the last lines of his report, his notepad resting unceremoniously on top of Pimblett's forehead.

I was expecting to see the horribly bent torso, but the

spine had been flattened and under the sheets the body looked almost normal – except for a pair of blueish feet sticking out.

'I understand this was a mere formality,' the mortician said, leafing through his report. 'The chief constable told me you knew what killed this man. Is strychnine what you had in mind?'

'Yes,' I replied, 'but we also want to know whether you found anything else. Anything untoward.'

'Well, the lad was developing a bad case of arthritis – no wonder in those damp cells – but other than that he looked very normal. No signs of violence or struggle.'

McGray was looking at the feet with a slight frown.

'What is it?' I asked. Right under the edge of the sheet, by the man's ankle, there was a thin, neat scar; a perfectly curved line.

McGray drew the sheet back to inspect the man's calf. I walked around the table and saw that the entire circumference of his ankle was etched with a most intricate design: a snake, twisted and knotted in a disturbing yet beautiful pattern. It would have taken a lot of skill and a very sharp scalpel to mark the fine scales and the little fangs.

It looked just like the technique used to draw on Greenwood's inner thigh, only this design had been cut deeper and was much more complex. They both had been marked with the same creature, which was surely no coincidence.

McGray looked at it, enthralled. 'How come ye didnae mention this?'

The man shrugged. 'Most of these lowlifes have

tattoos or marks of some sort, and that's not a particularly big one. Is it something of consequence for your investigation?'

'It's beginning to be,' McGray said, and then whispered to himself, 'So . . . he worked for the witches . . .'

19

I had completely forgotten about wiring some money from London, and when I mentioned the issue to McGray he did not react in quite the way I had expected. His eyes widened as if I'd unveiled a barrel of whisky, and before I finished talking he was already trotting towards the telegraph office.

'I was thinking o' that last night,' he said. 'It was going to be my first stop today, but then all this pile o' shite happened.'

'Your first stop?'

'Indeedy. D'ye have Oakley's telegram?'

'Of course! I should have thought of that myself. I do have it. It seems all I do these days is carry documents for you.'

'Good. Ye said it was sent from Lancaster, so –'

'They might still remember the sender.'

'Aye, but don't say it now as if it was yer idea.'

I was glad Lancaster was not a large town. Its wire office had only six telegraphists and they all sat along two desks in the same room. Four of them were women, which seemed tremendously unusual; engineers did not like to leave their precious inventions in the hands of females. These ladies, however, were not deterred: sporting snow-white blouses and very straight skirts, they seemed completely at ease tapping the transmitters, and the air rang with the sound of electric pulses at a frantic rhythm.

It was one of the women who came to assist us. 'Can I help you, gentlemen?'

Before anything else I requested my money, and saw her eyebrows rise when I mentioned the sum.

Once I had the notes neatly folded in my wallet, McGray showed his badge and put Oakley's telegram on the counter. 'One more thing, lass. We're CID. We need to ken who sent this message to Edinburgh.'

'Do excuse me, you need to . . . ?'

'Och, we need to *knoooow* who sent this.'

I turned to the clerk. 'Miss, you can see there is no signature. All the sender gave was an initial. Is it usual for you to send out telegrams without a proper return address?'

The woman nodded as if speaking to a young child. 'Very common, sir. People try to send as few characters as possible – it's cheaper.'

McGray rolled his eyes. I blushed a little and whispered, 'What? In all my life I have never needed to count the words in my telegrams.'

'Well,' the woman said, 'without a proper signature it could be difficult to track, but not impossible. I can work out the cost from the number of letters and look at the date in the ledger. The payment will be registered there.'

So she did, and after a short wait she came back carrying a thick ledger. 'You're lucky, sirs. The message was paid for by a Miss Redfern.'

McGray inhaled sharply. 'Hear that, Frey?'

I nodded, feeling at last like some pieces were coming

together. 'So it *was* the Redfern in Pimblett's file . . .' I mumbled, and heard again the eerie words of Judge Spotson in my head. We were on the trail of a witch after all.

'We need to find that woman,' McGray told the telegraphist. 'It's vital. Any information ye can give us . . .'

She was already turning the pages. 'I can definitely help you there. Miss Redfern has an account with us. She's a very regular customer. I'll give you her address.'

It was no surprise that Redfern had been Pimblett's most assiduous visitor. She would call almost fortnightly, always at different times and days of the week, so none of the guards, despite their long shifts, had been fully aware of the frequency. Only a couple of them remembered her clearly, and they described her as a short, thin woman in her sixties or seventies, with a remarkably forceful voice.

They barely had time to tell us, for McGray had rushed back to the castle only to fetch a warrant and a couple of sergeants as backup. The chosen ones were Thatcher and a younger officer they called Kenny.

'What are you expecting to find at Redfern's lodgings?' I asked, as I saw the sergeants picking up their truncheons and charging their guns. 'We should not need reinforcements to question an old lady.'

McGray chuckled. 'Did ye think we'd need muscle to question that wee lass Oakley?'

I had to nod. 'Touché.'

We set off as the day was drawing to a close, with Thatcher on one side and Kenny on the other. A dry, icy wind scoured the town, turning the layers of snow into solid blocks of ice. However, I could barely feel the cold and I cannot fully credit my coat for that; suddenly I was feeling anxious. I had no idea what we were about to encounter, and the darkening sky, still moonless, seemed like an ill portent.

The street we went to was aptly named Shambles, and despite being a few steps from the sumptuous town hall it was a depressing sight: a long row of run-down shacks, some of them barely standing. Most of the windows were boarded up or covered with filthy rags, and the crumbling chimneys spat black smoke as the people warmed their lodgings with whatever fuel they had to hand.

We marched down the slushy road, our shadows projected as long stripes by the single working street lamp. The few wretched occupants we encountered ran away when they saw us, shouting and swearing, a couple of them so intoxicated that they tripped and had to crawl to the safety of their dens; even a stray dog ran from us as quickly as its bony legs allowed. Some faces appeared behind the windows, peering at us with suspicious eyes, probably wondering if we were coming after them.

Among the Shambles one building stood out, a storey taller than the rest and boasting the only full set of windows with their glass unbroken. The walls, though as dirty as the others, appeared to be thicker and stronger. This must have been considered the mansion of the block.

'There's nobody home,' McGray said; all the rooms were in darkness. He knocked anyway, but the door gave way with a creak.

Thatcher had brought a lantern, and when he lit it we saw what had been a thick latch, still boasting a mighty padlock. The iron had been ripped from the wood and was hanging by a single nail.

We drew our weapons, and after a deep breath McGray kicked the door aside.

Thatcher lit the room, revealing that the place had been turned upside down. Wrecked furniture, splinters and shards of glass lay all around.

'We are not the first here,' I mumbled. 'Do you think that the Redfern woman left before this happened?'

McGray assented. 'Aye, hence the padlock. That doesnae look like a lock to put up when ye go out to buy tatties.'

We stepped inside cautiously, probing every shadowy corner as the light moved around. McGray found an oil lamp on the floor, cracked but still working. He lit it and I saw him sniff the air.

'Smells . . . herby here.'

I agreed. 'Like an apothecary's.'

'Look upstairs,' McGray told the two chaps, 'but be careful.'

We searched the ground floor, kicking aside chairs and rubbish as we went. I recognized the smashed remains of a few bird cages; some black feathers still lay around. There was a large back room used as a pantry, entirely taken up by shelves and cupboards, once crammed with jars and bottles that now were shattered on the floor. Herbs, powders and unknown liquids were spread all over, giving off that strange musky smell.

'See any foxgloves?' McGray asked, but before I could answer we heard a piercing cry from upstairs, then hammering steps storming down.

It was Kenny who'd screamed, and he came to us looking as pale as a ghost. 'Sirs, you have to see the loft.'

He rushed upstairs and climbed up through the hatch.
We found Thatcher there, trembling as he shed light on
the bizarre room.

In its centre there was an enormous pewter pot, wide
enough to have a bath in, but instead of water it was full
of ashes and the charred remains of an outlandish collection of items. I recognized book covers, pieces of distorted
clay figures and quite a few animal bones – I'd rather not
speculate whether they had been burned dead or alive.

That, however, was not what had made them scream.
My eyes drifted to the opposite end of the loft, and I
instantly felt a chill rising up my spine.

A raven had been nailed to the wall, the poor bird's
blood dripping on to the wooden boards. Pinned to one
of the wings there was a piece of paper, with the most
horrendous message written in blood:

> *You whores are next*
> *I KNOW*
> *Joel*

We all stood still for a moment, transfixed by those
ghastly words and the sacrificed raven.

I gulped and was the first one who managed to speak.
'Nine-Nails . . . is this a spell? A ritual?'

McGray looked at the pot. 'Could be, but I doubt it.
Looks more like someone was getting rid of evidence.'

I walked closer to the bird and examined it carefully.
'The blood is not congealed yet . . .' I forced myself to

touch the plumage with my fingertips and could not repress a gasp. 'This is lukewarm! Lord Ardglass must have been here minutes ago.'

McGray looked staggered.

'Youse heard the dandy!' he told the officers, not wasting a second. 'Our man could be near. Go and search the surroundings. Knock on every door if need be. Come back here in half an hour if youse don't find him.'

Off they went. McGray and I stayed and rummaged through the cold ashes, but everything there had burned beyond use. If they had been attempting to destroy any evidence, they had done so quite effectively.

I did, however, find something fresh on the floor: a shattered bowl which had contained sugar and a red onion, the root squashed by someone's muddy boot.

'Look at this,' I said. 'That charm we keep finding . . . It was also in Oakley's bedroom.'

McGray took a good look. 'I'm more and more convinced it's a protection charm. No other reason the witches would have it as well . . . And it explains why Joel would've trampled on it.'

I arched an eyebrow. 'It makes no sense. Were they trying to protect Ardglass? And now he is chasing and killing them?'

I was going to elaborate, but McGray pointed at the broken bowl.

'What's that?' he asked. Next to the shards of clay there was an envelope.

I picked it up and my pulse hastened. 'It looks like the envelope Ardglass asked me to hand him at Oakley's house.'

'I'll have to trust ye; I didnae see it properly.'

I looked at it more closely but I did not need to ponder for long. Our horrible encounter with Lord Ardglass was imprinted on my memory; I could almost hear his voice demanding the envelope, feel my hand pulling it from beneath the black cat. Every detail rushed back to me, even the touch of the paper in my hand. 'This is it, I am certain,' I spluttered, opening it, 'but – damn! It is empty.'

Nine-Nails frowned, looking around, and our eyes fell on the raven and the bloody note nailed to it at the same time. I held the envelope up, next to the blood-smeared warning. The papers were the exact same yellowy shade, the exact same texture.

'Envelope and letter cut from the same sheet!' said McGray. 'Of course! A fugitive wouldnae carry pen and paper, so he used whatever he had to leave his message . . .'

McGray was right. He pulled the paper from the wall and turned it over to reveal cramped lines of handwriting.

'What was written on there that was so important to him?' I asked, as McGray brought the gas lamp nearer.

'It's signed by Redfern. "Miss R", just like the telegram.'

We read it in silence. It was an ordinary, seemingly routine communication: Redfern stated that her 'business' was doing well and that the winter was setting in.

However, reading on, embedded in one of the middle sentences, was the key:

. . . Last night I saw an old man of the Lancaster gentry. He brought good business but was aghast to come round. I bet the likes of him rarely set foot in a place like Shambles St . . .

'That's how damn Joel found them,' McGray said, pointing to the line. 'Redfern gave away the name of her street. A terrible mistake to write that down . . .'

We satisfied ourselves there was nothing else of relevance in the loft, and went downstairs. McGray was restless and walked out to the street, and I followed him solely because the house was as cold as outside.

I saw that there was light coming from the adjacent shack, where McGray had already gone. He knocked but did not wait for a reply; he simply opened the brittle door, which had no lock, and entered the one-room dwelling.

There we found a very malodorous woman, whose face was so dirty I could not possibly guess her age. She jumped into a corner, crouching on a filthy old mattress and covering her face, as if the very light of the lantern hurt her.

'*Leave me alone!* I haven't done nothing! *Nothing!*'

'We're not gonnae harm ye,' McGray said, as gently as he could. 'We just need to ask ye a few questions.'

'You peelers always say that!'

'How do you know we are – peelers?'

'Your boys just came here. I'm not a fool. You're looking for her. But I don't know nothing.'

'Give 'er a sixpence,' McGray told me.

'Excuse me?'

However, the woman had already uncovered her face, and her eyes lit up as I tossed the coin into her hands.

'Do you know the woman who lives next door?' I asked.

'Aye . . . I mean, I've seen them.'

'*Them?* Who else lives there?'

'No one else, but the hag gets loads o' visitors . . .' Her mouth twisted. '*Clients.*'

'What sort o' clients?' McGray asked.

'All sorts. Gentlemen, ladies, washerwomen . . .' Her tone darkened as she confirmed our suspicions. 'She did dirty works for them. Everybody around here knows she's a witch.'

McGray could have punched the air in triumph, but I was not excited at all. I only asked dryly: 'And she surely charged good money for her services?'

'Oh yes! How else could she have such a fine house?'

I felt sorry for the woman. To her, any brick building with more than one room was a palace.

McGray leaned forwards. 'Did ye see her receive many clients lately?'

'A few, as usual, but it all went quiet yesterday afternoon. Last person I saw going in there was a young woman.'

'Did ye get a proper glimpse? What did she look like?'

She shrugged. 'About as tall as me' – so medium height for a woman – 'kind of skinny, brown hair, lil' too fancy for this neighbourhood, if you know what I mean. And very fidgety. She kept looking round when she knocked. Well, most folk coming to *her* look nervous.'

'She sounds like our lass,' said McGray. 'How come they're not here any more? Did ye see them leave?'

'Yes. A couple of hours after the lass arrived they both left with their bags. Looked like they were going on a trip. T'was all very hasty.'

'Do you have any idea where they might have gone?'

'No, no. I never had any dealings with her. She's a witch, I told you.'

'After they left,' I said, 'did you see who broke in?'

'Ye *must* have seen,' McGray stressed. 'It happened in the last hour. And ye must've heard too. These walls o' yers are paper thin.'

The woman hesitated. 'Well, I saw a man go in, but . . .'

'What?'

She shuddered. 'He saw me sticking my head out the window. My Lord, he had those dreadful red eyes; I thought he was the Devil. And he shouted at me, "Mind your own business, bitch!" Then I heard hurly-burly in the house, smashing glass and things thrown round. I didn't look again. You see, this isn't the nicest place to live; we learn very soon to stay out of trouble.'

'Indeed,' I said. I gave her another sixpence and just as we left we saw Thatcher trotting back. Kenny was nowhere to be seen. I was going to ask about him, but then I saw that Thatcher was pulling a young boy by the arm. The child's filthy face reminded me of our own Larry, the former chimneysweep who now helped my housekeeper.

Thatcher was panting, his bursts of steaming breath glowing in the lantern's beam. 'This boy says he saw a man leaving *the witch's house.*'

McGray extended his palm at me and I had to give him another coin. I had run out of sixpences and all I had to give him was a shilling. He did not give it out straight away but waved it in front of the boy.

'See this, laddie? The more ye tell us – so long as it's true – the sooner this'll be in yer pocket.'

The boy sneered, an expression that did not belong on a child. 'You speak funny, mister.'

McGray laughed. 'Well, if ye don't want it ...' But before he could shove the coin into his pocket the boy jumped forwards.

'He went to the shipyards!'

'How can ye tell?'

'He ran to Wood Street and he was carrying a big bag.'

'Not exactly conclusive,' I remarked.

'No,' Thatcher jumped in, 'but I sent Kenny down that road. If we run, we can –'

Nine-Nails had already tossed the shilling into the boy's grimy hands and was running towards the main road. 'Take us there, Thatcher!'

'Your loss,' said the child, pocketing the coin and running away as soon as the policeman let go of him.

I sighed, looking at the receding shadows of Nine-Nails and Thatcher. 'Come on, Ian,' I told myself as I sprinted off. 'At least this will keep you warm ...'

20

The wind now blew mightily, whistling as we raced along the gloomy, icy streets. More than once I felt my feet skidding on the hardened snow and managed to keep my balance by sheer good luck.

'Skerton Shipyard,' Thatcher announced as the narrow alley broadened.

Before us were curved embankments descending sharply to the River Lune. The waters were turbulent under the harsh wind, large waves crashing against the brick walls of the banks.

We stopped to look around, but the road along the river was deserted. Any workers would have run for shelter after dusk. In front of us were the open gates of the shipyard, where a mass of scaffolding clustered around two unfinished hulls.

Next to this there was a line of sad brown warehouses along the piers and docks, their windows like little glowing squares reflected on the choppy waters. Any of them would be a feasible hideaway.

'Where do we go now?' I panted, but then the wind brought the answer.

'More policemen!' a man yelled in the distance, and then we heard a second voice, a woman's, begging for help.

A man came running up to us, his arms flailing. He

waved at us desperately, beckoning us to follow. 'There's a wounded peeler! Hurry!'

So we did, and not a minute later we found a young woman kneeling by a man's broken body. We instantly recognized him as Kenny.

There was a nasty blow on his forehead, to which the lady was pressing a now sodden handkerchief. His eyes were wide open and spasms shook his hands and feet.

Thatcher blew his whistle once and again, the call cutting the air like a clean knife, as McGray and I kneeled down beside Kenny.

'Ye all right?' McGray asked.

'What a stupid question,' I said. 'Let me look at that wound. I am a doctor . . .'

'Nae, ye never graduated.'

I glared at him. 'Do you honestly want to discuss that right now?'

I carefully pulled the cloth away to see the bashed skin. The blood flowed instantly.

'Well done,' I told the woman. 'Keep up the pressure. We need –'

Kenny's quivering hand grasped mine. The young man seemed fully conscious. He opened his mouth and gagged. I was going to tell him to relax but then his words came out: 'He went there.'

He raised his arm to point at one of the nearby buildings, less than a hundred yards away. It was a very old warehouse with small windows boarded up, and it looked no different from all the similar structures surrounding it.

McGray leaped to his feet and ran towards it. I protested, but then Thatcher dropped the whistle and chased after him. In a blink I was left with a wounded officer and two confounded passers-by.

I heard the swift steps of another officer, the only one who'd responded to Thatcher's call, approaching at full speed.

'Help these people to a hospital,' I barked, showing him my badge, and before he could ask any questions I ran to the old warehouse, following the light of Thatcher's lantern.

I cannot believe I got there so quickly, for I could still hear the echo of the battering McGray was giving the front door. There was a final creak of collapsing wood and then I saw the light vanish into the decrepit building.

The twenty steps that I still had to run felt like an eternity, but I finally made it to the entrance. Before stepping in I looked back and managed to glimpse the policeman and the man moving Kenny, the terrified lady following close behind. I felt terribly guilty for leaving them to their own devices, but the sound of frantic steps from the darkened warehouse reminded me of all that was at stake.

I looked inside, but the place was so dark I could see only patches of unpaved ground. The light of the street lamps filtered through the gaps between the window boards, barely enough to reveal an enormous storeroom, entirely empty. A wide timber staircase was its sole feature. I did not like all the shadows around me, and readied my weapon as I went further in, step by cautious step.

The sound of more footsteps came from above, and then I heard a whistle of astonishment that could only have been uttered by McGray.

I climbed the stairs, tripping twice in the almost total darkness, but then I saw the gleam of Thatcher's lantern and my jaw dropped.

The upper level was cramped with sacks, crates and barrels of all sizes, some of them piled up to the roof. I recognized the same herbal odour as in Redfern's house, and also the stench of caged animals. I saw a few crows and cats, but also magpies, snakes and even a grey baboon. Next to their cages stood an intimidating African idol.

'What is all this?' I muttered. 'Have you not found Ardglass?'

'Doesn't seem to be here, sir,' said Thatcher, scrutinizing the scene with bewildered eyes.

McGray, however, looked like a child in a sweetshop. I saw him tearing open a jute sack, from which he extracted a fistful of odd roots, which were naturally shaped as human bodies.

'Asian ginseng,' I said, utterly unimpressed.

'Aye, an aphrodisiac. Very pricey.' McGray moved to an open crate and rummaged through its contents.

'McGray, if Joel is not here we should resume our search.'

But Nine-Nails was not listening. He lifted a jam jar half filled with fresh leaves – and something that moved. I had to blink to make sure it was not an illusion: a tiny frog, with skin as yellow and bright as a lemon's rind.

'Just like Spotson said,' I whispered.

McGray was awestruck. 'This wee thing is so poisonous ye'd die from touching it with yer fingertip.'

'Then do not hold it so close to me,' I snapped. 'I must insist we . . .' Then I saw a crate containing what looked like cheap tea tins. I opened one, to discover it was full of dried foxgloves: flowers, leaves and chopped stems.

'Yer favourite,' McGray mocked.

'Sirs,' said Thatcher, coming to us with a thick account-ancy book, 'I just found this. You'd better have a look.'

McGray was having a field day looking around, so it was I who leafed through the book. To my surprise, it was one of the tidiest ledgers I had ever seen, with detailed accounts of expenditure, income and profit margins.

'They are running a nice little business here,' I said. 'A trade in poisons and hallucinogens and charms . . .'

'Who would have thought?' McGray added. 'A web of witches, trading black magic.'

I chuckled. 'There is hardly any magic here, but it is impressive nonetheless: very sophisticated chemistry. I would not blame the unlearned folk for thinking all this is supernatural – *you*, Nine-Nails, have no excuse. I believe that . . . Oh, for goodness' sake, McGray, stop pocketing stuff! This is evidence. We must have Massey seize all this merchandise.'

He ignored me and went on stuffing his every pocket with herbs, sachets and amulets. He sensed my recrimi-nating stare.

'What? I'm doing field research!'

I shook my head and searched around with Thatcher. In the furthest corner we found what would have been a little office, where an old, dusty desk had been pushed to one side. There was an improvised bed, a bundle of blan-kets and a few logs in a small burner. One of them still glowed.

Lying nearby were the ends of a loaf of bread, an empty

bottle of red wine and the discarded bones of two roast chickens.

'That was an expensive meal,' I said. 'McGray, you should –'

Thatcher gasped, suddenly as pale as parchment, and he pointed ahead. On the opposite side of the room there was a door to a wide cupboard . . . but it was ajar.

My eyes descended slowly, and I felt a cold wave of fear when I saw the tip of a large foot sticking out. Someone was still there.

I gulped, losing my focus for an instant. I was going to aim at the door and shout to the man to come out, but before I could do anything the world erupted into chaos.

The cupboard door was flung open with an explosive movement. Then Thatcher yelled and dropped the lantern, which showered sparks as it shattered on the floor. Then I could see nothing. There was a savage growl and the wooden floor creaked under the stomps of what seemed a wild beast.

Thin strips of light came in from the street through the boarded-up windows, and I could make out only fleeting hints of pale skin and the flashing spark of two sharp black eyes. He was a mighty thug who looked like a circus weightlifter: a wall of muscles, gigantic in all three dimensions, and I caught a slatted glimpse of a thick moustache all waxed and curled up. He was wielding a thick bludgeon, and as we saw it we instinctively jumped backwards, my body colliding with McGray's.

All this happened in an instant, and before we could react the behemoth struck a mighty blow on Thatcher's shoulder. I heard the chap's bones cracking and his anguished scream as he fell to his knees. The giant kicked him aside and then ran at us, his stamping feet shaking the entire building.

We aimed our guns at him and McGray fired, but just as he pulled the trigger the brute knocked over a tower of boxes, and an avalanche of witchcraft paraphernalia rained down over our heads.

Glass jars and boxes hit my head and I fell flat on my chest, my gun sliding out of my hand. I felt for it frantically, but then my fingers landed on something soft and slimy. I shrieked. Had I just squashed the poisonous frog? How many seconds would I have if –

I rubbed my hand on the floor, desperate, and as I did so I felt the grip of my gun. Just as I touched it a mighty hand grabbed my leg and dragged my entire body from under the rubble.

I slid through broken glass, herbs and slimy articles, until the man lifted me in the air and I found myself hanging by a leg, upside down, swinging from side to side like a trophy salmon.

I saw his towering bulk, a triumphant grin and him wielding the truncheon to strike a final blow to my head. I was resigned to a smashed skull but, with all his might, McGray threw a tea tin that hit the brute in the temple.

Though the man seemed hardly to feel it, for a split second he turned to see where the object had come from, and then a large bottle smashed right into his face. An oily liquid splashed all over him, and as he roared his grasp loosened.

My cheekbone hit the wooden floor and I heard more

bottles shattering. I crawled away, whimpering, hearing his enormous feet crushing everything in their way.

McGray screeched: '*Shoot him!*'

I groped around on the floor desperately, cutting my fingers more than once on shards of glass. I saw a jar rolling away, shimmering under a strip of light, and in it the bright yellow frog. It hardly registered, for I could hear McGray shouting again, amidst the din of crashing wood and glass. I looked up and caught a glimpse of the bludgeon falling towards Nine-Nails, who dodged it by mere inches, throwing whatever he could lay hands on at that mountain of a man. Right then I felt the cool trigger brush against my thumb, just as McGray tripped over a sack of herbs and fell on his back.

'*Shoot 'im, ye bleeding sod!*'

I grabbed the weapon so tightly my fingers ached, my eyes fixed on McGray's shadow, now crawling across the floor. The man's massive back blocked my view, and in the second it took me to point the gun he struck two deafening blows. McGray hollered.

I fired without really aiming, and the explosion of the shot obscured every other noise.

There was an eerie pause. Neither McGray nor the circus freak made a sound. Thatcher whimpered in the background, and then, as if a bubble had burst, I heard a grunt and saw the man's broad hand rising to squeeze his right shoulder. The truncheon fell and bounced on the floor.

Just as I pulled the trigger again the man turned, his now bloodstained hand describing a great arc and hitting my wrist, sending my shot to the ceiling. Then he trudged to the staircase. I stood up and fired again, but an instant too late.

'Ye all right?' McGray said, springing to his feet, searching around for Thatcher.

'I can walk,' said the young man, 'but I won't be –'

'Good. Get yerself some help.' Nine-Nails tossed debris aside and somehow found his gun immediately. He barked at me without pausing, 'If ye'd taken one more second, my brains would be mush!'

'You are welcome!' I snapped, following him down to the empty ground floor.

'He's gone.'

The front entrance was deserted, but then we heard the creak of another door, flapping in the gusts of wind.

We rushed outside, to a main road, too wide and too straight for anyone to hide so quickly. Simultaneously we caught a glimpse of a large carriage heading east, swift and thunderous, and then the circus freak making his escape in the opposite direction. McGray swore and ran after him without hesitation.

I was puzzled by that carriage but I could not have caught it, so I followed Nine-Nails along the deserted avenue.

The man was surprisingly fast, but on the open road there was nothing to hide his silhouette. McGray fired a couple of times, but his aim was so erratic I could not believe it.

'Are you all right?' I asked him, nearly out of breath, but he did not reply.

We ran on, until the road bent slightly northwards and for a moment we lost the man around the corner. By the time we reached it he was entering a small side road.

The sign read *Bridge Lane,* and behind a row of ter-
raced houses we encountered a thick brick wall. The
man was climbing it with an agility unthinkable for
someone his size, and by the time we reached the wall
there was but a trail of his blood left on the disturbed
snow.

McGray jumped up, easily grabbing the top of the wall
and then pulling himself upwards. He had to lend me a
hand and as he pulled me up I felt the cold bricks grazing
my entire body.

He did not offer to help me jump down, and I fell on all
fours like a clumsy toddler. I scrambled up and as I ran
forwards I saw that we were in very luxurious walled gardens: snow-dusted lawns lined with privet, leafless rose
bushes and frozen fountains.

I saw a line of tall townhouses to our left, all their windows lit, and beyond them loomed the castle walls. We
were running along the back of the road where old Judge
Spotson lived.

'He's going to the priory,' McGray yelled as I caught
him up.

'That is right beside the castle!' I cried, looking at the
cluster formed by the priory's bell tower and the castle's
turrets. It was as though the man was heading straight for
the police headquarters.

I could not see him any more. Neither could McGray,
but he was following the unmistakable deep footprints
in the snow. The gardens ascended a gentle slope; nonetheless we soon found ourselves out of breath. With every
stride I felt more and more hopeless, as if my entire
existence had been nothing more than that futile chase.

I grunted and cursed, but just as my knees began to burn we reached the courtyard of St Mary's Church.

The thick door was partly open, showing a warm glow within.

We found the nave in complete silence, the echoes of our careful steps the only sound. We were finally in a well-lit place, with countless candles burning on each side of the pews, their golden flames flickering in the wind we'd brought in.

On the granite flagstones there was a clear trickle of blood.

The tiny drops drew a twisted track all along the aisle, and we followed it across the choir stalls. There were Gothic carvings of bats and gargoyles perched above each chair, and in the quivering light their eyes almost looked alive.

As we advanced I looked around, my gun at the ready, expecting someone to jump from behind the columns and pointed arches.

'*Don't move!*' McGray shouted, startling me, and hurled himself forwards.

Past the choir stalls the trickle of blood became smudged, as if clumsily mopped, until it disappeared completely. I only saw it out of the corner of my eye, for my attention was on McGray. I felt a twinge of fear in my chest when I saw movement in front of him.

A cloaked figure, thin and undeniably female, had been lurking at the altar and was now running for dear life, clasping a bloodstained bundle of rags. Had she just cleaned up the trail of blood? We had a glimpse of a small hand, bony and as pale as a corpse's, grasping the edge of the stone arch that led to the bell tower. The figure disappeared in an instant.

McGray grabbed one of the thick candles, the wax dripping on his bare hand, and marched on.

'*Stop!*' he roared.

We filed up the spiral staircase, the woman's steps echoing ahead of us. She was breathing laboriously and letting out a faint, wicked laugh. It was the sound of an old woman, but eerie and cruel, and hearing it in the darkness made me shiver.

'Are ye Redfern?' McGray shouted. 'Where did yer bully go?'

The laughter turned into a frank cackle, ever nearer, as we reached the top steps. That tower was the highest point in Lancaster, and when we stepped out the wind blew so strongly it made McGray stagger.

The candle went out immediately, and in the moonless night, so high above the street lights, everything turned black. But the darkness did not last long.

There was a sudden spark, and before I could take in what I was seeing there came an explosion of light and fire.

McGray jumped backwards, pushing me back with his arm, and I nearly fell down the winding staircase.

In a blink the belfry was ablaze, violent flames bursting from the bells themselves and shining in the strangest shade of emerald. I felt the wave of heat on my face, almost burning my skin and blurring my vision. McGray pulled me aside and we both crouched against the damp stones, hearing the roar of the fire, feeling the scorching heat pass through our coats and burn our backs. I feared the flames would char our bodies, but the initial wave soon receded. McGray was the first to rise and I heard him whistle in awe. I turned around but instantly had to shade my brow with the back of my hand. Through half-closed eyes I saw the fire, and despite its intensity I could not look away. I was rapt by the flames, so terrible yet so beautiful. I will never forget that fulgent shade of green.

McGray had to nudge me. 'Where did she go?'

I looked around; the stones of the belfry were now brightly lit but we could see no one. We walked around the fire, squeezing against the balustrade and inspecting every corner.

'She's gone,' Nine-Nails whispered.

'She cannot be! Where to?'

I looked down, to the courtyard and surrounding gardens, but saw only a young watchman, looking up at the fire in utter astonishment.

Over the roar of the fire we heard a sharp caw and then saw a raven, its wings blacker than the night, flying away from the tower. I watched it go and then I gasped.

'McGray . . .' I mumbled, pointing. I was so astounded I could not say another word.

Somewhere in the distance, miles away, a second fire cut the darkness, as green as the flames by which we stood. It was above the horizon, and my troubled mind thought it was floating in the sky.

Beyond, just as McGray came to watch, a third green spark appeared, so far away it was but a faint little star against a black background.

We held our breaths, speechless, and with a shudder we realized that something terrible had just been unleashed.

21

Nobody had to extinguish the flames – they simply receded, leaving the bells glowing as if they'd just been taken out of a blacksmith's furnace. Neither McGray nor I managed to move until the flames were gone; we remained staring alternately at this and the more distant fires, and then we had to shake the bewilderment out of our heads. Things had taken a far more mysterious turn, and now we had a lot of work to do.

Searching the church must be the first thing, so we rushed to the castle and brought as many guards as they could spare. One small group was sent to the shipyards to search the old warehouse, but most of them were told to help us at the priory.

When we returned we found a little crowd already gathered around the courtyard, staring in amazement at the top of the tower. I could not blame them: the bells were like embers against the dark sky. Nobody seemed to regard the ungodly hour and weather, and we had to elbow our way through the throng.

''Tis the Devil's work!' I heard a rustic woman say, a scared little boy clinging to her skirts. Then came the drunken cries of a middle-aged man, who stood precariously on top of a bucket as he shouted his lungs out.

'The end of the world!' he roared, waving a nearly

empty bottle of spirits. 'Repent! *Repent!* You filthy, sinful wre–'

McGray silenced him by 'accidentally' nudging him off his perch, then winked at me, as if it were the height of wit.

'Disperse this mob,' I told the officers, and they began sending the people forcefully on their way – with a kick in the behind for the intoxicated preacher.

The crowd scattered quickly, but I knew that in the morning everyone in Lancaster would be talking of nothing but the strange green fires.

The abbot, a middle-aged man as tall as he was wide, came to aid us with an enormous set of keys. We searched every corner of the church and its surroundings: the organ, the choir, the sacristy . . . Nothing and no one untoward was found.

The only traces of the huge man and the old woman were the half-erased track of blood and the rags used to clean it, which we found half charred in a corner of the belfry.

It was in the small hours, well past three o'clock, when I saw McGray lean against a granite column and surrender to a deep yawn. I was not feeling too well either.

'We should go for a rest,' I told him. 'The officers can manage without us until morning.'

He shook his head, but then he yawned again and I had no trouble pulling him out of the priory. Even the freezing air of the small hours was not enough to cut through his fatigue, and when we arrived in the inn he landed on his bed like a log. Unusually, he was snoring in seconds.

I took off my overcoat, but before hanging it on a chair I had a look at all the trinkets I'd been collecting: Oakley's telegram urging her to go to Lancaster, Redfern's letter smeared in crow's blood, Joel's portrait . . . and then my notebook, still open at the page where Miss McGray had scribbled *Marigold*. I thought how things were spiralling out of control: we'd started off chasing a single madman, investigating a single murder, only to plunge ourselves into the swamp of intrigues of the Ardglass clan. And if that were not enough, their family affairs now turned out to be somehow linked to this tangle of dark 'magic' and an underground coterie of smuggling witches.

I decided I would not think about any of that just then, and shoved the portrait and other items back into the coat pocket.

Despite my total exhaustion I did not sleep much, mostly because of Nine-Nails' rumbling snores, and by six o'clock I could not take any more tossing and turning. I got up and found the innkeeper receiving a cartful of groceries, so I ordered a hearty breakfast.

My appetite was finally restored, and I devoured fried eggs, bacon, cheese and scones. I was particularly delighted by the latter, because it was impossible to get hold of decent scones in Scotland.

I was buttering my second helping of the delicious fruity bread when McGray joined me. His hair was dishevelled, his eyes red, and the creases in his overcoat, which he'd not taken off throughout the night, showed perfectly on which side he'd slept. Still, the words he chose to greet me were: 'Ye look ghastly.'

I did not lie. 'I had a terrible night.'

'How come? Did I snore?'

'Snored, talked, belched, farted – apart from your ears,

there is not a crevice in your body that did not produce some sort of noise.'

'Honest? What about –'

'Nine-Nails, allow me to finish my breakfast before you boast all the vulgarity I know you are capable of.'

McGray devoured a meal even vaster than mine, and I was glad I'd risen earlier, for seeing him wolf down half a dozen fried eggs, with yolk dripping from the corners of his mouth, was so abominably off-putting I would rather share the table with a dung-splattering piglet.

I may have told him as much, not that anything would put me off those delicious scones, but his mind was on more pressing matters.

'We need to go back to the warehouse,' he said, smacking his lips. 'Search it properly.'

'There are constables taking care of that. I told them to wake us up if they found anything relevant; if they had, we would know by now.'

'I want to check myself. Those laddies could overlook something.'

I nodded. 'Indeed. You are the witchcraft-nonsense expert.' I pushed my cutlery away, a little reluctant to mention the last ordeal of the night, but I had no choice. 'In the priory . . . What do you think we saw? And don't tell me –'

'She turned into a raven.'

I shook my head, then sighed. 'Why, of course. Because there is *no other* feasible explanation.'

'Some o' the Lancashire witches admitted in court they had the power to turn into animals. Crows and cats and dogs.'

'Where did you read that? In the latest penny dreadful?'

'Actual court proceedings,' McGray retorted. 'They've been published. Some o' those women honestly claimed they were witches and could harm people just by looking at them.'

'Let us discuss that later,' I said, too impatient to listen to such folktales. 'The woman we saw, do you think she was Redfern?'

'Aye, she must have been, erasing the tracks o' that giant bastard who must be her minion, just like Pimblett was. They must need muscle to run their business.'

'Indeed. An ageing woman would not be able to run that warehouse by herself. How many more people are we going to end up chasing?'

McGray looked stern. 'The only one I need to catch is Lord Joel Ardglass. Alive.'

I sighed. 'Is that really all you can think about?'

'What d'ye care?'

I became exasperated. 'Nine-Nails, we are on the verge of uncovering a potentially dangerous gang. These people have very dubious intentions that we do not fully understand, and their reach seems to extend from here to Scotland. Does that not worry you?'

He went on eating, deaf to my words.

'And all you think about is your reckless personal crusade. Your sister scribbled some nonsense and may – *may* – have spoken a couple of words, but that does not mean that Joel can help her case or will even tell us anything. Even if we do manage to –'

McGray banged his knife and fork on the table, his face red and his nostrils swelling like a bull's. He glared at me and I thought he might stab me with his cutlery, but then something strange happened. His snorting gradually subsided into suspicious sniffing and the wrath in his eyes gave way to a puzzled stare.

'Do ye smell that?'

I had just perceived it. 'Something is burning. What could –'

Right then a thunderous scream came: *'Fire! Everybody out!'*

The dining hall's door opened with a thud, letting in a billow of black smoke, and the innkeeper came barging in, his face pale.

'For goodness' sake,' I mumbled wearily, gathering two more scones as I stood up. The other guests and staff screamed and ran frantically, pushing and shoving me a couple of times. 'All we need now is a little cloud of rain following us around.'

McGray was not yet as weary as I. He ran to the inn-keeper. 'Is it serious? We can help youse.'

'Tis the main staircase, but I don't think –'

McGray rushed there and I followed. Those were the steps that led to our chambers, the carpet and the oak handrail roaring in flames.

'At least this one looks normal,' I remarked.

McGray was already running to the main entrance. *'Bring snow!'* he shouted, and then pointed at two strong-looking guests. 'You and you,' and then he looked at me, 'and Frey, don't just stand there like Marie Antoinette eating cake.'

He knocked the scones out of my hand, and I could

well have shot him for that, but the people's screams were becoming ever louder.

We ran out to the street and the cold air hit me without mercy, for I'd left my overcoat in the room. People were shouting and alarmed guests and maids were still storming out, as we gathered snow from the ground with our bare hands.

Other guests, passers-by and a policeman came to aid us, and we ran in and out, carrying snowballs and throwing them into the fire. The cook also joined us, bringing buckets of water from the kitchen.

'Is anybody trapped up there?' I asked the innkeeper, but he shrugged with a terrified scowl.

Very soon I felt the sweat dripping from my temples, yet my hands were so cold I no longer felt my fingers.

With the welcome help it must have taken us less than ten minutes to extinguish the fire, but it felt like an eternity. As I ran back with a last load of snow I found McGray and another two men trampling on the dying flames.

The innkeeper came up, red and sweaty, and almost crying at the sight.

I stopped him. 'Excuse me, Mr . . . ?'

'Jones.'

'Did you see how it started?'

'Oh, I don't know what happened, sir,' he whimpered. 'I passed them stairs and they looked fine, then I walked back 'cos I'd forgot a key, and they were like this!'

McGray rushed upstairs, each stride spanning three steps. 'Could it be . . .'

I ran behind him, and heard his angered swearing as we found the door to our room wide open.

McGray had barely crossed the threshold when he let out the angriest cry. '*Och, sons of bitches!*'

I peered in as he shouted, and the sight of the place left me aghast: somebody had broken in, the linen had been tossed about, the wardrobe and all the drawers were open, and I found my coat crumpled on the floor. All the contents of my pockets – the letter, the telegram, even my wallet – were scattered around it.

'They searched ye well,' McGray said as we both kneeled down. 'Did they take anything?'

I picked up my wallet and found it still full of large notes. 'It was not money they were after.' I looked through the other articles, and very soon we understood the cause of it all.

Joel's photograph was gone.

22

'Another bloody search,' I moaned, exhausted, after we had gone through every bedroom, corridor and hall. We'd also questioned a couple of people, but soon realized it would be impossible to find the culprit.

'What a perfect plan,' McGray said as we took one last look at the disordered bedroom. 'Set the fire as a distraction, take everyone out o' the inn, do yer business without worry and then run away hidden in the hubbub.'

'Do you think it could have been Joel?' I asked. 'He is the only one who'd not want that picture seen.'

McGray pondered. 'Aye, but if that's the case, how did he find out we had it?'

We heard a throat clearing. It was the innkeeper, coming in with a sheepish look. 'Sirs, may I have a word?'

'Only if it is urgent,' I said, but then the chubby man hesitated.

'*Well?*' McGray snapped.

The innkeeper started. 'Oh, well, I sort of forgot to tell you that there was this other guest, a young lady . . . She came to me yesterday and asked me if you two were policemen.'

McGray grabbed him by the collar, too violently even for him. '*What!* How could ye forget to tell us that?'

Mr Jones gulped. 'I didn't think it was important, and then you two were away all day . . .'

'What did she look like?' I asked, although I could have uttered the answer myself:

'Short girl, slim, brown hair . . . very well mannered. She came here with her grandmother.'

'What did you tell her?'

'The truth. That I didn't know for sure. I assumed she'd seen the policemen who came to fetch you in the morning. The ladies took a room not long before you did, the one right next to yours.'

McGray and I exchanged worried looks.

I remembered what the filthy woman at Shambles Street had told us; she'd seen Oakley and Redfern going out with packed bags. Then I recalled our first night at the inn, when we'd heard two women arguing.

'McGray, you asked them to be quiet,' I said. 'Banged on the wall . . .'

'Aye, Oakley must have recognized my voice.'

'And then we both mentioned Joel's portrait before sending the coats to the laundry . . .' I looked at the innkeeper. 'We need to inspect their room right now.'

We rushed to the reception, grabbed the appropriate key and the innkeeper led the way back upstairs. He knocked very gently.

No reply. McGray then hammered the wood with his fist. '*Open up, bitches!*' He waited seconds before snatching the key and unlocking the door himself. He kicked it open and stormed in. He roared, '*Damn it!*'

The place was empty. Neat, but empty.

On the made-up bed lay a bundle of sterling notes and a handwritten message, which McGray seized and read aloud:

'"Dear Mr Jones, sorry about the fire. We have left

enough money to cover the cost of any damage, as well as the comfortable rooms provided . . ."' He looked up. 'No signature.'

'Let me see,' I said. The hand was rather elegant, although the smudged ink told how hastily it had been written. I arched an eyebrow. 'Why do they say *rooms*?'

Mr Jones was already counting the notes. 'Oh, they were travelling with a male servant. A mighty feller, taller than you and with a back wider than them door frames.'

I rubbed a hand over my face, my stomach burning with frustration. 'I know this will be an utter waste of time, but did they give you names and addresses?'

'It'll be in the log,' the chubby Mr Jones said. 'I'll fetch the book.'

While we waited I cast a tired look over the neat room, shaking my head.

'Ye all right, Frey?'

'It escapes me . . . Why would they not want us to find Joel? Why, if he is trying to kill them? And this is a desperate act.'

McGray sighed, at a loss. The innkeeper returned with the tatty guest log and showed us the relevant line. The women had signed in as Mary and Jane Smith. Hardly believable.

Nine-Nails snorted. 'Clean this room for me, Mr Jones. I'll take it for the night.' He strode out, I grabbed my overcoat and we made our way back to the priory.

'I like the irony of it,' McGray was saying as we walked up the icy street. 'Tonight I'll be sleeping in the bed of the very witch we're looking for.'

In fact – he would not.

*

I felt rather dizzy, standing at the edge of the belfry in the daylight.

McGray was stretching out the map he'd ripped out of a book from the castle's library.

'Would ye say it was east-south-east?'

I was holding a small compass I'd snatched from Massey's office. 'Possibly. I was not precisely focused on the cardinal points last night.'

The evening wind had cleared the air, giving us an unblemished view of the horizon in all directions. We would have to make haste though, as there were black, threatening clouds coming from the east.

'It must have come from that hill,' I said, indicating a smooth mount a few miles beyond the edge of Lancaster.

McGray checked the map. 'That's called Black Fell. There's nothing round there. Not even farms. What about the other wee light?'

I took a few steps to my right.

'That one was more towards the south.' I squinted, trying to see the outline of a distant hill. I could just make it out, but only as a pale shadow, barely darker than the grey of the sky. 'There.'

McGray frowned. 'Cannae see. Are ye sure?'

'That is the direction,' I said, a little surprised; McGray had very good eyesight.

He ran his fingers to the edge of the map. 'That could be Winfold Fell. Although I must say . . .'

'What?'

'Pendle Hill's that way.'

I cackled. '*Pendle Hill!* Do you mean . . . the Pendle Witches' Pendle Hill?'

'Aye.'

'That is ridiculous! You cannot possibly see that far from here.'

'Course not. Pendle Hill's thirty, maybe thirty-five miles away, but look at the map. Ye've just pointed directly to it . . . well, to some mount that's halfway there.'

'Mere speculation.'

'Aye, but even ye should admit it makes sense.'

I did not answer – but he was right. Those women had left undeniable traces of witchcraft. Now they were lighting mysterious fires that got closer and closer to a town famous for its ancient witches. Even I could not call that a coincidence. I watched McGray scrutinizing the horizon, and the yearning in his eyes scared me.

'We are not going there,' I said as firmly as I could. 'I would not go even if we had strong evidence that Ardglass was heading that way. We have already done much more than we should.'

McGray inhaled, readying himself for a heated argument, but Thatcher came up to interrupt him. 'Sirs, we found something in the crypts. You must see it.'

The young sergeant had his arm held in a sling, his shoulder wrapped in bulky bandages.

'Ye should have a rest, laddie,' McGray told him as we descended from the tower.

' 'Tis all right, sir. Bone's broken but I'm fit enough for searching. Kenny is the one suffering, terrible blow to his head.'

'Will he recover?' I asked.

'Aye. The doc said he'll be fine, but he won't be able to work for a few days.'

We entered the nave and then descended further down. Some narrow stone steps led us to the underground crypts reserved for the higher priests.

The stones around us were centuries old, and the damp air, loaded with dust, was a torture for the lungs. We followed the white glow of a lantern and found a couple of young officers, as well as the chubby abbot, looking at a pile of stones smashed on the floor. The rubble had fallen off a wide niche, leaving the cavity completely exposed. The carved plaque, though eroded by time, still read *Lord William Ambrose.*

'We found them stones like that,' the older officer said. 'We tried to put them back but they all crumble in our hands.'

I picked up a piece of rubble; to my astonishment it felt really light. It was porous too, and it crumbled between my fingers with very little pressure.

'This is not granite or sandstone,' I said, crushing it a little harder. 'This is pumice.'

The abbot was scandalized, fanning himself with both hands.

'This is desecration –' he began to say, but McGray pushed him aside, snatched the lantern and shed light into the niche. As he began to rummage through the dusty contents the abbot shrieked. 'Inspector, this is a sacrosanct place! We come here only to inter our most saintly brothers.'

'Well, there are witchcraft artefacts in yer sacrosanct place,' said McGray. He pulled out a green glass bottle and held it close to the light. Clearly another witch bottle: inside it I could see the shadows of bent nails and rotten herbs.

McGray was about to crack the cork but I managed to stop him. 'Do *not* open that damned thing in a confined space!'

Again the abbot cried, '*Upon my honour, show some respect!* This is the resting place of some of the most devout souls of the Anglican Church.'

I raised an eyebrow. 'That tomb is for a lord, not a cleric.'

The abbot defended it with pride. 'Lord Ambrose was one of our most earnest benefactors during the early days of the Reformation, when Lancashire was still full of Catholic heathens. He deserved his place here.'

'In other words,' I added, 'he was one of those who buy their way into heaven.'

'He might not be resting that peacefully,' McGray said, looking back at the open tomb. His shoulder was blocking my view, and when he moved aside I felt yet another shudder.

Lord Ambrose's skull had been ripped off the skeleton, and now rested upside down. Yet what really upset me was that the eye sockets and the spinal cavity were stuffed with rusty needles, thorny sprigs and dead flowers, like a vase from the underworld.

I plucked up a petal, brown and brittle, and upon inspecting it I could not repress a tired groan. 'Oh Lord . . .'

'What is it?'

Very soon I would wish I'd lied.

'I think these are marigolds.'

23

McGray was all astonishment. 'Are ye serious?'

'They might be dead,' I went on, 'but these flowers are definitely not ancient. Someone must have placed them there rather recently . . . within the past few months, for certain.'

That only fuelled McGray's agitation, and to the abbot's dismay he plunged half his torso into the alcove. The alarmed priest yelled and tried to pull McGray's arms; Nine-Nails did move away, but only in order to backhand the man's face so hard it wobbled.

'*Nine-Nails!*' I shouted, catching the fat abbot before he collapsed. 'You just attacked a citizen!'

He was already back in the niche. 'If ye care so much, go rub his cheeks with almond oil. Ye'll need a couple o' flasks for each cheek.'

We heard the clatter of bones being thrown about, then Nine-Nails let out a repulsed cry. He jumped back out, and I saw his hand was covered in a black, slimy substance.

'What's this shite?'

I approached, wrinkling my nose in disgust as I smelled the mysterious oil. 'You'd better wash your hand . . .'

'Why? Is this poison?'

Before I could answer, a very tall officer with a grating voice came up to us. 'Sirs, Thick Crispin wants to talk to you. Says it's very important.'

'Thick Crispin?' I asked, before McGray reminded me that was the name of Judge Spotson's grandson.

'He will have to wait,' I said, but then the chap himself came down, his eyes so wide he reminded me of the flower-stuffed skull.

'Inspectors, I must have a word,' he gabbled, tripping on the rubble and nearly falling on his face. 'In private, if possible.'

'Go away,' I said.

'Please, sirs . . . It's about the . . . the frogs!'

I turned to him so quickly my neck almost snapped. 'What?'

McGray spoke in the gravest tone. 'Everybody out.'

The abbot was indignant. 'I will not leave you alone here, to further desecrate the –'

'*Get out!*' McGray roared, his voice resounding through the crypts, and the officers left immediately, dragging the priest out. As the echo of his high-pitched dissent died out we were left in a gloomy silence.

McGray wiped the black slime on the side of his coat, leaving a mighty stain, and held the lantern up to shed light on Crispin's face. 'Well?'

The young man's lip was trembling as much as his voice. 'Last night my grandfather had a moment of clarity . . . or so it seemed.'

'You have our undivided attention.'

Crispin shoved his shaking hand into his pocket and produced a crumpled piece of paper. 'He was very agitated after you visited. Didn't sleep well . . . and he usually sits around all day, but that afternoon he paced all over the house. I saw him clasping his head – he does that a lot these days, when he's trying to remember things . . .'

A long pause followed.

'He did remember?' McGray whispered.

'Yes. He was looking out the window when that fire erupted. That green fire. Did you sirs see it?'

'We saw it,' I said.

'Well, my grandfather was shocked, truly shocked. It was as if that fire brought back his memories, all at once. He shouted for me, asked me to bring him some paper. He babbled a lot about frogs. He would not speak the words, he only wrote them down. He said that a lot of the frogs . . . came from here.'

He handed us the note, but did not let it go when Mc-Gray grasped it. 'Grandpa did ask one thing from you . . . before going all scatty again.'

'Aye?'

Crispin whispered, a quivering little voice that barely made sense. 'You must not tell anyone it was him who disclosed this. You must swear; that's what he asked.'

I frowned, staring at him suspiciously. 'Do you know what this is all about?'

Crispin shook his head. 'No. It all sounds like nonsense to me, but I've learned to tell the difference; I know when Grandpa is with us and when he's not. This seemed very important to him; I told you, he didn't even dare say these words aloud. He wouldn't let anyone bring the note but me.'

'We can keep a secret,' McGray said, his voice reassuring. 'Trust me, I have a very dear one too. Although she cannae speak to me these days.'

Crispin nodded. He gradually loosened his grip, but before we could thank him he was gone.

McGray stood in silence, simply staring at the stone steps. It was as though he had suddenly forgotten where he was. I had to snatch the piece of paper and unfold it. The spidery writing, undoubtedly that of the frail old man, bore doom:

Cobden Hall,
Pendle

'*We are not going to Pendle!*'

My shout attracted all sorts of stares from people on the street and I could not blame them; I was beyond red, turning a strange shade of purple, and arguing in tones reserved for London's most drunken East End crooks.

McGray had ignored me all the way across town, walking impassively towards the train station, and his game of selective deafness made me irate. Only when I started uncharacteristically shouting did he look at me, but even then it was barely a glance out of the corner of his eye.

He ignored me as he enquired after horses, carts or carriages we could hire. Nobody wanted to take us through the Forest of Bowland; the roads, they said, were terrible, infested with robbers, and there were hardly any inns or shelters to break the journey. Some of those drivers, claiming to be true human barometers, augured terrible snowstorms (they could feel it in their bones, they said) and those hilly, desolate moors were the worst place to be marooned during a blizzard.

When they heard we were supposedly heading to Pendle they all suggested we take a train to Preston and then a reasonably short trip by stagecoach, but McGray would hear none of that.

'What's the bloody use o' that?' he had grumbled. 'We want to follow those beacons.'

'No,' I snapped. '*You* want to follow them. I want to get hold of a cudgel and beat you back to sense.'

Another stagecoach driver refused to take us, but suggested we ask 'Benjo' — but only if we were absolutely desperate.

No wonder, for Benjo was a nasty-looking old man, who reeked of a most off-putting mixture of beer and sweat — at least one, if not both, of those constituent parts being stale. He did not want to drive us either, but he did offer a carriage: a rattling, creaking piece of wreckage, which he was willing to sell us along with a famished, diseased mule.

'You must be joking,' I spluttered. 'That bloody beast should be shot and put out of its misery. I doubt it will even survive the trip.'

'Take it or leave it, boss,' Benjo said.

McGray appeared to be seeing an entirely different animal. 'Frey, pay the laddie.'

It was not a large amount, but I chuckled nonetheless. 'You must have had a lungful of mushroom powder in that warehouse if you believe I would ever hand you money for such a rotten cause! We have nothing to suggest that Joel has even left Lancaster. We are *not* going to Pendle.'

Nine-Nails grabbed me by the collar, gnashing his

teeth and pulled me away to whisper: 'The beacons point there. The mad judge says all the frogs and trinkets came from there. Joel left a note saying he knew everything. He must know it's all happening there. *We have to go there.*'

I pulled away, his expression making me terribly uneasy. 'Nine-Nails, your eyes are crazy. Joel might have meant anything by that note. He is insane, have you forgotten? Besides, we are now in English jurisdiction. The sensible thing to do is to assign a dedicated inspector to go down there and carry out an official investigation. In the meantime we should stay here; there are many trails and places we have still not investigated in proper depth. Even back in Edin-bloody-burgh!'

McGray again snorted, '*Pay him!*'

'Pay him yourself if you are so desperate.'

'It's not just the money I need. Ye've seen we're not chasing just a wee lass any more. I cannae do this alone.'

'Then you cannot do it at all, because I am *not* following you.'

He chewed his lip, a fervent glow burning in his eyes. Something I'd only seen in him once, when he was kneeling by his sister's side. 'I've never been so close to finding what's wrong with Pansy.'

'McGray, you are not –'

'*She talked!*' he snapped, an unnatural frenzy taking hold of him, and his booming voice attracted the attention of everyone around. 'After five years she bloody talked! And she chose to speak to that murderous, mad bastard! Why would she do that? And then she wrote in *yer* bloody notebook! *Why?* Now I'm only a blasted coach trip away from finding out.'

'You are not close at all,' I said, so coldly I could scarcely believe myself. 'I told you before: you should have never taken on this case. I have followed you too far already and I will not plunge myself any deeper into this mess. Not even if you drag me by force.'

McGray assented. 'As ye wish . . .'

He moved swiftly, faster than I could react. All I remember is a flashing image of his fist, barely an impression, right before my vision blurred and all I saw were stars.

The entire world reduced to numbness, mental and physical, everything happening as if I were watching from miles away. I felt my body being dragged, as my brain reluctantly took in what had just happened.

Nine-Nails had punched me! Right in the nose too!

As the seconds passed the pain took over, intensifying until my face felt as if it were splitting. I was holding my nose and groaning as McGray snatched my wallet and emptied my pockets, and I could not put up any resistance when he placed me in the carriage. A moment later he was whipping the lame mule, dragging us miserably into the Lancashire wilderness, to those snow-blasted moors where all we'd find was darkness.

24

The pain in my face was excruciating for a good while, making me wish Nine-Nails had knocked me out entirely. By the time I managed to open my eyes and consider my options it was too late: Nine-Nails was driving so fast I could not possibly jump out without smashing myself to ribbons on the rocky road. Even if I could, he had also taken my badge, wallet and gun, and we were too far from Lancaster for me to reach the town before the infuriatingly short winter day came to a close.

All I could do was wait. I would have to follow McGray, but I was adamant that I'd desert his stupid quest as soon as the first sensible chance came.

Resignedly, I looked through the carriage window. We were ascending into the hills, heading straight towards the black clouds we'd seen from the bell tower. I saw the clean skies to the west and my heart sank. The watery sands of Morecambe Bay reflected the golden rays of sunlight, their usually dull, muddy colours turned auburn. Nearer to us, yet already minuscule to the eye, were the brown and grey streets of Lancaster, clustering around the small mount on which stood the towers of the castle and priory. I could imagine what the green beacon would have looked like the previous night; for anyone standing where we were, it would have seemed a bright ball of fire floating in mid-air.

We soon reached the other side of the hill and I lost all sight of Lancaster. The drive must have lasted two or three hours before McGray finally slowed down. He stopped the carriage beside the ruins of an old barn and I heard him jump down from the driver's seat, then his muffled steps on the snow.

'Will the countess have supper?'

'*Supper!*' I cried. 'I want to tear you apart!' Unfortunately my voice came out very nasal, my nostrils full of clotted blood.

'Aye, ye sound really menacing.'

That made my blood boil. The carriage creaked like a brothel's old bed as I alighted, and the strong, icy wind was like daggers hitting my still tender face. I had to wrap myself in my coat as I looked around. Even though McGray had stopped at the summit of a hill, all I could see was mile upon mile of rolling, barren emptiness, extending to the horizon and beyond. A few lonely shrubs stood above the thick layers of snow. Constantly battered by the wind, they looked like dark, bony hands all praying in the same direction.

I found McGray sitting on a stone, munching on a greasy meat and potato pie and washing it down with a flask of ale. Partially sheltered against the lichen-spotted wall, he was oblivious to the wind, the snowflakes that were beginning to fall, and the fact that he'd effectively kidnapped a colleague.

His utterly blasé attitude did nothing but worsen my temper. I felt my lips twisting involuntarily, showing my gnashing teeth as I snorted in wrath.

'*You* . . .' I growled, but I heard the adenoidal sound of my voice and had to stop to blow my nose. '*You* . .' I repeated, my voice now believably enraged, '*wretched* . . . *twisted* . . . *filthy* . . . *sheep-offal-stuffed* . . . *hare-brained Scot!*'

At last he looked me in the eye. 'Cannae tell why, but I kinda feel something's bothering ye.'

'*How could you do that?*' I hollered, thrashing at the air in a paroxysm of fury.

McGray sneered, and spoke only when the echoes of my screaming had died out. 'Och, look at yerself, sobbing and drumming yer heels 'cos I stole yer pudding.'

'*Stole my –*' I had to force myself into composure, as the agitated movements made my face ache more. 'How can you act as if nothing – How can you –' I tilted my head. 'Where did you find pies?'

'Bought them off an auld lady when ye were sobbing. And her ale's not bad at all. C'mon, have a bite.'

He threw me a soggy pie, which I did not bother to catch. The greasy lump of dough hit my chest and then fell to the snow with a dull thud.

'Yer gonnae regret not eating that.'

He'd prove to be right, and very soon, but even if I'd known it then, I was so angry I could only kick the pie away.

'Give me my gun.'

'Och, what d'ye want that for? Are ye gonnae walk all the way back to Lancaster?'

'Well, I should be able to if I so wish! *I am being held hostage!* People in London will hear about this. As high as Commissioner Monro.'

McGray bit into his pie and spoke, spitting crumbs. 'Jesus, I forgot how touchy youse Southrons are. A wee smack on the face and ye cry I *assaulted* ye.'

I was going to argue, but the terrible wind made me sneeze like I seldom do. I blew my nose again and pitied my handkerchief, smothered in coagulated blood and the fruits of painful expectoration. I threw it away.

'I will wait in the carriage,' I said. 'You may freeze to death out here if you want. At least I could then retrieve my money and take that flimsy mule to the nearest civilized spot.'

The cracked wood made for meagre protection, but welcome all the same. I would not want to have spent more than a few minutes in that unforgiving weather, and the way McGray endured it reminded me of those wretched drunkards we usually saw sleeping in the frosty alleys of Edinburgh's Old Town.

Full of ale and meat pies, McGray resumed driving and we descended across the eastern side of the hill. It was only a short time before the last gleam of twilight faded and the night settled, together with thick snow. The black clouds were now directly above us, obscuring everything around us and making the world a tenebrous cave. I realized we did not even carry a lantern.

McGray had to stop and take the carriage off the road. We stood on a sloping terrain, using the very thick trunk of an old oak to shelter the mule from the cold. McGray had trouble tethering the animal to the tree; he was trying to use the minuscule spark of a match for a light, but the wind was merciless and in the end he carried out most of the task blindly.

'Cannae even see the bleeding road,' he said as he jumped into the carriage.

'So this is how your epic quest ends,' I mocked.

'Stranded in the middle of bloody nowhere, in a carriage that is virtually a crate with wheels, pulled by a pathetic creature that is not going to live through the night.'

'Say another word and I'll throw ye out,' he warned, huddling up in the opposite seat, where he fell asleep within the minute.

I had never seen him sleep so soundly, or even two full nights in a row, and it surprised me that it should happen under such dire circumstances.

In fact, I envied him. The bitter cold and his deafening snoring did not let me rest, and very soon every joint and bone in my body either ached or had become numb. I spent hours shifting around on that hard seat, feeling the annoying draughts that filtered through the cracks in the carriage. Nevertheless, my eyelids eventually felt heavy, and I welcomed the delicious drowsiness and the promise of some repose.

I must have slept for a while, although it felt like a blink. Then, before I had the chance to dream, something seemed to emerge from the impenetrable darkness. A gentle glow, passing through my eyelids like the morning sun.

Only it was green.

I opened my eyes immediately, but even then all I could see was a blurred, hazy radiance. A drop trickled down and I realized I was looking at the carriage's steamed-up window. I leaned forwards, rubbed the condensation away and then saw, clear cut against the blackness, a line of green globes of fire.

They were marching down the road, mere yards away from us, in a silent procession going east. I tried to count them, but the lights meandered and crossed each other as they moved ahead. I gave up on the exact number, but estimated there must be a dozen of them.

I nudged McGray, desperate to alert him, but he was sleeping too deeply and would not wake up unless I shook him hard. He did not even move when I looked into the side pocket of his coat, desperate to find a weapon. His heavy arms were crossed tightly across his chest. The guns must have been in his inside pockets.

Again I looked at the lights, now fading into the distance; they'd be gone as swiftly as they had appeared. Recklessly I opened the door, the icy air striking my face, and jumped out of the carriage.

I trudged along the road, my boots sinking into the snow, watching the now distant glares. I was going to shout, to order them to reveal themselves, but then I remembered the horrible heat I'd felt in the belfry, the green fire burning through my clothes, and then Redfern's cruel cackle resounded in my head, as clearly as if she were standing by my side.

Unarmed and with an unconscious companion, I decided to remain silent, despite the frustration clutching at my chest.

My face was now numb, the night breeze a deadly shroud, and I plodded back to the carriage. McGray had noticed nothing. Even the cold draught had not stirred him.

I stayed awake for a long time, my eyes wide open, expecting more green glows to come from any direction, not really knowing what I'd do if they came for our carriage. Every gust of wind and every ruffle of branches startled me, and I became even more anxious when tiredness made my eyes watery. I tried hard to stay alert, but despite my efforts I slowly drifted away.

I heard blows and grunting, and before I opened my eyes I thought I was back in London, in the modest Suffolk Street lodgings I'd missed so much since moving to Edinburgh, and that Joan was mercilessly tenderizing a steak in the kitchen.

Nothing to do with my reality: I stretched, feeling my body as numb and stiff as a great-grandfather's, and had a look through the carriage's window. It was very early morning, the skies completely overcast, and the dull light that filtered through the clouds rendered the world in all the hues of blue and grey.

For the first time I had a clear view of where we had stopped: we were in the middle of a narrow valley, with steep hills on either side of the road. The snow had hardened and flaked off in places, showing that underneath the ice those slopes were entirely covered in purple heathers. One would have thought that the hills would protect us, when in fact they'd done the opposite: the wind tore along the chasm, hitting us even harder than if we'd spent the night in the middle of the open moors.

Despite the whistling gusts I found the source of the noises that had woken me: McGray was kicking the rump of the old mule, which now lay sadly on the ground, half buried in layers of snow. No wonder it had not lived through the night, after its ailing legs had been made to run at a gruelling pace up that steep hill.

For a moment I felt sorry for the beast's cruel fate, but then I realized what it truly meant: we were effectively stranded in the middle of Lancashire's wildest moors, miles away from anything, and with no means of transport but our own feet.

Instead of renewed fury I felt an irrational impulse to laugh.

'Oh! So it did die,' I said, my voice gloating with vindication.

McGray gave it a last kick, then grabbed my collar and pulled half my body out through the window. 'I should've given yer seat to the nag!'

He left me balancing precariously on the sill, and I nearly fell on my face. I pushed myself back into the carriage, conscious of how awkward my movements must look, and stepped out. The snow was deep, my feet plunging several inches, but the edges of the road were still visible. The path was smooth, showing no footprints or any trace of the dark procession I'd seen at night. I was going to tell McGray about it, but decided not to. Those lights had been heading in the very direction I was trying to avoid; if I spoke, I would only reaffirm McGray's demented drive.

'We can easily follow this track,' I said instead, smoothing out my coat. 'If we make our way now at a good pace, we should be back in Lancaster before nightfall. We will have lost an entire day because of your unmitigated stupidity, but at least –'

'We're closer to this wee village,' McGray interrupted. He was seated on the dead mule, examining the crumpled maps he'd torn from the library books. Strangely, he was squinting and holding the sheet mere inches from his face. 'Slaidburn.'

'Slaidburn? Is that not the village where . . . ?'

'Where Pimblett was born, aye. It would take us a wee bit out o' the way, but we can get there in a couple of hours, even at yer pregnant snail's pace. We might find some help. And maybe even find out a thing or two about Pimblett. It looks like one o' those places where everyone knows each other; someone may be able to tell us how Pimblett ended up working for the nasty auld witch . . . and for Redfern.'

'Where exactly are we?' I asked, and McGray pointed at a little canyon.

'Trough of Bowland.'

I looked at the map and immediately snapped, 'That village is to the east. I want to go west – *back!*'

'D'ye still think anybody gives a toss what ye want?'

'I am not going,' I affirmed. Even as I spoke I realized how illogical I sounded, but somehow I could not possibly retract. 'I'd rather walk thirteen miles west than six miles closer to your mad witches.'

'As ye wish,' McGray said, standing up and heading east, undeterred. 'Just remember ye have no weapons, money or badge. I wouldn't be surprised if ye get beaten or murdered or – *desecrated.*'

Exasperated as I was, I had to follow him, trotting pathetically until I caught him up. 'You cannot possibly imagine how much I want to punch you in the throat right now.'

'Well, ye can always try.'

'I am not going to –'

'Afraid?'

'Shut up! I will delay my pleasure simply because if we

meet a wolf or a murderous thief I will need something to distract them with.'

We forged on, hoping to reach the village as quickly as possible, but it was as though the skies were determined to dissuade us. The wind and snow became a proper blizzard, hitting us in the face without pity. I crouched and wrapped my face as best as I could in my furry collar, marching behind McGray with my eyes open only enough to make out his footprints. With every breath I felt the freezing air burning my nostrils, and my stomach growled with unbearable hunger. I yearned for the greasy pie I had recklessly thrown away.

'We have to find shelter!' I yelled when I realized I could no longer feel my feet, the inside of my boots now as cold as the snow on which we were treading. I thought of those ghastly stories about explorers in the Alps: gangrenous legs and toes so badly frozen the flesh and bones snapped like glass.

McGray did not reply or slow down, so I yelled again.

He turned back, but not because he'd heard me. His gaze was fixed on the road, in the direction we'd come from.

'What is it?' I asked, but again he did not reply.

I looked to see what he was staring at, but in the blizzard the world was nothing but a blur of white. A moment later a hazy, milky shadow appeared on the horizon, just emerging from behind the nearest mount. As soon as I saw it I noticed the barely audible sound of hooves and wheels.

'Is that what you heard?' I asked, but McGray shook his head. He seemed genuinely confused.

'Nae, I heard . . . someone screaming.'

'Screaming? I heard nothing.'

'Someone was calling my name,' he muttered.

'I am absolutely certain I did not hear –' I gasped. The outlines of the incoming carriage had become clearer and I had to rub my eyes to confirm the vision. 'McGray . . . that is the same carriage we saw outside the warehouse.'

'What? Are ye sure?'

'Indeed. It was a black landau; definitely not the type of transport you'd expect to see on a road like this.'

McGray sheltered his eyes with his four-fingered hand, squinting and frowning as if his eyes could see only blurred shadows.

When I looked again the carriage was much nearer. I could even make out the expensive-looking trunks tied to its roof, but my heart jumped when I saw the voluminous silhouette of the driver. He was swathed in a thick, hooded cloak, but one did not need to see his face to deduce it was the gargantuan man we'd shot in the quays.

'The circus freak,' I hissed as McGray unholstered both weapons. *'Give me my gun!'*

'Nice try, lassie. Step aside.'

I hardly had time to move; the carriage was but twenty yards from us. McGray planted himself in the middle of the road and shouted at the driver to stop, but the man came on relentlessly. I jumped aside, glancing at the galloping horses and their steamy breath as they darted towards Nine-Nails. I winced as I pictured them knocking him over and stamping their mighty hooves mercilessly on his body. Why would the man who'd tried to kill us stop now?

McGray fired twice but missed the thug, and both bullets hit the corner of the carriage. Then there was loud neighing, as the man pulled the reins so hard I thought he'd strangle the horses and the carriage would shatter under its own momentum. The beasts stopped, one of them delivering a wet snort only inches from Nine-Nails' face. He wiped the mucus as casually as if it were soapy water, his other hand holding the gun firmly. It was a strange image to say the least.

'Can we ask ye —' There was movement inside the carriage, but all I could see was the back of a dark figure, bending down. 'Can we ask *youse* a few wee questions?'

My ears were suddenly deafened by the blustery weather, while my eyes went from McGray's heaving chest to the driver's thick, quivering hand. *Why had he stopped?* Why not finish it all when McGray had so willingly placed himself in front of the wheels?

'*Get down!*' McGray roared.

Again, something stirred in the carriage: a slim, female figure emerged, cautiously peeping through the window that faced the opposite side of the road from me. It was clear to me it was Oakley, but McGray's expression shifted to an inexplicable mixture of surprise and what could have been fear.

'*What?*' he gasped.

I could see the girl's back. She raised an arm swiftly and from that moment it was like she'd cast a curse. McGray shouted as something flew towards him: a dark bottle Oakley had thrown. It fell by Nine-Nails' feet and exploded in flames so violent the blizzard could not smother them. McGray's clothes caught fire – green fire, which he desperately tried to extinguish with his bare hands, the pistols falling to the ground.

'Drop!' I yelled, sprinting towards him, but I could not get to him. The troglodyte driver had alighted and he struck my still tender face with the back of his hand, making me see stars and throwing me backwards on to the snow.

Through watery vision and the blizzard I could barely see the shadow of the giant, marching with enormous strides. McGray had dropped to his knees but did not have a chance to put out all the flames; the giant grabbed him by the collar and lifted him with one arm as easily as he'd heft a bundle of clothes. McGray was still ablaze when the man lifted his free fist and punched him mightily in the face. The blow echoed so loudly even I felt it, then a second strike followed, on the same cheekbone, and I saw McGray spitting blood.

The driver tossed him to the ground, where McGray lay motionless. Then the giant bent down and picked up both guns, aiming one at me while he went through McGray's pockets. I saw him snatch money, our badges and a couple of small vials that McGray must have taken from the witches' warehouse.

'What do you want?' I asked, my voice trembling with rage and cold. 'Are you following Lord Ardglass? Or are you running from him?'

He ignored me, pulling his hood up to keep his face concealed. As soon as he had pocketed the loot he jumped back on to his seat and spurred the horses. Again I expected their hooves to trample on McGray's body, but for a second time they defied my logic; the driver moved aside and carefully, almost meticulously, rode around Nine-Nails and the small green fire that still burned, oddly, on the snow itself.

'*Go back!*' he roared in a rasping voice, the two short words barely audible in the gale.

I watched the carriage wheels make deep marks on the white road, rushing away, leaving us alone and helpless in the harsh snowstorm.

25

It was as if they'd brought the worst of the elements with them, for as soon as they disappeared the wind hit even harder, bringing more snow to batter us mercilessly.

I groaned as I moved, clumsily bringing myself to my feet and taking faltering steps towards McGray's body. He was as still as a corpse, and no matter how angry I'd been I could not help gasping in dread when I saw him. He lay on the ground, his eyes wide open, and I feared the worst until he drew a deep, sudden breath. The marks of the fist spanned from his cheekbone to his jaw, the skin already swelling and his lip burst. There was still a small green flame burning stubbornly in the folds of his coat; I smothered it with a handful of snow, and found that the fabric was not charred but rather smeared with a black, slimy substance.

The larger flames, where the bottle had hit the ground, trembled violently in the wind yet did not die out, and under the green glow there was a dark stain. I threw on more snow and when the fire was out I found that the stain was another slimy spill. I instantly thought of the resinous substance McGray had found in the ancient crypt. Had that tomb been in fact a storage place?

I felt the stuff with my fingertips, as the snow had rapidly cooled it down, and cautiously smelled it. That was no magic: it had the strong scent of gunpowder, and the slime must be a blend of oils, tar and maybe pine resin. When lit at the right angle, it shone with specks of glitter, which must have been the finest shavings of metal. I tried to wipe it off, but the nasty substance stuck, leaving a greasy film on everything it came into contact with.

I heard McGray take another troubled inhalation. I looked back at him and gasped. It was snowing so copiously that his hands, feet and half his face were already buried under a white sheet. We had to move now or that pass would become our grave.

I had to lift his torso – no mean feat – and lean his head forwards, for he was probably choking on his own blood.

As I held him I could no longer contain the most frustrated groan. I was marooned, lost, unarmed, in the midst of one of the worst blizzards of the century, with an injured man who could not even crawl . . . I had to shake my head and put those thoughts aside or they'd overwhelm me.

'Think, Ian,' I said aloud. 'One thing at a time . . .' I struggled for a desperate moment, but I finally managed to focus on our most vital need. 'Shelter,' I murmured, 'or we will freeze to death.'

I looked around, but there was not a feature or tree or rock we could use. I groaned again, and before the gloom took over I stood up, took a deep breath and pulled on McGray's arm. I had not expected him to be quite so heavy. I had to bend, put his arm around my shoulders and pull him upwards, grunting as I heard my spine crack. Another deep breath and I took my first step, with Mc-Gray hanging as limply as a sack of potatoes, his boots dragging as I made my gruelling way forwards.

The movement roused him, but not entirely, and he began to moan. Suddenly he opened his eyes, lifted his chin and babbled in a panicked voice.

'I saw her! *I saw her!*'

'You had a privileged viewpoint,' I said, struggling under his weight.

'She wasn't the witch.'

'Who was she, then?' I listened carefully, but McGray babbled and stammered. 'I am not that proficient in your dialect yet.'

He swallowed painfully – I could tell that talking was draining all his energy – but he managed to utter a single word: 'Pansy.'

I nearly tripped, my legs tangled in his.

'Pansy!' I cried. 'That is nonsense. Your sister is safely locked in the asylum, back in Edinburgh.' McGray was shaking his head, grumbling again, and I sighed with impatience. 'Do trust me; she is in a nice, warm room, perhaps in a soft bed, and someone is bringing her a tray with a hearty dinner . . .'

I realized what was behind my own words. I was starving! No wonder I struggled to drag bloody Nine-Nails along, for the last thing I'd eaten had been the large break-fast at the Lancaster inn. Again I thought longingly of the greasy pie McGray had offered, and was tempted to run back to wherever it was and dig it up.

I cannot tell for how long I walked, or even whether I followed the road at all. My every thought was focused on the next step, my boots sinking deeper and deeper into the snow. It could have been minutes or hours, but it seemed as if my entire life had been nothing but that painful march. Just as I felt McGray's body slipping out of my weakening grip I made out a grey shadow in the distance, behind a sudden indent in the terrain.

It was an ancient oak, with leafless branches that looked like bony hands and claws, ready to catch us and drag us underground. Its gnarled roots clasped the cracks and edges of a jagged rock, forming a deep, wide hollow between the stone and the ground.

I nearly yelled in victory and moved on with renewed energy. The last few yards I dragged Nine-Nails by the wrists, past caring, and pushed him as well as I could into the deeper corner of the sheltered nook.

There was just enough space for us both, and I had to curl up, my back bent snugly against the damp roots and soil. Tightly wrapped in my snowy coat, my nose leaking like an open tap and my body shivering from head to toe, I was the very image of misery.

All we could do now was wait, with nothing to look at but the vastness, the whiteness, the emptiness of that place. I tried to think of a lower moment in my life, but to no avail; I'd never felt so isolated, so doomed, so lost. Not even as a child, right after my dear mother's passing, when I would crouch under the table in a very similar fashion.

I rubbed my arms and chest, and tried to send my mind to merrier thoughts, desperate to keep myself warm and sane.

I thought of my initially pleasant Christmas: the blissful train journey to Gloucestershire, which I had spent in a delightful private compartment, alone with a cigar, a brandy and my belated correspondence.

My dear Uncle Maurice and Elgie, my youngest brother, had met me at the train station, and I felt a pang of nostalgia thinking of that moment; those two rogues were the only relatives whose presence I could tolerate with equanimity, and seeing them after many long weeks in Scotland had brought warm feelings to my heart.

Then the deer stalking, the food, my young brother's superb violin playing . . .

I tried hard to stay on the good memories, but I could not help my mind going back to the unfortunate encounter with my elder brother and my former sweetheart.

Laurence and Eugenia had arrived unannounced, allegedly to give our father a pleasant Christmas surprise. The old Mr Frey had indeed been stunned, but not as they had intended. Laurence had always been his favourite son, the one with the chief post in Chancery Lane, the high connections and the house closest to his; but none of that mattered that day. Father made it perfectly clear that he could not approve of one of his sons 'stealing a brother's mare'.

Eugenia nearly fainted when Father called her a trollop, and the old man refused even to sit at the dinner table with them. The lovebirds, now crestfallen, had been forced to eat their Christmas dinner on their own, at the long-abandoned dowager's house, and to spend the night there too, since there were no late trains they could catch.

I still cannot believe my father took my side. He even shared a glass of fine whisky – 'the one good thing that's ever come out of bloody Scotland', he'd said – while giving me the most affectionate speech his manners had ever allowed: after reaffirming that he thought I'd thrown my career into a spittoon, he'd grumbled a long sentence that could be loosely translated as 'you make your own choices, and my not liking them does not mean you are wrong'.

That is the one honest conversation I've ever had with my detached father, and I cannot believe I owe it to the whims of Laurence and Eugenia. Now I know that their engagement will always be as annoying as a pebble in my shoe, and all I can do is to avoid seeing and thinking of them. I hence welcomed the end of my holidays; I'd returned to Scotland thinking I would be safely isolated from the matter, but I had been wrong. I remembered how enraged I'd felt when McGray brought it up, so casually, in front of that rough, swindling Madame Katerina. *The rascals!*

And now I understood how he'd come to know: Joan, my housekeeper and the world's most pre-eminent gossip, had known about the entire affair from the very start, and it would not be a surprise if she had diligently communicated it to the old butler, George, who in turn must have told the juicy tale to McGray. I could picture them both laughing over the dirty linen of the 'soft Southron', the jilted upper-class snob, the flimsy lover who'd not been able to keep his 'lassie'.

The thought made me growl, and I glared at McGray, wanting to punch his already sore face.

It was good to feel angry, I thought. At least that would keep me warm.

26

No blizzard can last for ever. Not even that one.

The winds slowly died down and the clouds eventually dropped all their snow on the moors, but by that time the sky was already dark.

As soon as the clouds parted I heard the squawk of a raven, and then saw the bird flying boisterously into the now clear sky. Its winding trajectory took it east, towards a gentle slope that ascended in front of our shelter. It led to a high peak, its thick coat of snow gleaming subtly blue under the sliver of crescent moon. It was an ominous landscape, with the oak's twisted branches swaying above us, and even I felt its influence: I thought of green torches, black cats and cawing ravens. I would not like to venture down those wild roads at night, and I feared what new adventures Nine-Nails might drag me into when he woke up.

I looked at him, curled up on the ground. He'd looked utterly broken, even diseased; entirely at odds with his usual resilient self. Now, after a few hours, he was sleeping deeply, snoring like an expiring bull, as he'd done on the two previous nights.

'Two . . . nights,' I whispered, suddenly frowning.

It struck me again quite how odd that was. Nine-Nails seldom slept more than two or three hours, and when he did, it was usually followed by two or three days of uninterrupted vigil.

That was not all. He had been behaving – if possible – more erratically than ever: I would have never thought him capable of punching a helpless abbot or taking pleasure in kicking a dead animal, and I had provoked him much more bitterly in the past without getting my nose crushed. His obsession with finding Joel had been fervent, but throwing us into that ludicrous pursuit across the moors of Bowland, without having a trace to follow or even thinking of the practicalities . . . that had been downright stupid.

He was always reckless and impulsive, yes, but not to such an extent. It was as if something had amplified his fixations and blocked the trickle of common sense that had kept him alive in the past.

To crown it all, his good eyesight and his usually proficient shooting had become pathetic: I recalled him squinting to read the maps, and he'd failed to get a clean shot in at the vast body of the moustachioed circus freak, even when aiming from the most favourable distances. He'd managed to hit him in the shoulder, but that must have been a mere graze, otherwise he could not have taken McGray down so easily.

'What if . . .' I whispered again, an idea now taking root in my mind: what if the witches had cast some . . . 'spell' on him? I was not thinking of an actual charm, of course, but some clever hoax like the foxglove tea. There were countless hallucinogens those witches could be using: belladonna, opium, mandragora . . . However, I could not think of any way in which those drugs could have been administered. Food or drink were out of the question, for we'd both eaten from the same sources – and as

Oakley's poison had proven, my system was prone to much more violent reactions. I thought of the pie I'd not eaten, and remembered that McGray had bought them off an old woman – but I discarded that idea; Nine-Nails had been showing strange symptoms even before he ate the pies.

I dwelled on the problem for a good while but could not come up with any plausible theory. Then I remembered the old hag we'd nearly caught at the church and, just as one recalls an undesired melody, I heard the rough voice of Madame Katerina: *Witches can curse you simply with their eyes; one glare and you're lost.*

Just then Nine-Nails moved, startling me.

He stretched as leisurely as if arising on a pleasant Sunday morning, and yawned with his mouth so wide open I could see all the way to his uvula. When he spoke his voice sounded hoarse and worn out.

'*Fr . . . Frey?*'

'Yes. Were you expecting somebody else?'

He looked around, groping at the stone and roots around him. 'Where are we?'

'In Kensington Palace.'

'Huh?'

'I do not have the slightest idea,' I snapped. 'I was too busy dragging your oafish frame to safety.'

'Did they go away?'

'Yes, McGray, they did. Why they did not kill us, I cannot possibly tell.'

He stretched his arms and back, every joint creaking. 'I feel like a bloody elephant charged against me . . . Cannae believe ye moved me here under that bloody storm!'

I kept my arms crossed. 'What is truly astonishing is that despite this freezing cold I can still smell your wakening breath.'

McGray touched his cheek and moved his jaw sideways. 'Ouch! That devilled swine did ken how to blow a right hook.'

His face was now even more bruised than mine, the flesh less swollen but turned into all the most ghastly shades of black, purple and green.

'What?' he asked, seeing I was smiling wryly.

'I wish he'd finished the job once and for all.'

He looked at me and sighed. 'Has His Majesty decided to throw another tantrum?'

'Can you blame me? You have nearly dragged me to my death!'

'Och, there ye go again. Appease yerself! I've taken my beating too.'

'I do not give a pox what beatings you take! In fact, I would like to see you take a little bit more.'

McGray was searching his pockets.

'They took the guns,' I grunted. 'And the money. And our badges. You truly excelled yourself this time.'

He ignored me, distractedly scratching his leg inside his boot. 'I still have the map and some matches.'

'I still have a compass,' I said, feeling it in my breast pocket.

'That's all we need,' he said resolutely, pulling himself up and clambering out of our hideaway. 'Tell me where's east.'

I blew out my cheeks. 'You cannot be suggesting we go on right now!'

'Why not? Finally there's a wee bit o' moonlight. The sooner we get to Slaidburn, the sooner –'

He fell silent.

I was going to ask why, but I did not need to. Almost immediately my eyes saw a small speck of light in the distance; I had to blink to assure myself it was actually there.

It was a quivering flame, a torch, ascending across the hill along a twisted track. The light was golden, but just as I registered that fact, an emerald flash arose, so briefly I would have missed it had I blinked.

'Did ye see that?' McGray asked, already striding towards the glow.

'I did, but –'

McGray was moving fast, and I had to leap out and clasp him by the shoulder.

'You are not thinking straight!' I hissed. 'We cannot confront anyone as we stand. We are both beaten, we have no weapons and –'

He pulled away, and I could see that fire in his eyes I have come to fear. His mind was set, and only death could break his resolve.

I had no other choice but to follow him, not even able to grumble.

We advanced furtively, maintaining a prudent distance from the torch. As we drew closer I saw it lighting the white snow around it, and casting sharp shadows of the figures that held it.

There were two of them, covered in what looked like black rags that dragged on the ground. One figure was slightly broader than the other, and to me they both seemed female.

There was another green flash in the flames, and then a second fire appeared atop the hill. It too glimmered alternately yellow and green, and the torch responded, as if the flames were conversing in some sort of spine-chilling Morse code.

We followed the tracks of disturbed snow, but the fire in the heights became brighter and brighter, and we had to hide behind a large bush. That one was a beacon – perhaps one of the lights we'd seen from Lancaster, but I could not be sure.

Our eyes stayed on the two figures as they ascended the last twenty yards, now heading straight towards the fire.

A hunched figure seemed to emerge from behind the pyre, but silhouetted against the light it was nothing but a black shadow.

'I cannae see,' McGray whispered. 'Who's that?'

I half closed my eyes, straining to distinguish any feature, but all I could see were dark outlines. The two women planted their torch on the ground and then bowed so low I thought they could have kissed their own knees.

'What are they doing?' McGray asked. 'It's all a splodge to me.'

'Your eyesight has grown terrible,' I hissed. I was about to comment further on his weird symptoms, but then my heartbeat quickened.

The third figure, much shorter than the women, suddenly seemed to sprout from the earth, like a rising mast, and then the wind brought us the echoes of high-pitched howling.

The women threw something that exploded in pink

and red flames; the now towering figure hit them away, and then extended a pair of long arms, looking like a black crucifix, that made the women ululate. The sound was horrible, sending a chill down my spine.

McGray jumped up like an arrow, and before I could stop him he was running towards the macabre scene.

I grunted, sick of running after him, but I could not leave him to his fate. I imagined those shadows striking him and throwing him into the fire, and I left the safety of the bushes to run in pursuit. By then the three figures were embroiled in a savage fight, dark blurs rolling and dashing dangerously close to the flames. A small bundle was jumping about; it was a black cat, hissing and running for dear life.

The taller figure, square-shouldered, was wrapped in a thick overcoat, the black folds flying about as the women hurled themselves against it. A deep, enraged voice yelled back at them, a sound I recognized though I'd heard it only once.

Lord Ardglass.

He saw McGray running to him, and I caught a clear glimpse of his bloodshot eyes, looking like a demon's in the firelight.

'*Back off!*' he spat.

The slimmer woman turned back, and I saw clearly the youthful features of Miss Oakley. It was just for a split second, but time enough for Joel to land a mighty punch on her temple. The girl screamed and fell sideways, crawling away as the other woman brandished a small vial as if it were a weapon.

Joel must have known what it contained. He looked at

the little bottle with frightened eyes, even though he was armed with a large knife. It was a glass blade that reflected the glimmering fire, a hellish vision that was unnervingly familiar to me. He threw stabs to keep the woman at bay, but she was slowly gaining ground, ducking the blows and shouting unintelligible words, maybe hexes. She pushed the vial at Joel, and he had to take a step back, closer to the flames. The woman cackled then, a horrible, piercing sound I recognized immediately. That was the woman we'd seen at the church. The infamous Redfern. The very sight of her made me shudder: her creased, grey face, her bulging eyes burning more furiously than the green fire. She held her bony hand up high, and Lord Ardglass watched the sinister vial in terror.

McGray went straight to the pyre, pulled out a blazing log as long as his calf and ran towards Ardglass. Redfern showed her rotten teeth in a twisted grin as she stepped back to let the two men fight each other.

Joel threw a stab that McGray dodged by mere inches. Then Nine-Nails whirled the flaming torch around, the burning end reached Joel's hand and the dagger flew out of it.

'You bast–'

McGray hit him in the chest and Ardglass fell flat on his back. He rolled and crawled swiftly away, avoiding the blows McGray threw at him.

Redfern raised her bony arm, about to throw her potion, and I realized with a chill that she was *not* aiming at Ardglass.

I sprinted as fast as I could, yelling at McGray, but he

was too busy charging against Joel. I stretched out my arm but managed to grab only one of the folds of Redfern's sleeves, just as she threw the vial at McGray. The tiny bottle barely missed him: it hit the base of the pyre, the glass smashing and releasing a cloud of fumes that burned my eyes and nostrils, despite the distance.

Redfern let out a cry like an eagle's and turned to me. I had a fleeting vision of her long, repugnant nails before they reached my face and scratched my cheek. Without thinking I thrust out my fists, not knowing where I hit her, but she fell backwards and all I saw then was her body rolling down the hill, until it became lost in the darkness.

'Ma'am!' Oakley shouted, still creeping miserably over the snow. '*Wait!*'

She began to moan then, as she realized the old witch was gone.

I grabbed her by the wrist and hissed at her. 'You have a lot to explain!'

There was a gunshot behind me, and when I turned I saw McGray falling to the ground. His leg was bleeding and he groaned in pain, but he never dropped the burning log.

Lord Ardglass was standing up, pointing at McGray the same large-calibre gun we'd seen in Edinburgh. Again I had to jump forwards before I could even think what I was doing. I clutched Ardglass's wrist and the gun fired twice into the sky.

He punched my face, right on the open scratches, and I lost my balance. As I fell backwards I saw the log's green fire hit Joel in the stomach, and he also fell to the ground.

The gun slipped from his fingers and a large boot kicked it into the pyre.

It had been McGray, his eyes shining with renewed rage.

Ardglass looked around desperately as McGray stomped towards him. Suddenly Joel gasped and crawled with spasmodic movements. Too late, I saw him grab the shiny glass blade.

Oakley had strayed too close to him. Joel grabbed her by the hair, pulled her up and held his dagger to her neck. The girl's face was distorted in terror, her eyes wet and her lips trembling. I remembered her terrified face when we'd first questioned her; now her worst fears had materialized.

'*Drop that!*' Joel said, his eyes fixed on the flaming torch. 'Or I slit her throat.'

McGray was holding the log high, ready to strike a mighty blow, his chest heaving.

'You need her alive,' I spluttered, feeling as if my face were about to explode. 'You would have shot her and the old witch otherwise.'

Joel sneered. In the green, flickering light, his teeth made me think of a hound's fangs. 'You think you're so clever, boy. Are you willing to test your theory?'

As he said that he plunged the tip of the blade into the girl's skin. She shrieked in agony as a trickle of blood ran down her neck.

'*Don't!*' McGray shouted, and Joel cackled at him.

'You shouldn't worry so much about the likes of her. Hasn't this little witch tried everything against you?'

We did not reply, which pleased Lord Ardglass exceedingly. 'I thought as much,' he said. 'Following me will bring you nothing but disgrace.' Then he drew the knife to Oakley's cheekbone, softly caressing her face with the blade, smearing her skin with her own blood. '*I said, drop that!*'

Oakley yelped and my heart skipped a beat. McGray had to oblige, tossing the log at Joel's feet.

'Good boy. Now, as I told you before: *don't bloody follow me!*'

He showed his teeth as he said that, retreating into the shadows and dragging the poor girl with him.

'Why are ye doing this?' McGray asked.

Joel was already far from the fire, but I could still see his unsettling grin, and the wrinkles around his eyes and mouth looked like deep, sharp cuts.

'Boy, have they not told you I am *mad*? Just like your little sister.'

McGray gnashed his teeth, and with his deep frown and glassy eyes he looked as if Joel had really stabbed him.

He made to follow them, but I held him back. Weak and weary, Nine-Nails fell to his knees and I saw tears pooling in his eyes.

Soon they were gone. We heard Oakley's voice again, sobbing and then screaming. She let out one last shriek and then the world became silent. I tried not to think what could be happening on those dark moors.

We were left all alone on that icy hill, lit only by the dull moonlight and the beacon's waning flames.

27

'We need to find shelter,' I urged, leaning closer to McGray and looking at his bleeding calf. 'And I should look at that wound.'

He did not move. His stare was lost in the vast darkness ahead.

I pulled at his forearm, but surprisingly it was much more difficult to make him move now, when he was conscious, than when he had been lying in the hollow like a dead billy goat.

'We have to move!' I snorted. 'Joel or the damned witches could come back, and we are not exactly well hidden . . .'

McGray's stare was still fixed ahead, and he slowly lifted his arm, pointing downhill. My eyes immediately fell on another speck of light on the lower slopes.

'Oh Lord,' I moaned, drained to my very core. It was definitely another torch, albeit not green – and it was ascending in our direction.

I pulled McGray's arm more urgently, shook him, then pointed at the golden light.

'We have to go!'

McGray did move, but sluggishly, dragging himself to his feet with my help. He leaned on me and I nearly fell under his weight. As I struggled to take a first step I saw that his face was peppered with sweat and his entire body was shaking. That crushed any doubts I could have had: this was *not* Nine-Nails McGray. They had done something to him, rendered him helpless.

We must have moved but a couple of yards when I looked again. The torch was approaching at a slow but steady pace. I knew it would reach us before we could escape from the beacon's light.

'It's useless,' McGray said, realizing it too, and then dropped on to the snow, grasping his injured leg.

I swallowed, part of me yearning to collapse like him, to give in and let those witches give me final rest. I looked around desperately, trying to think of anything I could do. I saw Joel's gun lying among the blazing logs, its edges already glowing; I tried to get to it nonetheless, but the heat burned my hands before I could even touch it.

The torch was now less than ten yards away. I could see the outline of a veiled head and thought perhaps it was Redfern, returning with another vial of acid to throw at us.

'Use a torch,' Nine-Nails snapped, his face now distorted by pain.

I tried to pull one of the logs out of the pyre, but they were mighty hot. I could not believe McGray had actually wielded one. I ran to the one he'd used, cool enough now from lying on the snow, but the oily substance still kept its flames green and surging. It was quite heavy too, and I had to use both hands to lift it. I stood in front of Nine-Nails.

'*Back off!*' I shouted, swinging the torch. To my dismay the flames were already waning, but I had no time to resort to anything else; the dark figure was so close I could hear their muffled steps on the snow and see the bony, blotched hand that held the torch. A second hand emerged from under the black rags, armed with coarse, claw-like finger-nails, and very slowly pulled back the tattered hood.

McGray and I held our breath as we watched that face emerge; first a saggy neck, the skin as pale as that of something that dwells underground, every inch wrinkled like ancient bark. Then a mouth, half open, with a set of blackened teeth bent in all directions. Then the tip of a crooked nose. Finally, a pair of eyes so sunken and surrounded by folds of skin I could barely see the spark of their pupils.

It was not Redfern but a woman I'd not seen before, surely one of the oldest people I had ever met.

'Who are you?' I barked, not believing that such an old, frail woman could frighten me so much.

There was a meowing, and I saw the large, glimmering eyes of a cat, rubbing itself against the folds of the crone's cloak. It was the same black cat I'd seen fleeing from the fight a few minutes ago.

'Who are you?' I repeated, and then waited, but the woman said nothing. She raised her hand, showing us her leathery palm, as if asking for patience. I pushed the flames closer to her, but she did not move or blink. She simply stared at me with sad eyes I would never forget.

'What do you want from us?' I shouted.

Again, no reply. I felt as if those eyes were drilling into me, searching for something under my very skin, and I had to look away for an instant. When I looked again her eyes were fixed on McGray's. He was staring back as if in a trance.

The extended palm moved then, as furtively as the cat, both approaching McGray like predators. I blocked their path with the torch.

'*Get away!*'

They halted, but did not retreat. The cat hissed at me, while the woman kept her eyes on McGray. I pushed my torch at her again, deciding to burn her hands if I had to, but then McGray grabbed the log and tried to pull it out of my grasp.

'What are you –'

He took hold of the torch; I felt it slipping out of my hands and then he threw it out of my reach.

He was going to take the woman's hand. I hurled myself between them, but McGray pushed me aside with renewed strength and I fell on my rear.

'What on earth are you doing?' I squealed, seeing McGray join hands with that crone.

'This one's different,' he mumbled.

'McGray, you are not yourself! These witches have done something to you!'

He was deaf to my words. The woman tugged his hand slightly, but just then there was a simultaneous movement: the woman's face and the cat's head turned suddenly, looking at the opposite side of the hill. I saw nothing there.

The crone pulled McGray more persistently, then threw her torch into the beacon's flames.

'We have to follow her,' Nine-Nails said, struggling to stand up. I had not realized how much his calf was bleeding until he stretched his leg and I saw the red patch on the snow where he'd been sitting.

'I'm not following that crone,' I insisted, but she and McGray were already staggering away.

The woman whimpered as she looked at me, her eyes imploring, her knotty finger indicating the spot her cat was still staring at.

Three, then four flames appeared in the distance. They were all green, like the ghostly torches I'd seen the previous night.

'We'll move faster if ye help!' McGray snapped.

I looked between him and the lights, grunting in frustration. In the end I decided to go with them and help the old hag move him, but only because I'd rather take on one witch than four.

I took a quick look back, just as we stepped into the deeper darkness, and saw that the cat had stayed behind.

We rushed along almost blindly, entirely at the mercy of that old woman, who seemed to know by heart every rock and feature of the terrain. We followed a twisted path, but not once did we stumble across an obstacle or a patch that was not smooth.

The woman was panting now, and she whimpered again when we heard female screams from the top of the hill. She did not breathe easily until we reached a small cluster of pine trees. I heard the trickle of a little stream, but under the evergreen canopies and a weak moon I could not see it. The land did descend abruptly to its banks, but the woman led us by an easy route. I felt flat stone steps under my feet, taking us to what I thought at first was a pile of rubble. It was in fact a tiny stone dwelling, ensconced in an indentation of the land.

The woman dashed forwards much faster than I would have thought her capable of, and opened a creaking door I could not even see. She pushed McGray in and I followed, groping about until my forehead hit a wooden beam – the entrance was barely four feet tall. I did not have time to moan, for the crone pushed me in as well and then shut the door.

Suddenly we were trapped in absolute darkness.

I cannot tell how long we waited in that place, only that it felt like hours. I could hear nothing besides McGray and the woman breathing, for none of us moved a muscle. We simply crouched there, expectantly. My nostrils became filled with herbal scents, not too dissimilar from what I'd smelled in Madame Katerina's rooms.

At last there came a scratching at the entrance, and I saw the old woman light up a homemade match. I had a first glimpse of her jar-lined walls as she bent to open the tattered door.

The cat had returned, purring loudly as it walked in. The woman let out a relieved sigh, and after locking up again she reached for an improvised oil lamp (a rusty tin pot with a wick made of thick string). The light bounced off hundreds of glass jars, containing everything from herbs and powders to crawling bugs and slithering reptiles. The ceiling was low and slightly domed, and there were no windows. The building could have been an abandoned kiln or a place to store grain, but this woman had made it her home, and it looked nothing like the lodgings of a beggar. There was a neat pile of blankets for use as a bed, another bundle where the cat curled up, and a small stone hearth. She had a fire lit in no time and then hung a pewter cauldron over it.

'Who are you?' I asked again, but the woman was busy at work, carefully gathering jars and pouring their contents into the pot. I could not help regarding her with suspicion. 'What are you doing?'

She mixed dry leaves and oil, her back turned to me, and I could not think of anything to do or say. I was not even sure we should have followed her; for all I knew she could be preparing every manner of venom and explosive, ready to murder or torture us.

'Why should we trust you? Are you not one of them?'

I did not know myself what I meant when I said *them*.

'Can you understand what I am saying?'

She turned slowly, her eyes as sad as before, and she pointed at McGray's leg. Only then did I realize that he'd dropped to the floor, his back resting against the crooked wall and his outstretched legs covering almost the entire length of the room. His trouser leg was soaked in blood, yet McGray seemed to be sleeping peacefully, his chest swelling in long, slow breaths.

I kneeled down swiftly, tore away the ghastly tartan and inspected the wound. The bullet had gone in and out cleanly, missing the bone, but it would soon get infected, unless . . .

Just as I thought that, the old woman threw a damp cloth into my hands. I was unsure whether to use it, until the sting of some sort of alcohol hit my nose. The woman certainly knew how to disinfect wounds. After wiping away the blood I applied a tourniquet, using strips of

McGray's own trousers, and just as I tied the cloth the old woman pushed me aside.

Before I could protest she was already applying a green unguent to the wound, an oily mash of herbs that smelled of camphor and mint. McGray grunted a little but then settled back to his slumber. The woman finished by wrapping the leg with a clean bandage, so neatly I could not have done much better with my Oxford training.

She stood up and went back to her small fire, where she began to boil potatoes as if it were a normal evening.

The fire soon warmed up the little place, and the smell of boiling vegetables reminded me how starved I was. Even the dull aroma of unseasoned starch made my stomach growl, and when I saw the old woman put two large potatoes into wooden bowls my mouth began to salivate.

Brusquely, she landed one of the bowls on my lap. I was so famished that the sad spud was the most tempting of dishes; I still looked at it with distrust.

The old woman noticed this, and she pinched off a piece of potato and shoved it into her mouth, chewing slowly, her eyes challenging mine. The instant she swallowed I dug my fingers into the bowl and devoured the potato desperately, licking my fingers and smacking my lips in a way that would have made McGray blush. Each mouthful was like a gift from heaven, the soft pulp warming and restoring. Unbelievable that a humble potato, grown from mud trampled on by pigs and chickens, could become someone's salvation.

I did not look up until I had eaten the very last shred of potato peel. I found the crone kneeling by Nine-Nails: she was crushing the other potato and then feeding the mash into his mouth, as carefully as a very experienced nurse.

As I watched them an irresistible slumber began to take hold of me. I did not know whether it was something in the food, or the herby smell of the place or sheer exhaustion, but my eyelids were suddenly so heavy I could not struggle. It was but a moment before I drifted off, and the last thing I heard was the empty bowl falling from my hands.

28

I woke to the sound of scratching, and then the tinkling of glass. When I opened my eyes I saw the black cat playing around with an empty jar, rolling it across the floor with its paws and then chasing it. There was no trace of the crone but a pot of porridge was simmering over the fire.

Nine-Nails was lying in the exact same position, so pale and still that my heart jumped. I was going to rouse him, but then he inhaled long and deeply – not even babies sleep so soundly, and for a moment the fact made me hate him.

I was about to slap him, but then the door opened and the old woman returned, carrying a basket full of roots and frosty weeds.

She helped herself to porridge and then poured me some. It looked like sludge, but I was still very hungry so I ate without a murmur.

'Are you never going to tell us who you are?' I said, but I met the same silence as the night before, which did not improve my mood. 'Can you not speak at all?' I snapped.

She turned her face away, as if my words had been a splash of water. There was a slight, almost imperceptible tremble in her hands. I had hit the nail, and I immediately felt a pang of guilt.

'At least you understand me, I suppose.' I shook my

head, saying the first thing that came into my mind. 'What can I call you? You must have a name.'

She did not react for a moment, and I was beginning to think she did not really understand my words, but then she stretched out an arm and pointed at one of the jars. I strained to see but did recognize the dry leaves inside.

I wrinkled my nose. 'Nettle?'

The woman did not nod or assent, but simply resumed her meal. I did nod.

'Nettle it is – whether you are hinting at the truth or simply humouring me.'

We ate the rest of our oats in silence, and when Nettle was finished she poured another portion and began feeding McGray.

I took a look around, and the obvious hit me. That room was like a smaller, cosier version of the warehouse in Lancaster. Exactly at that moment, as her arm stretched out with a spoonful of porridge, I saw a dark shape on her wrist, faded and distorted by the folds of her leathery skin: it was a very old scar, showing two intertwined snakes, each head biting its partner's tail to form an eight.

'You are definitely one of them,' I said, 'but why would you look after us?' I felt the bowl becoming cold in my hands. 'You are *not* trying to harm us, are you?'

That was the first time I received a clear response from her. Nettle looked straight into my eyes and then shook her head. She also pulled down her cloak, concealing the old mark.

I would have to believe her.

McGray chewed the food lethargically. I still could not

believe that a shot in the leg, painful as it would be, could leave him prostrated like that – not Nine-Nails McGray.

I arched an eyebrow as I looked at the old crone and her collection of jars. Perhaps destiny had brought us to the place we most needed.

'If you understand their witchcraft,' I began, feeling utterly ridiculous, 'you might be able to help us.' Nettle did not seem to hear me, but I'd realized by now that was simply her way. 'I believe . . .' I had to take a deep breath. 'I believe McGray, your current patient, has been . . . well, bewitched in some way.'

Nettle turned to me as if she'd heard an explosion. Even the cat appeared to stare at me. Nobody in my life had looked at me with such intense, undivided attention.

'He . . . he has been acting oddly,' I added. 'He very rarely sleeps, but now he falls like a bloody log whenever he can; he is a remarkable shot but he now misses the most ridiculously easy targets; he has never been a feathery dove, but now he is irascible and throws punches and kicks at the slightest provocation; his eyesight seems impaired; and' – I thought of what he'd said about his sister – 'I believe he is seeing and hearing things that are not there.'

Her sunken eyes, with their half-hidden pupils, could not have shown more concern. She stood up and began to rummage through her jars, dropping a couple that smashed on the floor. I saw her produce a black wax taper, then a dry twig of something that could have been thyme.

Nettle tied the twig to the little candle, her bony fingers unsteady as she worked a tight knot.

Then she moved her lips. I thought she might finally

say something, but she only hummed from the bottom of her stomach. It was a deep, guttural sound that echoed around the walls and made me shiver. She took the taper and herbs over to the hearth, and very gently spun them over the flames, humming and humming, until they caught fire.

The cat sat by her, very still, its green eyes hypnotized by the little ritual, as the musky fragrance of burning leaves slowly filled the room.

She turned around, and I nearly gasped when I saw her eyes, turned up and showing their veiny whites. She waved the little bouquet, the smoke drawing erratic shapes in the air as she advanced, her humming growing ever louder, interrupted only when her breath ran out. Then she resumed, louder still.

I heard McGray stir. His face was distorted, his nose wrinkled, as if the herbal scent disturbed him.

Nettle leaned over him. Her black rags, hunched back and wiry grey hair obscured my view, but I heard McGray snorting madly. I rushed up, fearing she was doing something horrible to him, but when I looked I saw Nettle hovering above him, barely touching his chest with just one finger. I tensed my legs, readying myself to jump at her if she tried anything untoward.

She poked McGray's coat, at the fabric over his pockets. Then the cat moved, as stealthily as if hunting a mouse, and used its paw to pull a fold of fabric. It pummelled its paws on it eagerly, but suddenly jumped away, hissing, as if pricked by a thorn. It ran into the furthest corner, where it curled up into a ball, hiding its head.

Nettle pulled the fold and her humming stopped

immediately, as soon as her fingers touched a seam in the inner lining.

'Of course!' I whispered. I recognized the stitches: that was the spot the girl at the inn had mended – allegedly because the garment was so worn out it had torn. I felt my jaw drop, a million questions rushing into my mind. 'How did you know that was there?' was the first I could utter.

Nettle drew circles with the taper over and over, building up a small cloud of smoke over the fabric. She dug her nails in and ripped the patch off, and a little cloud of dust emerged, mixing with the smoke; underneath it I saw a dark bundle roll down, and Nettle took a step back, letting out a frightened moan.

The object looked like a tiny, blackened chick, so tiny I thought it must have been sacrificed before hatching. I could not help my curiosity and leaned forwards. On closer inspection I realized that it was actually a hummingbird, crushed flat like a pressed flower. Tied to it there was a round slice of some dried fruit. Or it could have been some type of cactus . . .

Nettle pulled me back, groaning in angst. She pointed at the bird, then her nostrils, then tapped her temples.

'Does that make people see things?' I said. 'Is it a – *jinx*?'

I thought it must be, for Nettle would not touch it. She pierced it with a rusty poker, and then, holding it at arm's length, and before I could protest, she threw it into the fire together with the candle and the twig.

'*Wait!*' I shouted. 'That was evidence!'

I tried to pull it out of the hearth, but Nettle moaned again and grabbed my arm. She sounded desperate, letting out a sound close to a scream, and I felt her eager nails even through my thick sleeves. I retreated, out of pity more than anything else, and the old woman stood in front of me, with both palms held high and the most frightened grimace.

'I understand,' I said. 'I must not go any closer.'

Nettle slowly drew her hands away, casting me a distrustful look. She gathered more twigs and herbs from her jars and returned to McGray. The scent was so strong I could perceive it yards away: a rather sickly sweet blend of liquorice, rancid tobacco and something else I could not identify. Nettle waved the herbs above McGray's face; he turned his nose away, groaned and kicked about.

Suddenly he jumped up, startling us, roaring as a spurt of bile jetted across the room. It was horrendous, ghastly, and shockingly . . . it was black.

I felt powerless, watching as Nettle pulled at McGray's torso and helped him bend forwards, to empty his insides on to the floor and not on to himself. He coughed and gagged, and I felt genuinely sorry for him.

Nettle beckoned me with her knotty hand and I helped her drag McGray's body, now completely spent, away from the nasty pool of blackness. She opened the door, letting in the icy air, and then began mopping up the bile with the hem of her ragged cloak. That made me feel even more revolted than the vomit itself.

I installed McGray in a corner, where he fell into a deep, yet disturbed slumber. I could see his pupils flickering madly beneath his eyelids, and his weakened jaw moved as if he were trying to speak.

He was a sorry sight, but the old woman mopping up

the sick was even worse. I felt my spirits sinking into a dark, cold place I had not visited in the years since my mother passed away. I wanted to escape from that horrendous place, to eat, to wear clean clothes, or at least to be able to breathe warm, clean air.

I had to turn my back to them, feeling the despair clutching at my chest, and ended up facing the hearth. From a prudent distance I watched the little hummingbird, and it held me engrossed as the flames consumed it.

I wondered what other secrets that old woman kept, how she'd learned all she knew . . . and how she'd ended up a mute, miserable hermit.

One of the tiny wings sprang up as the fire crackled, and there was a sudden flash of colour: an intense, dark red, which made me think inescapably of congealing blood.

29

McGray had the most troubled sleep, yet I could not help the ghost of a smile: that probably meant he was returning to his normal self.

In the windowless kiln it was impossible to tell the hours of the day, so I walked out to check as well as to breathe some much-needed fresh air. The sky was for once clear and blue, and the sun finally shed golden light on to the fields. I knew the warmth would not last, so I rejoiced in it.

Nettle came and went, fetching herbs, digging up roots, washing her ragged cloak in the icy waters of the stream . . . That was her life, a meagre, hardworking existence, scraping food from the forest and the moors in utter solitude.

Quite laboriously, she cooked some sort of broth out of melted snow, wild seeds and a single carrot, and when she shared it with us I felt a gratitude I had never known before. That woman was as poor as one can imagine, and as ugly as an old boot, but she was all charity and kindness.

She fed McGray at first, but after a few slurps he managed to hold the bowl himself. I could see him swiftly coming back to life, and the first words he uttered could not have been more eloquent: 'Have ye ever felt as battered as if someone had run ye through a butter churn filled with porcupines?'

I chuckled. 'Is that how you feel?'

'Nae, that's what ye look like.'

Even Nettle smirked.

'That I must grant you,' I said, all bitterness. 'Unshaven, soiled, half starved, beaten, scratched and having worn the same undergarments for the past five days . . .' I pointed at my bruised nose. 'Oh, and *this* was your doing.'

McGray grinned. 'Aye, it felt really good. I've always wanted to punch yer snooty face, especially when ye wrinkle yer nose in that shite-sniffing way – *like now*! I had shown restraint 'cos I pity yer delicate constitution.'

I raised an eyebrow. 'I thought it was the jinx that made you do it!'

McGray turned sombre. 'Well, aye and nae.'

He stood up – although he had to crouch under the low ceiling – and limped towards the hearth. He picked up Nettle's iron poker and started digging in the ashes. All that remained of the charm was a minuscule skull, and McGray pulled it out and passed it from hand to hand as it cooled. Nettle did not try to stop him, so I guessed whatever nastiness it had carried had already burned away.

McGray sat by the fire, examining the charred remains of the hummingbird.

'What a peculiar curse this was,' he said. 'Like nothing I've ever read about. It wasn't even unpleasant at the beginning.'

I leaned closer. 'Tell me more.'

McGray looked between the charred skull and the fire, deep in thought, before he replied.

'I can only describe it . . . well, as if there was a fever in my very blood. I was like a locomotive without brakes.

Everything I wanted to do I could do, and if something or someone wanted to stop me I could crush it without remorse. I do remember it all though . . .' He stared intently at the tiny skull, its sockets as small as the eyes of needles. 'It makes me cringe now . . . punching that abbot, setting off without a plan, standing in front o' that blasted carriage . . .'

'Punching and kidnapping me?'

'Frey, I've already told ye how much I enjoyed that. This didnae put anything into my head. It was all me, all my will and wishes, only amplified, made reckless. I wouldn't even stop to wonder why the change. I didnae *notice* any change, until . . .'

I ventured: 'Until you began seeing and hearing things?'

He looked down. 'Aye, it all went to hell very quickly after I thought I'd heard *and seen* Pansy.'

I was glad he realized it had been nothing but a vision, but it was not the time to gloat about being right. 'That was Oakley, of course.'

'Aye, it couldnae have been anybody else, but ye mentioned a few times that my vision was blurry. I could only see shapes, and without being able to make out all her features, I thought the lass looked just like Pansy.'

'It is all right,' I said. 'They are both thin, dark-haired; besides, it all happened very quickly.'

McGray pressed his forehead with a weary hand. 'And it was something I *wanted* to see.'

I felt my mouth relax into a triumphant smile. Could Nine-Nails finally be allowing some rationality into his stubborn, superstitious head?

'A hummingbird . . .' he whispered, now holding the

skull a couple of inches from his eyes. 'A sacred bird, without shadow.'

I sat back, feeling utterly defeated. 'Oh, here we go again . . .'

'These wee fellers symbolize joy, renewal . . . peace. Murdered hummingbirds are meant to inflict acute damage. To derail yer spirits.'

Nettle was nodding and I was gnashing my teeth. I could not believe I had even considered that McGray could be finally showing some sense.

'Do you not think that perhaps that stupid bird was simply impregnated with something that gave you those symptoms?'

'And what precisely d'ye think that "something" was?'

'I do not know – I left all my toxicology books in London – but I can tell you there was some sort of fruit or cactus tied to it, and when it burned it flashed a strange colour. There are countless substances that –'

'Yer forgetting Nettle here took the spooks out o' me.'

'The – what did you call them?'

'Spooks. The jinx.'

I snorted. 'Inducing vomiting in a frail person with a strong smell? Hardly a feat.' I looked at her out of the corner of my eye. 'No offence.'

'It was black vomit,' McGray reminded me.

'You could have swallowed blood when that brute beat you.'

'Or perhaps ye . . . Bah! Yer hopeless.'

He shoved the skull into his breast pocket: a memento he would probably add to his collection of sinister trinkets – if we ever managed to return, of course. He searched his other pockets and produced the crumpled, torn map he'd stolen in Lancaster.

'Oi, hen, tell us where we are.' Nettle frowned and turned her face away. 'Och, come on! We won't tell anyone yer house is here, I swear.'

Begrudgingly, but still much sooner than if I'd requested it, Nettle stopped her work and came to peruse the map. She pointed at a small brook, the squiggly blue line flowing from a mount called Winfold Fell; I guessed that was where we'd encountered Joel and the other witches.

'A little further from the roads than I expected,' I said.

'Aye, but not too far from Slaidburn or Dunsop Bridge. We can still get help there. Unless . . .' McGray looked at Nettle, a cheeky glint in his eyes. 'Unless Nettle here can suggest another destination.'

The old woman needed no encouragement this time. She reached for a jar full of dried peas and began placing them on to the extended map. One on Lancaster, one on Pendle Hill, one on Beatrix Fell.

'Those are the beacons,' said McGray as Nettle placed more and more peas, some of them even off the sheet, where Yorkshire and Cumbria would have been. Nettle then picked up other seeds, like peppercorns, star anises, and others I had never seen.

Her cat came closer, sniffing at the seeds and touching them with its paws, yet never moving them. After a moment it sat up very stiffly, its front paws right next to a peppercorn that marked a small village: Slaidburn.

Nettle nodded, caressed the cat and then poked at the mark for Slaidburn rather vehemently, and then at some spot further south, where she placed one last pea.

'There is nothing there,' I said, but McGray looked pensive.

'That's just off the slopes of Pendle Hill.'

'The witches' hill?' I asked.

'Aye. D'ye need more convincing? Joel's definitely going there.'

'It is not convincing I need now,' I retorted, but McGray was already on his feet, as if acute poisoning and the graze of a bullet had been mere trifles.

'Ye coming or what?'

I blew out my cheeks. 'Nine-Nails, have you not regained your smidgen of good sense? This woman might well have drawn the map to our deaths.'

He laughed heartily. 'Och, can ye be any more theatrical? Come on. If ye live through this, ye might have a future writing tacky novels.'

I had forgotten how cold it was outside.

McGray wrapped himself in his overcoat, letting out a hearty 'Brrrrrrr'. He was still limping a little, but I was surprised by how quickly he was recovering.

He turned to look back at Nettle. 'Och, hen, thanks for yer – *What?*'

She grasped his arm and pulled at him gently. Her cat was jumping about enthusiastically, leaving a meandering trail on the snow. Nettle followed it and made her stumbling way to the foot of a gnarled ash tree. The bark was almost as pale as the surrounding snow, with black buds waiting patiently for warmer days to burst into new foliage. Nettle leaned down, kicking the snow aside, and then dug with her bare hands. McGray helped her, and soon they reached the frozen soil. Nettle used a stone to crumble it and uncover some round, filthy object.

At first it looked like an oversized turnip, but it was in fact a bundle of rags, which Nettle retrieved with great effort. McGray helped her, and Nettle began to undo some very tight knots. It looked as though that object had been buried for years, for the fabric tore with the slightest pull.

Nettle untied fold after fold of cloth. The innermost layer looked surprisingly clean; it had been dusted with a white powder, which turned out to be ordinary flour. That had effectively sealed the pack's contents from the elements, and we nearly gasped when we saw a very fine pouch made of dark leather, with a shiny brass buckle.

I stretched my neck to see as Nettle opened it and poured its contents out. The first thing I saw was a bouquet of assorted herbs and dried flowers. There followed some bizarre items like locks of human hair, a mummified frog, and others I was unfortunately becoming familiar with, like bent nails and a very old red onion. Finally I heard a clanking, and what Nettle produced left me open-mouthed.

It was a gun. A very fine revolver with an ivory grip, the metal as shiny as if she'd just taken it from a merchant's shelf. There was also a smaller pouch full of bullets.

McGray seized the lot before I could stop him, and examined the weapon with the excited eyes of a child on Christmas Day. 'This'll really smooth our way. Thanks, hen!'

She also produced a small twig of lavender tied to a dry bay leaf, and put them in my breast pocket with motherly care.

I wanted to give her something, anything, as a thank you, but except for those dried flowers my pockets were empty.

Almost by a miracle one of my cufflinks still clung to my shirt. It was a fine, small piece of gold. I took it off and offered it to the woman, but she shook her head and made to turn away.

I grasped one of her hands – her skin was drier and more calloused than I'd thought – and I forced the cuff-link into her palm, wrapping her bony fingers around it.

'Do take it. Please.'

She assented in the end, waving her other hand, asking us to leave. We hopped on slippery stones across the stream, and as we climbed the slope towards the road I looked back one last time.

I saw the old woman standing very still next to her stone shed, the cat lying along her shoulders, both of them watching us intently. Inexplicably, part of me felt sorry to leave.

When I looked ahead I found McGray smirking at me.

'Och . . . ye like 'em older.'

'Pox on you.'

We soon reached the end of the woods and the view opened to the barren moors. A thick cloud had begun to cover the sun, the receding rays casting a weaker light on the snowy hills, but we had no trouble spotting the road that went east.

We descended the gentle slope, all covered in bright snow. I looked at the smooth, pristine . . .

'Frey, look,' McGray said, exactly at the same time as I saw it.

The snow was not entirely undisturbed. There was a deep, messy trail, almost a dent in the otherwise pure whiteness. It went all the way from the woods we'd just left down to the road. As we approached we saw dark speckles smudged along the crumpled snow.

'Blood?' McGray asked as I knelt down to inspect it.

'Yes,' I said, after touching and sniffing one of the droplets. The track was wide and easy to follow, until it reached a thick tree stump. There, clinging to the trunk's splinters and waving like a standard under the breeze, we found a filthy apron, ragged and soaked in red.

McGray took a deep breath, then walked closer to the garment and we both looked at it carefully.

'It belonged to a slender woman,' I said, looking at the straps.

Nine-Nails picked it up by a corner and brought it closer to his eyes, so that I thought his eyesight must have gone bad again. 'Here,' he said, showing me the material.

Delicately embroidered in lilac thread there was a minute stem of foxgloves.

'Oakley's,' I murmured, the memory of her shrill screams disturbing me as much as when I'd heard them. 'Do you think she's . . . ?'

McGray looked around. The ground surrounding the tree was mushy, as if it had been trampled repeatedly for a good while. There were spots of blood all around, and Nine-Nails shuddered.

'Aye. I hope it was quick . . .'

We had not walked a full mile when the first snowflakes began to flutter around us, the clouds clustering together again. There was but a thin strip of sky visible on the horizon, tinted in red by the last rays of the sun.

'Already twilight?' McGray exclaimed, plunging his boots into the deep snow as we descended along the road. Other than his slightly slower pace, nobody could have told he'd been shot the night before.

'Yes,' I grunted, 'you slept for *quite* a while.'

'Och, Frey, ye sound like a wounded kitty.'

'I am beyond wounded,' I retorted, arduously dragging my legs. 'I have never been in such a disastrous state in my whole life.'

'Not all of us can say that, dandy,' he said, looking at his right hand with bitterness. 'Things should improve once we get to Slaidburn. We can have a proper rest tonight and tomorrow morning we can go on to Pendle . . . now that we ken there's definitely something wicked happening there.'

I snorted. I did not want to reveal my intentions just yet, but I could not humour McGray as he made plans for his crusade.

'I am not going to Pendle.'

McGray did not seem to register my words. I had to repeat myself, much more firmly this time. He cast me a perplexed look. 'Don't be ridiculous. Ye've been reciting that like a bloody parrot since this all started.'

'I have stomached enough,' I snapped, my contained fury finally rising to the surface. 'As soon as we reach that godforsaken village you will go on by yourself. I am heading back to Edin-bloody-burgh.'

McGray halted. 'Yer deserting?'

'One can hardly call it that. When I submit my report,

Campbell will agree with my decision. This is English jurisdiction. We should never have ventured this far.'

'Ye sound like that pathetic Messy back in Lancaster, sloping yer shoulders whenever some responsibility falls on them! D'ye not care about this mad lad killing and torturing people wherever he goes? Are ye not even slightly curious about the nasty trade these crones are carrying out?'

I rubbed my face in frustration. 'Nine-Nails, this is not about Joel or those blasted witches. This is about *your* family!'

His chest heaved.

'I am sorry for your sister,' I spluttered. 'I truly, truly am, but I cannot follow you any longer. Face it: this is a stupid quest for the vaguest of clues. For all we know, Pansy could have simply asked Joel to bring her some warm milk. And even if she *did* say something of import, that does not mean she will *ever* repeat the accomplishment.'

McGray grabbed me by the collar, his steamy breath bursting out like the vapours of a train engine. I could see the cold understanding in his eyes, the anguish, the wrath at words that perhaps he himself had thought but refused to acknowledge. He could have ripped me apart with his bare hands.

I still found the courage – or the madness – to whisper out my most heartfelt words. 'You believe it is worth killing yourself for that, and I will not even attempt to persuade you otherwise, but I am not going to follow you any more.'

He spoke in an ominous tone, and as the sun descended it was almost as if his words darkened the entire land around us: 'Ye've no idea what it is like, do ye? To be clinging to a last shred of hope, and then to have someone like ye rub my face in how pointless it could all be.'

'McGray –'

'*I have nothing!* I've nothing left, but the slightest chance to bring her back. When ye realize something like that – it breaks ye to the bones.'

He chuckled bitterly. 'How could ye understand? Ye don't even like yer own folk; ye come from a pack of bloody wolves that stab ye in the back at the first chance. I bet ye didn't even like yer own mother.'

That felt like a physical blow. My mother had passed away more than two decades ago, yet I had never forgotten the horrendous days that preceded her death. Whenever I thought of it I felt a surge of tears I had soon learned to repress, even as a young boy.

I preferred not to share that with McGray. I had probably injured him far more with fewer words. However, no amount of empathy could make me change my mind; this mission was meant to fail, I knew it, and I would not become another casualty in the tragic history of the Ardglass family or the McGrays.

I gulped painfully. 'Now that we have established where we stand . . . we should move on. The sooner we are in a civilized place, the sooner we can each go our separate ways.'

'Before we reach that point I want ye to remember that I wasnae hexed, blootered, drugged or impaired in any way when I did this . . .'

I flinched, anticipating a good beating, but for some reason he changed his mind. He released me and pushed me away, hissing.

'Go wherever ye fucking want, ye pretty London boy.'

His voice sounded so vicious, so full of resentment, I would have preferred the actual blow.

He resumed his march, impassive, and as I watched him walk away I noticed that the snowflakes had become thick and heavy. I did not want to follow Nine-Nails, but I'd need to find shelter soon, and Slaidburn was the nearest place.

Just as I started after him we heard a throaty shout, closely followed by the rattle of wheels. The sound came from ahead, beyond the next bend of the road.

McGray raised his hand to his breast pocket, caressing the weapon. His tension lessened only a little when we saw the source of the noise. It was a cart, old and creaking, laden with at least a dozen barrels of beer. A sickly mule pulled it at a sluggish pace, and the man driving it looked just as miserable: hunched, skin and bone, and with one of those drowsy grimaces that spread apathy simply from looking at them.

McGray planted himself in the middle of the road and waited patiently until the cart reached us, the snow quickly piling on our shoulders. The mule decided that walking round Nine-Nails would be too much of an effort, and stopped in front of us as the driver let out a mighty yawn. He dragged his voice after spitting out some snowflakes. 'What?'

'What's yer name, laddie?'

The man took his time to reply. 'Floyd. Why you ask?'

'We need a ride,' McGray said. 'We're going to Slaidburn.'

That Floyd looked us over carefully, our filthy clothes and sorry faces. It took him an infuriatingly long time to respond, as if speaking required Herculean strength. 'Nah, I just came from there ... and I don't want any trouble.'

He spurred on his sad-looking mule, but it did not manage more than one step; McGray held the beast by the mane as he brought out Nettle's gun.

'A ride, laddie,' he growled, and I heard the click of the safety catch. 'Else I'll give ye a big trouble in the middle o' yer bloody head.'

The veins in Nine-Nails' temples were pounding, and I feared he'd do something stupid, but even that filthy carter had enough sense to give up the reins.

Nine-Nails installed himself on the driver's seat as Floyd got down.

'Where ye going?' McGray demanded.

'Err? I thought you –'

'I need someone to pour me a beer,' McGray said, and the carter did not waste his chance. Much faster than I would have thought him capable of, he clambered back on as McGray turned the wobbly cart around.

After my passionate speech I was sure he would leave me there, and I would not have blamed him. I still cannot believe he had the compassion to turn back and whistle.

'Hop on, lassie, or ye stay here for ever!'

I chuckled. 'And follow you where you are heading? Are you mad?'

'Please yerself,' he said, already spurring on the mule and riding away. He snapped at Floyd, 'Throw him yer stinking rags. He'll need them in this weather.'

Floyd pulled a dirty blanket from under the seat, together with a sack of bread and a flask probably full of ale, and threw them at my feet. The bread was so stale it sank like a stone into the snow.

McGray shook the reins and the mule took its first weary steps, the wheels rattling as they gathered momentum. Just then the wind hit me hard, as if trying to awaken me from my stubbornness. The cart was gaining speed so I had no more time to think. I had to jog ridiculously and leap on to the back of it, clinging precariously to one of the leather straps that kept the beer barrels in place.

Nine-Nails was already helping himself to the tankard of beer he'd been handed. Floyd sneered at me.

'Look a' that! Your high-born chap decided to –'

'Don't push yer luck, laddie, I've only just met ye,' McGray snarled.

I settled down between the barrels, preferring that to sharing the front seat with Nine-Nails.

The trip was very short, but so tense and silent it felt like it took hours. McGray focused on driving the mule, his face so broody I did not even attempt to speak.

We had both crossed over a line from which there was no return, and realizing it made me feel strangely . . . saddened. I wondered whether we'd ever trust each other again.

30

The vast, empty moors slowly gave way to sparse wood-land. Oaks and firs flanked the road, but under the darkening sky we could barely see their outlines.

The more we advanced the more uneasy I felt, yet I could not tell the reason. There was something in the air I did not like, like a dark premonition that came on the icy wind and the earthy smell of the woods, but I shook my head and cast those thoughts aside.

We finally saw the first lights of the village emerge. A small cluster of golden sparks turned, as we approached, into square windows, their glows reflected by a pebbled street and the sandstone walls of ancient dwellings. I felt as if we were walking back into the past, for those regions of England have changed very little since the Reformation – and I expected to find the residents thoroughly superstitious.

Slaidburn was little more than one long street, so it was easy to find our destination. In the dim light we made out the tattered sign of the village's inn. Though it was cracked and weather-beaten, one could still read *Hark to Bounty Inn*.

'This is the place,' I said, somewhat relieved, for part of me had never believed that Nettle's advice would lead us anywhere. The window glass was misted, but I could see a roaring fire inside. 'At least it looks warm in there.'

McGray whistled as he alighted. 'Blimey! I saw this building drawn in an auld book. This is the inn where they
locked the Pendle witches on their way to Lancaster!'

'I hope they have washed the linen since,' was my
laconic remark.

McGray did not bother to abuse me. He was busy pulling Floyd down off the cart.

'We might need yer rickety piece o' shite,' he said, taking off his boot and pulling out a thick wad of notes.

'You had that on you all this time?' I asked in
astonishment.

'Course I did! I put most of yer money here before we
left Lancaster, while ye were crying in the back of the
coach. It's not the first time I've travelled dangerous
roads.' He turned to Floyd. 'Here, for yer trouble,' he said,
and he tossed him a liberal amount of sterling.

'Excuse me!' I protested.

Floyd was already counting the notes with greedy eyes.
'My! 'Tis enough to buy me own cart and give old Mr
Brewer t'middle finger!'

'Then sod off and be merry,' McGray concluded, and
before I could say another word Floyd was off.

'Nine-Nails, in the future, do refrain from squandering
my money.'

'Shut it!'

He went to the inn's main door, which he found locked,
even though all the ground-floor rooms were lit. I looked
up and saw a light coming from one of the upstairs windows, but it went out almost as soon as I had raised my
head.

'There's folk in there,' McGray grunted, pounding on

the oak door, but there was no answer. In fact, the village was completely deserted, as if people had left in such haste they'd had no time to extinguish their candles.

McGray knocked again and we waited, but there was not a sound until a couple of crows landed on the inn's roof, flapping their wings and cawing at each other. Nine-Nails looked at them with suspicion and was about to say something when the door burst open, almost hitting him in the face.

A middle-aged woman came out at a run, waving madly, her face distraught. She wore a stained apron and her nervous hands clasped a dirty cloth.

'Have you found them children?' she urged.

McGray frowned. 'Children?'

The woman halted, looking at the cart and then at us with befuddled eyes.

'Can we help ye, lass?' McGray asked, but the woman was frantic.

'Where's Floyd?' she asked, still staring at the cart. I opened my mouth but McGray rushed to speak.

'We . . . we found this thing abandoned on the road. We guessed it came from here. Who's Floyd? He yer husband?'

The woman looked disgusted at the very suggestion. 'God, no! He brings our ale, but the whole town's looking for our poor children. *Our –*'

She broke apart then, surrendering to tears and covering her face with the greasy rag. McGray patted her on the shoulder. 'Calm down, hen. We're CID, we might be able to help youse. Can we go in?'

He was not really asking for permission; the woman

was so distressed McGray led her by the arm back into her own inn.

We had barely crossed the threshold when a very tall man blocked our way. My heart jumped as I caught sight of that imposing figure, expecting a waxed moustache and a menacing crone lurking behind. It was not the case, and I looked at him with relief, despite the threatening face he turned on us. The man had fiery eyes, weathered skin and a blond, bristly beard. I could see beads of sweat all over his forehead.

'What the hell have you done to my wife?' he barked at us.

I realized we must look like filthy tramps, and even on his better days I could not blame anyone for looking askance at McGray.

'All right, all right,' McGray said, gently pushing the woman forwards. 'We found yer missus outside; she was asking us about some missing children.'

The woman buried her face in the man's shoulder and wept on. He half closed his eyes, all suspicion. 'You're not from round here.'

'Indeed we are not,' I replied, offering a hand the rough man did not shake. 'We are CID inspectors. We are stranded and could use some assistance.'

'We have enough trouble already.'

'And perhaps we can help youse,' McGray offered.

'We're full,' the man retorted.

I took a peep over his shoulder. There was a large sitting room with several tables around the fire, and the meaty smell of a stew wafted into the porch, yet there was not a soul there.

'This is not a particularly thriving business,' I remarked.
'I said we're full!'

He pushed his wife aside and took a step forwards. I
saw McGray reaching for his breast pocket and I had to
tug at his arm.

'We don't need more trouble either,' I whispered. 'We'd
better leave, we might have better luck elsewhere.'

'Listen to the pretty boy,' the innkeeper grunted. 'We
don't like no foreigners here.'

Nobody moved for a moment, until the silence was broken by the steps of a young man, obviously a servant, who
came past carrying a copper bath on his shoulders. He also
looked at us in confusion, before addressing the huge innkeeper: 'Where d'you want the bath, Mr Greenwood?'

I could not believe my ears, immediately remembering
Joel's first victim, the death which had triggered this
entire expedition.

'Greenwood!' McGray cried, unable to conceal his
surprise.

The innkeeper looked more suspicious than ever.
'What does my name have to do with you?'

McGray cleared his throat. 'Are youse in any way connected to a Miss Elizabeth Greenwood – a nurse in
Edinburgh?'

It was as if one of the beer barrels had shattered
between us. Mr Greenwood gasped, his wife's weeping
stopped and she turned her head to McGray, her eyes
bloodshot.

McGray nodded sombrely. 'I see youse are.'

Husband and wife exchanged looks. They were terrified, hands, lips and legs shaking.

'What shall we do?' the frightened woman burst out, but Mr Greenwood squeezed her shoulder.

Most reluctantly, and after a full minute of internal struggle, the man stepped aside and let us pass.

'They bring news of our daughter Lizzy,' he told his wife in an unnecessary loud voice. 'Fetch 'em something to drink.'

'Where are yer stables?' McGray asked.

'Just leave the mule where it is!' Mr Greenwood blurted. 'We'll send someone to take care of it.'

Mrs Greenwood brought two pints of dark ale and a small drummer of brandy – the latter for me – and carefully placed the glasses on the table.

'Have a seat, missus,' McGray offered, but she looked nervously at her husband.

'She's all right,' he said, lighting up a cigarette. 'She has work to do. Go check that stew; the inspectors will be hungry.'

The woman looked appalled. 'The gentlemen won't be staying, surely!'

Mr Greenwood grunted through his teeth, 'Do as you're told.'

She curtsied, but as she walked away I noticed her trembling ankles. Mr Greenwood's eyes followed her, and he did not speak until he was certain his wife had gone.

'It's bad news about our Lizzy, isn't it?'

McGray took a swig of ale to clear his throat. 'I'm afraid so. We're very sorry.'

The man stared into his glass, biting his lip. He drew in smoke slowly, looking up and blinking anxiously to dissipate tears, which he hardly managed even after downing half the pint in one gulp.

'H-how did it happen?'

'It is better that you sent your wife away,' I admitted. I'd given bad news to relatives more times than I could remember, but it had never become easier. 'Your daughter was murdered by one of her patients – an inmate in the Edinburgh asylum.'

Mr Greenwood again looked up, his pupils flickering in anxiety. We gave him a few minutes to compose himself, but the poor man's distress worsened. He was breathing raggedly, and covered his brow with a shaking hand.

'W-why would anyone do that? Was it just the madness?'

'To this date,' I said, rather embarrassed, 'we are not sure.'

'But ye might be able to help us,' McGray jumped in. 'Can ye tell us a wee bit more about her?'

Mr Greenwood cleared his throat. 'We haven't seen her in years. We . . . we didn't part on good terms.'

McGray leaned forwards and whispered, 'We ken she gave birth at some point. Was that why youse quarrelled?'

It was as if someone had slapped Mr Greenwood in the face. 'How could you possibly know that?'

'Post-mortem,' I said. 'The fact caught our attention, given her marital status.'

Mr Greenwood shook his head, frowning in sorrow. 'That's where all her problems started, the silly girl. We were sitting at this very table when she told us. I was furious. Her mother smacked her . . .'

'Did youse kick her out?' McGray asked.

'You must understand, Inspector, that we are very well known in the region. We're not rich but at least we're respectable. We couldn't have borne people gossiping behind our backs, calling her names . . . whispering that she'd lain with every man who'd ever spent a night in this inn. I would never have anyone call my child a wh–'

He bit his knuckles.

'So youse kicked her out,' McGray repeated.

Mr Greenwood banged his fist on the table. 'She knew very well she couldn't stay. She knew the sort of life she would have had – her and her baby. When we suggested that she leave she was only too keen.'

'Where did she go initially?' I asked.

'For once the bastard who impregnated her did something useful. He and Lizzy exchanged letters and she told him everything. The damn fool would not marry her. Instead he sent her the address of some woman in Lancaster who could employ her – how very kind of him!'

'Who was this woman?' McGray asked promptly.

'Never saw her in the flesh, Inspector, but she was called . . . Something Redfern.'

I inhaled and nearly cursed, but Nine-Nails silenced me with a glare. 'What sort o' job did she offer?' he asked.

'Lizzy said the woman was a midwife. She had agreed to take care of the pregnancy very quietly, and then take Lizzy on as her apprentice. She was aware of Lizzy's story and didn't mind; it was all very convenient. My daughter even had time to pack and leave just before her belly betrayed her.

'We saw her once again. My wife and me went to Lancaster to pick up the child – a girl. Lizzy was so much changed; she had gone too impetuous, too independent to listen to our advice. That evil witch had filled her head with stupid ideas: how she didn't need nobody, how she could maintain herself and all that fancy liberal shite. Her plan was to save up and buy a small house, and then send for the girl and claim she was her niece.'

I thought of the tidy cottage we'd visited, where Joel had accosted us and where I had drunk the poisoned tea. Oakley had told us she rented a room from Miss Greenwood.

'She nearly took that plan to its conclusion,' I said. 'I wonder why she went as far as Edinburgh.'

Mr Greenwood shrugged. 'Even in Lancaster people suspected the truth about the pregnancy, and apparently this Redfern woman had some connections with the Scots, so I assume that's how Lizzy ended up there. Not a bad deal, I assumed; she didn't write or reply to our letters, but she always sent enough money to pay for the child. I bet the thug that fathered her couldn't have done no better.'

There was a hint of pride in that sentence, but it came with as much guilt.

'From what you tell us,' I said, 'you knew who the father was.'

'Yes. Just a womanizing lowlife from the village, a good fifteen years older than Lizzy. He had left when his mother, a seamstress, died. He was still rather young and there was no one to take care of him. One day, years later, he came back, all grown up, with shiny new boots and full pockets. We all suspected he'd got into dodgy dealings, but even though we all distrusted him he did catch the eyes of our silly girls. He came, he got them in trouble and he left again!

'We did hear of him working somewhere in Edinburgh, and I suspected that might be the reason our Lizzy went there. I thought at some point he'd marry her, but a year or so ago my wife heard the bastard was in jail.' He laughed scornfully. 'Serve him right.'

McGray tilted his head, surely thinking the same as me. 'Was this man, by any chance, called Harry Pimblett?'

The man's eyes opened wide. 'Lord, you two seem to know even more about it than me!'

McGray and I looked at each other. So the father of Greenwood's child was the very man we'd found dead in the Lancaster prison; the man who had served Lord Ardglass for years and whose former master had then travelled hundreds of miles specifically to murder him.

Greenwood and Pimblett, so deeply connected to each other as well as to Redfern and Oakley. And somewhere into this mysterious network, somehow, fitted the Ardglass family.

'You should probably know that he is also dead,' I said. 'Murdered . . . by the same man who took your daughter's life.'

Mr Greenwood shuddered, and despite the dim light from the fire I saw all colour disappear from his face.

'How did you find us?' he spluttered, and I could tell he too was beginning to understand.

'We've been following the tracks of the murderer,' said

McGray, 'and, well . . . we heard from a very good source that he'd be in this village.'

'Oh dear Lord . . .' Mr Greenwood burst out as he covered his mouth, rose to his feet and turned his back to us, resting both hands on the mantelpiece.

McGray stood up and went over to him. 'What's the matter?' he asked softly. 'Is it what I think?'

Mr Greenwood nodded vehemently, and then spat out the words as if they'd been burning him. 'It's no coincidence that you gentlemen appear the night after Lizzy's child went missing . . .'

'So it was *her* child!' McGray cried.

'We were told the child had passed on,' I said, remembering Oakley's statement. *The poor creature died* were her very words.

'You were told lies,' Mr Greenwood said. 'The girl, Daisy, was living happy and well here with us, until . . .' his voice trembled and the poor man bit his knuckles, 'until last night . . .'

I caught a glimpse of Mrs Greenwood, gazing at us from the kitchen doorway, shedding copious tears and squeezing her apron so hard the cloth was turning to shreds. She'd heard it all.

Our eyes met and she jumped back, letting out a piercing, anguished wail. From the kitchen we heard the clatter of pans and shattering glass.

Mr Greenwood ran to her and we followed, only to find the woman kneeling on the floor, dangerously close to the burning stoves, anxiously rocking a small wicker cradle. A few pink ribbons swung in the air, as well as a tulle rose that was about to come off. There was a frightened young maid at the back of the room, her back pressed against the wall, her hands clasping a ladle.

Mr Greenwood hastily kneeled by his wife's side. The woman whimpered and cowered as if she expected him to slap her, but instead he put his arms around her, with a tenderness I would not have expected from him, and murmured soothingly in her ear.

McGray came to me and also whispered, 'I thought the lil' girl was a good few years auld.'

'So did I . . . Then again . . . she did say *children.*'

The shaking woman managed to stand, and McGray helped Mr Greenwood to bring her back to the table in the main room.

'You shouldn't have listened,' he was telling her as they passed in front of me. 'You shouldn't, you silly bird.'

I looked at the scared maid. 'Girl, bring her a glass of any spirit you have.'

She nodded clumsily, but still managed to put a small glass on the table just as I joined them.

'It was that horrible man,' Mrs Greenwood was saying, slowly rocking backwards and forwards. 'He came last night asking for a room. We didn't know any of this would happen; he was a very elegant gentleman, although his clothes did look all mucky.'

'Did he give his name?' I asked.

'Yes, sir. He said his name was Ardglass.'

'He gave his real name,' McGray whispered. 'Just like in Lancaster Castle. He didnae want to hide away . . .' I saw his eyes flickering with anxiety. 'Go on, hen.'

'Well, sir, we gave him a room and served him dinner. He was very polite all the time – until he saw our girls.

Daisy was running around with her toys and Hannah here was feeding the little one. The man asked if – if one of them was called Daisy! It gave me the creeps when he said that, I'm telling you! My God, the way he looked at them ...' the woman shivered. 'He knew everything about them, everything about our Lizzy! *How can that be?*'

She was falling apart, so McGray encouraged her to take some drink.

I had a disturbing image of Joel squeezing all this information out of Oakley, and perhaps Nurse Greenwood too ... the young women telling him everything through agonizing pain.

'That we can explain to youse,' McGray said sombrely, perhaps with the same image in his head, 'but first I need ye to go on. Tell me, who was this other girl?'

'Primrose. An orphan baby, sir,' she said, clearing her throat after a short sip. 'We care for her too. This man asked me which one was Daisy ... I wouldn't tell him, of course, not for all the gold in the world. I told him in those very words, and he jumped on me' – Mrs Greenwood gulped, placing a hand on her belly – 'and he punched me right in the stomach; he threw me aside and took them both!'

She covered her mouth and cried miserably on her husband's shoulder.

'I was out,' Mr Greenwood said. 'Tending to the bastard's horse. I heard the screams and ran in here, but Ardglass used those moments to run away through the back door. All we heard was his horse galloping down the main road –'

'And the girls screamed,' Mrs Greenwood moaned. *'They were screaming!'*

The maid looked away, wiping tears with her apron. Even Nine-Nails shuddered, thinking of the scene.

'What do you think he'll do to the children?' Mrs Greenwood wondered.

Even McGray, cold-blooded as he could be, turned away.

I had to take a deep breath. 'I honestly cannot say.'

31

'We might be able to help,' said McGray.

Mr Greenwood was helping his wife upstairs. 'Almost all the men of the village are out there, looking for them. I don't think much more can be done.' He looked at the maid. 'Hannah, give the gentlemen something to eat. Then I want them out.'

'*Out!*' I squealed. 'Are you mad? It is snowing hard!'

The couple went up without responding, and young Hannah curtsied and ran to the kitchen.

McGray sat back down at the table, took off his boots and stretched his legs, massaging the bandaged one. 'Well, drinks and a free dinner are better than nothing at all.'

I paced around. 'We could call for reinforcements. This is still within the Lancashire jurisdiction. We could send word to Lancaster and Massey might send officers from the nearby towns.'

McGray raised an eyebrow. 'Och, I thought ye'd had it! What happened to being sick o' chasing Joel?'

'I did not say I would help you chase Joel. I said I would help these people look for their girls.'

'Same thing, Pythagor-arse. Joel took them.'

I sat down. 'Indeed, and I begin to see his pattern.'

'Och, aye! I thought ye were quicker than that.'

'Let me bloody finish. We have had barely any time to speculate.' I looked into the fire, my mind going back to the very start. 'Insane as he is, Joel is after all those witches, that is a given. I remember how nervous Oakley was when we questioned her . . . she must have known Joel would come after her.'

'Aye, that's why the lass ran to Lancaster. Redfern sent her that telegram we found . . . She has to be some sort of elder witch. Both Oakley and Greenwood must have been her novices. Pimblett too.'

'Indeed. Now, why would a crazy man set off on such a witch hunt? They must have wronged him – or his kin.'

'It must have been something really bad! See how he got rid o' Greenwood and Pimblett. Cannae think of a worse way to kill a person. And that raven he left at Redfern's house with the warning – even *I* felt revolted.'

I assented. 'That would explain why Oakley did not ask us to protect her. She would have had to explain the witches' doings to us. That is why she poisoned us with the tea . . . and then, since she was staying in the room adjacent to ours, she most likely bribed or coerced that young maid to hide the hummingbird charm in your clothes. Still . . .'

McGray finished my sentence. 'That doesn't quite explain why she warned Joel on the train to Lancaster . . . or why she stole his photograph from our room. She doesn't want us to find him.'

'Most likely because he would tell us things about them,' I said. 'Details about their black market or their sisterhood?'

McGray pondered. 'Aye, that has to be it. These witches seem to really fear him. Oakley went to Redfern looking for protection, yet for some reason Redfern thought all they could do was run away. Joel must know something terrible about them.' McGray massaged his eyelids, frustration taking over. 'Damn him! He's been the bloody pacesetter all along. He took these children before we even found out they existed.'

'And nothing guarantees this will be the end of it,' I muttered. 'He might want revenge against all the witches in the land.' I thought of the handful of peas on the map and felt a wave of fear. 'In that case, we – I mean, *you* could spend months on this hunt.'

'Nae . . . he's been ahead of us all along but not any more. At last we have some forewarning. We ken he's going to Pendle Hill: according to Nettle that's his final destination. And d'ye remember the judge's note? Cobden Hall, in Pendle!'

I sighed, not believing what I was about to say.

'I hate to admit that both statements make sense now – but you are not as ahead as you think. If Joel took the children last night, he might be in Pendle as we speak. And you are in no state to run there right now; your leg is still recovering and you would not want to be worn out and famished when you face him . . . or whatever you might find in Pendle Hill.'

As if to support my point, McGray's stomach growled violently.

'All right, we'll eat and try to rest a wee bit, but then we're setting off to the nearest town. We'll definitely need reinforcements.'

'Stop saying *we*. I might help you find those reinforcements, but I am not following you any more.'

Hannah came back with a tray laden with steaming food, and McGray did not even register what I'd just said.

'Is there a telegraph round here?' he asked the girl.

'No, sir. For that you need to go to Whalley or Clitheroe. I can see that someone in the village gives you directions if it's urgent.'

Our eyes were fixed on the bowls of hot stew she was placing before us.

'It's not as urgent as this,' he said, grabbing a spoon and gorging himself like a hog in fattening season. My own manners were not any better; Nettle's potatoes had barely taken the edge off our hunger, and I had not appreciated how thirsty I was until I had a first taste of thin ale. I'd always thought of it as a vulgar, positively medieval drink, but I must have emptied two pints in less than seven gulps.

We indulged in bread, tender meat and potatoes, and the girl kept refilling our bowls and glasses quite diligently.

McGray finally let out the loudest, longest and most pleased of belches, his mouth and cheeks reverberating.

I fanned a hand before my nose. 'You are about to bring the plaster off the ceilings . . .'

Mr Greenwood came back then and sat next to us. He looked as if someone had beaten him with a truncheon.

'Ye all right, lad?' McGray asked. The man nodded, but his voice said otherwise.

'Gentlemen, I'm afraid I can . . .' He gulped. 'I can only allow you to stay here for tonight, and all you can have are the sofas in the smoking room.' He drew out a handkerchief and mopped sweat off his temples. 'You – you have to understand. Our rooms upstairs are in no state to receive anyone.'

I was about to say that even the most poorly made bed would be heavenly, but Greenwood seemed too affected to be questioned.

McGray thought the same. 'All right,' he said softly, 'we won't disturb youse. Tomorrow we'll rise very early and see if we can bring officers from Clitheroe.' He threw me a recriminating stare. 'I can assure ye that at least *I* will see we find that bastard and yer girls.'

One would have expected those words to be reassuring, but it was as if he'd threatened Mr Greenwood with a gun. He covered his mouth with the handkerchief, his eyes terrified.

'I appreciate your intentions . . .' Again a difficult gulp. 'But we're fine.'

He rose immediately, hitting the table with his thighs and knocking over the glasses, to rush to the main staircase by the entrance hall. We followed him, dumbfounded by the sudden change in his mood, but did not have a chance to speak. Mr Greenwood roared when he saw the young manservant. He had been waiting by the door since our arrival, next to the copper bath and three buckets brimming with still-hot water.

'So where do you want the bath, boss?'

'*Sod the bath!*' he shouted, his face flushed with rage, and ran upstairs before anyone could say a word.

I must have been desperate, for I raised a hand swiftly. 'Oh, boy, in fact, I – I could really use a good soak . . .'

*

What a delight it was to scrub away all that caked dirt, grime and sweat.

Since Mr Greenwood wanted no one to disturb the upper level, Hannah and the manservant installed the bath in the pantry, and I had to wash myself surrounded by beer barrels and hanging joints of salted meat.

As soon as I stepped in I realized the bath must have been meant to ease Mrs Greenwood's nerves; the water had been boiled with lavender and rosemary, and their sweet scents rolled up in a heavenly wave of calmness.

Hannah kindly offered to wash my clothes and claimed she could dry them quickly with the hot iron. I initially thought of refusing – I could not trust anyone after what had happened to McGray's coat – but then I remembered how long it had been since I'd worn anything clean. Quite frankly, I'd rather confront a deadly, possibly poisonous amulet than put on those underpants in their current state.

Off she went, and I surrendered to the delights of hot water and soap. For a few minutes, at least. Then the door burst open and McGray came in to help himself to a bottle of wine and some jars of pickled fruits.

'*Get out!*' I howled, automatically pulling up a towel to cover myself.

'Aye, everybody wants to see ye wrapping yer bosom.'

He went away but left the door ajar, a nasty draught hitting me straight in the face. I called Hannah three times, but she must have been taking care of my clothes. I had to get awkwardly out of the bath to shut the door and made sure that this time the latch clicked. I left nothing to chance and blocked the door with a big sack of flour.

A wise choice it was, for five blasted minutes later they tried to break in again. There was a broomstick resting against the wall. I grabbed it and banged on the door.

'*Do you bloody mind?*'

I tossed the broomstick aside and tried to relax, only to be interrupted again by a shy knocking on the door.

'*What now?*'

Hannah's nervous voice came from the other side. 'I brought your clothes, sir. Shall I leave them by the door?'

I grunted something that must have sounded affirmative, and I heard her pull up a chair, where I later found my clothes carefully folded and still warm from the ironing. The girl had not managed to remove all the stains, but I could not have felt more grateful. I told her so once I was dressed; she came with a cup of tea and showed me the way to the smoking room, where she'd improvised two beds from the tattered sofas.

I found McGray there, fishing the last chunks from a jar of pickled pears. The wine bottle was uncorked but he had barely touched it. He'd been given a change of clothes, including a pair of plain baggy trousers that had probably belonged to Mr Greenwood in slimmer days.

Far from looking relieved, there was something rather odd in his expression. His jaw was slightly tensed, and his frown was a touch more deeply wrinkled than usual. I am surprised I noticed at all.

As I walked in he looked sideways, as if straining to hear something.

'What is –'

He raised a hand, now looking at Hannah as she unfolded a clean sheet. I said no more and waited patiently

307

until the girl was finished. She made sure we did not need anything else, curtsied and left. I was going to speak but McGray raised his hand again.

I mouthed 'What is it?' but McGray kept looking sideways, not blinking. The room was so silent I could hear the rustle of my clothes as I breathed.

McGray put out the single oil lamp and the room sank into darkness. I could see nothing while I waited for my eyes to adjust. Eventually I made out McGray's shadow, silently drawing out Nettle's gun. I cannot tell for how long we waited, but it must have been a good while. Finally I saw McGray turn his head – he'd heard something.

He stood up very slowly, but halted altogether when we clearly heard wood creaking.

The noise had come from upstairs, and another creak soon followed. There were measured, careful steps, making their way across the first floor . . . yet they made the ceiling vibrate.

McGray went to the door, synchronizing his movements with the noise upstairs, hoping to conceal the sound of his own steps. I imitated him and stood beside him as he turned the handle with the deft touch of a surgeon. He waited for the precise moment and opened the door with a swift, decisive movement. The wood creaked, but so did the steps.

I drew in an apprehensive breath, and time seemed to stretch painfully until we heard the next step.

McGray had opened the door only a few inches and I had to crouch to peep through the gap. We were looking into the room where we'd been sitting earlier. They had extinguished the fire, but a few embers still glowed. The pathetic light did not reach across the room, where the kitchen door was completely shrouded in darkness.

The steps continued, growing louder but also becoming more spaced out; more cautious. Suddenly I felt that it was not the sound alone that approached but something ominous, making the air oppressive.

Have they poisoned us again? I thought, but all my doubts would soon be cleared up.

I expected to see the glow of an oil lamp or a taper, but there was none. I expected perhaps to see Mr Greenwood, lurking in the darkness for some gloomy purpose, but he did not come.

A shudder ran through my entire body when a black shadow finally appeared, a large mass that obscured the entrance and then blocked the dying glow of the hearth. I blinked, trying to make out any features, but when I saw them I wished it had been an actual spectre.

It was that gargantuan man, as tall and broad-shouldered as we remembered him. The man we'd found in the warehouse, the one who had beaten McGray to a pulp on the road.

He looked directly at us. I was convinced he had seen us and was gathering strength to thrust himself against us, but after an instant he moved on.

The man walked straight towards the kitchen, but just before his massive frame was swallowed by the shadows I heard McGray click the gun's safety catch, and then he kicked the door open.

'I'm pointing at yer brains, laddie,' said Nine-Nails viciously. 'Move and yer dead.'

32

The man stood as still as stone.

'What the hell are ye doing here?' McGray demanded, moving forwards. I reached swiftly for the oil lamp and lit it.

As I illuminated the room we saw the thug's back, so broad he probably had to twist his waist to pass through doorways, and his beefy arms, thicker than my thighs. I was so glad McGray was armed and back to his senses.

Nine-Nails howled, *'Tell us what yer doing here, ye prick!'*

The man turned around, and as he did so he began to laugh. I was expecting the waxed moustache and round face we'd seen in Lancaster, but there was none of that. Instead I saw an entirely new face, dark haired and dark-skinned, with ruddy cheeks, a broad nose and tiny, black eyes staring fiercely at us.

'Who the hell are you?' I asked.

I'd never seen that man before in my life, but McGray gasped, so utterly shocked I feared he'd drop the revolver.

The scoundrel was opening his mouth, but before he could say a word we were attacked from the side.

A shower of hot liquid hit us, the smell of cheap tea hitting my nose, and the split second we looked sideways was enough for the giant to lift the table and use it to strike McGray's arm.

I glimpsed the shadow of an old crone swathed in

black, and behind her the slim figure of a younger woman still clasping a large teapot.

'Oakley!' I yelled. 'We thought you were dead!' but then a fist the size of a frying pan struck the side of my head and threw me flat on my chest. The punch had not even been intended, but came from the man's arm whirling while striking Nine-Nails.

The oil lamp rolled across the room but did not go out, and from the floor I saw McGray and the giant embroiled in a ferocious battle, throwing fists and chairs, making me think of a pair of fighting bears. A muddy boot landed inches from my face and I had to crawl away on all fours, still dazed by the blow. Then I heard choking and saw that McGray had seized the brute by the neck, his arm tightening around it.

The gun lay right next to McGray's foot. We both must have seen it at the same time, for he kicked it in my direction. I stretched out my arm but I was not close enough. I dragged myself forwards desperately, catching a glimpse of the bully's face, which was just beginning to turn purple. The very second my fingertips touched the gun I saw the empty teapot flying like a bullet to hit Nine-Nails in between the eyes and smash into smithereens. He shouted, lost his grip and the bully freed himself. As he struggled to breathe, he threw himself towards the gun and managed to push it away before McGray attacked him again.

'*Catch those bitches!*' McGray roared, a trickle of blood on his forehead, and I saw the women running to the entrance.

I could not leave him to the mercy of that beast, but

then a thick hand gripped me by the shoulder and pulled me back.

'Do as he says,' the coarse voice of Mr Greenwood told me, as he hurled himself forwards to join their fight.

There was no time to think. I ran to the porch, where I found Mrs Greenwood. The woman was shaking as she handed me another gun.

'My husband's,' she said, and I grabbed the weapon without slowing down.

The gelid night air stabbed me, but I had no time to go back for my coat. I heard neighing from the stables and immediately ran there, my feet skidding on the snow, now hardened by the wind.

The stable door was wide open, flapping in the cold draughts, and I caught sight of the black cloak of the old woman sneaking in. I followed with long strides and the first thing I found was the large carriage we'd encountered before. It had been there the whole time! The women, however, were not in it. Instead, they were jumping on to the tattered cart McGray and I had stolen.

Oakley, wrapped in a black cloak and hood, was standing on the driver's seat, leaning over the beer barrels.

'*Stop!*' I shouted, running around the carriage and readying the gun, but before I could take a proper aim Oakley had unfastened the barrels and old Redfern pushed them off. The casks fell, rolling towards me, and all I could do was jump aside, but one of them still caught my calf and I fell forwards.

Oakley let out a mocking cackle, sharp and loud like a raven's caw, as she whipped the mule mercilessly and the cart darted out.

I shoved the gun into my breast pocket, jumped on to my feet and then atop one of the rolling barrels. Right before I lost my precarious balance I leaped forwards and miraculously managed to grab the very edge of the cart, my feet dragging on the slush as the wheels rolled into the main road.

The old woman dug her nails into my arms and I screamed. *'Damned old witch!'*

I had no choice but to endure the pain as I tried to pull myself on to the cart. The woman withdrew her nails to slap me, freeing one of my arms. I took the chance and hit her with the back of my hand, sending her frail body away. She fell on her back, wailing in pain, and from the reins came Oakley's even more desperate lament.

The crone curled up, moaning, and I had enough time to pull myself forwards. I leaped on to the driver's seat, but Oakley had kept her hooded eyes on me, and before I reached her she struck me with the whip. I ducked just in time to save my face, but the whip did lash my chest, precisely as the wheels bounced over a pothole, and I too fell backwards. I screamed as the entire world whirled around me, thinking that my body would roll out of the cart. Somehow I managed to grab the wooden surface, my body sticking out over the side, the bushes beside the road suddenly lashing me.

With wounded leg, whipped chest and scratched arms, I do not know how I gathered the strength to pull myself upwards. I bellowed from the bottom of my stomach, a wild sound I had never uttered before, that made the old woman shrink even more.

I reached for the driver's seat. Oakley whipped me

again but this time I did not even register the pain. I clutched her wrist, which was surprisingly thin, and it was easy to pull the whip out of her hand.

She let go of the reins, then started to give me a good beating with her arms and legs and knees. The mule became frightened and began to run erratically, the cart hitting stones and tree stumps, and bouncing so violently we nearly flew off the seats.

'*Stop it, you stupid girl!*' I roared. 'Do you want us all to die?'

I did my best to contain her, but she was the wildest creature and I only had hold of her right wrist.

We came to a bend in the road and the entire cart tilted, nearly capsizing, and I felt our bodies sliding off. I thought we'd fall right in front of the wheels, but then the cart wobbled upright again. I could not see the road or even think under the woman's relentless blows.

'You'll excuse my manners,' I said finally, and then smacked Oakley's hooded head very hard.

She cried out, more in anger than pain, and I had time to grab her. I held her tightly against my chest with one arm, while looking for the reins with the other. The girl struggled and kicked about, but her arms were firmly locked. I was surprised by how small and thin she really was.

I groped for the reins, and found them dangling very close to my own feet. I brought the cart to a halt, so suddenly the momentum nearly threw us forwards. As soon as the wheels stopped I jumped down, dragging Oakley with me, dumping her on to a bank of snow, bringing out the gun before she could do anything.

'Do not try another trick.' I gasped for breath. 'I am *so* sick of running after you.'

She crouched miserably, holding her hood with trembling hands, and the most spiteful words came out of her lips.

'You filthy, disgraceful wretch!'

I heard her clearly, but it took me a moment to take in the sound. I inclined my head and took a faltering step, then stammered, but all lucid words had deserted me.

'How can . . . How can this –'

'You heard me,' she growled. 'Did you not, Mr Frey?'

I inhaled deeply, not believing my ears, my heart pounding harder than when fighting her on the cart. I swiftly pulled the hood off her face and the girl looked up, tears of rage oozing from those fiery brown eyes.

The eyes of Caroline Ardglass.

33

I had arrested many a high-born person in my career, but never a young lady and her elderly nanny.

Miss Ardglass was deeply distressed, but I could not risk her doing something reckless again, so I had to make her drive the cart at gunpoint, old Bertha sitting next to her all the time. It was the most awkward ride, nobody daring to speak, and I felt hugely relieved when we made it back to the stables.

We found the inn in a dreadful state. There were shattered windows, glass and debris all around the porch, and the snow by the main entrance had been kicked about and turned to slush. A long carving fork had been driven into the door frame, right next to a fresh splatter of blood. I feared what we might find inside.

'Ladies first,' I said, pushing Caroline by the shoulder. 'And if your minion is on his feet, tell him to behave.'

The girl sought Bertha's hand, and they made their sorry way into the entrance hall, their legs shaking.

Caroline's voice also trembled. 'Hello?'

I heard a coarse male voice and saw a big shadow coming from the sitting room. I tensed all my muscles, but thankfully it turned out to be Mr Greenwood.

'Oh my, the ladies have returned!' The man was covering his eye with a steak, his shirt was torn and his knuckles were grazed. He saw me aiming the gun at Caroline's back. 'I hope they didn't give you too much trouble.'

I simply grunted. 'Where is their man?'

'Oh, we took care of him.'

Mr Greenwood led the way to the dining room and the mayhem there shocked me. The table was broken in half, two of its legs had been ripped off (possibly to be used as truncheons), there was a huge hole in the diamond-paned window (possibly the result of a flying chair) and there were ashes scattered all over the place (probably flung at somebody's eyes).

The huge man – Jed – was sitting on the floor, his hands tied with a leather belt and his dizzy head swaying slowly from side to side. There was a deep cut on his forehead, the blood now wiped off, and with his flaccid cheeks and jutting brow he looked like a sad bulldog. Mrs Greenwood was standing next to him, holding McGray's gun with an unexpected firmness.

'A job well done,' she said bitterly, her eyes going from Jed to Miss Ardglass.

'Where is McGray?' I asked.

He came in from the kitchen, helping himself to whisky straight from the bottle. Other than fingermarks on his neck and a very slight limp, he looked surprisingly fresh.

'What took youse so lo–'

He saw the women's battered faces. Caroline's cheek was red and swollen, and Bertha was pressing my bloodied handkerchief to her burst lip.

McGray strode towards me and punched my arm with all his strength. 'Och! Ye a lady beater now, Frey?'

'*Excuse me!*' I yelped, rubbing my sore arm. 'These women are about as much ladies as I am!'

'That's what I've been saying since I met ye!'

'Don't even start, Nine-Nails.'

'No wonder he was left at the altar,' Caroline added.

'*I was not left at the* –' Then I snorted, my patience gone. 'Never mind. Shall we ask the delightful ladies how come they have been following us the entire bloody time?'

'They threatened us!' Mrs Greenwood barked, showing her teeth. 'She told us to send you away or we'd never see our children again! The evil little witch.'

Bertha went red. 'Don't ye talk to my lass like that, ye auld cow!'

Both women burst into cursing and slander, until McGray raised his arms and hollered from the pit of his stomach: '*Quiet!*'

The yelling did stop, but they both went on murmuring spiteful things at each other. McGray picked up the only two chairs that were not broken and offered the seats to Caroline and Bertha.

'Sit down, ladies. I knew it was youse when I saw yer war dog, Jed. He's a character in Edinburgh – everybody kens Lady Glass keeps him handy to deter her well-earned enemies.'

That sentence seemed to wound Miss Ardglass deeply. She was already distressed, but those words completely crushed what little strength she had left; the girl frowned, sobbed and burst into tears.

'Serves you well, you little witch,' Mrs Greenwood mumbled.

McGray snatched the gun from her. 'Oi! Go get us some tea.'

'But . . .'

'Now!'

Mrs Greenwood walked away, Bertha watching her with a smirk. McGray drew a handkerchief from his breast pocket and gave it to Caroline. She was about to wipe her tears, but then she sniffed the cloth and had to toss it aside.

'As conceited as ye,' he told me. 'Now, Miss Ardglass, I guess it was *ye* who set me on fire on the road.'

'Yes, I had no choice. You were in our way and would not move.'

'And it was yer bloody carriage at Skerton Shipyard the other night.'

'Yes.'

'What the hell were ye –'

'And it was us who set fire to the corridor in the inn,' she snapped, 'to get into your room and retrieve my father's photograph before you two paraded it all over Lancaster.'

'Wait a minute,' I said, taking off my jacket, still damp with the tea Caroline had thrown at us. 'I'd rather you tell us your story from the very beginning – and your father's. Spare no detail, please.'

'It all started around six months ago,' Caroline said, all of us staring at her – even Hannah, the young maid, who was pretending to sweep up the glass and splinters. 'My father had one of his spells of lucidity one night and he came across a strange book in his bedroom; it was full of notes written by that new nurse, Miss Oakley. Those pages are unique, Mr McGray. They were witchcraft notes, but they were not written in Grimorium.'

'Grimorium?' I asked.

'Aye,' said McGray, with an enviable light of understanding in his eyes. 'For centuries witches have written in code. When they write a potion's recipe and say *add eye of newt* or *toe of frog* they don't really mean that.'

'Indeed,' Caroline added. 'They might mean mercury salts – or copper sulphate to tint their fires green.'

'Did Oakley's notes have a cipher?' Nine-Nails asked, with an almost academic interest.

'No, Mr McGray. As my father told me at some point, not a single witch has ever written down a cipher to the code. It is almost an entire language, but it exists only in their heads and they have passed it on for generations. Witches are not allowed to register their knowledge in anything other than that encryption, but Miss Oakley must be a very inexperienced witch. She broke the rules and left all that knowledge exposed in plain English. When my father found that book he realized the witches had been performing . . . *works* on him.'

She covered her mouth, a deep frown etched into her otherwise smooth skin.

'Works?' I repeated, but again McGray was a step ahead. He looked shocked.

'They turned him mad! Didn't they?'

Caroline nodded anxiously.

'My father had a long time to read those notes. Pimblett must have been the one who started it, putting nasty herbs and mind-altering powders into my father's food and drink. And when he was moved to the asylum the nurses went on. They didn't want him dead; they only wanted him mad – they'd use ground cacti and fungi to make him see things, or turn him violent, herbs to stupefy him, sometimes chemical powders or foxgloves to keep his body weak and docile . . . They controlled him like a marionette for years!'

'Miss Ardglass, wait a moment,' I said. 'How do you know all this? I thought you had not seen your father at all since he was admitted to the asylum.'

'You are right that I was not allowed in, but I still found a way. Very early on I began visiting him at night, every new moon, so nobody would see me crossing the gardens – I'd wear this very cloak and I'd tell my grandmother I was going to one of our country cottages, or to London, and she never suspected a thing. It has been six years, so I was eventually spotted by some of the inmates, but apparently they thought I was an apparition, some tortured soul that would only come out when there was no moon in the sky. Nobody believed them, of course. I was safe.'

I looked at her black cloak, and for the first time noticed the very common clothes she was wearing, as if trying to pass for a girl of modest means. It was no wonder that the innkeeper back in Lancaster had confused us with his description: two slender girls, both with brown hair, both with good manners, both travelling with an older woman and an ogre . . .

'What else did the witches do to Joel?' asked McGray.

'Well, he came to know the exact substances and doses they had been using on him, but he never told me anything more specific than what I've already told you. He said I'd be safer that way.'

'Did ye see any potions, amulets?'

'Only once, not long ago. He asked me to help him search his bedroom and we found a dead hummingbird stuffed with herbs. It was an alarming little thing to behold. My father threw it into the fire immediately. He knew what it was but again he preferred not to tell me, for my own safety.

'He said he'd use the witches' own methods to protect himself. He asked me to bring him things to which he had no access in the asylum: strange herbs, chemicals, red onions I had shipped from Spain . . .'

McGray was engrossed. 'Did it work?'

Caroline bit her lip, tears again coming to the surface. 'At first I thought he was going terribly mad,' she said, 'worse than ever before, asking me for all those items, but then . . .' She sniffed and wiped the tears away. 'It seemed to work! He improved so much. He even laughed at times! He hadn't laughed in almost ten years. He never laughed much, not even before his madness took over . . .'

We had to wait for a moment, while Caroline gulped painfully and Bertha held her hands with motherly affection.

'If he was feeling better,' McGray said at last, 'how come he didnae tell people? Denounce the harpies?'

'I asked him that very question,' answered Caroline. 'In the end he was so sharp and well he could easily have walked out a vindicated man. But he simply told me I should wait . . . and I did. I could not tell anybody; I was not even supposed to be there!'

'And I assume he hid the book from Oakley,' I said. 'Did she ever try to find it? Tell the other witches it had gone missing?'

'I don't know,' Caroline began. 'I wouldn't think so . . .'

'Oakley probably tried to keep it quiet,' McGray interrupted, meditative. 'Ye don't want to upset a gang o' cunning witches – but I'm getting ahead o' myself.'

'Did you ever suspect he was planning to escape?' I asked her.

'No . . . Well . . . no.'

I tilted my head. 'You do not sound very convinced.'

'I never thought he'd escape, Mr Frey. I hesitate because the last time I saw him he acted very strangely. He told me not to visit him the next month . . .' She sobbed, but this time she managed to speak through the tears. 'He said he loved me, that he'd always loved me. He was so earnest; he hugged me like never before and then sent me away.

'The next new moon was New Year's Day. The night he . . .'

She looked away.

'Why did the witches use Joel?' McGray asked. Mrs Greenwood was pouring cups of tea for everyone.

'At first he was not entirely sure,' Caroline said, 'but soon after he found the book he asked me to investigate why they might have selected him. Of course I couldn't ask my grandmother for help, so it took me a while. Sometimes I had to go away to do the research, also under pretence, but I found the first glimpse of an answer in our own home, in an inventory of my grandmother's assets. I found a relatively recent acquisition she'd never mentioned to me: it was a large country manor with some fifty acres of land around it – in Lancashire.'

McGray looked up. 'Was it called Cobden Hall?'

Caroline looked surprised. 'So you know about it.'

'We've been making enquiries too. Please go on.'

'I investigated more, although I never dared go to the place itself, not even after I found that the house and the land had belonged to our distant ancestors, when the family name was still Ambrose . . .'

I remembered the grave we'd found in the crypts of Lancaster Priory, and that eerie skull stuffed with marigolds and pins.

'My many-times-great-grandfather,' Caroline went on, 'lost the property in a very tragic turn of events. Everything was auctioned and ended up in the hands of a man named Oakley. Nobody knew him or how he'd made his money, but he settled into the manor and his family lived there for a very long time.

'My family slowly gained back money and prestige. The Ambrose barony is now extinct, but my grandmother got hold of another title by marrying into the Ardglass clan.'

'How did your grandmother manage to regain the property?' I asked, and Caroline smiled crookedly.

'My grandmother has a talent for snatching properties by dubious means.' She looked at McGray. 'She even tried to seize your house at Moray Place, even though your father had paid her more than half already.'

McGray smiled bitterly, surely revisiting unpleasant memories.

'Apparently it was quite a scandal,' Caroline continued. 'My grandmother must have declared something in the

Lancaster courts a few years ago, but I could not find any record of those proceedings. I travelled myself to Lancaster last November and hired a lawyer to look for them, but all he found was an entry in the property registry, stating the hall and all its land passed to my grandmother in June of 1882. I was appalled when I read that date. It was within weeks that my father's mind began to crumble. Within a few months he was a different person, and by December he was in the asylum.'

Again she needed a moment, and Bertha encouraged her to have some tea.

McGray was stroking his chin. 'So Lady Glass upset the witches by snatching Cobden Hall – something odd has to be going on there, that's clear – so the witches decide to take revenge by turning him mad . . .'

'That's what I imagine,' Caroline said.

McGray pushed his tea aside and took a sip of whisky instead. 'Something doesn't quite fit here, lass . . . Does yer grandma have properties across Britain? I thought she mainly hoarded Scotland and a wee bit o' London.'

Caroline assented. 'That is correct. Cobden Hall was a very odd investment for her.'

'Did she do much with it?' I asked. 'I suppose not, otherwise you might have heard of it.'

'That is the strangest part. My grandmother didn't do *anything* with it. She didn't let the manor, or the farming land. All she did was strip it and sell the furnishings and fittings. From her ledgers it looked like she made a small fortune from the Elizabethan and Jacobean items. As soon as she had sold everything she forgot about the place. She loves her profits, so I found that very odd. She has not been to the manor in years, and in all that time she's not even sent any of her brokers to inspect it. Anything could be happening there . . .'

McGray was in deep thought. He stood up and began pacing.

'That truly makes no sense. Could it be that . . . ? Perhaps the witches threatened to do something worse to her if she didn't let them use the property?'

'Possibly,' I said, 'and that might also explain why they did not kill Joel but went to so much trouble to keep him mad all these years. As a sort of guarantee.'

McGray was still pacing. He was about to say something but then changed his mind.

'What is it?' I asked.

'Besides Lady Glass not making sense . . . This Pimblett man . . . I recall from those files that he was yer father's butler for a long time, wasn't he?'

'Yes, for many years, yet he left as soon as my grandmother arranged to send my father to Dr Clouston. He didn't even leave a note; he simply disappeared one day. My grandmother was furious.'

'Although, knowing her, probably secretly pleased she didn't have to pay him,' Bertha tutted.

McGray nodded, his eyes stern. 'From what we've seen, he must have been in the witches' service for quite a while too . . .'

'Wouldn't surprise me if he joined them as soon as he left Slaidburn,' Mr Greenwood ventured.

McGray furrowed his brow and I knew what he was thinking.

'It seems that they were planning this long before Lady Anne took possession of the manor,' Nine-Nails said.

Caroline looked at him with alarmed eyes, her chest suddenly swelling. 'Well, my father always was a little prone to depression, but . . . Do you mean to say . . . it was not *only* revenge for losing the land to her? Why else would they do it? Why would someone spend all those years spying on him?'

'And then send two lassies to continue the job,' McGray added. 'It's a lot of effort. And then the marigolds . . .'

I knew he was thinking of that ancient skull too.

'The marigolds?' Caroline asked.

McGray and I exchanged worried looks. It was a malevolent shadow we were discovering around the Ardglass family.

Nine-Nails shook his head. 'Never mind, lassie. Let's cross that bridge when we get to it.'

'It's not a trifling detail,' said Caroline.

'Course not, lass, but I cannae give ye an answer. Youse, on the other hand, still have a few answers I need. For instance, how come ye decided to follow yer dad's footsteps, even if it meant attacking two CID inspectors?'

Her face went pale.

'And how did you know where he was heading?' I added. 'You claim you had no knowledge of his plans, yet now I see we have encountered you at almost every step of our – and *his* – journey.'

Miss Ardglass opened her eyes wide. 'What are you implying, Mr Frey?'

I could feel the tension rising in the room, the frowns of the Greenwoods tightening as I spoke.

'Did you assist Lord Ardglass in any of his crimes?'

'Of course I did not!' Caroline spat. 'I told you already! I never thought he'd escape, and I certainly never dreamed he'd harm anybody! I was genuinely shocked when you brought us the news that morning.'

'Perhaps,' McGray said. 'But youse did follow him quite closely. How?'

She gulped, suddenly shrinking into her seat. Bertha patted her hand.

Miss Ardglass took a deep breath. 'There is no point concealing it, I suppose,' she said. 'As soon as you left us that day I took a carriage and went to one of grandmother's empty cottages. My father used to play there as a child, and that was the spot where we handed him to Doctor Clouston. My grandmother never let the place again; I imagine it brought her bad memories. I somehow knew my father would go there. It was mere intuition.'

'Why did you not tell us?' I interrupted. 'We explicitly asked you if you knew where he could have –'

McGray held me back. 'So ye went to the cottage and found him there.'

'Yes. I didn't believe he'd done it. I kept telling myself he couldn't have.'

'And he admitted he . . .' McGray looked at the Greenwoods. Their faces were mortified. 'He admitted he was responsible for Miss Greenwood's death?'

Caroline struggled to speak. 'I didn't believe it until I heard it from him.'

'*You scum!*' Mrs Greenwood roared, hurling herself forwards, her nails ready to strike, but her husband seized her by the shoulders. 'Your bastard father killed our poor girl!'

Caroline jumped up. '*Your precious daughter poisoned my father for years!* She got what she deserved!'

McGray tried to appease them, but they went on yelling, their faces red, spittle flying. Nine-Nails stepped back and we watched them let all that steam off, expecting them to tire at some point, but they could have continued until dawn.

Nine-Nails aimed into the fireplace and shot. Only then did the women stop. There was a moment of silence, but then Mrs Greenwood burst into tears; she covered her mouth and again cried miserably on her husband's shoulder.

'Sit,' McGray told Miss Ardglass, whose chest was still heaving, but he had to push her by the shoulders to make her obey. 'Now, focus, lass. Ye spoke to Joel. He told ye where he was going, right?'

Caroline grunted. 'Yes. He said he'd go to Lancaster, to find Pimblett . . . God, I tried to persuade him not to, I honestly did! But he said his life was already ruined. He made me swear I wouldn't follow . . . but I had to do something.

'Bertha and Jed wouldn't let me come alone. We took the next train, where I saw Mr Frey vomiting like the Trevi Fountain. Of course I warned my father, and he probably hid in the coal car. When we alighted Bertha saw him very briefly.'

'He was all covered in charcoal,' said Bertha.

Caroline's eyes went from McGray to me and back. 'After that, we found you were at the same inn. All we had to do was follow your tracks to know where my father was heading.'

'Our tracks?' I echoed. 'How could you possibly have followed us all the way here?'

Miss Ardglass sneered. 'Are you that much of a fool, Mr Frey? You two are unmistakable: a lanky Londoner who fancies himself a duke, travelling with a scruffy Scotsman who wears ridiculous clothes ... We simply had to ask. Wherever you went, people remembered.'

'She does make a fair point,' McGray whispered.

'Indeed,' I said, 'you *do* wear ridiculous clothes.'

Caroline went on. 'We managed to follow you to those warehouses by the port. It was a miracle we found my father storming out of those buildings. We barely managed to get him into the carriage before you two and that moustachioed brute came out.' Her eyes became sombre. 'My poor father was *not* happy to see me. I'd never seen him in such a vicious temper. He said spiteful things and I even thought he'd lost his mind for good. He had taken a lot of strange artefacts from that warehouse – a glass knife, weeds, weird lamp oils ... He gave me a strange "fire bottle" and said I should throw it at the witches if they ever came near me.'

'Of course,' I said. 'It was you who attacked us on the road.'

'Shall I apologize?' she mocked.

'I ken how much an Ardglass apology is worth,' Nine-Nails said.

'We did all we could *not* to kill you,' Caroline went on. 'You were standing in the middle of the road like an idiot – Jed nearly destroyed the carriage to stop on time. And I did try to throw the bottle a little off.'

'*Tried!*' McGray protested. 'I bloody well caught fire!'

'Moving on,' I said, before another burst of emotion overwhelmed us, 'did your father tell you where he was going?'

'No, again it was you gentlemen who guided us.' Caroline laughed quietly. 'Mr McGray harassed almost every coachman in Lancaster to find transport to Pendle. As soon as we heard that I knew he'd be going to Cobden Hall. Although I didn't know he'd be coming to this village. We stopped here because of Pimblett's connection with the place – and because we needed shelter.'

'You only just missed your monster of a father,' Mrs Greenwood snapped.

Caroline drew in an indignant breath, but went on, 'When we arrived the entire village was in turmoil. As this – lady said, the children had just been snatched and all the men were preparing to go and look for them. They turned us away when we requested a room; I knew the predicament they were in, but we had no option and had to force our stay.'

'They terrorized us!' Mrs Greenwood told us.

'We may have been blunt but we offered you good money,' Caroline hissed, before turning to us. 'We asked them to tell no one we were here. I assumed you two would come along at some point, and I was right. It was infuriating to have to stay put while you ate *our* dinner and His Royal Highness soaked in *my* lavender bath. I had no idea the children's kidnapping was in any way connected to my father.'

Mrs Greenwood opened her mouth to speak but her husband raised his hand. 'The girl's telling the truth. They didn't know Lizzy's child was in question and we didn't tell them our names when they arrived. They didn't hear our story until you inspectors questioned us. When I went upstairs the miss here was distraught. She said that if we got rid of you they'd take us to the children. They said they could get to them, on the condition that you two didn't know of their presence . . .' He looked at Miss Ardglass with contempt. 'I didn't like that deal at all, and I would have preferred to tell you everything – but she claimed she knew where the children were.'

I arched an eyebrow and turned slowly to face Caroline. 'Miss Ardglass, *do* you know?'

She did not reply, but looked down so swiftly she might as well have crouched like a cornered cat.

McGray smiled. 'Aye, I think the lass might have been telling the truth for once . . . or at least part of it.'

34

'*Tell them!*' Mrs Greenwood hollered. '*Tell them now!*'

McGray's patience had run out. 'Mr Greenwood, control yer bloody wife; next time she yells like that I'll punch *yer* face.'

The man did squeeze her arm and McGray turned back to Caroline.

'Miss Ardglass, I need ye to tell us what ye think yer father did to those children . . .'

I smiled bitterly. 'And the sooner you tell us the better. We do not want to lose innocent lives to one of Joel's psychotic episodes.'

Caroline jumped up, rushed over to me and gave me a mighty slap.

'Watch your words! It is my father you are talking about!'

I stretched my jaw, my skin burning. 'With all due respect, miss,' I hissed, 'your father is a confessed murderer.'

She raised her fists and McGray had to step between us. '*Och, stop it!* I don't want youse girls having a catfight right here.' He looked at Caroline. 'The bloody dandy's right. Yer dad's a dangerous lunatic.'

There was poison in Caroline's eyes. 'So is your sister.'

Nobody moved. Not even the Greenwoods, who knew nothing about Amy McGray, but Nine-Nails' expression was enough of a briefing. He drew in a long breath, and it was like the absolute silence between lightning and the strike of thunder.

Then, startling everyone, he thrust his arm out and grabbed Caroline by the throat, pushed her backwards, knocking over the chair, and pinned her against the wall.

'*How dare you?*'

Bertha yelled and punched him all over, shedding desperate tears, but she was harming herself more than she did the tall Scot. Neither Mr Greenwood nor his wife moved a muscle, so I had to step forwards.

'McGray, let her go!'

'I've cracked people's bones for less than that,' McGray whispered between his teeth.

Caroline's face was losing colour, but her eyes were as full of rage as McGray's. It looked as if she did not – or rather *could not*–feel any pain.

'We are partners in disgrace, Mr McGray,' she spluttered. 'Whether you like it or not.'

I pressed my gun against Nine-Nails' back, making sure he heard the click of the safety catch.

'*Let – her – go.*'

After a seemingly never-ending pause, he obliged, leaving Miss Ardglass coughing from the depths of her throat, as Bertha helped her back to a seat.

McGray walked to the furthest corner of the room and must have gulped down at least a quarter of the whisky in one go.

I leaned in close to Caroline. 'Are you able to talk at all?'

She looked up, glaring at McGray with teary eyes.

'I know your sister talked to my father. If you help me, I am sure I can convince him to tell you everything.'

Nine-Nails turned his head slowly. I could only see one side of his face, but the spark in his eye was evident.

'What d'ye mean by *help*?'

'Do not listen to her,' I said immediately. 'She is crafty. She will tell you anything you want to hear.'

'My father is going to Cobden Hall for revenge,' Caroline continued, her voice quivering. 'If he gets there, I'm sure those witches will kill him, but if we cut him off before he arrives, we might still save him. I know exactly *when* he'll be there, but there is little time left.'

'What about the children?' Mr Greenwood asked.

'Yes, what about our children?' seconded his wife.

'My father would never harm them,' Caroline said. 'He must have hidden them somewhere safe. I don't know where or even why, but I am sure they're fine, and I am *sure* I can persuade him to bring them back.'

There was a gleam of hope in everybody's eyes, except mine. I was outraged.

'Do you want us to take you to your father?' I said. 'Perhaps in a luxurious hansom carriage? And then, after he surrenders the girls, will you expect us to let you both go on your merry way?'

She looked defiant; my words were like wind hitting stone. 'Yes.'

McGray turned. 'It's a tempting deal, lass.'

'*What?* Nine-Nails, are you completely insane? These people have been aiding and abetting a murderer. They lied, stole evidence, assaulted two inspectors – shall I continue? If you are in your right mind, you must realize it is our duty to deliver them to justice before they think of another creative way of fooling us.'

There was a collective cry of *What?*, *No* and *How dare you?*

McGray approached Caroline with imposing steps. 'Are ye sure yer dad'll tell me what Pansy said?'

'If I tell him I owe you – of course.'

'And we want our lil' ones!' Mrs Greenwood jumped in.

'I told you,' said Caroline, 'I am sure they're fine.'

'And I hope that's true,' McGray said darkly, 'because if he's done anything to them, or if he refuses to tell me anything when I ask . . .' he pointed his finger at her, so closely he almost touched her between the eyes, 'I'll kill him myself.'

Caroline held his manic stare, and Nine-Nails did not wait for her response to his threat.

'How long do we have?' he asked.

'Not long,' said Caroline. 'Before dawn, I'd say.'

It was as if the world had stopped, awaiting only Mc-Gray's answer. I was shocked, yet hardly surprised, when he shook hands with Miss Ardglass.

'We have a deal, lassie.'

I choked and stammered before yelling, 'You cannot make such a deal! It is illegal. *Illegal!* And you are a bloody officer of the CID!'

All eyes fell on me. All of them indignant.

'If you think the pretty boy will give you trouble,' said Mr Greenwood, his fist stamping his palm, 'we can take good care of him. Especially when the brewery lads return – they're large chaps, and they don't have to look for the children no more.'

McGray stroked his stubble. 'Aye, but we'll have to tie
him up until yer lads arrive. I don't want him to do anything stupid.'

They approached me, ready to put their plan into
action, and I howled: *'Wait a bloody second!* Am I the only
person in this room who believes murder and torture
ought to be punished?'

Caroline looked at me with the most turbulent eyes. I
had seen that expression before, and it made me feel an
awkwardness that was disturbingly familiar.

'No,' she said, 'but you are the only person here who
doesn't love someone.'

Never, in my entire life, had anybody's words wounded
me so deeply, so swiftly. I lost all control of my facial
expression, which I regained upon seeing my dumbfounded reflection in the window.

'Nine-Nails,' I said, 'strangle her.'

'Ye try to strangle her and I'll make ye wear yer pair as
earrings.'

'I say we lock him in one of the rooms,' said Mrs Greenwood. Her husband was already untying Jed's fat wrists
and McGray was coming to seize me.

I lifted Greenwood's gun and aimed at McGray's face,
the barrel inches from his nose. 'Lay your filthy hands on
me and I swear I'll do it.'

'Yer outnumbered, laddie!' he said with a chuckle.

'Yes, I can count, but I will not be roughly handled by ·
any of you like a goat. I shall make my own way.'

McGray and Mr Greenwood marched behind me.
I went upstairs and stepped into the first guest room I
found open. An unfortunate choice, for the window was

missing one of its diamond panes, letting in a frosty draught.

'The gun,' McGray said.

'I cannot believe you are doing this,' I said. 'I can tolerate your stupid occult nonsense, but you are taking part in an actual . . . conspiracy . . . obstructing the course . . . is anyone listening to a bloody word I'm saying?'

'The gun, *now*, or instead of a room we'll throw ye into the privy's pit.'

I handed over the weapon as Mr Greenwood drew a set of keys from his pocket, and I watched the door close slowly, leaving me in the cold, damp darkness.

It was evident that the room had not been occupied for a while. The Greenwoods used it for storage, and under a bundle of clothes I found an old overcoat. It smelled like mouldy bread, but I wrapped myself in it nonetheless.

I heard muffled voices downstairs, and could not repress my curiosity. I was so glad I was alone with nobody to see me; I could lie flat on my chest and press my ear against the floorboards – as Miss Ardglass had surely done.

Mrs Greenwood was yelling again, babbling unintelligibly before being cut off.

Miss Ardglass then went on to talk about the things Joel had discovered about the green beacons, and how witches used different colours to communicate across the country. McGray asked something, but with his accent I could not make out his words; Miss Ardglass carried on talking about a visual code, and I remembered the flickering flames we'd seen on the moors, right before our violent encounter with Joel and the two witches. From McGray's description – the flashings of green we'd seen in the fire's usual yellow – Caroline deduced that Joel had deceived Redfern and Oakley, using their own code to make them think there was another witch waiting for them on that hill.

Green, she added, was an alarm signal, used to summon all the major witches for an emergency Sabbath. According to Oakley's book, their ancient codes dictated that whenever the green beacons appeared, all witches had three days to travel to the meeting; that was how she'd worked out the exact time Joel would be at Cobden Hall.

I thought of the lights I'd seen on the road from Lancashire, that night right before I fell asleep in the decrepit carriage. No wonder the witches were having a reunion: with a psychopathic lord killing them like flies, and the police having discovered their enormous stock of smuggled artefacts in Lancaster, they were all flocking to that lonely spot near Pendle.

I did not envy the people downstairs, about to follow the merciless Joel and face all those witches with their myriad poisons. I heard them preparing weapons and charging rifles, and suddenly felt a pang of unmitigated guilt. Only God knew what they were about to confront, and they'd need as many helping hands as possible. I lifted a fist, ready to bang the floor and tell them I'd join their doomed party, but then came a piercing scream.

I heard it clearly through the cracked glass, the eerie lament brought on the wind. I could not tell whether it was a male or a female voice, but then I heard it again, this time much closer.

It was a high-pitched screech but indisputably male.

Everyone downstairs stopped talking. They'd also heard it.

I stood up and went to the window, feeling the cold draught on my face. My heart skipped a beat when I saw all the green, yellow and red fires twinkling in the distance.

They were coming.

35

I rubbed my eyes, thinking it might be a nightmare, but I could not fool myself.

They were indeed coming. From the south-east, from Pendle, forming a neat file of multicoloured torches as they marched towards us.

I dropped to the floor, banging with my fists and shouting my lungs out.

'The witches are coming!'

McGray shouted back. 'Can ye see them?'

'Yes. More than twenty lights.'

I heard the dismayed cries of Bertha and Mrs Greenwood, and barely made out Caroline saying, 'I did not expect this!'

There was a female cry, hoarse and nearby. I leaped back to the window and saw one of the houses catch fire. The flames were mostly gold and orange, but the occasional sparks of green sent everyone into panic.

I squinted and managed to see the silhouettes of a woman and a young boy rush out from the blazing house, their terrified voices echoing in the darkness, along with the loud cawing of a raven. I felt like Rameses witnessing God's plagues.

The flames on the roof lit the main road, and it shocked me that nobody in the village came out to help. I could not even see any curious faces peering through the windows.

Then I saw a black carriage, its polished surface gleaming in the firelight. It was escorted by four mighty Percherons, the exotic horses ridden by men almost as large as their beasts, and followed by a parade of smaller horses, all carrying figures swathed in black cloaks.

'Dear Lord,' I muttered, thinking that each person out there would be armed not only with guns but also with vials of things worse than strychnine.

I heard that male wail again, but it did not come from the east. It came from the opposite direction, from the road McGray and I had come along a few hours ago.

There was a lone rider there, the horse galloping at full speed, pulling a thick rope. The grey horse halted right in front of my window, and I followed the thick cord until I saw a dark figure crouching on the trampled snow. It was a man, his limbs trembling as he tried to move. I recognized the hunched back and bony features of Floyd, the cart driver. His was the crying voice we'd been hearing, as he was dragged along the roads like a sack of flour.

The black carriage approached, and the accompanying riders positioned themselves around it. There was an unsettling, almost soldierly precision to their movements.

A short, dark figure alighted, aided by one of the tall men. I could tell it was a woman, dressed all in black, her pale right hand the only skin I could see. Her left hand was engulfed in a thick leather glove, like a falconer's.

The woman walked up to the crouching man with a noticeable limp, and then she spoke, her resonating voice instantly taking me back to that dreadful night atop Winfold Fell.

'Is this him?'

'Aye, Miss Redfern,' someone replied. That was the first time anyone had confirmed her name. 'Says they were heading here.'

Redfern kneeled down, grabbed Floyd's hair and lifted his face. 'Is that true?'

Floyd moaned. He was in a very sorry state, his face covered in ghastly bright-red blisters, which reminded me of the acid burns I'd seen in medical school. Redfern slapped him, then pressed her gloved thumb against one of the blisters, and I could swear I heard his skin sizzle. Floyd howled in a pain I could not even imagine, his anguished voice tearing the night air, his legs writhing in despair.

'Is that true?' she repeated.

Poor Floyd nodded, and Redfern bent closer to him, her hooded ear listening intently. She rose like a dart, held her left hand high and the raven landed on her glove. One of the men handed her something – I guessed it must have been a little note – which she fastened to the bird's leg before tossing it back into the air. As the raven flew away Redfern nodded to the men. Two of her guards banged on the inn's door with their enormous fists, and she bellowed: 'Give us the Ardglass woman!'

McGray's thundering voice responded at once. 'Sod off, youse rank bitches!'

There was a general uproar, high-pitched cackles from beneath the black cloaks and deep, cruel laughter from the broad-shouldered guards.

'I don't like to ask twice, Nine-Nails McGray,' Redfern said, her voice imposing even over the clamour of her helpers.

I would have given anything for a gun; from that window I would have had a perfect shot at the witch's head. I cursed them all downstairs.

I heard McGray uttering a frantic 'No!' followed by Mr Greenwood yelling, and then a rifle shot came from one of the windows, missing Redfern by a mere inch and hitting the carriage.

The witch nodded, stepping back. All the men drew out guns and rifles, and without a second command a rain of bullets fell on the inn's door and windows. I had to cover my ears, even at that distance, and the deafening shots prevented me from hearing what was happening below.

I feared looking, but could not help it: four big men kicked the main door open while the others continued their relentless shooting, and eventually I heard a scream. It was Caroline, her voice desperate as one of the men dragged her out. The shooting stopped and then I could hear McGray grunting.

The other three men were struggling to remove him; two of them kept a firm grip on his arms while a third one stood behind, holding Nine-Nails by the neck and occasionally punching his kidneys.

Caroline looked in panic at the multitude of torches around her, but the girl went still when she faced Redfern.

The old woman was pushing her hood back, for the first time showing her white, wiry hair and her bony, angular face. With her high cheekbones and soft jaw she appeared to have been very beautiful in her youth. Like Oakley's, her manners were not those of a pauper.

'Where's your father?' she asked.

Caroline spat on the crone's face, who wiped herself with a ragged sleeve, and then struck Miss Ardglass a terrible slap.

'We'll find him anyway, dear. Save yourself some pain.'

'Go find him then.'

Redfern held her by the hair. 'There's only one reason I don't give you the lashing that you deserve. Mrs Marigold wants to see you.'

I could not believe my ears: Marigold, the very word written by McGray's sister. And then the skull in the crypt, its eye sockets stuffed with dry marigolds.

'She might show some mercy if she hears you were a good girl,' Redfern went on.

Caroline held the crone's stare. I could not tell what her expression was; however, even from the upper floor I saw a set of stained, uneven teeth as Redfern grinned.

'Have it your way,' she concluded.

The hag searched in the folds of her cloak. She produced a little vial and something that looked like a jute pouch, on to which she poured a few drops. 'Hold her still,' she said, and a second guard had to step forwards. Caroline was twisting and kicking savagely, and I clenched my fists in burning frustration as I witnessed what followed.

Redfern struggled, taking a few of the kicks, but in the end she managed to cover Caroline's head with the pouch, her gloved hand pressing the material firmly against the girl's face. McGray howled dreadfully and Caroline continued to struggle, but very soon her voice and body lost all strength. Her limbs and head fell slack, and the men carried her to the carriage as if handling a rag doll.

'Pray it be only laudanum,' I mumbled, still appalled by Floyd's blisters. I spoke so softly that someone standing next to me would have struggled to hear; nevertheless, Redfern looked up. I instinctively jumped aside, my back against the wall. She could not have possibly heard me, I knew it, yet I did not dare move back.

McGray shouted then. 'Let the lass go; she has no idea where the madman went.'

Redfern did not bother to reply. 'Tie him up. And gag him, I can't stand his accent.'

'What do we do with all the others inside?' a deep voice asked.

I very slowly leaned back towards the window, and I saw Redfern being helped back into the carriage, looking at the inn over her shoulder.

'Burn it all.'

The cloaked women advanced, hurling their green and red torches at the shattered windows. Mrs Greenwood cried out in terror, as did her maid. I did not hear her husband, or Jed or Bertha.

As the flames began to spread the snow on the main road glowed. I had a perfect view of the entourage as they left: the women's cloaks were not rags but fine black velvet, and the men's horses were some of the finest beasts I'd ever seen, just like the ones that pulled the carriage away. I looked about, but McGray was gone and I could not tell what they'd done with him.

The fire advanced swiftly, but I only realized it when the smell of charred wood reached my nostrils. Suddenly I felt the floor hot through my shoes. The building was on fire, I thought with a wave of fear, and I was locked in that room.

'It was the witches!' somebody shouted from the street, followed by many other panicked voices, yet nobody came to help. How could they leave their neighbours to their fate?

You are on your own, Ian.

I threw myself against the door, again and again, but it was solid oak, with large, thick hinges. When my shoulders were sore I kicked repeatedly, but to no avail. Even one of the witches' burly guards would have struggled.

There was a burst of flames towering as high as my window, lighting up the bedroom as if it were midday. Luckily it was just a flash, but it cracked the window glass and I felt its heat as if I'd briefly opened a furnace.

'Death by fire . . .' I muttered, despair taking hold of me. I looked out through the window.

The witches and their men were now just a faint cluster of sparks in the distance. Only then did people flock out of their houses. The villagers ran about like crazed ants, calling for water and throwing snow at the windows.

'Mr Greenwood!' someone shouted, but there was no reply.

I pictured them all lying on the floor, the flames licking at their lifeless bodies – the keys to my room next to them, now red hot.

There was smoke coming through the shattered glass, making my eyes sting as I watched the mayhem down below. All the village men were still away, so I saw mostly elderly men, a few women and young children, perhaps as terrified as I was, and their water buckets and their fistfuls of snow seemed a pathetic response.

I had an awful image of my skin charring and blistering, my eyeballs boiling, and the fear made my chest ache. Then I looked at the window's metal frame and immediately made up my mind: I'd rather jump and break all my bones on the pebbled street than meet such an excruciating death.

The pane's diamond lattice was too small for even a baby to pass through. I looked for anything in the room I could use to break it. All I could find was a long candle holder made of pewter, and I banged the life out of those frames.

'There's someone up there!' people shouted as they saw the glass shards raining down.

A series of coughs racked my body. The smoke was now so dense I could barely see outside.

Through my panic I became aware of a lone rider galloping into Slaidburn. With the smoke and my teary eyes I could not make out any detail, but I heard exclamations of fear as the people made way for the horse.

'Oh no . . .'

I hit the lead with renewed strength, finally bending the metal, sweat trickling down my forehead and back.

The rider halted by the entrance, nobody daring to speak or even look at him. He drew something out of his breast pocket, which must have been a gun, for everyone yelped and the man went inside without hindrance.

An instant later I saw Mrs Greenwood dashing out, bending double and coughing. The next thing I heard was banging on my room's door, three loud, insistent thuds, and then a gunshot that sent the latch flying.

The man threw the door wide, splinters scattering everywhere, and it was as if someone had opened the entrance to hell. A blast of unbearable heat, closely followed by a cloud of heavy, black smoke, entered the room. I took a breath, but the singeing hot air was itself like fire and I began to choke.

The corridor was brightly lit, and against that light I saw the dark, tall figure of the man we'd been chasing all along.

'You!' I roared.

'Follow me or you're dead.'

I crouched, backing away, and Lord Ardglass grasped my arm and pulled, but I instinctively resisted. His eyes were bloodshot.

'You have seconds to decide, boy! I will *not* die for *you*.'

Indeed I had no choice. We sprinted out of the room and on to the staircase, which had already caught fire in places. The flames danced and the smoke curled upwards. Joel dragged me down those stairs, our shoulders brushing the ignited walls more than once, the wooden steps cracking under our feet. It was so hot I could not tell whether my skin burned or not, let alone register what was happening beyond the banisters.

I saw the entrance as a black square in the pure blaze, and focused all my thoughts on getting there, counting each painful step. I heard sizzling that might have come from Joel's clothes, or my hair, or anywhere. That nasty sound injected a terrible fear that propelled me forwards. Suddenly I found myself in the dark outdoors, the chilly air hitting me but failing to dissipate the infernal heat my face had absorbed.

There was no time even to look at the frightened crowd, for Joel pressed his gun against my neck, so hard I thought it would pierce my skin.

'To the horse,' he snapped, and he pushed me towards the animal, which stood strangely still amidst the surrounding mayhem. I saw Joel's leather bag, embossed with that decorated A, tied to the saddle.

I had to jump on to the horse and Joel mounted behind me.

'Ride,' he ordered, and pushed the gun into my flesh even harder. 'Try anything and I *will* empty this into your neck.'

I spurred on the horse. I had no chance to look back, no chance to see what had happened to any of the people in the inn. I could not even glance at the building or see whether the fire had spread to the adjacent houses.

As I galloped away from the village the world became darker and colder, and I felt as if we were falling into an immense, black abyss.

36

As soon as the lights from the village had completely faded Joel punched me in the back and pressed the barrel against my neck a little harder. He barked in my ear: 'What did they do to Caroline?'

'They took her with them.'

'I know that much. Did they harm her?'

'I cannot tell,' was my honest answer. 'From where I stood it looked as though they used laudanum to sedate her.'

'A bag over her head?'

'Yes.'

Joel's voice became even more strained. 'They must want to play with her before . . .'

He did not finish that sentence.

'They wanted to know where you were going,' I snorted. 'Hardly a surprise, since you have been killing them by the day.'

After that I tried to ask questions, but every time I uttered a word Joel punched my spine again.

We rode almost blindly for more than two hours. The crescent moon could not be seen; the scant light came from the few stars that were not concealed by thick clouds. Nevertheless, Joel seemed to anticipate every bend and corner on those narrow country roads, pulling the reins himself whenever we needed to turn. Although we were going south-east we never saw or heard the witches' procession; perhaps Joel was purposely taking a path to avoid them.

In the dim light I finally saw the silver outline of a long, snowy mount, rising from a gentle slope in the east, and then breaking into a sharp precipice in the west. It was a solitary hill, its summit the highest point on the horizon. Needless to say I was looking at Pendle Hill, the place Joel had been heading for all along. I could not count how many times I'd said I would never go to that spot, yet I had inescapably gravitated towards it.

We were a couple of miles from the hill when the horse began to pant in exhaustion. Joel reined in next to the ruins of a low stone wall. A thick ash tree had grown right next to it, the gnarled bark almost embracing the granite.

Joel hopped off. 'Climb down, boy,' he commanded. 'Let the beast rest.'

So I did, but did not repress my acrimony. 'You seem so compassionate . . . to beasts.'

Then I thought of McGray's mount, its breath steaming in the cold, life leaving its fine body.

He kept the gun aimed at my head, a pair of piercing pupils fixed on mine.

'I'm not compassionate; I pay eye for eye,' he whispered, making me feel a sudden chill. In the shadows his face looked ghostly grey, like that of a reanimated corpse. Other than his old photograph and that blurry reflection in a window, I had never seen him so close. I could tell that the weak, sickly young man was long gone. Now, in his fifties, his face had hardened, looking leaner and more angular. He did not have many wrinkles, but those few were set like fine yet deep scalpel cuts around his mouth and in between his eyebrows. It was as though his features had been affixed for years in a single, angry frown.

I could not hold my tongue. 'Your daughter is hostage to those witches, but I suppose it is all worth it, since you got your idiotic revenge.'

Joel inhaled through his teeth, hurled himself upon me and I became petrified, assaulted by the memory of the dying Nurse Greenwood. Before I could step back he punched me hard on the cheekbone.

He was ten times stronger than Caroline, and I staggered, but I still managed to harden my countenance.

'You hit like your daughter.'

'You arrogant little brat,' he hissed. 'Don't come preaching about compassion to me. *Those damned harpies ruined my life!* My hands never touched their businesses yet they decided to take revenge through me and my folk! When I found Oakley's little book and realized all the dreadful works they'd been performing on me ...' He nearly gagged, choking on unmitigated rage. 'The very nurses who were meant to look after me were the ones keeping me insane!'

'Your daughter mentioned how they used cacti, chemicals ...'

'Yes. And they even fooled the good Doctor Clouston. That damned Greenwood kept me on the edge. The filthy witch! Pretending to be always sweet and kind to me ... I remember thinking she was very pretty.'

'We were wondering ... did they use you to keep Lady Anne away from –'

'Cobden Hall? Yes. Greenwood told me before the

strychnine worked its magic. My mother wanted that manor back in the family, but that's been the witches' lair for centuries. They threatened to kill me, and curse Caroline and do terrible things to my mother if she used the property. Now they run all their affairs from there, and it even bloody suits them that their lair is owned by somebody else. If their trade were ever made public, my mother would be accused of overseeing it. *The cunning, scheming harpies!* When I learned all this . . .' Again the rage took over and he had to pause, snorting and gnashing his teeth. He finally managed to spit the words out. 'My insides went on fire.'

I saw his clenched fists and the swollen veins in his neck.

'That is all I can feel these days, boy, this scorching hate in my chest that overtakes any other emotion, and I abhor them for that too. I can picture every torture, every torment inflicted on their flesh, but nothing seems enough. Strychnine poisoning? A few minutes of pain and then it's all over.'

He smiled darkly and his final words were bloodcurdling. 'If they didn't make me lose my mind with their potions, they have certainly done it now.'

'I regret nothing,' Joel said, 'not even Pimblett's death. He was the worst of all, the perfidious bastard. He pretended to be my friend for years! I shared my deepest secrets with him, not knowing that he was keeping record of my every word and step, storing it all in his twisted little mind until he could wield it all against me. No, boy, I regret nothing.'

He stared at Pendle Hill, motionless, and I could hear his deep, earnest breaths.

'I do curse myself for dragging Caroline into this,' he went on. 'I did all I could to keep her out, but she would not yield. I even threatened her the last time she saw me. All fruitless. She has too much of my blasted mother in her. It seems I was not meant to have a tame daughter.'

Joel's lip trembled, for a fleeting instant he looked like the feeble young man in the photograph. He was going to speak again, but then swallowed, as if gulping some words down.

'You could have stopped,' I said, 'when you realized she would not back off.'

Joel shook his head. 'No, I could not turn back. Precisely *because* of my Caroline. There is a final detail you don't know yet. Have you not wondered why these witches went so far against us Ardglasses?'

I raised my eyebrows, thinking of McGray's words. 'As a matter of fact, that is one of the questions I have yearned to ask you. They have devoted a lifetime to harming and spying on you. It all started long before the Cobden Hall issue. Why?'

Joel nodded. 'More than a lifetime, boy. This is far beyond a dispute over a mere plot of land. This has spanned generations.'

'Miss Ardglass did tell us that your ancestors lost land to the Oakleys,' I said, 'and she mentioned that your family name used to be Ambrose ... I happened to come across the grave of an Ambrose, in Lancaster. McGray opened the crypt and we found traces of —'

'Witchcraft?'

'Indeed.'

Joel exhaled. 'Damn witches. They took care of every little detail. See, before I tell you more, you must know theirs is not a trifling organization. Witches are very rare, and few know of their existence – a very *privileged* few.

'Prime ministers, royal families, the wealthiest industrialists, the witches know them all and do jobs for them. They have been receiving messages for Queen Victoria from her dearly departed Albert for nearly thirty years! They are the last vestige of those village healers whom people resorted to in medieval times, back when everyone in this island was a devout Catholic.

'Cobden Hall belonged to a particularly pious family. During the Reformation, when the monasteries were being dismantled and desecrated, they bought all the stones and glass they could. They brought sacred items from the monastic houses in Whalley, Preston, even York. They pretended to have converted, of course, but they kept their old faith zealously. They invited priests to celebrate secret masses ... under the very stones that had once made their temples, praying to virgins and crucifixes made from the ingots their old relics had been melted into. They also welcomed the old-fashioned healers, mostly women, and they performed all sorts of jobs: blessings, cleansings, births ... even jinxes and clairvoyance.

'Everyone in Lancashire knew what happened inside those walls, but nobody challenged them. This county was fertile ground for the old ways, far from the grip of London and the Reformists. I suppose people found a more immediate comfort grasping rosary beads or staring at the image of a saint than from the more abstract concepts the Lutherans preached about.

'Lord Ambrose was the one person powerful enough to challenge them, and he eventually brought them down. He could never prove their secret Catholic rituals – nobody would testify against them – so he accused them of witchcraft. Lord Ambrose was one of the magistrates who prosecuted many women to please James I, so he had plenty of cases on which to base his lies. Six women went to the gallows, but during their execution they cursed him.

'Well, not only him. In front of the crowd they cursed him and his descendants. Thirteen generations would meet nothing but pain and suffering, and then the Ambrose line would come to an end.

'According to legend, Lord Ambrose died while the women pronounced that very curse. His own son was murdered, allegedly by a resentful mistress, and his grandson was famously insane; he died aged twenty.

'The decades passed, then the centuries, and the curse faded in the people's memory . . . but not for the descendants of the surviving witches. They continued to perform jobs for anyone who had enough gold or connections, or indeed anyone who could offer them protection. They lurked underground all this time, passing on their wisdom and learning new tricks, and gaining access to an ever more powerful clientele. And they managed it all by exerting the power of their . . . reputation.'

'Their reputation?' I asked.

'Indeed, boy. Curses are most effective when one *makes*

them happen. They had cursed the Ambrose family, and the best way to ensure that people feared them was to ensure that their curses came to fruition.

'They watched us carefully. If you read our family history, you will not find a single happy ending. Untimely deaths abound, and those who did live for longer had miserable, pointless existences. That's what they intended for me.'

I frowned, finding the whole story difficult to believe. 'How could this go on for so long without anybody doing anything about it? Were your relatives not aware of the witches' interventions?'

He smiled bitterly. 'The witches got what they wanted: the Ambroses became known as a jinxed family, and of course there was this family legend about us being the targets of black magic. Not everyone took it seriously, though. I didn't, until . . . well, let's say I should have kept my eyes more widely open.

'We learned a few protection methods, which again were regarded as quirky family lore. We applied them with varying degrees of success. My own mother deploys protection charms in all her properties —'

'Bottles filled with bent nails and foul liquids?' I put in, and Joel raised a brow.

'So you found them!'

I wrinkled my nose. 'I wish we had not.'

Joel sighed. 'Indeed, I wish I'd never had to tell you all this. Now my daughter is in their hands . . . She is the thirteenth, you know. I counted the generations. Now I suspect there is a good reason she has not found a suitor: the witches want our lineage to die with her. Do you understand me now? My Caroline's death would be the ultimate proof of their powers.'

Again I could not believe it. 'Do you mean to say their very powerful "clients" have been following the history of your family? Expecting you to die miserably and your daughter to pass away without offspring?' He assented. 'Would they really go to such extremes simply to build up a legend around themselves?'

Joel smirked. 'Entire religions have been based on weaker, foggier stories. It's not what you can do, it's what others *believe* you can do that gives you power.'

He spoke those words most earnestly, but I could only shake my head again. Perhaps it was because of my very rational frame of mind, but despite Joel's explanation I could not understand the full extent of the witches' influence. Unfortunately, I would very soon become fully aware.

We were silent for a moment, while I processed Joel's long story. He used that time to rummage through his leather bag. He produced a half-burned cigar and lit it up.

'They took Adolphus with them, didn't they?' he asked.

'Yes.'

Joel frowned, then muttered: 'This might still work.'

Then he turned back to the bag and pulled out a large bottle, its stopper sealed with wax. I heard the clink of glass; the bag was packed with dark articles.

'Did you take all that from the witches' warehouse?'

'Indeed.' Joel began to splatter the tree's leafless branches with the oily contents of the bottle. Just as I noticed the acrid stench of that slimy substance I'd seen before, Joel ignited a match and threw it into the fuel. The tree caught fire at a preternatural speed, and the flames sent green and golden glimmers all across the plains.

'What are you doing?' I asked in alarm, expecting to see a hundred green torches flocking in our direction at any moment.

'Don't worry about it, son. Not yet.'

'What do you mean, don't worry? Is this not one of those beacons the witches run to?'

'You are learning swiftly. Yes, but I know how to trick them now. Did you not see me lure that bloody pair of witches to the top of Winfold Fell?' he smirked. 'The stupid fools were expecting to find one of their own, begging for help. I knew they'd be taking that road, close to one of their beacons, so I settled myself there, ousted the mute hag who watches over that pyre and then lay in wait for them. What a pleasure it was to see their flabbergasted faces when I appeared!' He looked into the dancing flames, basking in the cruel memory.

I remembered Oakley's bloodstained apron, the red spills around that lonely tree stump.

'Did you enjoy killing Miss Oakley?' I could not help asking. 'And what have you done with those children?'

Joel arched an eyebrow, an eerie smile playing on his lips. 'Are you worried about them, boy? It does you credit. You are right, I want the blasted witches to come, but we will not be here when they arrive.' Again he plunged his hand into the bag, and this time produced another two guns, which he waved at me before pushing them down into his belt. 'I will trust you with one of these when the time comes. Right now I cannot; you are too prudish with the law.'

'What do you mean, when the time comes?'

'I brought you because I might need an extra pair of hands,' he said, as he tugged the reins of his horse, guiding the animal to a nearby tree and making sure that a mass of bushy wilderness kept his mount concealed. We would never see that horse again.

'An extra pair of hands!' I protested. 'I will not assist you in any –'

'Boy, you are not in a position to dictate what you will or will not do,' he said, as he counted the bullets left in his gun and passed the straps of the leather bag around his shoulder. 'Now follow me; it will not be a long walk.'

'Walk where?' It was foolish to even ask that question, as I already knew how Joel would respond.

'We're going into the witches' den.'

37

We followed a twisted path, which was no more than a track trodden by sheep and cows. The night was eerily silent, yet my ears constantly expected the squawking of a crow or the meowing of a black cat.

'Since I might die because of this,' I whispered, 'I must ask you this question.' Joel said nothing, which was the best invitation I'd ever received from him. 'Inspector McGray dragged me here because of his sister, because a nurse claimed she heard her talking – to you.' Joel kept on walking, not even turning his head. I had to spell the question out. 'Did Miss McGray really speak to you?'

Joel snorted. 'Oh, not you as well!'

'Miss McGray has not spoken in years.'

'Indeed, she had not.'

'Oh! So she did talk to you!'

'That's none of your business, boy.'

'It bloody well is now! I would be sleeping in a soft, warm bed, without my entire body being covered in bruises and scratches and burns, had that little brat not decided to suddenly open her bloody –'

Joel seized my jaw and covered my mouth, his leather glove squeezing my face like a clamp.

'*Be quiet,*' he hissed. 'It is not far now.'

He turned on his heels and within minutes we reached a dense stand of oaks and birches, growing around a low stone wall. We were at the very edge of Pendle Hill, its snowy slopes ascending steeply but a few hundred yards away. Between us and the peak there was a small valley, flanked by very tall trees, and in one corner, nestled snugly among the trees, stood the gloomy mass of Cobden Hall.

There was light coming from its many windows, and I could see that it was a very odd building, its L-shaped layout a rather incongruous mixture of architectural styles.

The shorter wing had arresting windows with pointed arches, the granite carved into the intricate shapes of an ancient cathedral. The longer, larger wing looked a few centuries newer, its tall chimneys and decorated gables undeniably Tudor.

There were two carriages parked by the entrance. One of them was Redfern's, newly arrived. The other, however, was larger and well polished, so that it reflected even the faint glimmer from the windows. It had been pulled by four magnificent horses, their coats as white and pristine as the snow around them.

I was going to ask to whom those could belong, but Joel raised a hand, bidding silence. Then I saw the bright, yellow eyes of a cat. Its black fur was visible only against the snowy ground.

The little animal walked past us, and Joel would not move until it was lost in the shadows. Crouching, he walked along behind the wall, until we found a small, round structure made of eroded stone. It reminded me of the abandoned kiln that the witch Nettle called home, but it had no apparent entrance, or flue. It rather looked like a solid mass of rock with no purpose.

Joel took off a glove and dusted the snow away, feeling the stone underneath with his fingertips. At a certain point he stopped, scraped off frozen moss and then felt the stone again.

'This is it,' he mumbled, touching a large, round rock, as big as a beer barrel.

I realized it was a large lump of pumice, porous and light enough to be lifted by a single man. It reminded me of the crumbly debris around Lord Ambrose's desecrated tomb. Joel pushed it aside, and I saw the deep blackness of a wide well. Joel produced a little taper, which, when ignited, glowed with a small yet persistent blue flame.

'If they see this,' he whispered, 'they may think it's carried by one of them, for a little while, at least.'

In that cerulean light I saw a neat set of stone steps, descending steeply into impenetrable darkness.

'Follow me, boy,' Joel said, going down the first few steps but holding the gun firmly. 'Do *not* try anything funny, please. I honestly don't want to have to shoot you.'

I followed him down, into the damp, fetid air of what turned out to be a narrow tunnel. I had expected it to be a dank little hole, but those underground walls were lined with granite slabs, their polished surfaces reflecting the unsteady glow of Joel's candle. The stones rose in a soft curve to a pointed-arch ceiling.

'They used this tunnel to bring in priests to celebrate Mass,' Joel told me, and then the gracefulness of the passage made sense: one would not expect the reverent Catholics to make their priests slither through a grubby mud tunnel. 'This was built just as they expanded the original wing,' he added. 'These hidey-holes are always

364

easier to insert into a building during its inception. The Oakleys knew about it, but never told the other witches of its existence.'

'How come *you* know about it?'

There was a chilling draught, which made me shiver along with Joel's answer.

'I had it from that Oakley girl. She used to live here until my mother took the property off her family – the information I managed to squeeze out of her . . .'

I thought again of the torn apron, and a dozen ghastly images of Joel torturing the young nurse rushed into my head. I forced myself to push them aside. 'Do you really believe the witches have not found this tunnel yet?'

'I do not know, boy, but this was designed to fool the best Crown searchers during the Reformation. I would not expect someone to stumble across it . . . unless they're consciously looking for it.'

'I hope you are right,' I murmured, 'or our visit here will be quite brief.'

We continued along the passage, which ran in a very straight line. Joel's taper illuminated the few yards ahead of us, and beyond the light the tunnel disappeared into thick shadows. I thought of a wolf's throat, waiting patiently for us to tread well inside, and then its jaws closing upon us when it was too late to turn back.

That moment came sooner than I expected, and I saw the abrupt end of the tunnel: a spiral stair, its steps as regular and smooth as those at the entrance, ascending through a narrow opening. I was feeling increasingly apprehensive: I felt we must be underneath the very core of the manor, and I had no gun in my hands, or any means to defend myself.

Joel went up very slowly, each step a calculated, careful movement. I hesitated, but then the blue light shining on the granite stone became weaker, fading as he took the taper away. I nearly gasped, imagining myself trapped alone in that place and in utter darkness, and so I rushed forwards.

I caught the flame's last glimmer, but for a terrifying second I found myself blinded. I had to grope about, my hands anxiously feeling the cold walls around me until finally they opened up into a damp chamber.

Joel was standing there, looking upwards and admiring the hollow in the dim light.

The place must have been two or three yards long, and just as wide, but it was its vaulted ceiling that amazed me: it was a mosaic of saints, angels and Virgin Marys, carved in all types of stone. I saw marble, sandstone, granite of all shades. The pieces, mostly busts and faces, had been cut out into shapes that fit snugly together, like an ancient jigsaw, leaving no empty spaces.

Even though the chamber was empty, it was evident we were in a small chapel, and I felt a tingle all over my skin. I have never been of a spiritual disposition, but even I could not fail to be moved. It was as if that place were still crammed with the souls of all those dead priests and their secret congregation. I pictured them risking everything to save their relics, even if they had to cut off the heads and forget the rest, and then lovingly carving and fitting them together in that safe haven. I could imagine the clandestine Masses, that little chapel ablaze with candles and a flock as jam-packed as the saints who looked at them from above.

'This was an old fireplace,' Joel said after a moment. 'The centre of the building must be much older than Tudor or Elizabethan. This would have been one of those big open hearths, built to heat the entire building in the Middle Ages. In Tudor times those went out of fashion, so it would not have been at all suspect to cover it up when this wing was redesigned. Clever people.'

I was surprised by how learned Joel turned out to be. The man was incredibly intelligent, but that only made his actions more upsetting.

Joel walked around the chapel, holding the light up close to the walls and feeling the bricks with his fingertips.

'There has to be a way in,' he whispered, but so softly I had to guess half his words.

He prodded a section where the stones seemed particularly eroded, and then blew the candle out.

Not a single thing could be seen. I swallowed, if only to remind myself that there was something else in the world other than that blackness, and then I heard a very gentle rubbing.

A thin, dim line of light appeared before my eyes, as Joel opened a door I had not even seen. I thought it would be an exit, but instead that door led to a sort of empty wardrobe built into the wall.

The golden light came from the back wall of that cavity, through two horizontal cracks, just a fraction of an inch wide and expertly blended into the pattern of bricks: spyholes that looked into the manor.

The chapel was connected to the main building through that little passage, less than two feet deep. Perhaps it had also served as a watchman's post, or a 'fake chamber' – if someone discovered the spyholes and made their way in, they would only see the first small section and think that was the actual hideout, while the main chapel remained hidden behind it.

I saw Joel's black outline, his long fingers bidding me to come and have a look. I did not want to stand so close to him but my curiosity was greater than my fear. We squeezed together in that dusty cleft, pressing our faces against the surprisingly warm stone, peeping through the slits.

The smell of burning wood hit my nose, and together with the amber glow told me we were standing right behind the wall of another, albeit smaller fireplace.

The one that warmed the study of Britain's most feared witch.

38

It was an ideal spying hole: the fire lit our view, and it also kept people away; not even scullions like to spend too long cleaning the ashen depths of a hearth.

Squinting, for my pupils were wider than the slit, I saw a room that could at once have been a library, a veterinarian's operating room, a chemist's lab and a botanist's greenhouse.

The fireplace and a dozen candles lit shelves packed with enormous books; pots with mushrooms, cacti and other fleshy plants; cages for rats, ferrets and crows; vases containing slithering snakes, frogs and spiders. Along with the smell of burning wood came the aromas of countless different herbs, minerals . . . and also the ghastly tang of fresh blood.

I heard a slow, yet constant drip, and a repugnant splatter, as my eyes moved towards a large work table. A chilling sight it was, covered with a disarray of herbs and flasks, as well as sharp instruments and sopping red rags.

A giant shadow was projected over all the artefacts, far larger than the body it mimicked: that of a very old woman, barely five feet tall, with a wide waist and short, stumpy arms, which moved spasmodically over the table. I could not quite see what she was dissecting, but her wrinkled hands were soaked in dark, slimy blood.

A black cat jumped on to the table, gingerly approaching the crone's hands, which offered it a revolting piece of whitish meat.

I forced myself to look up, to that ancient face. She had leathery skin, gnarled as the bark of a tree and stretched over sharp bones. Her eyes were mere slits surrounded by folds of skin, sunken in deep sockets, making her face look like a living skull.

If someone had told me that the Devil was a woman, I would have definitely believed it.

For an instant I thought she had wings, but it was the shadows playing a macabre trick: perched on her left shoulder there was an enormous, hairy bat. Its coriaceous black wings were tipped with long, sharp claws that clung to the hag's clothes. With a coat of golden fur around its neck, and large, glassy eyes, it looked more like a fox with wings. It was the largest bat I'd ever seen, and my memory went back to my childhood years, leafing through my grandfather's zoology books.

'Mrs Marigold?'

It was the deep, deferential voice of one of her muscled servants, standing by the door.

The witch lifted her face. Nothing could be seen of her eyes, and only a tiny glimmer revealed she had any.

'You got this letter,' the man said, handing her a fine envelope. 'And that lord is here . . . Cecil or what's his name.'

I had to cover my mouth to repress a gasp.

Could he actually mean Robert Cecil – Lord Salisbury? If so, that witch was about to receive our prime minister!

She wiped her hands with a greasy cloth, and spoke with a rasping, commanding voice: 'Brought the lady?'

'Aye.'

'Damn, I told him not to! Bring him in. Only him.'

As the man left she carefully tore the envelope open; however, she ignored the letter, which she tossed aside, and instead focused on the wrapping. She flattened it and passed the paper over a candle flame. As she did so, brown letters seemed to appear as if by magic.

How many means of communication did they have? Cats, ravens, beacons, secret vinegar writing . . .

Marigold covered the work table with a black cloth, rinsed her hands in a small basin and then sat on an old, very ornate oak chair.

The guard returned, and I strained to see whoever entered the room. Having recently met the prime minister in person, I knew what to expect.

Thankfully, it was not him.

A much younger man, thin and with a feeble frame, came in. His very fine suit seemed completely out of place, as did the top hat he clasped nervously.

He looked around the room and gulped, but was not nearly as shocked as I had been. I could tell he'd been there before.

'Come,' Marigold said, her blotchy hand beckoning the man closer. 'Quickly, William. I can't have you here for very long.'

He obeyed, as sheepishly as a young boy. As he walked right past the fireplace I recognized the familiar brow, its lines so soft it did not project any shadows around those scared eyes. My mind flew back to my brother and father discussing politics, and I remembered that name. The man before us was indeed a Cecil, but not the most prominent one. We were looking at the prime minister's second son, a lord in his own right, yet Marigold had addressed him by his given name, as contemptuously as if he were a homeless drunk.

His trembling mouth tried to speak, but Marigold jumped in first, startling him.

'I told you not to bring your woman.'

Lord William Cecil barely managed to reply. 'She . . . she insisted.'

'Then she must be more frightening than me,' Marigold mocked. Lord Cecil shifted his weight from leg to leg, and the witch enjoyed his discomfort. 'Are you absolutely sure you want to do this?'

He wiped cold sweat from his forehead, his eyes fixed on the hairy head of the enormous bat. 'Indeed, ma'am.'

'I told you. If you have children, they'll be miserable souls.'

'My wife is desperate.'

'You don't know what desperate means, son.'

She stared at him, utterly motionless, and then the black cat jumped on to her lap, licking blood off its whiskers.

'Your children will have untimely ends, gruesome destinies. And you still want them? Is this to preserve your ancestry? To keep the mighty bloodline?'

Lord Cecil stood still like a stone, barely even breathing.

Marigold stroked the cat. 'You aristocrats disgust me.'

The shaking man seemed puzzled, not knowing whether to speak, stay still or go. Marigold did not speak until the man's nerves seemed about to collapse.

'We'll help you, but only because I owe your father.'

She owed his father! Britain's prime minister. Not only did he know about the witches, but he'd done *favours* for them! I gasped, and Joel elbowed me in the ribs to keep me quiet.

I could not tell what was going on in Lord Cecil's head. He seemed relieved and terrified in equal measure.

Marigold stood up. The cat jumped down and sprinted towards the same shelf the old crone was headed for, where countless jars were neatly aligned.

'It's an easy job,' she said, looking at the handwritten labels. She opened a large jar, sniffed the contents and then poured some crushed herbs on to her palm. 'One of my sisters will visit your wife soon. In the meantime, make her a brew out of a spoonful of this, with plenty of honey; it should be the first thing she drinks in the morning and the last thing she drinks at night. It will prepare her.' Unceremoniously, she poured the powder into Lord Cecil's top hat. He looked at her with pathetically grateful eyes, as if he would drop to his knees and kiss the hem of the hag's skirts.

'How can I ever repay you?'

Marigold smirked. 'Oh, we'll let you know, William. In due course.' Then she grabbed his arm, her eyes widened a little and I managed to see a hint of grey pupils. 'There will be problems,' she said, erasing the man's smile at once. 'And they'll come soon. I warned you well.'

Saying no more, she turned back to her seat, but the bat kept its sinister eyes on Cecil, its furry neck contorted at an impossible angle.

'Wha– what shall I do when . . . when problems come?'

She waved her hand dismissively. 'If you can't handle it yourself, you know how to find us.'

'The green?'

'Yes, the green. Now *go*.'

Cecil could say no more. The tall guard, who had been there all the time, pulled him by the shoulder as if man-handling a begging child. They left and soon Lord Cecil's whimpers faded away. The door, however, did not close, and a female figure appeared.

It was Redfern, her cloak still damp from melted snow-flakes. She rushed to greet Marigold, bowing low and slowly, offering a hand engulfed in a black leather glove.

The witch shook her hand hastily. 'Did you bring them?'

'Yes, ma'am. They're outside.'

Marigold snapped her fingers and a procession of sorry figures came in.

First came two of her guards, snorting and jerking as they pulled along Nine-Nails McGray. He was gagged and blindfolded, still putting up a fight, even though his heavy steps revealed that he was exhausted.

One of the men kicked his calf as they both pushed him to his knees, not a yard from where Marigold sat.

Behind came another man, slightly shorter than the other two, carrying Caroline's inert body. I heard Joel inhale sharply as he saw his daughter; her head, still wrapped in the filthy bag, dangled limply from her slen-der neck. Joel's hand scratched at the stone, and I had to squeeze his shoulder to remind him of the thin ice on which we stood.

Then, after them all, came somebody else, guarded by

a fourth brute. It was a young woman, her head bent in shame, her small, pale hands tightly interlaced in front of her. I blinked in disbelief when I saw her face.

Miss Oakley.

I'd been certain she was dead! Why had Joel not told me? I could only wonder what had happened on that hill. How had her bloodstained apron ended up there?

'What a nasty pile of filth,' said Marigold, her voice sending McGray into a fit of rage. The guards kicked him right in the spine. 'Keep him quiet. I want to talk to this little traitor first.'

She pointed at Oakley, and the girl's legs nearly failed her, her face as white as bones. The guard behind her thrust her forwards and she barely managed to keep her feet as Marigold addressed her.

'*This is all your fault, you useless swine!*'

Oakley's lip trembled. She did not even have a chance to move when Marigold jumped to her feet, as quick as a fox, to strike her with that long hand, her nails catching the skin, leaving three long scratches on Oakley's cheek.

The girl fell sideways, screeching in pain, and curled up on the floor, covering her head with shaking hands.

Marigold hovered over her, the bat's wings spread as the animal tried to keep its balance.

'I couldn't care less about that stupid Pimblett – but *Greenwood*! Greenwood is dead. One of my most promising girls! And her death brought these police bastards upon us! Now they've even found our most precious stocks! How could you be such an imbecile?' She grabbed the girl by the hair, pulling her head up. 'At least have the decency to look at me when I speak!'

Oakley's chest was heaving. Terrified as she was, there was a spark of fury in her eyes.

'Our most important rule,' Marigold barked. 'Only write in Grimorium. Keep it all in your damned head otherwise. Two hundred years of our work, and you left it all in the open. I wish I had left you and your bastard child to die in the slums when you came begging for help. Your wretched parents must be turning in their grave.'

'I'm sorry,' Oakley managed to say, but there was only anger in her voice.

'Not sorry enough,' Marigold retorted, 'but you *will* be. You know what we do to witches who go astray, don't you?' Marigold produced a long, shiny glass knife from the folds of her skirts, and Oakley's eyes nearly fell out of their sockets. 'Yes, you do know. We cut their tongues out and send them into the wild, my dear.'

I shuddered, thinking of poor old Nettle, and how the only sounds she could utter were groans from her throat.

Marigold pushed Oakley away. 'We'll deal with you properly in due course.'

Then the witch turned to McGray, the sharp knife reflecting the many quivering flames in the room. Her eyes widened gradually, from mere dark slits to yellow, veiny globes. She pointed at him with the knife and the guards pulled away the blindfold and the filthy rag from his mouth.

Nine-Nails shook his head and moved his numb jaw sideways. When his eyes met Marigold's he made a frank retch.

'Yer one ugly bitch.'

She smirked, taking a small step closer to him, the

knife aiming directly at Nine-Nails' right eye, but he did not move an inch.

Marigold brought the knife closer and closer to McGray, and just as I thought it would pierce his cornea she pulled a green apple out of a pocket, and with a swift movement she cut out a wedge, which she fed to her repulsive pet.

'No, I won't spoil you yet. First I want you to tell me a few things. How did you find our warehouse? Was it the imbecile Judge Spotson?'

'Bugger off,' McGray answered, but it was as if Marigold could read his mind.

'We didn't give him the proper dose, then,' she said. 'We have controlled the Lancaster judges for a long time: they give us leeway to do our business through those ports. Occasionally we have to compromise, like when a shipment of opium was discovered by a damn customs officer who wouldn't take a bribe. Pimblett had to be the scapegoat and claim he'd been working alone. Unfortunate man; we had agreed to reward him most handsomely when he came out of jail.' She shrugged. 'Better for us; saved us quite a bit of money at the end of the day.

'Spotson was particularly helpful that time. He had to be; he owed us a few favours. Oh yes, we have boosted many, many careers in the past century. Sadly, we have to silence people when they're of no use to us any more, but we have to do it discreetly. We prefer to kill them, of course, but we can't do it all the time, or the new judges wouldn't want to help us.

'Spotson must remember more than I would like . . .' She scratched the furry head of her bat. 'I suppose he is

old and frail enough to die without arousing much suspicion.' She turned to Redfern. 'Make sure it happens soon.
We can't take more risks right now.'

Marigold went back to McGray. 'My last question,
before we let you – rest in peace.'

She ran a knotty, twisted finger along McGray's jaw, a
repulsive nail pressing just hard enough not to tear his
skin. 'Why, young man, are you so interested in our affairs?'

He held her nasty stare. 'Doing my job, ye stinking hag.'

Marigold laughed. 'Yes, doing your job. A little too
well. We know how your . . . police works. Why follow
Ardglass all the way here and so desperately? You went
well beyond the line of duty.'

Her fingernail stopped and she pressed harder. A second
later I saw a trickle of blood running down Nine-Nails'
cheek.

'I came all the way here . . .' he began, ''cos I wanted to
say *how now* to Lancashire's ugliest midnight hags.'

She slapped him, but McGray's head did not even
move. Then she tossed the apple aside to seize McGray
with one hand, wielding the knife with the other. The
blade rushed towards McGray's eye, catching the light of
the candles before –

'His sister spoke to Joel!' Oakley screeched, and Marigold's head immediately turned to her.

'What?'

'This man's sister is also an inmate in Lord Ardglass's
asylum.'

A wide grin appeared on Marigold's face, wrinkling
that dry skin like sheets of parchment. The bulging eyes,
mad with delight, were bloodcurdling.

'Tell me more, dear,' she whispered, dropping McGray's face and once more leaning over Oakley. 'What makes that "talk" so special?'

The girl cowered. 'That girl's crazy. She hadn't spoken a word in more than five years. I heard the head nurse telling Dr Clouston that Miss McGray had spoken for the first time. She had spoken to Ardglass. I am sure Mr McGray wants to know what she said. Everyone in Edinburgh knows he's obsessed with his mad sister.'

Nine-Nails growled. 'Ye bitch! How come Joel didnae shove some poison down yer bloody throat?'

Marigold was clicking her tongue, looking back at him with the most derisive stare. 'Is that all?'

McGray did not have to reply; his grimace was eloquent enough.

'Then I seriously overestimated you,' Marigold said. 'On good grounds, though. You have a reputation, Adolphus, of being far too interested in us witches. My girls heard many times about the nine-fingered man who was too keen to find witchcraft books, demonologies, cures for curses . . . At least now I'm sure you're no threat.'

Marigold went back to her ornate chair, all of us staring at her expectantly. Nobody spoke or moved until she bid so, and she seemed to take her time. She wiped the knife before pocketing it, and then interlaced her fingers, studying Oakley, McGray, and then Caroline.

When at last she did speak, her words were poison.

'Prepare the Ardglass girl for the stake. I want it done with before dawn.'

Joel could not hold back a hiss, and I knew I should not even attempt to silence him. I saw the black cat pacing alarmingly close to the fireplace, its big, yellow eyes perusing the fake brick wall.

Fortunately Marigold was much too busy to look at her cat.

'And the Scot?' asked Redfern as soon as the large man had taken Caroline away.

'Kill him as soon as you can,' Marigold said, as if ordering milk in her tea. McGray seemed rather unaffected, but he did react upon the witch's next words. 'And send someone to take care of that insane sister of his, as a matter of urgency. Ardglass might have shared our secrets with her too.'

'*The fuck, ye will!*' McGray roared, so loud I thought the walls shook, and struggled as the two men forced him out. 'I'm gonnae kill ye myself, ye auld crock! I'm gonnae kill all o' youse!'

McGray's raucous yelling took a while to fade; his booming voice must have been heard throughout Cobden Hall.

We could still hear the echoes as Marigold snapped at Oakley, for the girl was still crouched miserably against the crammed shelves.

'Get out of my sight! You're a disgrace to us all! You'll be lucky if you and your bastard brat live to tell the tale.'

Oakley dragged herself out of the room, her legs barely responding, her wails mixing with McGray's distant echoes.

Redfern was the only one left. Old as she was, her skin appeared smooth next to Marigold's, and her commanding tone seemed reduced to the weepy voice of a teenager: 'What shall we do about that beacon?'

Marigold slapped at the bat, and the animal flew up to perch upside down by one of the ceiling beams, wrapping itself in its sinewy wings.

'That blasted beacon!' she sneered. 'Appearing when we least needed it.'

I assumed they were talking about the fire Joel had started by the ash tree.

'Are all our sisters here?' Marigold asked.

'Nearly all, ma'am, but we're still missing a few.'

'And the ravens?'

Redfern frowned and her crow's feet deepened. 'We sent a couple, ma'am, but none has returned yet.'

The oldest witch scratched a wart on her chin. Now that everyone had gone, she allowed herself to show some self-doubt.

'Did you say Ardglass was fluent in the code?'

Redfern frowned again, visibly embarrassed. 'Enough to fool me, ma'am.'

Marigold rolled those hideous eyes. 'We can't risk it. Send three men – men only. If it's a trap, we can spare brainless muscle.'

Redfern bowed again, and like the others she walked away. Mercifully, the black cat ran after her.

Marigold remained in her chair for a moment, her fingertips pressed together and her eyes now dark slits again, almost as if she could retract them back into their sockets at will. We could have waited there for a very long time, but then there came the roar of a very familiar, very Scottish voice. Then thumping, female shouting and cats hissing.

The witch leaned forwards, as the panicked voice of one of the thugs called out.

'The Scot's escaping!'

Marigold jumped to her feet, grabbed a bloodstained cleaver from her work bench and hurried out.

Joel groped about and I heard the tinkle of metal. He was pulling on rusty iron rings nailed into the stone. 'Step back, son.'

As I did so he was already pulling the entire wall, also made of pumice, which opened inwards to create a gap barely wide enough to let us through. Some burning ashes stuck to our boots as Joel sprinted through the fireplace and into the witches' lair.

39

I leaped after him, the flames licking at my trousers, and I had no choice but to pat them out with my bare hands.

Joel did not lose an instant. He was already throwing jars into his leather bag. One of them was full of little spiders, and I caught a glimpse of the characteristic red spots of black widows.

'Witches,' I said scornfully, staring at that collection of sinister paraphernalia. 'They do not do magic! It is all trickery and show and lies.'

'It's not that black and white, son.' Then he looked at me with the sternest of expressions. 'We're getting Caroline.'

I had to laugh. 'That is bloody suicide!'

He aimed his pistol directly at my face. 'I said it would pain me to shoot you, not that I would not do it. Step out and do as I say.'

I stood my ground.

'Your friend is out there too!'

Just as he barked that, I heard McGray hollering again.

'That "friend" has got me cornered in this blasted place as much as –'

'*Step out!*' he roared, pushing the gun against my chest, and before I knew it I was out in a gloomy corridor, the yelling of women and thugs coming from all directions.

A very tall man approached, a wall of muscles emerging out of the darkness. I barely registered the waxed moustache we'd seen in Lancaster, and his eyes had not even time to widen before Joel shot him right between them.

The man fell on his back with a resounding thud, and there was an immediate uproar of voices. The shot must have been heard throughout the manor, for there came a crescendo of heavy footsteps; I could even feel the wooden floors shaking. We both sprinted away aimlessly, neither of us knowing the building's layout.

'How many are there?' I panted.

'No idea,' Joel said, finally handing me one of the three guns.

We reached a corner of the corridor, just as a small figure rushed into Marigold's office: Oakley, jumping over the large corpse without even glancing down.

I thought she caught a glimpse of me, but she disappeared through the door and then I heard her gasp, surely at the open fireplace.

'Is she running away? What the –'

Joel slapped the back of my head and pressed a finger to his lips. He was not looking at me though; his eyes were fixed on the next corner, further along the corridor, where I could hear female whispers. He moved as silently as a hunting wolf, his gun held tightly, and I readied myself too.

We sneaked forwards carefully, and as soon as we reached the corner Joel leaped ahead, pointing his guns at the two women we found there and shouting madly.

'Where's my daughter?'

A plump, middle-aged woman stood there, white faced, with a young girl crouching right beside her.

'I know you both!' I cried, pointing my weapon alternately at each of them. I recognized the tight blonde curls of the maid at Spotson's house. 'So it was you who has been poisoning the old man!' My eyes then went to the other girl. 'And you washed McGray's clothes! You planted that accursed bird in his coat!'

'These witches get everywhere,' Joel snapped. '*Where's my daughter?*'

'We're saying nothing,' the woman said; 'she'll be dead soon,' and then she hollered her lungs out, in a voice so deep and powerful my ears ached. '*Ardglass is here!*'

Joel struck her in the face with one of the guns, the woman fell backwards and the girl ran like the wind, shouting 'Ardglass' again and again. Joel shot at her but missed, the bullet hitting the wall as the slender figure fled; he looked down at the plump woman. She was pressing a hand to her cheekbone, blood trickling through her fingers.

'Speak!'

The woman spat at him, and I knew that Joel was going to shoot her. I pushed his arm and the bullet hit the floor.

'*Damn it, boy!*'

'I will not stand by and watch you slaughter people!'

I saw that uncontrollable rage in him again, the blood rushing into his face as he slowly directed the gun towards me. The woman began to rise and this time I aimed at her.

'I did not say *you* could move!'

'These whores deserve no –'

I punched him right on the nose, so hard I heard his

septum crack, and so unexpectedly I sent him tumbling against the wall.

'I am sick of you all!' I was incandescent. 'You and *fucking* Nine-Nails. If you threaten to – *I said you could not bloody move!*'

As I shouted I plunged my hand into Joel's bag, pulled out the jar of black widows and made to throw it at the portly witch.

'There they are!' someone yelled.

Three gigantic men came running from the direction the girl had fled, followed by another young witch, and instinctively I threw the jar at them. The glass shattered on the first one's massive chest, shards and spiders flying in all directions, and the ruffians lost all their bravery. One dropped his gun and another one shrieked, as they all retreated, trying to bat the black widows away.

I caught but a glimpse of that, for Joel and I turned and ran, this time taking a different turn and finding a narrow flight of stairs.

In the distance, even through the thick walls, the voice of Mrs Marigold could be heard, howling about both Joel and McGray being at large in the manor. She mentioned Caroline and then Joel halted, listening.

'Did she say "bring her down"?'

Those had been the words. In fact, she sounded too close for my liking.

Joel ascended, skipping steps and panting, breathless and reckless. I saw that same frenzy, that irrational drive I'd seen in McGray and Caroline. Joel was not even deterred when the steps, voices and even the cats' meowing could be heard but yards from where we were.

We reached the top of the stairs, which opened into a long, wide corridor. To our left there were wide windows with pointed arches, overlooking the manor's front lawns and letting in weak rays of moonlight; to our right there were thick oak doors, at least a dozen of them.

The place was deserted, but the voices sounded awfully near; they must all be behind one of the closer doors. The nearest one, though, was ajar, just enough to show that behind it was a broom cupboard.

My heart leaped when a chink of light began to show around the second nearest door. I scarcely had time to tug at Joel, so desperately that in one swift movement I managed to thrust both him and myself into the small cupboard, exactly as that other room opened.

Joel pulled the cupboard's door to, but the strap of his bag got caught, leaving a gap which exposed us to the hallway.

It was too late to do anything about it. Witches and guards were rushing down the stairs, each woman carrying a fir branch, and each man carrying either a pistol or a rifle.

We held our breath. We could even smell the herby scent of the witches' clothes and the stinking sweat of their protectors.

Marigold came out too, escorted by four particularly large men.

'And Redfern,' Marigold was saying. 'Where the hell is Redfern? Tell her to bring the Ardglass girl down! I want her in the courtyard as soon as the pyre is ready.'

A sound came from the floor, so faint yet so damning. It was a soft scratching at the door, and looking down

I found a black cat, its paws on the wood, trying to poke its little nose and whiskers into the cupboard.

Joel was about to kick it but I stopped him. All we could do was stand still as a dozen armed men marched past mere inches away from us, and pray they were too busy to look at that blasted feline.

Each person's step, each ruffle of their clothes resounded in my ears like a physical torture, and so did every scratch from those tiny paws.

And so we waited. Their numbers waned, until one last straggler, a teenage girl, ran awkwardly after the main crowd.

I had time to take a blissfully deep breath, and then Joel kicked the door open, sending the hissing cat into the air. The animal landed on its feet and ran to the stairs.

Through the windows, a few sparks caught our attention.

The sky had cleared, with only thin strips of cloud glimmering under the crescent moon. There was a very faint glow on the horizon, a line of indigo announcing that the sun would soon rise. In the middle of the court-yard there towered a post, already surrounded by a huge pile of logs and straw, dark against the silver snow, and there were men and women throwing more and more fuel on to it. There was a circle of witches around the pyre, each holding in her left hand a bushy branch of fir. They were lighting them up, passing the flames from torch to torch, blue balls of fire appearing all over the courtyard.

'Just when we needed a heavy snow,' Joel said, glaring

at the skies. There was no chance whatsoever of a miraculous storm smothering the bonfire.

'We cannot stay here,' I urged, prodding his arm. In all honesty, I did not have the foggiest idea as to where we should go, or what we should do.

As I ran behind Joel despair began to set in my mind. How could we possibly save Caroline? Or find McGray? Or even just get out alive for that matter?

We crossed the corridor and entered a large room, which must have been the end of the wing, for it had wide windows on three of its four walls. The stone arches and stained glass had obviously been salvaged from a church or cathedral, but the imposing structures housed a stark, empty room. The wooden floorboards bore marks of heavy furniture removed a while ago – most likely by Lady Anne, trying to squeeze profit out of the residence before being chased away.

'We should go back,' I said, feeling alarmingly exposed in that bare room. 'If one of those thugs finds us here, there is no place to –'

I was interrupted by shooting. It came from the storeys above us: a succession of blasts, echoing like thunderclaps and followed by a female shriek. There was a collective cry from the grounds and Joel and I ran to the windows.

Through the stained glass – a fragmented piece which must have been part of the Virgin Mary's robes – I saw the coven in turmoil: the witches' faces were lit by the blue flames, and they were all looking up, pointing and shouting in fear.

There was another shot, and then, mere inches from the glass I was pressing my nose against, a body fell.

I saw barely a blur, but the glimpse of a dark-haired head stuck in my mind. The body hit the ground, and even under the dim moonlight and the glimmer of the torches, the splatter of blood seemed intensely red.

It was a man's body. A tall man, wearing a familiar overcoat.

From above, from where the shots had come from, a woman bellowed in a voice that sounded like the cry of an eagle: '*The Scotchman's dead!*'

My blood ran cold.

'That cannot be,' I mumbled.

The witches cheered and someone shot the burst cadaver for good measure, but the noises came to my ears like distant echoes, as if someone had just knocked me on the head.

Why did he not listen? I thought, shock and anger clutching at my throat, my mind racing. He'd brought it all upon himself: the trip to Lancaster, the obsession with the occult, the lonely years of being avoided and mocked by everyone . . . all out of devotion to the young sister whose cure he'd never found.

I had a strange feeling I had not expected; a cold void seemed to creep from within, as I realized that Adolphus McGray had destroyed himself, and now his sad life would see no redemption.

'He did not deserve to end like this,' I found myself saying, my face frozen in front of the glass.

Marigold was coming out then, easily recognizable as she carried her winged pet on her shoulders, making her look far taller and scarier than she would on her own – all part of her sense of theatre. She walked past McGray's body, spat on it and then went on towards the pyre. She raised her wrinkled hand and waved at her coven, and they all began to dance around the stack of logs and straw. Their fir branch fires drew circles in the air, as the witches sang a macabre hymn in unison; their sharp staccato high notes were like stabs in the air, as unsettling as Mozart's most chilling requiem.

One of the guards came out carrying Caroline, which sent the women into an otherworldly ecstasy. The girl was still sedated, her limbs dangling limply as the man carried her towards the pyre.

'Not my daughter!' Joel shouted, punching the window and turning around. He sprinted across the empty room, so resolutely a bullet could not have stopped him.

It took me a moment to react, for my mind was still struggling to take in the image of McGray's dead body on the snow; my eyes were still fixed on him and the horrible splatter around his head. It must have only been a few seconds, but they felt like an eternity. Then something, and I still fail to tell what, pulled me out of the shock and I saw the guard climbing the mound of logs with Caroline in his arms, to tie her to the central post.

I ran after Joel, back into the long corridor, where I found him subdued by an enormous guard. The man held him by the torso with one arm, and with the other he clenched Joel's neck so tightly that Joel was gagging and I heard both guns thump to the floor.

I ran over to them, and with the butt of my gun and all my strength I struck the giant's temple.

The blow barely disturbed him, his grip on Joel weakening only a little. I had to strike him again, and then a third time before he let go of Joel, who was already stretching out his arms towards the dropped weapons.

The man swung his thick fist, a blow I dodged by sheer luck, and then Joel did what I'd tried to avoid: he shot the man in the back, and I had to jump backwards or his hefty body would have crushed me as it fell.

The unfortunate guard writhed and screamed, for the bullet had hit him right in the spine. I could not help feeling sorry for him, but before I could say anything Joel shouted, 'Damn!'

And again he ran off. Through the arched windows I saw that the pyre was beginning to catch fire. The witches were dancing around it, then bending down to rub their coloured torches against the logs. Over the blue glow I could see Caroline's black cape. She was still unconscious; her chin lay slack on her chest.

I stumbled down the stairs, the echoes of the chanting becoming louder as I descended, drumming in my ears. Real, tangible horrors were happening out there. The fire about to melt Caroline's body, McGray's corpse, Joel's shattered life – these were no vague, distant legends. I had spent all this time trying to persuade Nine-Nails that such things did not exist outside his occult books, only to find that the folktales had been masking something far, far worse. These people were monsters, not empowered by magic or mystic charms but by their twisted minds, by their poisons, their organization and their secret knowledge. After a wrong turn I found myself in a corridor I did not recognize, and Joel was nowhere to be seen. I was lost. Lost and alone, for McGray was dead, Caroline would soon follow, and her enraged father was running recklessly around that blasted manor.

I felt the urge to go out there and do something, but what could we do, even if we got to the fire in time? We were outnumbered; they would shoot us before we took three steps, and then perhaps throw us into the fire too. Should I flee? Should I try to at least save myself?

If I could find a way out, I might have a chance. I decided to follow the chanting, going down a corridor and around a corner, and as the singing grew louder the rooms became colder. I was on the right track.

Finally I made it to a wide entrance hall, the place scoured by wintry draughts and lit by the fire outside. To the right I could see the broad arch of the main gate; its oak doors were open wide to the snowy field.

A dark figure came out of a nearby door. I gasped, but it was only Joel. I ran to him and managed to intercept him a few steps from the main entrance.

'Let me go!' he roared, punching and kicking out, a man possessed like none I've ever seen.

As he pummelled me I tried to talk some sense into him, but then a shot silenced us both.

For an instant I thought a bullet had hit him, but then I heard a familiar voice. Female.

'Stay where you are!'

We slowly turned to the hall's main staircase, and saw Oakley coming down. She was wielding a large gun, and even from that distance I recognized the weapon that Nettle had given us, the weapon McGray had once held.

Joel spat in rage. '*You little bitch!* We had an agreement. My daughter for your life and your child's.'

Oakley looked sickly pale; her hair was dishevelled, her eyes sunken and framed by dark rings.

'I'm doing what I have to,' she hissed.

I could not contain myself either. 'You killed McGray!'

'There's nothing I wouldn't do to bring my child back.' She came closer, gnashing her teeth before she concluded, 'Cheat, lie, steal or kill.'

All of a sudden the glow outside became brighter. We could not help but turn to see the blazing pole and the crowd of men and witches around it. As the fire caught hold Mrs Marigold's bat became startled and spread its wings, the translucent skin spanning more than two yards, and the animal opened its rat-like muzzle as if to roar, showing off its long fangs.

The flames now burned furiously, spiralling and throwing smoke and green sparks up to the sky. Then, brought to us on the icy wind, came a tormented cry: a long, piercing howl that filled the air, louder than any chanting.

Caroline had awoken, and her body, dwarfed amidst the fire, now twisted and contorted in agony. The witches cheered, filling the air with an infernal racket.

An uncontrollable chill ran through my body, and I could not do anything to stop Joel, who hurled himself forwards in a reckless sprint.

'Stay here!' Oakley snarled, pressing the gun against my back. 'If you know what's best for you.'

I hardly registered her words, my eyes fixed on Joel. He ran to his daughter, and what a disturbing image that was: his black outline against the green and blue fire, shooting coldly at the heads of anyone before him – and beyond him, atop the seven-foot pyre, his beloved daughter burning alive. I could see the flames curling up her clothes and crawling swiftly towards her head, still wrapped in that jute pouch. It must have been soaked in oil, for it caught fire in an instant.

At once the eerie cheers became shrieks of panic, shooting came from everywhere and Caroline's cries became agonized, as men and witches alike fell to the ground.

I heard Marigold roaring an unintelligible order, but before she could even complete the phrase the guard closest to her came to her rescue. The tall man grabbed her by the arm and neck, huge leather-gloved hands grasping the pale, leathery skin. The witch choked as her man pulled her aside, and he threw her towards a quartet of guards who surrounded her like a protecting wall.

Joel did not get far. A shot hit him in the shoulder, and I saw a spray of blood. He did not stop, but almost instantly a second bullet caught him in the stomach, and then a third in the leg. He fell flat on the snow as a multitude of women ran to him, all of them wielding daggers, ready to rip him apart.

Marigold's protector approached as well, his boots sinking deep into the snow. They looked like a colony of black vultures about to peck and dismember a dying animal.

Behind them, Caroline let out one last, tearing scream, and then her head fell forwards as the fire engulfed the cloth bag around it.

Then Marigold roared in victory. '*The Ardglass clan is de–*'

A choke.

Then a hacking cough.

The witches halted, looking up, and then the guards opened their flanks to let everyone see what was happening to the most feared witch in the country.

She was gagging, a hand around her neck and the other stretched out, as her stout body slowly sank to the ground. The bat flapped its wings madly, until Marigold in her distress slapped it away.

The witches dropped their knives and ran to her aid. All chanting had ended. Joel's shaking body lay on the ground, quite forgotten by all hands except one. The tall guard who had just approached stood by him, then leaned down, grabbed one of Joel's arms and dragged him into the manor.

As the witches and guards gathered around the choking Marigold, this man strode up to us quite impassively.

He pulled back his black hood, but I already knew who it was. Nine-Nails opened his hand and, horribly smeared into his leather glove, I saw a tiny, shiny dead frog.

'Run, lassies,' he said, 'or we stay here for ever.'

40

McGray took off his poisoned glove, tossed it away along with the ghastly yellow frog and picked up the injured Joel. Flabbergasted, I trotted along behind him and Oakley.

'How did you do that?' I spluttered, as Oakley led us through the now familiar corridors. 'How did you get out there?'

They did not have time to answer. We could hear the enraged shouting of men coming back into the manor, their thumping footsteps ever closer. They'd been fooled for a precious few seconds, but now we had to flee.

'My girl,' Joel whispered, his mouth tainted with a trickle of blood.

We made it back to Marigold's study, stepping over the corpse of the moustachioed guard, and from behind the door came a strong oily smell.

When we walked in I saw that all the floors and furniture were covered in the witches' sticky oils. However, the mess was nothing to what I saw next.

Crouching behind Marigold's work table, swaying in confusion, was Caroline Ardglass.

She jumped up, aghast at the sight of her wounded father, and went to him with clumsy steps. She managed only to caress his cheek, and then dropped to her knees.

I caught her before she hit the floor, and perceived the nasty stench of laudanum still oozing from her hair.

I stammered. 'If she is here – then who was burning?'

'Redfern,' McGray answered quickly. 'Oakley here helped me get loose. Then we went to the room where Redfern was "preparing" Caroline, and we used her own laudanum to sedate her.'

'Didn't you hear Marigold shouting that Redfern could not be found?' said Oakley. 'Under the laudanum bag no one could see her face. You'll have to carry her,' she told me, already squeezing herself into the gap behind the fireplace. 'I gave her some smelling salts, but Redfern always used the stronger stuff.'

Caroline did not resist as I guided her to the fake wall. Oakley extended her hands to receive her on the other side, but I faltered. I did not trust that young woman at all.

'Make haste,' McGray said, and once again I had to surrender to fate.

I handed Caroline over, then squeezed myself into the hidden chapel, and turned back to receive Joel's bleeding body from McGray's arms.

Nine-Nails was the last one to come through. With his gloved hand he picked up a handful of red-hot ashes and threw them on to the oil. I caught a fleeting glimpse of bursting flames, just before he pulled shut the stone door and sealed it. There was a moment of darkness but then Oakley lit a candle stub.

'Quickly,' she said. 'This won't burn for long.'

We heard muffled screams behind the thick stone walls, but they faded away as soon as we descended into the long tunnel.

'You played your cards well,' I said to Oakley, recall-
ing Joel's words, 'never letting them know about this
passage.'

She grunted. 'My mother always told me that witches
never forgive. If things ever went wrong, this truly was
her only way out.'

I followed the waning flame of her candle as we rushed
along. Caroline managed the first few yards, but after that
I had to carry her.

'How is he?' Caroline asked. Despite my most gentle-
manly efforts I had to hold her close to me in that narrow
tunnel, and could not help feeling her pounding heartbeat against my own chest.

'Holding on, lass,' McGray replied, and I heard Joel's
troubled breathing. 'Barely.'

Oakley dropped the tiny candle, but as the fire died
out I saw the faintest of gleams bouncing off the stones.
We had reached the end of the passage, and the earliest light of dawn was trickling through. I could not
remember ever feeling so relieved by the simple sight of
daylight.

The relief did not last long. After Oakley climbed the
stone steps, the light showed us Joel's clothes, his shirt
soaked in red. Caroline gasped and again, all decorum
aside, I had to bring a hand to her head and gently make
her look away. It was unfortunate that McGray and Joel
ascended first, for Caroline had a full view of the trail of
her father's blood.

We emerged by the stone wall. My memory of being
there as Joel opened the passage was as blurry as if it had
happened days ago.

McGray laid him on the ground, resting the poor man's back against the trunk of a thick oak.

'We cannot stop now, we are still too close,' I muttered, looking back at Cobden Hall. The bonfire was still roaring, throwing a column of black smoke towards the indigo skies. There was also smoke coming from broken windows. We were still so near I could perfectly see the silhouettes of witches and men running about.

However, nobody was listening.

Caroline pulled herself free and dropped to her knees. Of all the horrors she'd witnessed, the maimed body of her father must be by far the worst. She took one of his long hands and kissed it, heedless of the dirt and the blood.

Joel took in painful, whistling breaths. 'My poor creature,' he began with tremendous effort. 'You must love me so much.'

She fell apart, pressing his hand against her cheek and sobbing as she felt it go colder.

I felt so sorry for her, but part of me could never forget that he was a murderer. He had poisoned and tortured. He had dragged us all into that mad quest, and we were not safe yet.

'I did everything for you,' he said. 'I tried to get rid of them before they reached *you* and made your life miserable.'

'You should have told me,' she sobbed. 'We could have gone away. I would have taken you anywhere.'

'Don't ever think what *could* have –'

He coughed and spat blood; I could tell that one of the bullets had hit his lungs. Every breath seemed an agony, but to my surprise he raised his eyes to McGray, and then said the same words he'd uttered back in Edinburgh.

'You'd do anything for her, would you not? Your sister. If you could have her back, you'd do anything.'

McGray was just as astonished. 'Aye.'

'So you understand me.'

'Cannae condone what you've done, but aye, I see why you went this far.'

He was touching the stump of his missing finger, mortified. How much of himself could he be seeing in Joel? Did he now fear that he might become something like him? Perhaps he already had and I myself was too blind to see it.

Joel had another fit of coughing. Caroline produced a handkerchief and wiped the blood from his mouth.

'Amy . . .' he began. 'She told me . . .'

There was more coughing. None of us could tell whether he'd manage to utter the next word, and McGray was holding his breath.

All his searching, all his anguish, all these years looking at Pansy, longing for a word, for answers . . . It all came down to this moment.

I shall never forget the look on his face, distorted by all those emotions rushing in as he stood there, powerless, hanging on the next word of the dying Joel Ardglass.

Joel inhaled most painfully. We all thought that was the end of him, but he managed to whisper: 'She told me – *don't do it.*'

McGray frowned deeply, as if he'd heard the most unbelievable lie.

'In a rant,' Joel added, 'I told her what I was up to . . . I told her about the witches, about Marigold, about every-thing. And she said – *don't do it.* Wonderful girl. She tried to warn you too.'

Tears pooled in McGray's eyes. He pulled at his hair in frustration, surely a million questions rushing to his head. And no time left to ask them.

'Will she speak again?' he said. A pointless question, but that was all he managed to say.

Joel smiled. 'She'll be fine. I left her some charms . . . to protect her.'

A lonely tear ran down McGray's cheek, but his voice did not falter. 'What d'ye mean? Was it a witch that turned Pansy insane?'

But Joel did not reply. He gulped painfully and looked back at Caroline. 'You're so beautiful too . . . My beautiful gir–'

His voice failed then. He could not even cough any more.

'Stay with me,' Caroline implored. She squeezed his hand, as if desperately trying to keep him in this world, but he could not be helped. 'Stay with me for ever.'

Joel looked up, at the dim stars still visible in the dawn-ing sky, and for a brief moment there was peace in his eyes. That blissful expression settled on his face, then the spark faded, and he never moved again.

41

Poor Caroline did not have a moment to grieve.

Out of respect I let her close Joel's eyelids, but we could not spend another minute there. Right away I pulled her upwards, easily. It was as though she'd lost all her will; the only trace of spirit was her hand, still clenched around her father's. She did not let go even when McGray lifted Joel's lifeless body; she held the pale, icy fingers as she trotted to keep up with Nine-Nails' strides.

We all followed Oakley, who made her winding way north, taking us through the wilderness rather than along the roads. The sky was lightening unnervingly fast, and with each step we took I expected to see or hear the witches' men, coming to get us – and make us pay for Marigold's life. Would they already know it was Redfern they'd burned? That it was not Nine-Nails lying dead in the courtyard? We could not possibly tell. Yet.

'Where are ye taking us?' McGray asked.

'If Lord Ardglass kept his word, there should be help on the way.'

'Help?' I repeated.

'Yes. We had a plan.'

'Pray explain.'

Oakley did not slow down as she spoke. 'You two surely remember that night, the night Lord Ardglass lured Redfern and me to that fire on Winfold Fell . . .'

'Course we remember,' said McGray, and Oakley shuddered.

'Lord Ardglass dragged me away and was ready to kill me. He nearly made me swallow a nasty strychnine pill . . . I begged for mercy, told him I had a daughter to look after . . . and he made me an offer.'

'An offer?' I echoed.

'Yes. He asked me to get the witches off his daughter's track. In exchange he would pretend to kidnap my child – and my best friend's – from the Slaidburn inn. Lord Ardglass would make it look as if he'd taken them as part of his revenge. He'd give his name, make it clear it had been him. We also left my apron in the open, stained with raven's blood, so that you two' – she looked at McGray and me – 'would think me dead and stop following me. Then I was supposed to go to Cobden Hall, and tell Redfern and Marigold some makeshift story to take their attention away from Miss Ardglass. Lord Ardglass would eventually give me the girls, and we'd stage my death and then I'd be free! I could escape with them and go wherever I wanted. It was a good plan. He kept his word and did his part, taking the children just before Miss Ardglass arrived in Slaidburn. I was going to do *my* part too, I swear! I went to Mrs Marigold, but she was furious and didn't let me speak! Redfern had told her all about my notes left in the open. They said they'd do horrible things to me and my child. Before I could explain, somebody else came in to say they'd found the trail of Miss Ardglass . . .' her voice faltered, 'so they locked me up and went after her. And I feared the worst! I feared Lord Ardglass would think I had betrayed him, and then – well, you saw what he did to my dear friend Elizabeth . . .'

Caroline staggered. She dropped Joel's hand and I thought she would hurl herself at Oakley, but the poor girl was utterly drained, body and soul.

Oakley glared at her. 'I feared the absolute worst. No – I was almost certain. I could see Lord Ardglass in my head, thinking I'd failed him, doing the worst things to our little girls. But then some of our sister witches saw this beacon by the edge of Pendle Hill. The same beacon Lord Ardglass had agreed to light up when the children were safe with the exiled witch.'

'Nettle,' McGray said, and Oakley nodded.

'Yes, some people call her that. I could not be sure Lord Ardglass had gone on with our scheme; however, as long as there was hope, even a fool's hope, that the girls were alive, I had to do what I could. That is why I decided to help Mr McGray free himself from the guards' grip.'

'Fire bottle,' he added.

'Then he asked me to take him to Miss Ardglass. I knew Redfern would be in the small parlour where they prepare people for the pyre – rubbing them with oils so they burn faster. I took a bottle of Redfern's own laudanum and threw it at her. There was only one guard . . .'

'A piece o' cake to knock down,' McGray added with a note of pride. 'We had an unconscious brute and an unconscious witch in front of us, so I immediately thought of swapping us all.'

I looked at the plain trousers he had put on at the inn. 'Do you realize that *not* wearing tartan just saved all our lives?'

He looked at them dejectedly. 'Aye, I'll let ye have that this once.'

Oakley continued. 'As Mr McGray swapped coats I ran to Mrs Marigold's study to fetch the poisonous frog.' She nodded at me. 'I believe you saw me going back there.'

'Yes,' I replied, 'I did.'

'Then Mr McGray took Redfern's body to the fire, with her face covered, while I took the *real* Miss Ardglass back to the passage, and then used the unconscious guard to create a distraction. I nearly tore my arms off dragging him to the roof, where I shot Mr McGray's gun before throwing the body to the ground. That allowed the real Mr McGray to fasten Redfern to the stake without people paying too much attention to him.'

'Then I planned to find my way to Marigold and touch her with the wee frog,' said McGray. 'She probably would've suspected something, but Joel's shooting gave me the perfect excuse; I pretended to be protecting that auld hag. I'm only sorry I couldnae get to him sooner.'

'I told Lord Ardglass to stay where he was,' Oakley said, 'but he didn't listen.'

McGray looked at the lifeless body he was carrying. 'He thought his lass was dying.'

'However,' Oakley went on, 'he reminded me of our agreement. He mentioned it before running out to his death. That's why I think Nettle will meet us here. Lord Ardglass must have thought the same as me: *do my part of the deal and hope the other one does as well.*' She brought a shaky hand to her chest, her eyes now flickering all about the woodland. 'She should be around here . . . or not too far, good Nettle. I'm so happy she lives so close to Slaidburn. No hands could be tenderer.'

'We are several miles from her hut,' I remarked. 'It is

not an easy distance for a woman her age, let alone carrying two children along.'

'She'll be here,' said Oakley, but with a hint of desperation in her eyes, as though trying to convince herself more than anybody else.

We all looked around anxiously, all except for Caroline, who took Joel's hand again and rubbed it gently, as if trying to keep it warm.

The sound of a cracking twig came from the distance, loud in the quiet morning. It could have been anything, or anyone, but none of us dared say a word.

McGray held his breath, taking a small step back. I followed his gaze and saw the black coat of a rather big cat. I touched the butt of my gun, ready to take the animal down, but as it approached its features became familiar.

'That's Nettle's cat,' said McGray.

Oakley assented, her face glistening with hope. She ran to the cat, kneeled down and took it in her arms. By then we could already hear the footsteps of a dozen feet.

'She's not alone,' I gasped, fearing Nettle would arrive with an army of tall men behind her.

Her hunched, stumpy figure did appear, blurry at first in the morning haze, and a tall man to her right. To her left, however, came two shorter female figures.

Caroline looked up and opened her mouth, but struggled to make a sound. She finally let out a deep cry: 'Bertha!' and she ran to the silhouettes with her arms wide open. 'I thought they'd burned you!'

I first saw the haggard face of Mrs Greenwood, but then I recognized Bertha, receiving Caroline into a tight embrace, her elderly voice sweet and welcoming.

'Dear child, they didn't. Only nearly. They shot poor Mr Greenwood, but Jed took his wife and me out of there just in time.'

The cat jumped out of Oakley's arms and she rose, just as Nettle came up, carrying a little bundle of blankets.

'Primrose! My girl!' Oakley burst into tears of joy, taking the baby with motherly tenderness.

McGray's face showed the merest hint of a smile. 'Good to see ye, hen,' he told Nettle, and the elderly woman squeezed his arm affectionately.

Then Bertha saw Joel's body, and her reaction was second only to Caroline's, whom she embraced more tightly.

'Oh, my dear, I am so, so sorry.'

Caroline buried her face in Bertha's shoulder, and at last allowed herself to cry. She let out a torrent of tears she had surely been repressing all this time.

They were all so emotional I was the only one left to think of the practicalities.

'We need to move on,' I told Jed. 'How did you come here? Do you have transport?'

'Aye, boss. We took a cart. I think the same one youse two stole before.'

'Yes, that's the one,' said Mrs Greenwood, carrying a sleepy five-year-old with pink ribbons carefully braided into her dark hair. Daisy. The little girl already bore an uncanny resemblance to the late Elizabeth Greenwood, but her wide blue eyes suggested she might grow up to be even more beautiful.

Perhaps I'd been too miserable for far too long, but the sight of that innocent child, her entire life still ahead of her, full of possibilities, filled my heart with inexplicable warmth.

'Very well,' I said. 'Take us there. The further and sooner we go, the better.'

We started off, but Oakley, Nettle and Mrs Greenwood lagged behind.

'What are you waiting for?' I asked, all impatience.

'We stay here,' said Oakley, and Nettle nodded fervently.

'Excuse me?'

'We have a place to go. A fresh start for us all.'

I was about to protest, but McGray spoke to me in a manner that admitted no objections.

'Let them go, Frey.' And then concluded: 'This is not our jurisdiction. Don't ye keep saying that?'

With no arguments – or support, or even energy – I obliged.

We marched on through the woods, a very sad parade led by Jed and McGray, sharing the load of Joel's body, followed by Caroline and Bertha, and then me. Ian Frey: always alone.

I turned back once, but Mrs Greenwood and the former witches were already gone; they had vanished, as if they had never existed. The only trace they left behind was the black cat, seated proudly on a tree stump, its watchful eyes making sure we went away.

Epilogue

Oakley's garden was lit by the dancing flames of a small bonfire, surrounded by nothing but slush and upturned soil. The plants had been dug over mercilessly: no bulb, root or stem had been forgiven, and they'd all been piled in the centre of the patch.

I had not bothered inspecting the place. We might well be burning frozen potatoes, but I would take no risks; I did not want anybody scavenging for potion ingredients.

Constable McNair was still throwing lashings of fuel oil on to the heap, for the foliage had been terribly cold and damp, and now the plants singed and crackled, their woody shapes slowly shrinking: a mesmerizing sight. As I watched I felt a little like the subjects of James I, burning whatever I could not understand.

The fate of that house was uncertain. Elizabeth Greenwood had left no will, and her daughter, just like Oakley and little Primrose, might never be seen again. I assumed that after a few months the property would go to auction.

I wrapped my fur-trimmed overcoat more tightly around myself. I had indulged in a new one, and as I sniffed the odd scents of the burning herbs I thought of the terrible ordeal I had gone through.

More than the things I'd seen, I was haunted by the little pieces, the oddities that had lurked in the background during that black week.

I could not tell how Madame Katerina had foreseen my

being poisoned – not only that, but she had also foretold the very remedy that could have mitigated my symptoms. I also remembered her more ominous words when touching Amy's writing: *the most powerful of them can turn into animals, birds and balls of fire. And they hide in every nook and cranny, everywhere in the land. Beware of them, my dear.*

Nine-Nails had at some point nagged me about Redfern's escape from Lancaster's tallest tower, right after setting the bells on fire. We had followed her there, seen the flames erupt, and then thoroughly searched the scantest surface where any person could have stood. I remembered the instant we both crouched, protecting our faces from the fire. Redfern could have used those seconds to rush away. Nevertheless, I could not prove it, and Nine-Nails clung to that fact.

Even though I'd never think of the witches as actually magical, I could not deny – or underestimate – the extent of their secret wisdom, the ancient lore they'd kept to themselves for centuries, and which was unlikely to die out because of our little intervention. Their two leaders had perished and their main coven had been discovered (and half of Cobden Hall had been consumed by the fire McGray started), but I knew it was just a matter of time before they regrouped, recovered and perhaps decided to strike back – with redoubled efforts.

Those grim thoughts were interrupted by a cab's creaking wheels. I looked up and saw a one-seater coach halt by the front door, next to my own rented cab. The door opened and down came Nine-Nails. One of the many things that still upset him was his dead horse. We were at the very spot where Joel had shot the poor animal, and

McGray had so far refused to purchase a new mount. Philippa, my very expensive Bavarian mare, had almost been lost too. Amazingly, the good Dr Clouston had saved her. He'd recognized her after dropping us at Caledonian Station, while McGray and I hopped on to that infamous train. My poor mare had been trotting about, terribly scared, on the road by the station – Joel had probably jumped from her back and left her to her own devices – and Clouston's brawny driver, Tom, had managed to calm her and take her to the asylum's stables. I'd been elated when the tall man knocked at McGray's door and handed her back. Nine-Nails, however, could not share my enthusiasm; he'd only snorted and scowled in a way that very much resembled the sad expression he wore now.

He approached with weary steps, his square shoulders hunched dejectedly, which had become the norm ever since we'd returned. He had finally bought another over-coat, the old one having been used to fake his fall from the roof of Cobden Hall. The new garment was of a ludicrous cut and rough material, yet an immense improvement on the tatty bundle of moth-eaten crust he used to wear. Although, if he could have somehow retrieved his old coat from the corpse, I have no doubt that he would still be wearing it. I told him as much, but he was in no mood for jokes.

Nine-Nails had been left in a ghastly state. Utterly spent, he had sat as silent as the grave in the carriages and trains back to Edinburgh, his eyes wide, his stare lost in the distance as the countryside passed us by.

We greeted each other with a brief nod. I was expecting him to say something, but he just stood beside me, silently, watching the garden burn. With a shudder, I realized how much this posture resembled that of his mad sister.

Part of me felt truly sorry for him. I understood his despair, how galling it must have been to be so close to the prospect of his sister's condition improving, only to see it snatched away from him in a blink. Amy had not spoken again, despite Dr Clouston's best efforts, and with Joel now dead, any hope Nine-Nails might have held – of elucidating the nature of Pansy's condition, or even the possibility of her recovery – seemed gone.

'Did you go to the asylum?' I asked. He nodded, but I had to press for more information. 'Did you find everything in order?'

'Nothing new,' he said, kicking a few dry stems into the fire. 'We found nothing. No charms, no onions, no amulets . . . Joel did say he left protection for her. Ye were there, he *did* say it!'

I sighed and spoke as tactfully as possible. 'Yes, he said that. Nevertheless, he was dying. He might have been delirious.'

McGray bit his lip. He knew that. I could tell he was more aware of harsh reality than his wayward actions might suggest – and it was tearing him apart.

'If he said he left protection,' he muttered after a while, 'it might be that the witches also drove Pansy mad.'

I frowned. I had contemplated that possibility, but I thought I'd wait for McGray to be a little more recovered before we discussed it. However, there was something I did need to ask: 'Do you think the witches will come after her?'

McGray rubbed the back of his neck, visibly tired. 'Cannae tell. Marigold gave the order to Redfern, and both of them are dead. They could well have snuffed it before giving the order to someone else.'

He was not convinced though, and neither was I. What burning uncertainty now must haunt him. One more burden added to his weary load.

'I might bring Pansy to the house,' he said. 'So that only my most trusted folk look after her. At least for a while.'

I knew that Dr Clouston would strongly disagree, but that was another issue I did not want to discuss right then.

'Did ye talk to Campbell?'

'Indeed,' I grunted. 'What a colossal waste of time.'

'As usual.'

'He did manage to get a report from the Lancashire constabulary. It looks like the legal owner of the witches' warehouse was Pimblett, and now that he is dead it will go to auction. They searched the place while we were around, but only to verify nobody was there. After that they "locked" it. They waited five bloody days before deciding to inventory the blasted contents! Naturally, when they went back the place was completely empty.'

'The witches still pulling strings?'

'Perhaps. They could as soon have rolled out a red carpet, or hired the hags a bloody freighter to ship their contraband out of the country. And Judge Spotson was found dead, but a few days after we left Lancaster. It was a stroke, apparently. Not at all unusual for someone his age –'

'Yet too convenient.'

McNair was picking up his shovel and pick. 'All done, Inspectors.'

'Good job, McNair,' said Nine-Nails. 'Ye can go now. Ye look shattered.'

And he did. The young man had sweated profusely digging up the shrubs; some of their roots had been more than three feet deep.

'Did ye see Lady Glass?' McGray asked next.

'I did. She was home alone and still quite distressed. She said that Miss Ardglass had gone on a long trip. The girl intends to spend most of her time on the Continent. Bertha will chaperone her.'

'Doesn't want to spend too much time with her grannie after all she's done.'

'That is one factor, but Caroline also fears – understandably – that the witches might come after her.' I shook my head, thinking that Caroline's life story was becoming eerily similar to her father's; the curse perpetuating itself. 'I believe they will. They may wait years; they are a patient lot. But yes, I do not think they will leave Miss Ardglass alone. Or even us.'

McGray raised a hand. He was too weary to discuss those matters. However, he had one more question.

'Did ye tell Campbell about the prime minister's son?'

I chuckled bitterly. 'Of course I did. I even put in writing every detail I could remember about Lord William Cecil's meeting with Marigold. I typed it all out and gave Campbell a carbon copy . . . which he burned in his office hearth right in front of me. He said I should not open – in his very words – a can of royal worms.'

McGray assented. 'Typical Campbell. I want the other copy in my files.'

'Why, I am so flattered,' I mocked. 'I will have my contribution immortalized in your library of the occult.'

He turned away, in no state to refute my sarcasm. 'Just leave the damn thing on my desk.'

I saw him walk away slowly, dragging his boots, exuding misery but also provoking a spark of anger – which I understood all too well.

Just as part of me felt his tragedy, deep in the back of my mind I still could not forgive him. He'd led us into the worst dangers in the most reckless, selfish of ways. He had taken his beating, but so had I, because of a matter only vaguely connected to me. Now I was in as delicate a position as him and the Ardglass clan; I'd played a part in a daring strike against the witches' web, and as Oakley had said, they were anything but forgiving.

I am not one to kick a beaten man, so I would not make a great fuss about it any time soon, but I was sure my resentment would eventually come to the fore. Sooner or later I would explode against Nine-Nails, and I feared it might not happen at the best moment.

As his coach drove away I saw a lonely raven hovering above the gardens, so low I could see its fleeting plumage and glittering eyes. In old folklore it was thought terribly unlucky to kill a raven – now I suspected that the superstition might have been deliberately instigated by the witches.

I walked away, and as I breathed the cleaner air of the road I also rejoiced in my freshly applied cologne and the warmth of thicker clothes. For the past few days I'd appreciated cleanliness, good food, good drink and rest like never before, and I intended to continue to do so in the weeks to come. Once in the cab I lounged back in my seat, already savouring the prospect of a long sleep in a warm bed, Joan's best roast and a large brandy. I remembered I also had to visit Elgie, who'd been sending me daily messages about his progress at the Edinburgh Lyceum Theatre orchestra. I might even attend one of his upcoming rehearsals. He said they were performing 'the Scottish Play' . . .

I let myself doze as the blissful concerns of everyday life slowly managed to trickle back into my head. I passed out just as the carriage rode along Arthur's Seat, the ragged mount all covered in pristine snow. The last thing I saw was a thin, sharp ray of sunlight finding its way through the menacing clouds, as if promising a nice, quiet spring. Even that blasted winter would pass, and we would all live through it.

What a pleasant thought before falling asleep.

Author's Note

The subject matter of this book comes as no surprise: I lived within walking distance of Pendle Hill for two amazing years, which included the coldest March in half a century.

A lot has been written about the Lancashire witches (I'd particularly recommend the fantastic book by William Harrison Ainsworth), and I've tried to contribute something new. The witches I have described are partly based on the women sentenced during the seventeenth-century trials, but with a sprinkling of Latin-American lore and much of my Chemistry PhD background added in.

Fire always was going to be a key element. According to my late grandparents, witches appeared on the roads as balls of fire, and came at night to steal children. People said the best protection was to carry any metallic object shaped like a cross – even open scissors!

As regular fires did not feel supernatural enough, the many flame experiments from my university years proved very handy: copper salts are widely used in fireworks and produce my favourite shade of green. Some seventeenth-century texts also mention witches carrying fir torches with blue flames, which they coloured with a secret combination of saps and oils. Those witches might have been using methanol (also known as wood alcohol), a substance already produced in ancient Egypt for embalming corpses.

These thoughts evolved into my witches' 'visual Morse

code', which in Victorian times would have allowed them to converse across the country faster than anybody else.

Only well after establishing these communication rules, while looking for names for the witches' pre-eminent clientele, did I come across the very real stories about Lord William Cecil. He was the second son of Robert Gascoyne-Cecil, the then prime minister, and led a much quieter life as a vicar. However, he was well known for his eccentricities: many a guest saw him throw copper sulphate powder into his fireplaces in order to turn the flames green, claiming he was simply fond of the colour. I could not believe my eyes when I read that! Furthermore, Lord William's eldest son, Randle William, would have been conceived not two months after the events in this book take place – Randle and two of his three younger brothers met untimely deaths during the First World War.

The hummingbird charm, entirely fictional, was very entertaining to create. Hummingbirds are sacred in Aztec mythology, but here the bird would have been used merely as a showy carrier: the very fine plumage could be easily impregnated with hallucinogenic spores (as mentioned by Frey, the possible sources are countless; there are thousands of species of 'magic' mushrooms spread throughout the world), which would be released through clothes and inhaled whenever the person moved. The slice of cactus attached to it was peyote, a powerful psychedelic plant native to the north of Mexico and southern Texas. The witches' underground trade would have originated to procure exotic and powerful ingredients such as these. I also hinted at the hummingbird containing toxic mercury salts (mercuric arsenate, hence the red sparks Frey sees in the fire), which can be inhaled as well as absorbed through the skin. These would account for McGray's impaired vision and weakness, and would have eventually killed him.

The Grimorium code was mentioned to me by a Wicca practitioner whose name I'm not allowed to reveal, and although I could not find any reliable references in literature, the idea makes perfect sense. The word *grimoire* only became associated with magical texts when the witch hunts were at their peak and possessing such knowledge would have been dangerous. In French, Grimorium's root language, *grimoire* has also come to mean enigma or riddle.

The scatological contents of the witch bottle (my apologies) and their use for house protection are described verbatim from a medieval text.

The explosive bottle comes from childhood reminiscences: around Christmastime, back in the days preceding rigorous health and safety regulations, almost every Mexican child would play with these little gunpowder beads that look like chickpeas; you throw them hard on to the floor and they ignite. Curiously, they are called *brujitas* (little witches).

Finally, in Mexican folklore, marigolds (*Tagetes erecta*) are the flowers of the dead.